Edmond Sutherland was educated at Magdalen College School. He studied medicine at Oxford University, and after qualifying, he was later appointed research senior register and then consultant psychiatrist and postgraduate clinical tutor at Birmingham University.

He retired from medicine in 1985, subsequently studied fine arts for five years, and held a one-man exhibition in Oxford, which was well received.

This book is the second of a trilogy: *Watching, Withstanding, Waiting.*

My wife, Sheila Ann, has been a constant support while I have been engaged in writing this trilogy, and her suggestions have often been inspirational. Joanne has again assisted with secretarial matters.

Edmond Sutherland

WITHSTANDING

AUSTIN MACAULEY PUBLISHERS™

LONDON * CAMBRIDGE * NEW YORK * SHARJAH

Copyright © Edmond Sutherland 2024

The right of Edmond Sutherland to be identified as author of this work has been asserted by the author in accordance with sections 77 and 78 of the Copyright, Designs and Patents Act 1988.

All rights reserved. No part of this publication may be reproduced, stored in a retrieval system, or transmitted in any form or by any means, electronic, mechanical, photocopying, recording, or otherwise, without the prior permission of the publishers.

Any person who commits any unauthorised act in relation to this publication may be liable to criminal prosecution and civil claims for damages.

This is a work of fiction. Names, characters, businesses, places, events, locales, and incidents are either the products of the author's imagination or used in a fictitious manner. Any resemblance to actual persons, living or dead, or actual events is purely coincidental.

A CIP catalogue record for this title is available from the British Library.

ISBN 9781035831227 (Paperback)
ISBN 9781035831234 (Hardback)
ISBN 9781035831241 (ePub e-book)

www.austinmacauley.com

First Published 2024
Austin Macauley Publishers Ltd®
1 Canada Square
Canary Wharf
London
E14 5AA

As always, I am indebted to Magdalen College School for a sound basic education.

My thanks to Austin Macauley Publishers for their encouragement in publishing this book, which is the second in the trilogy, *Watching, Withstanding, and Waiting.*

Introduction

The clubhouse was substantial, and from the 'Long Bar', those relaxing had a panoramic view of the gently undulating, very private golf course. Even in the late autumn, as it was now, the fairways were in pristine condition, but then the summer had been kind to the green keepers. On the eighteenth green, having shaken hands and modest winnings discreetly exchanged, four golfers made their way to the bar to take proper refreshment. There were some members who did not disfigure the fairways by hacking divots from the fairways or, more regrettably, the greens, but who were members of the club who enjoyed the company of others and played games of pool or even engaged in a few hands of cards. Poker was the game of choice.

A local doctor was one of these clubhouse habitues. He had recently downsized his house to a more modest residence, which was evidence of his poor proficiency in cards or his limited understanding of his opponent's 'poker faces'. In either case, it had caused the lingering animosity of his wife, who was contemplating divorce. The doctor was again desperately trying to reclaim some of his earlier losses when the four golfers entered the bar. Such was his distressed concentration that he did not notice one of them clutch his chest, give a startled cry, and collapse.

Morgan, the bartender, witnessed the scene and raised the alarm immediately. The doctor, having reluctantly put down his cards, examined the prostrate figure and pronounced life extinct; an ambulance arrived promptly, and the body was removed. The fact that the person who had died was a Member of Parliament was thought, at the time, to be only incidental.

That was how it all began.

*** *** ***

Part One: Suspicions

Chapter One

Donald Muirhead, MBE, the Member of Parliament who had died, was considered 'a good egg' and had served his constituents conscientiously for several years, a steadfast backbencher never aspiring to government position. He had died at 4:35 pm on Wednesday, 15 September 2021, in the clubhouse of a golf course, part of a country club some 20 or 30 miles south-west of Birmingham. Of his death, there was no doubt. Why he was playing golf in Worcestershire was less clear. His constituency was hundreds of miles away; his place of electoral business was London.

Worcestershire seemed out of the way. This was a mystery that puzzled his wife and the police. His wife, Frances, was notified by the local police within hours of his death, but through her distress, she was not able to explain his presence in Middle England. 'No', as far as she knew, he was not a member of that golf or country club. 'Yes', he enjoyed golf and 'was a member of the local club in Cheshire that was within the boundary of his constituency'.

But Worcestershire? 'No', she had no idea what he was doing there. The police considered the matter curious but not worthy of further investigation. Later, the Home Office would rue that decision.

The coroner in Worcester was disquieted. Although the local doctor in the clubhouse had pronounced death at 4:35 pm and had given his opinion that the cause of death was 'a cardiac crisis', he was unable to issue a death certificate because he was not the deceased's regular physician, nor had he examined him previously. The hospital to which the body had been taken was also unable to issue a certificate for similar reasons. Therefore, the coroner ordered a post-mortem. This was carried out on the following Monday, 20 September, and the report indicated that death was due to acute coronary occlusion and, as a secondary cause, widespread arteriosclerotic disease. A death certificate was issued, and arrangements were made for Donald's funeral in the parish church of his own constituency and burial in the adjoining graveyard. His family had long since bought a plot. Between the vicar and an obliging cousin, arrangements were made for the final service.

Donald's death caused little comment in the corridors of power. He had never been considered a 'mover and shaker', more of a steady, reliable party member. Apart from an inconvenient by-election, life could proceed as normal. Three national newspapers printed obituaries, as did the local rag in his constituency. The regional news mentioned his name; his party association circulated a report of his 'good deeds and unselfish devotion to his constituents'. But elsewhere, the event caused little grief or even interest. Donald's wife, on the other hand, was devastated. And his three children were bereft and bemused, and his friends were suitably solicitous.

There was a large gathering at his funeral where the vicar spoke eloquently of Donald's 'contribution to society' and an obliging relative asked everyone to 'celebrate the life of a devoted family man who would be sorely missed and who was a thoroughly decent chap'. The service ended with the singing of *Jerusalem*, and as the congregation made its hesitant way out of the church, the organist played an arrangement of Elgar's *Nimrod*. It was all very dignified. In the church porch, the priest awaited worshippers, making their way to the graveside. This was his first post as vicar, although not his first funeral.

The Reverend John was a young, naturally good-humoured and cheerful, an energetic minister to his 'flock'. These excellent qualities had not yet been dimmed by the responsibilities of priesthood. Immaculate in his dazzling white Alb and purple stole, he did his best to compose himself and offer compassion and comfort to the widow and the children. It must be said, however, that he only partially succeeded in concealing his exuberance. Frances, however, was too preoccupied to notice, and the children were too awkward to know quite how to behave.

Eventually, everyone gathered at the graveside, and the vicar committed the body, after the time honoured and familiar words of the funeral service, 'to eternal and everlasting peace'. As the coffin was lowered, Frances finally broke down and sobbed brokenheartedly. With much embarrassed shuffling of feet, fascination with trees and fallen leaves and a surprising obsession with reading scripts on ancient tombstones, the mourners waited. No one took any notice of the well-dressed gentlemen at the edge of the crowd. After an appropriate time for reflection, the company turned and walked slowly between the dark, mature yew trees and through the lychgate onto the road leading to the hotel where the wake was to be held.

The road, which was a little more than a lane, led through an avenue of chestnut trees; their conkers lay brown and shining between the fallen leaves, and spirits slowly rose from the solemn mood of the funeral service and committal. The September sunshine, a timid warmth and the reds, browns and oranges of autumn acted together to engender a lighter atmosphere. Making their way towards the local hotel for refreshments, no one wanted to appear overly enthusiastic, and so the procession continued at a slow pace. Nevertheless, as they neared the hotel, only 100 yards from the churchyard, small groups began to form, and with relief, there was a discreet acceleration of pace, and people started chatting together.

The vicar accompanied Frances and her children. They did not speak.

The town in which the funeral took place, as already explained, lies hundreds of miles from Westminster on the banks of the River Dee in Cheshire. Because of its proximity to the river and eventually the estuary and sea, it had developed into a successful market town in a sprawling farmland, which was the constituency Donald had represented in Parliament for several years. Within driving distance of Chester, Liverpool and even Manchester, it was a popular centre for tourism, and some wealthy local businesspeople had built houses here. Market Square, as would be expected, was in the central area of the town, with the hotel in which the wake was to be held on its southern aspect. The hotel, built in the fifteenth century, had undergone so many modifications that the exact date was impossible to ascertain.

Local historians, however, pointed out that a house providing 'comfort to travellers' had been mentioned in several books printed in the seventeenth century, and the façade certainly had the appearance of antiquity. The low ceilings within, supported by heavy oak beams, again suggested an ancient period. The management, of course, advertised the historical importance of the hotel while at the same time emphasising the modern facilities that were to be enjoyed by the guests. As often happens, the modifications and alterations had resulted in a comfortable but confusing mixture of furnishings and interior architecture. However, the wake was held in a large room at the rear of the premises, simple in design but utilitarian in purpose.

An open fire kept the chill of autumn from the guests. Long trestle tables were covered with snacks, sandwiches, glasses of wine and soft drinks, and a small, discreet bar stood in one corner to supply additional beverages, for those requiring further easing of tension. From the huge picture window, guests were able to survey the pastures of Donald's constituency, and those with good eyesight could see the distant blue-grey hills with dark shadows discernible in the September sunshine. Gradually, the mood of the mourners lightened, and the vicar could be seen exchanging pleasantries with assorted ladies and gentlemen, laughing and enjoying himself modestly, of course. For those with a keen eye, he was rarely to be seen without a glass of something or other!

Frances nibbled, without appetite or enjoyment, a couple of sandwiches and smiled falteringly as the guests expressed solicitudes. She was trying desperately at the same time to reassure her children, who as teenagers, were unsure of their position in the social pyramid and were at an age where they were neither adults nor children. They resented sympathy, believing it to be intrusive or hypocritical; they took exception to unbecoming bonhomie, believing it to be irreverent. Frances' task was difficult.

"Mrs Muirhead." A hand was laid on her arm.

She turned without enthusiasm, expecting another expression of sympathy from someone she barely knew, only to face a middle-aged man she had never seen in her life before.

"I was extremely sorry to learn of your husband's sudden death. Please accept my sincere commiserations. My name is Hugo Stratton, and I bring with me condolences from Marcia."

That ensured Frances' full attention. "Marcia?"

"My boss."

Now she was lost completely. "Knew my husband, did you? And this Marcia?"

"I know Marcia, of course. But not your husband."

This made matters worse. How was it that someone, to all intents and purposes an unknown outsider, stood before her, explaining that he and his boss Marcia did not know Donald personally? What was this man Stratton doing in this hotel? This afternoon? At this wake?

"Who are you, exactly?"

Without answering the question, Stratton continued. "This is not a suitable place to explain my presence here, unannounced and uninvited. I wonder if I could impose yet more upon you and ask if I could meet with you tomorrow?"

Frances gave this serious thought. On the one hand, she was in no frame of mind to socialise with strangers, yet on the other, she was worried and just possibly had to be careful. Also, she had to consider her children's welfare; they needed to come to terms with the loss of their dad, and this might be done best with her alone. She had contemplated going on a short break with them. But...? Who was this Stratton? Come to think of it, who was this Marcia? Stratton, all the while, waited patiently for an answer. Then: "Mrs Muirhead?"

Re-engaging, she decided clarification would be helpful. She would speak to the children, who might welcome the intrusion, if only to understand more of their father's work. She need not have worried; what Hugo Stratton had to say was, of necessity, private. "Mr Stratton I am sorry, I was thinking. Today, I'm not receptive. You could come to the house tomorrow morning. Shall we say 11:00? You know where we live?"

Hugo Stratton knew where they lived and agreed to this 'excellent suggestion'. And so, it was settled.

By late afternoon, when the light was beginning to fade, the guests began to leave, and Frances stood with the children, smiling weakly as they received more good wishes and sympathy. Anthea, the oldest, now 17, was dressed in a new high-buttoned dress, which was suitably plain but nevertheless attractive. She smiled but looked down constantly and was obviously uncomfortable. The two boys, Robert (15) and Stewart (13), responded to the guests with unintelligible mutterings low in their throats, Robert constantly worrying at the sleeves of his suit and Stewart fidgeting continuously. The vicar ruffled Stewart's hair and was treated to a passionate grimace.

As they drove home, the family was subdued. Frances, reluctant to broach the subject of Stratton's visit, was surprised when Anthea finally mentioned it. She was enthusiastic. "I'd like to know more about Dad's work," she ventured. "Did this chap, Stratton, work with Dad?" And then, "That guy looked cool."

'Cool' was not a word that Frances would have used. She might have tried 'concerned' or 'interesting', even 'intrusive'. But 'cool' was not a word that came to mind. Of course, her daughter saw Stratton from a different point of view entirely, being much younger.

The boys frowned.

They all arrived home tired. The children were at boarding school and had been given special leave due to the circumstances of the death. This would only be the third night at home with Dad gone, and it would take some getting used to. To an extent, they might feel a great emptiness, even though they were in boarding school and Donald has spent much of his time in London. But the relationships within the family had been strong. Many years and much effort had gone into developing unique family bonds, and things would change. There would have to be a rearrangement of attachments, interpersonal relationships and even alliances. That would not be easy. For now, an early night seemed like a promising idea.

*** *** ***

The Muirhead family lived in a large house built by Donald's father, Andrew Muirhead, who had made a fortune during the Second World War by preserving fish caught by his fleet of trawlers sailing out of Aberdeen and producing tinned food for the nation. When the offshore oil boom filled Aberdeen with a new type of workforce and, as he saw it, the Americanisation of his beloved city, he moved to England, bought a farm with a huge acreage and set about fulfilling another life-time ambition, which was to breed a first-class head of cattle. In this case, Jersey cows.

After his death, his older son inherited the large farmhouse, the farm and livestock, but Donald, the younger son, was not forgotten. A large house had been built within the boundaries of the farm and given to him in perpetuity. He married Frances, a nursing sister in accident and emergency at a nearby hospital and raised a small family. This completed Donald's transition into adulthood and, with it came considerable responsibility that may have laid an increasing burden upon him later. Having gained a degree in politics and economics from a northern university, he then succeeded in converting a small, local business into a thriving concern, bringing employment and much needed prosperity to the area. He joined the local political committee, and it was recognised at central headquarters that having a local man put forward as a parliamentary candidate at the next election was a wise move.

His election as a Member of Parliament was a formality. Therefore, in his early 30s, he was a successful businessperson, a Member of Parliament with a very safe seat and a family-oriented person of some substance. Frances soon became accustomed to a 'weekend marriage' with Donald spending weekdays in London. The children grew, left for boarding schools and she gave herself over, publicly at least, to community welfare. Although Donald's death had been as deeply wounding as it had been unexpected, with the house, a healthy bank balance and the promise of further pensions coming, her future was secure.

Or so she believed.

The sound of car tyres on the drive at precisely 11:00 am announced the arrival of Hugo Stratton, and moments later, the sound of the doorbell galvanised the daughter, Anthea, into action. Dressed today in white shirt and stone-washed jeans, she hurried to the door and stood back to allow Stratton in.

"Miss Muirhead?" Stratton was politeness personified. He held out his hand. "Hugo Stratton. I've come to see your mother."

She put out her hand to be grasped, but now the difficult bit: she had to speak!

"Come in." She examined the doorstep minutely, perhaps for footprints. "Come in," she managed again, this time just a little louder.

"Thank you." Stratton was in. They went through to the large dining room, where Frances stood by the table, her face pale.

"Mr Stratton. And so prompt. Can I offer you coffee?"

"Thank you, if it's not too much trouble." And Anthea bustled away to make the drinks.

Frances and Hugo Stratton sat formally at the table. Frances did not offer the hospitality of the lounge.

Stratton pointed to the scene beyond the window, then changing tack, said, "When I approached the house, I couldn't help wondering about the name. 'Rubislaw House' is a most unusual name."

"It is. My father-in-law, Andrew, was brought up and worked in Aberdeen, the granite city. Most of the granite came from Rubislaw Quarry, and I suppose he wanted to bring part of Aberdeen with him. Hence the name."

Whether or not the subject had been deliberately introduced, it had a negligible effect on easing tension. Anthea re-emerged carrying a tray with three cups of coffee, even some sweet biscuits. Stratton murmured his thanks. For a few moments, the three sat without speaking, then Frances turned abruptly. "Why don't you join your brothers upstairs, Anthea? They are only listening to music, if that is what you call it. Turn on Robert's television. What do you think?"

"Okay, then. And it is music! It's Alexis Taylor," came the reply. Anthea slowly left the room and was heard mounting the stairs and shutting the bedroom door several seconds later.

"A shame," Frances conceded, "but you indicated that you wanted privacy, did you not?"

"Thank you. I did." Frances had her back to the window, her face in shadow. Stratton would have preferred to watch her expressions more clearly, but he could hardly ask her to move. Much of Stratton's training in secret services had been directed towards interrogation of subjects, hostile or otherwise. But questioning a family like this was difficult. He had to proceed carefully considering their recent loss. He wanted to gain their respect as well as their confidence. If that was his aim, he was disappointed.

"Mr Stratton, I am not a fool. Whether it is Donald's personal life or some other issue, I have no idea. But what I do know is that you are investigating some aspect of his behaviour. You might be from the police, the Special Branch, the intelligence services, or some such organisation. I don't know. Can we have it out in the open, please?" Frances looked directly at him, replacing her cup on its saucer firmly.

"Mrs Muirhead, I never for one moment considered you a fool. My purpose here was merely to offer our sympathy and secondly to ask you, as discreetly as possible, if your late husband had any major worries in his life." Stratton thought that covered it. Frances did not.

"If you mean, did he take his responsibilities as a Member of Parliament seriously, I can assure you that he certainly did. If you are referring to any intimate relationships within the family, that is none of your business. If he had worries, either with his constituency or his business, I am not able to comment as he scrupulously avoided speaking of such matters inside our home. So, I can be of little help."

"On the contrary, Mrs Muirhead, you have been most helpful. You have made it abundantly clear that your husband was a man of principle; I wish I could say the same of many of his colleagues in Westminster." Stratton smiled. Frances did not. Stratton decided that nothing further could be done without causing unnecessary distress or, more importantly, lingering suspicion. He changed the subject completely to ease the tension.

"You have a fine house with a view to…" He stopped just in time before making a most dreadful 'faux pas' "…To admire." He nodded past Frances towards the land stretching out before him. "I have never lived in the country; city man myself through and through, but I can see the countryside has certain attractions." Frances made no comment. She had decided that she had seen enough of this man and was not prepared to lengthen the interview, for that is what it was, with small talk. And if Stratton needed some information about the local party and its membership committee, he could get it elsewhere. Stratton realised the interview was over and stood.

"Mrs Muirhead, you have been, as I say, most helpful. Can I just repeat how sorry we were for your loss?" He did not say who 'we' were. Frances reluctantly shook his hand and went with him to the door.

"Thank you, Mrs Muirhead."

Frances swallowed. "Goodbye, Mr Stratton." The door closed behind him, and Frances now had extra worry to cope with as well as the sadness of her husband's death.

*** *** ***

Chapter Two

Hugo Stratton left 'Rubislaw House' and drove slowly towards the town and the hotel in which the wake had been held and where he had taken a room. However, instead of re-entering the town, he took a circuitous route through the countryside to the city of Chester, constantly checking his rear-view mirror and altering his speed at intervals. Training lasted a lifetime. The harvests had left the fields bare, most ploughed, and trees were beginning to lose their leaves, littering the earth with bright autumnal colours. Not someone given to artistic thoughts, nevertheless, Stratton could enjoy the countryside. There was still a modest warmth in the sunshine.

He drove past a group of industrial buildings on the outskirts and followed signs through the newly built suburb to the 'City Centre'; the traffic was unexpectedly heavy. He found a parking space only after some frustrated manoeuvring around the central shopping area. From there, it was a short walk to the small Italian restaurant chosen by his boss. She was easily recognisable, sitting straight but with elegance as always. Immaculately dressed, she was smiling not at Hugo Stratton but at a gentleman sharing her table. Stratton stopped. This was unforeseen. He was unsure how to go ahead, but Marcia, for that was her name, looked up and called above the chatter of other diners. "Hugo! There you are. Come and join us, why don't you?"

Mystified by this unexpected guest, Stratton sat with the two of them. Marcia explained the stranger's presence.

"Hugo. Allow me to introduce a local businessman. Mr Palfrey, please meet my colleague, Hugo Stratton." The two men inspected each other, Stratton more carefully and thoroughly. "Mr Palfrey is not joining us for lunch but has graciously kept me company until your arrival." Marcia was at her most charming.

"I can assure you it was no imposition," Mr Palfrey responded in kind, and Stratton smiled inwardly, for Marcia was an attractive, if mature, lady of a certain age. As if to correct any false impressions, Mr Palfrey quickly added, "I always make it a point of principle to join my dear wife at home every lunchtime."

"How considerate," Marcia murmured.

How henpecked, Stratton thought.

Mr Palfrey rose and took his leave.

"What was that all about, Marcia?"

"Local knowledge, nothing more. Mr, Palfrey is chairperson of the local Chamber of Commerce," Marcia said, smiling.

Marcia's same surname was never mentioned; perhaps it didn't exist, who knows? Or more probably, she did not want, or was forbidden, to give it. In this respect, she continued to embrace the secrecy of the Cold War's intelligence agencies. It was as if Gorbachev's glasnost, which had so impressed Margaret Thatcher and infected Western politics, had passed her by. She was the personification of discretion as head of a major department in the intelligence services, and Stratton, when he chose, was a listener and not a talker.

There were therefore many long silences between them, which did not have origins in truculence but were customary of professional observers. Having read the menu with a critical eye, Marcia called the owner to attend them. A young man, with the obligatory thin moustache to be expected on our southern European neighbours, stood at their table with commendable alacrity. Marcia had that effect on restaurant staff, or, come to think of it, all staff. She looked at Stratton.

"I have dined here before." Stratton never ceased to be amazed by statements from his 'boss'. "I can recommend the veal steaks and roasted vegetables in oil, butter and parmesan unless, like me, you prefer pasta, in my case, a spaghetti carbonara." Now Stratton had to decide whether this reduced his choice to two dishes or if he could choose for himself.

"The veal, I think." He took no chances and was rewarded with: "An excellent choice if I can make so bold, Hugo. Perhaps to accompany the food, we could risk a glass of Italian red. Not Chianti, please, something more full-bodied; you have that, Aberto? And of course, I will enjoy your special spaghetti." She could now settle; they need only wait for their meals and enjoy the glass of wine.

Stratton, on the other hand, was deeply uncomfortable finding himself socialising with his superior, because, to him, like everyone else in the department, Marcia represented authority—no, more than that... she was authority. She was remote, and that suited everyone. They knew where they stood. Here, he was unsure of the protocol but was almost immediately relieved of uncertainty, for Marcia reverted to office mode. After being served the wine, she made a judicious inspection of the room and decided that no one was within listening distance and, moreover, no one looked to be of any particular interest. Of course, you could never be sure.

"Hugo," she murmured. "Was your morning successful? Forthcoming, was she Mrs Muirhead?"

"Well, yes or no."

"You're not sure? Without doubt, I am amazed, Hugo; I know you too well for that."

Hugo chose his words with care. Marcia would evaluate every word, every phrase, every inference, whether voiced or not. "Not so much 'not sure', rather, 'cautious of a definitive conclusion'."

"How fascinating. Hugo, being overly cautious is not something that I associate with you!" Marcia sipped her wine. "Please tell me more."

"I'm sure I was welcomed, but on reflection, I think that the daughter, Anthea, may have acted as a friendly catalyst."

"How philosophical. Go on, please."

"I was served coffee, and we sat in the dining room, all quite informal. I felt no animosity whatsoever. Well, that is, not until the daughter was sent upstairs to keep company with her brothers."

"Authoritarian turn of mind, Mrs Muirhead, has she?"

"Not exactly that. She wanted to speak to me privately, and her daughter sensed the need to leave us."

"But there was no argument. Her daughter, even as a teenager, did as she was told."

"Yes," Hugo replied slowly and thoughtfully, "I suppose you could say that."

"I just have."

Their food arrived, giving Hugo a moment to gather his wits. Once the waiter disappeared, he continued. "Almost the moment her daughter left, Mrs Muirhead told me in no uncertain terms that she knew I was an investigative officer from one service or another, and she forcibly impressed upon me that her marriage and her intimate relationships were private and none of my business, that she knew of no worries her husband had above those that were normal for a Member of Parliament, and, finally, that he had no anxieties either over any business dealings or, at present, finance. I think it was a negative morning."

"On the contrary, Hugo, you have learned a very great deal. Mrs Muirhead controls her family, or at least her daughter and probably the other children as well. She is defensive of intrusion into her personal life and clearly obstructive or ignorant of her husband's business affairs. You and I both know extremely well that any business involves stress, and we must not lose sight of the fact that our good Mr Muirhead, MBE, MP, had numerous business interests in the capital. It would be surprising if he did not speak of those to her. If he didn't, why not? If he did, why does she need to be so protective of them?" Marcia sat back. "Thank you, Hugo. That has been a very productive morning's work. Now," she said, "let's eat."

Marcia enjoyed her meal and thanked Aberto profusely as she paid the bill. She left a substantial tip. As they walked back to their cars, Marcia explained that she was needed in London but asked Hugo to remain at the hotel for two or three days more. Apparently, there was to be a meeting of the local political party members, or at least those who, at such short notice, were available. The vacant seat needed a replacement, and if they did not want a candidate foisted upon them from the Central Party, they would have to nominate an outstanding candidate of their own and be quick about it. Of course, neither Marcia nor Stratton could believe this had not already been done in the central office. But that was not their concern. If he could become well known in the hotel, for that's where the members hold their discussions, he could become part of the background crowd, the furniture. And listen carefully.

Hugo accepted his orders. It would be helpful to get the feel of the neighbourhood and hopefully meet some of the constituents and party members. They drove off on their separate ways.

*** *** ***

As many of the party members were free the following afternoon, a Saturday, they met in Stratton's hotel in a 'function room' designed for such engagements. It was a large room conveniently situated at the top of the wide staircase with doors that could be firmly closed, ensuring those in attendance could have privacy. The members present, unfortunately only a few could attend at such short notice, sat at tables arranged in two lines facing each other. They included the local party chairperson, two party executives and some eager and generous party volunteers. Also among them, although always sitting apart, was the retired colonel, known locally as 'a character', or if one was ill-disposed towards him, as 'the toff with the whisky nose'.

He lived in a large, double-fronted, detached house on the outskirts of the town, and rumour had it that he was old enough to have had a batman while still a serving officer and that he and the batman now lived together, 'and the two were remarkably close'. However, that might have been an unjust and malicious scandal. Red of face, with a bulbous nose upon which could be seen broken capillaries, the colonel sat half asleep but would wake occasionally to make comments that were usually not apposite, often bizarre. Rarely did he contribute anything meaningful to the topic being debated. He knew, however, which way to vote.

Next to him, or closer than anyone else, a timid, pale-faced lady took the minutes. This was the secretary, Miss Ruth Miles, who was not comfortable with 'Ms', pencil poised and with horn-rimmed glasses perched on her thin nose; let's face it, everything about her was thin. Her pencil hovered in a nervous hand above her notebook; her lips were tightly compressed into a narrow line, better for concentration. It was said by those who had studied the poor woman over many years that her anxieties were such that her knees were more tightly clenched than her fists, and she had snapped many a pencil in two just holding it in a vice-like grip.

The main topic of conversation for the membership this afternoon was the sad demise of their Member of Parliament. It was decided quickly that a plaque bearing his name should prominently be displayed somewhere in the constituency. But where? The church would require diocesan approval or, at the very least, parish council blessing, wouldn't it? And the hotel was hardly suitable; he wasn't a mason, was he? They met at the hotel occasionally when, for some reason or other, the lodge was unavailable.

Somewhere in the market square was the best bet. But decisions of this magnitude required great thought. The matter was left pending until the next meeting. A letter of sympathy could be composed and sent to the widow. It was immediately agreed because if the secretary could do that, they hadn't got to do anything. They all turned and looked at Ruth. This was too much; she blushed, dropped her pencil and her glasses steamed up. Next, a letter to the local newspaper was needed, outlining the many attributes of their late and sorely missed Member of Parliament and one that would make the paper's short obituary appear pathetically inadequate. The chairperson could see her name 'writ large' and at once volunteered her services. The secretary dropped her pencil again, this time with relief.

The chairperson then brought them back to the considerations caused by Muirhead's death: proposals for a person who would be considered suitable as a candidate for the by-election. It was pointed out that they could not proceed further without advice from the party's Central Committee and that had to come from London. Best pend that. The meeting was officially declared 'closed'.

Adjoining the room in which the committee gathered, there was a small but comfortable bar named 'The Cocktail Parlour'. When not in use, which was often, a retractable grill was drawn down, thus discouraging petty pilfering. Not popular with the townspeople, this was where hotel guests congregated for a quiet drink, usually towards the end of the day and before or after dinner. On this afternoon, however, some members from the association meeting in the 'function room' were expected, exhausted and thirsty after their deliberations.

Hugo had anticipated such a post-committee gathering and had bought a local newspaper and made himself comfortable on a window seat, with half a pint of beer, sufficiently removed from the bar to avoid conversation with the barman. He read the paper and was managing the beer; he was not a regular drinker nor an afternoon drinker, but 'needs must'. Then he heard the committee start to leave.

He looked through the open door and saw them filing out with rather vacant expressions that schoolchildren have when leaving an examination room. But not all of them; there was a determined look in the eye of the colonel as he turned smartly into the 'Parlour' and, with his hand outstretched, approached the bar with single-minded determination.

"Your usual, sir?" Dale, the bartender, was working the optics already.

"Absolutely, old chap. Put it on the tab."

The colonel hoisted his abundant rump onto a barstool and, with a sigh of contentment, took his double whisky in one. Dale refilled the glass without request or comment. Next in was Ruth, the anorexic secretary, who timidly levered herself onto a barstool as far away from the colonel as possible. She was a spinster wracked with anxieties and unrequited love, coiled as tightly as a wound spring, pale of complexion and having yet another bad hair day. However, her temerity was rewarded when the colonel nodded to Dale and a large glass of sweet sherry was placed before her. She attacked her drink with surprising enthusiasm.

Two men entered, one tall with untidy hair and marginally too long to be elegant and at odds with his pin-striped, dark grey suit. There was no doubt, however, he carried with him an air of superiority. This was the local psychiatrist, Dr McIntyre, and with him was a small man of worried expression and diffident nature, Mr Simpkin, one of the eager if ineffectual volunteers. They drew up at the bar, and Simpkin was keen to buy Dr McIntyre's whisky.

Stratton let the group settle and start talking together before he moved slowly to the bar for another 'half'. He spoke to the colonel. "Excuse me."

"Sorry. Dammit! In the way, as usual? Sorry." The colonel moved his considerable frame together with his barstool a few inches to allow Stratton a glimpse of the bar. "Dale. Fella here in dire need of alcohol. Got your attention, have we?"

"Thank you," Stratton said.

"My opinion. Make a newcomer welcome. Not seen you in here before, am I correct? Cheers." The colonel raised his glass. Stratton responded in kind. "Don't let me interrupt your discussions," he apologised.

"Nonsense, here to relax. Nothing secret going on."

Stratton was pleased to be included so quickly; this is what he had come for when all said and done. He leant on the bar, reinforcing his inclusion.

It seemed the colonel had temporarily lost interest in local politics, but his companions were discussing the untimely demise of their Member of Parliament. The first to speak was the volunteer, Gerald Simpkin. He appeared anxious to speak, testing his status within the group, perhaps desperate to be included.

"I know his wife, or at least Avril, my wife, does," he explained with breathless excitement, hoping to garner some attention, possibly even esteem. "My wife is a keen lepidopterist; butterflies, you know?" Silence. *Damn it, overdone it again!* he admonished himself.

"She has asked Mrs Muirhead for permission to explore Muirhead Senior's farm to look for unusual species and to photograph any for her records," he finished lamely. The group looked at him; no one spoke. Stratton 'felt' for the poor man. "We went to the funeral and afterwards. A splendid turnout." This was better received, and after several heads nodded, Simpkins was suitably relieved.

Dr Andrew McIntyre spoke, his Scottish accent now only occasionally noticeable after living south of the border for twenty years or so. "I suppose the central office will be sending someone up as a suitable candidate for the by-election." He needed the MP and this committee on his side, but he had to be careful.

Sipping his whisky and looking over the rim of the glass, he said, "We must always remember that the services require constant development. The district is in urgent need of further facilities for patients with mental health problems who cannot wait forever for an appointment at the NHS. The waiting lists are longer than ever. Even before the closure of the large mental hospitals in the 1980s, the services were stretched near breaking point. Finances are urgently needed for an alternative service. And that does not even include social care. We will need someone who is sympathetic to that."

"And of course, COVID didn't help." Ruth, the secretary, ventured.

"Right," said McIntyre, much to her relief.

There seemed to be little enthusiasm for that topic. And the members started looking at their watches, making moves to go.

"Come on, Ruth." The colonel had woken up at this hasty exit, and pointing to her glass, he encouraged her, "Have another." She required little encouragement. "And what's your poison…?" he asked, turning to the newcomer.

"Hugo Stratton," Hugo supplied his name.

"Right. Stratton. Knew a chap in the army, name of Stratton. Big feller. Sar-major. Straight as a die. Damn fine physique on him." The colonel gazed vacantly into the distance, lost in memory for a moment, then recovering, said, "Come on, Dale. Services needed, there's a good chap." And then, looking around, he asked, "Gone, have they?" He seemed surprised. "Come on, Ruth, drink up. There's a good girl. What's your poison, Stratton?"

Ruth finished her drink, put her glass down and pushed it forward all in one movement. And at the same time, she said, "Really, Colonel. I shouldn't."

Dale went about his duties, hoping that 'this doesn't go on all afternoon'. Once the colonel got the 'taste', he could be here all evening, never mind all afternoon. And that damned secretary was easily led. He was pleased to see the newcomer, Stratton, go. He doubted if Ruth would stomach more than two or maybe three. An early afternoon seemed likely.

Later that afternoon, Stratton sat on the edge of his bed, gazing out of the window. The trees were really turning now. There was surprisingly little traffic noise. Take some time. Read a book he'd brought. Get ready for supper. He'd drive to London tomorrow, first thing. He'd had a restful time, which had been mildly interesting but not truly newsworthy. Was there anything here? Marcia was keen on something but hadn't told him what it was. And she was rarely wrong. So, there must be something. His memory was good. There was no need to make notes; he could relate accurately this afternoon's conversation. Was there anything? Worrier Simpkin's wife was in touch with Mrs Muirhead. So what? McIntyre, the doctor, was moaning about the services for mental ill-health. But wasn't everybody? Not a lot there, he wouldn't have thought. But he could be wrong.

*** *** ***

Chapter Three

Rita, on checkout today in one of Streatham's many 'minimarkets', noticed something odd about the couple as soon as they entered the store. She and her boyfriend, Dennis, watched repeats of the Sherlock Holmes series and Miss Marple and Hercules Poirot investigations obsessively every evening. Like Dennis said, "Why read the books if you can watch them on the telly?" However, his opinion may have been unduly influenced by the fact that one of life's skills had passed him by: he could not read. Occasionally, they watched *Line of Duty*, *LA's Finest*, *Shadow Play*, or *The Drowning*, but those weren't the same. "Couldn't understand 'alf of what was going on. Didn't 'ave to think, that was the trouble," Dennis said, and who was she to argue? Some of Rita's friends thought she was balmy, but what did they know?

Anyway, Rita kept an eye on the couple who had just entered the shop. Late middle-aged, slow, reading the contents of packages in detail; she made up her mind that they were not British. Her deduction was correct because when they spoke to her at the till, their accents weren't London, but 'more your French'.

"You have no gateaux Napoleon, Charlotte russe, Rum baba…?" And seeing Rita's vacant expression, Monsieur DuPont continued, "Cream cakes, perhaps?"

"We've got Swiss rolls, but they're jam, I think."

The couple didn't want Swiss rolls with jam. They paid for the other goods and left the shop.

Antoine DuPont was brought up in a rambling, run-down house in Saint-Denise, a northern suburb of Paris. His paternal grandparents were members of the French Resistance during World War II; eventually, a group of soldiers of the German Army took them into the courtyard and shot them, whether as a reprisal for their resistance during the occupation, religious beliefs, or mindless frustration and anger, it was not known. When tiny Antoine was four or five, his father lifted him and pushed his forefinger into one of the bullet holes. He looked at his finger when it came out; there was no blood, just white dust.

Later, when he must have been ten or thereabouts, he came home from school to find his mother on the front step, crying bitterly. She refused to give a reason, but a classmate told him in a malicious whisper a few days afterwards that his father had deserted his wife and 'run off' with a local shopgirl. He never saw his father again but experienced the same loss as he had with the grandparents he never knew and who had left no blood. Neither did his father. Just emptiness.

Antoine married Delphine, and they continued to live in Saint-Denis. Perhaps, unsurprisingly, both had been officers of the French 'Police Nationale', both in specialist units for counterterrorism. Since the Charlie Hebden murders and the wave of terrorist bombings in France in 2015, counter-terror was an ever more active branch of the police force. There had been increasing cooperation between law enforcement agencies from countries across Europe, and Britain was no exception, even though now Britain had distanced itself from Europe, politically. Marcia, a senior member of the intelligence agency, had been told of the DuPonts' imminent retirement and had persuaded them to open a small 'School of Anglo-French Languages' in Streatham.

They were to manage a large house on the corner of a backstreet in Streatham to be used as a lodging house for students newly enrolled in the intelligence services. Monsieur and Madame DuPont were under no illusions about the house. It was used primarily as a training and study centre for street surveillance and evasion. The DuPont's French origin was a useful cover for the 'The School', which had a modest turnover of residents and offered an ideal place for Marcia to hold meetings that needed privacy and which had, for the moment, no official backing. Having visited the 'minimarket', M and Mme DuPont returned to the house. Marcia was expected for one of her infrequent meetings that very Saturday afternoon.

Hugo Stratton and Nigel Mountford arrived at The School within minutes of each other. They parked in the back lane behind the house and walked through the kitchen together. Neither Antoine nor Delphine looked up as they passed. On the first floor, they entered a large room with an unusually small window. It was gloomy. A standard lamp stood forlornly, unlit.

"No change since the last time we were here," Mountford said. "Furniture just as basic. Hard wooden chairs. Standard lamp, no carpet. Curtains heavy enough, though."

Stratton lowered himself gingerly onto a chair. "Been a while. Must be six months since that debacle with Keenan and Donato*. I wonder how the group captain is faring now that the Whitehall committee has been disbanded."

"No idea," Mountford said. "I see she's added a small table and an internal phone. But it's so dark in here; God knows what the table's for. You'd not be able to write. Not a great deal of money was spent here." Mountford unimpressed, was, as usual, fidgeting with his tie, crossing and uncrossing his legs, then plunging his hands in and out of his trouser pockets.

As they tried to get comfortable on the heavy, wooden and unpadded chairs, they neither heard the footsteps on the stairs or in the passageway outside nor the door opening. Nevertheless, they both looked up, and there was Marcia standing in the doorway, looking at them and smiling in welcome. Stratton wondered how long she had been standing there. 'A powerful woman, no doubt about it.' He tried to form an opinion. 'Mature? Well, of a certain age; if that were too depreciating, then some might say worldly. Perceptive? Certainly. Kindly? Depended on the circumstances. Above all, loyal'. Her elegantly coiffured hair, a suit of the finest woollen fabric with a discreet pinstripe and her stylish 'low, kitten heels' emphasised her composure.

Stratton knew she had spent many years as an active agent, both at home and abroad, and now held an administrative position at Vauxhall Cross, the British Headquarters of the Secret Intelligence Service. And nothing else. Of her private life, he knew nothing, and to the best of his knowledge, neither did anyone else. He held her in the highest esteem.

"Hugo. Nigel. How lovely to see you together again."

She entered and sat at the table. "Furthermore, he has a part-time advisory role in a competent, thriving company of investigators located in Parson's Green. A company that might prove especially useful to us." Picking up the internal phone, she spoke to Madam DuPont in the kitchen. "Delphine, could you bring us up some tea? Have you got any of those delightful, homemade eclairs? You are an absolute marvel. Merci." Two minutes later, Delphine brought in the tea and a plateful of her 'delightful eclairs'.

"Thank you." Marcia was gracious as usual. Delphine didn't speak.

"Shall I be mother while you tell me of your inquiries?"

Nigel Mountford began, "I went to the golf club near Evesham, where Donald Muirhead died, as you asked. It is exclusive, and when I say exclusive, I

---

* See 'Watching' (First book in this trilogy)

mean very exclusive. I had to wave my Whitehall pass about, and vigorously at that, before they let me in. But I finally got to the bar where Muirhead had collapsed."

"I wonder if your Whitehall pass was altogether wise," Marcia mused, sitting at the table and pouring tea.

"No other way of getting in. Covered it by pointing out that Muirhead was, when all said and done, an MP, and letting them make the connection."

"Mmm." Marcia did not sound convinced.

Mountford paused for a moment, then continued. "Anyway, Morgan was the bartender who raised the alarm on the fatal day and, luckily, was on duty the day I was there. Told me what we knew already but added that Doctor Brightwell, a GP in Worcester, or Evesham, plays cards most afternoons and loses money most afternoons; he was the chap who pronounced death. The doctor is of no interest to us, that's for sure."

"Expensive, the club, is it?"

"Very. Membership is strictly limited. The green fees would be prohibitive to me and…" He was about to say 'you' but thought better of it.

"Lady members?" Marcia asked nonchalantly, as if considering applying herself and proving to Mountford, if no one else, that she could afford the fees.

"Oh, yes, they're in the twenty-first century." Marcia was busy passing the tea and eclairs around, and she had not been watching Mountford as he recounted this. She was listening carefully for a fluctuation of voice or some evidence of anxiety or undue scepticism. If she was, she heard nothing to support such worries.

The chairs were not conducive to relaxation, which did not seem to be their primary purpose. She said nothing for a few moments and then made up her mind and murmured, "And we come now to the nub of the matter, Nigel. What was our good, or perhaps not so good, Donald Muirhead, Member of Parliament, doing on this golf course just outside Evesham? Besides playing golf and having a heart attack, I mean. Are you any closer to answering that mystery, Nigel?"

Mountford shifted uneasily in his seat. Now that he was not holding forth about his inquiries in the Vale of Evesham, his fidgeting had begun again. He scratched his head, adjusted his tie and blew his nose…

"No, not really, Marcia. What I did discover, however, was that he was not a member of the club but was there at the invitation of a full member. He was often invited, and by the same chap."

"Mm. Is that helpful? Name, Nigel, did you get a name for this generous person?"

"Oh, yes. William Oldham, known in the club as Bill."

"Really, Nigel? How very English, wouldn't you say?" Nigel had no idea, having never thought about it. "And you say, domiciled in Bromsgrove…close to Birmingham…our second city, as it calls itself."

"That's what Morgan, the barman, told me."

"And Mr Oldham's business? Morgan was helpful there, was he?"

"No specifics. Thought retail or import/export. Vague really."

"Well, that covers about everything. Not a problem, Nigel; we can soon find out."

Marcia leant on the table and ate the last éclair. *Mountford is starting again, but hesitantly*, Stratton thought.

"Nothing in a bar is so conspicuous as standing there without a drink. So, I asked Morgan if I could buy a drink. No luck. Against club rules or something. But Morgan poured a pint of lager and pushed it across the bar to me, wiping the condensation off the glass as he did. Not my drink." Stratton did not think it would be. "But helpful in the circumstances. The bar was filling up, so I took a table and watched the golfers on the last putting green, if that's what it's called. Whatever. I sat there a while and was thinking of leaving before I became interesting to the others in the bar when a guy came over and asked if he could sit at the table. Fair enough; that was what I was there for. In any case, before I could really answer, he sat down."

"Spoken to the barman, Morgan, had he?" Marcia interrupted the flow.

"Oh, yes. I saw him come in."

"How long had you been sitting there, would you say, before he came in?"

"Ten minutes?"

"I see," Marcia said carefully. "Time for a phone call and a drive."

"Only if he lived nearby."

"I see," said Marcia again. "Go on."

"Brought a whisky, I think, from the bar and asked if he could join me. I said yes. European, I think; English was not his first language, anyway."

"Have a name, does he?" A gentle question.

"Leon Weber."

"Sounds as if you were correct in your assumption; he was not from within our shores." Marcia smiled.

"He asked if I were thinking of applying for membership. He told me he was on the committee."

"And you said?"

"Possibly. To be frank, I didn't want to go down that road; I know next to nothing about golf, and that would soon become obvious. He asked me what my handicap was."

"What did you say?" This sounded like a genuine inquiry from Marcia.

"Oh, I said about average."

"And did that satisfy him?" Marcia asked incredulously.

"Seemed to." Mountford found nothing strange about that.

"Well, well." Marcia sat back. "Just as well you didn't say you were keen to join the club."

"Then we started chatting. He told me Bill—I suppose he meant Bill Oldham from Bromsgrove—played regularly—off six, whatever that means—often invited Muirhead as his guest. Quite pally, I was told."

Marcia murmured, "But in any event, friendly, were they? This businessperson from Bromsgrove but whose business is still a mystery."

"The impression I gained was that he was well-heeled. Millionaire? Leon started talking about the course and the particularly difficult dog-leg par five, which sounded painful. It was then that I lost interest and decided enough was enough. That wrapped it up. Finished my lager. Said I had an appointment and left."

There was a pause while Marcia considered Nigel's story. She slowly refilled her teacup from the pot. Stratton noticed her attention to Oldham's wealth. While she contemplated Mountford's contribution, Stratton took the opportunity to stand, stretch his legs and walk across the room. Looking out of the narrow window, leaning against the frame, he saw that the sun had dropped below the rooftops opposite; their room was shadowed and even darker. The street was lined with parked cars but otherwise deserted. There were no pedestrians. The one car on the block tiles at the front belonged to Monsieur DuPont; Marcia would have parked in the rear access lane. Not a sound. The neighbourhood was certainly quiet.

Marcia abruptly emerged from her reverie. She seemed startled that Stratton was no longer sitting next to her.

"Hugo…Oh, there you are." She saw him standing at the window. "Are you with us? Or have you more important business to attend to?"

"With you, Marcia, with you. Stretching my legs. These chairs are hard." Stratton returned to his chair. "And it's getting dark in here."

"You're quite correct, Hugo." Marcia seemed unaware of the gloom but turned on the standard lamp. It made hardly any difference.

"Let us see what we have learned. Nigel, Hugo, draw up your chairs to the table. We can lean on it for support." Marcia eyed Stratton tersely. They sat to the table.

"If I remember correctly, Hugo, your inquiries in Cheshire were interesting, if not exactly revealing. Am I correct?"

"Yes," Hugo agreed reluctantly. "You found more value in my meeting with Frances than I did, I must say."

"I think it may be wise for you to appraise Nigel of the purpose of your travels in Cheshire."

Stratton was relieved. He could be concise. "I went to the funeral and wake of Donald Muirhead, MBE, MP, and introduced myself to his wife, Frances, whom I arranged to meet the following day. I did so at the family home and discussed the interview later with you, Marcia. You made some interesting deductions. Perhaps you'd like to repeat them." He looked expectantly at his boss.

"I would prefer at this stage that you and Nigel compare your impressions, and then we may be able to draw some preliminary deductions."

Hugo sighed. This was her style. Allow others to gradually recognise for themselves that there might be alternative interpretations to simple narratives. He had already experienced that many times; the latest was in the Italian restaurant in Cheshire.

"Nigel. When I visited the matrimonial home, called 'Rubislaw', can you believe Frances was polite and, I thought, welcoming? Her daughter made coffee and was then asked to leave us and join her brothers upstairs. She did it without a murmur. Marcia," he said with a glance, "thought that unusual for a teenager— I mean, for a young girl meekly agreeing to such a request without protest. Marcia assumes the mother to have a more dominant role than in a typical household."

He paused for Nigel to comment. Nigel did not.

"After the daughter left, Frances spoke to me emphatically, telling me that her husband had no more worries than any other conscientious Member of

Parliament. And if I was inquiring into his private life, either within the home or his business dealings, it was none of my business. I was shown the door."

Then Nigel commented, "So…protective of her home life. And his life and business."

"Precisely." Marcia smiled.

"However," Nigel continued, "the acquiescence of the daughter, a teenager or not, may not be that unusual."

Marcia frowned. Nigel was arguing with her. "Have experience of teenage young ladies, do you, Nigel?" she asked pointedly.

"No, not really." Nigel was unmarried and made no secret of the fact that he lived on his own. Marcia may or may not have known that.

"Precisely," Marcia repeated. She knew he lived alone!

I wonder if you have, Marcia? Both Nigel and Hugo thought together. They did not know that she spent her sixth form years at an all-girls school. And a boarding school at that. And as for children, well, who knew?

She continued, "Hugo, the following Saturday, you met with some members of the local political party for Mr Muirhead's constituency, I believe."

"That's true," Stratton agreed. "I met some in the bar of the hotel after their meeting." He then gave details of the conversation but made no attempt at interpretation.

"Shall we pool our knowledge, combine our intellectual resources and focus our minds on important possibilities that can be deduced from our travels?" she inquired.

Nigel Mountford had become unusually still, leaning on the table, his brow furrowed. He was clearly struggling to understand something fundamental. At last, he plucked up courage and asked with measured politeness, "Marcia, I'm at a loss to understand why an insignificant death in Evesham and a funeral in Cheshire have anything to do with us. We are civil servants, albeit with unusual objectives, but we are paid to protect our country. It is not clear to me yet why we are interested in this at all."

As is quite often the case, Nigel was exhibiting a prosaic turn of mind. If the truth were told, however, Hugo had been wrestling with similar thoughts but had managed to suppress his uncertainty. This illustrated the difference between the two agents.

"I congratulate you, Nigel," Marcia remarked, surprisingly. "It would seem quite different from the treachery and misdeeds that occupy so much of our time and energy. I think a moment for an assessment of our position is required."

Hugo and Nigel waited. They both knew there was more to this than met the eye, and now Marcia had decided to tell them. *And not before time*, thought Nigel. Hugo, on the other hand, knew this game already from previous experience.

Marcia started with a preamble. "The government has been concerned, and quite rightly so, with the disastrous effects of COVID-19, a pandemic that has, as you know, caused terrible consequences. The global death toll alone, estimated by some scientists and statisticians, is to be as high as 15 million, which is catastrophic. There have been many deleterious secondary consequences that are equally worrying. The economy, travel, industry, interrupted schooling and university studies and so on have all been adversely affected. However, one magnificent by-product, namely the development of vaccines, has added another useful tool to medical care and, indeed, has opened avenues of research that may lead to vaccinations for many other types of awful infections or infestations, even, I am told, cancer.

"The difficulties and successes encountered because of this dreadful virus have occupied the minds of the government. And, of course, the origin of the infection is a mystery, possibly of malicious intent. As well as that, the unrest and potentially universal cataclysm of the war between Russia and Ukraine, and make no mistake about it, that is what it is—a war—hardly bears thinking of. But governments must think! It is no wonder that officials in Westminster have been preoccupied."

"With you, Marcia, with you. The agenda is crowded," Hugo commented quietly.

Marcia murmured, "How succinct, Hugo." She beamed.

Nigel said nothing. He was waiting.

"While these events have been unfolding worldwide, governance has continued uninterrupted. The vigilance of our departments has not faltered. It was because of our surveillance that we were able to detect and prohibit the loss of information vital to British security from the Conference Centre in Hampstead. Keenan and Donato, who were part of that conspiracy, are now existing within our prison walls and will continue to do so for many years to come, and this is due in no small part to your actions." She smiled at Hugo and Nigel, and they nodded modestly.

"And, with all this preoccupation with a pandemic interfering with the smooth procedure of the government in mind, I made a note of some disturbing rumours that I have come across within the environs of Westminster, which at first sight may seem unrelated. But I am not so sure. Unusual and suspicious influences are being brought upon some of our Members of Parliament. You have, no doubt, heard allegations that agents have infiltrated Parliament; it has even been alleged that a Chinese agent has offered large 'donations' to a politician and aspiring politicians.

"Whether or not these allegations have any basis in fact, I have made it my business to identify potential recipients who, through their businesses, might be unduly susceptible to such influences and whose voting in Parliament may be compromised. I have approached the director of our department." She did not say which department. "And I have permission to recruit both of you for a limited period to investigate in depth one, and only one, Member of Parliament of which I had suspicions. Unfortunately, that Member of Parliament died near Evesham. Hence, Nigel, your journey to that golf club, the place of his unfortunate demise, and Hugo, your sojourn to Cheshire, and his constituency."

They looked at each other. Now, they had been told, in effect, that this was to be a small group investigating the business of activities of a single Member of Parliament or at least a deceased Member of Parliament. Both could immediately see more problems that his death would present.

"I see you both hesitate. Let me put your minds at rest. Firstly, this will do your careers no harm whatsoever, quite the reverse. And secondly, and to my mind, more importantly, Donald Muirhead's death makes things easier for us. No one is likely to consider that agents of our government would search a deceased businessman's dealings for anything except for probate purposes. Any influence he could have brought to Parliament would have died with him. But for us, the process, or the operational system of financing such an activity, if we can find it, may be invaluable."

"Modus operandi," Nigel ventured.

"Precisely." Marcia did not smile. "Therefore, let us turn to the inquiries you have both made and consider, if anything, now we are all fully aware of the suspicions I have, which gives us reason to pause. Nigel, your visit to the golf club has led us to believe that Donald Muirhead was a little more than 'just friendly' with an extremely rich businessperson from Bromsgrove and that as soon as you made your presence known to Morgan, the bartender, one Leon Weber hot-footed it to the clubhouse and looked you over." Nigel Mountford moved on his chair and looked steadily at the floor below him.

"And now, Hugo, you have been busy as well. First, Mrs Muirhead was not pleased to see you and, if I am not mistaken, exerted her authority in the house and showed you the door." Hugo could not argue with any of that, therefore he did not speak. "Turning to the members of the local party you met in the hotel bar, your summation would lead us to the conclusion that the colonel, Gerald Simpkin and Mrs Ruth Miles are 'bit players' in the general action. Ruth Miles, poor lady, may have her mind overwhelmed by the lack of amorous attachments, and for the moment we can disregard her.

"However, it is my feeling that Dr McIntyre may be of interest. As I read it, he was keen to know the name of the new candidate for the vacant seat and wanted him/her to know of his concern about building a new 'clinic'. I assume you both will require a little time to absorb the information we have discussed this afternoon, which is understood to fall within the restrictions of the Official Secrets Act. Could we meet here early next week after you have had time to consider my theory? Shall we say Tuesday?"

Both agreed Tuesday was an excellent day to meet. Marcia was delighted; she extinguished the light in the standard lamp, and they left by the rear door. Neither Antoine nor Delphine looked up as the three passed through the kitchen.

*** *** ***

After the meeting with Stratton and Mountford, Marcia returned to her very private hotel in Chelsea. Not open to the public, the hotel catered for ladies and gentlemen of a certain age and distinction who wanted good service and complete freedom from intrusion. Each suite of rooms was beautifully furnished, the cuisine excellent and the room service beyond reproach. She was extremely comfortable during the weekdays, but of course she had her cottage behind Wytham Woods, near Oxford, as her weekend retreat.

The morning's appointment with Stratton and Mountford had been productive, and she knew that she had their interests in the death of Donald Muirhead, MP, MBE. Her own interest had been engendered by two things. Firstly, as she had said previously, what on earth was Muirhead, who lived in

Cheshire and worked in London, doing on a golf course near Worcester? And secondly, she had heard repeatedly whispers of a self-important, career civil servant. Too often for her composure. It was with that in mind that she had invited a private secretary to a treasury minister for a drink this evening. Well, a rather upmarket drink, if the truth be known.

That evening, at precisely 7:00, Marcia presented herself at the bar of an incredibly famous and sophisticated watering hole in central London. She had made a special effort with her clothes and was wearing a most discreet perfume.

"Richard! There you are." She greeted the secretary with an embrace that was proper to the dignity of the club. "And how are you and the new minister?"

"Oh, you know." Richard was always guarded in response to inquiries about his ministry and his minister.

"I hear wonderful things about his development in government. You must be a godsend to him."

"Oh, you know," Richard muttered, "one tries to steer a cautious line. There's always trouble brewing somewhere. It is in the very nature of things."

"Not you, Richard, not you. You are far too experienced."

"Oh, you know. Sometimes see 'wrong uns' before they know it themselves." He was modestly humble.

"But your new department and your new minister have a clean sheet to develop your plans."

"Do not believe it. Always someone up to something. Forsyth, for example, and I will say no more."

And he did not. No matter how much Marcia probed, that was the end of that conversation. However, she was satisfied with her expensive round of drinks.

*** *** ***

Chapter Four

Retired Captain Reginald Henry Young was in his element. A warm afternoon of September sunshine stretched ahead, and his idyll would be uninterrupted either by Mrs Braithwaite, the live-in housekeeper, five years widowed, obliging but with a sharp tongue, or by his ample and commanding but charming wife, Diane. He held both ladies in the highest regard but occasionally with varying degrees of trepidation: Mrs Braithwaite, an excellent housekeeper and cook, regarded any tardiness to the table for Sunday lunch as a capital offence; and Diane, whose father had bequeathed to her the large, mock-Tudor house in which they lived and a small fortune, viewed any deviation from good manners as evidence of an accelerating decline in her quality of life.

During afternoons such as this, however, when Mrs Braithwaite was taking the day off and Dianne was at the church hall engaged in good works, Reginald was able to practise his newfound passion of birdwatching alone and at ease and allow himself to appreciate the fortune of having such a good cook and housekeeper and the comfort of such a devoted and loving wife. He was comfortably dressed in his usual striped blue and white shirt, with a white collar and cuffs and scarlet braces. He had dispensed with the regulation tie. Well, it was Saturday afternoon, wasn't it? He could gaze at the stream and fondly remember the chorus of frogs on a summer evening and a tiny waterfall that had mysteriously appeared over a fallen rock one night.

And another gin and tonic would add to the pleasure.

Although Reginald had retired twice, he had never considered relinquishing an active life. His first retirement was from the RAF police division with the rank of group captain and a distinguished service record; the second came after a conspiracy was discovered in Whitehall concerning the misappropriation of sensitive government research. He had played a small part in the apprehension of the miscreants and was subsequently highly thought of, but, of necessity, retired. After being married for 25 years, he and Diane had developed a mutually rewarding companionship. Diane accommodated Reginald's small idiosyncratic ways with fortitude, and he had learned that her Christian beliefs were of immense importance to her and that her devotion to him was just as steadfast.

Their marriage was secure and agreeable. They had discussed their future together. Having no children, which at times they regretted but which they now accepted philosophically, they could travel whenever the fancy took them, mainly in Britain, possibly France, staying at comfortable hotels, retreats and spas. Then, thorough exploration of church, local history, and industry, rural or urban, for Diane; and hostelries, golf courses, and his new passion of ornithology, for Reginald, they would later collaborate on essays for each location, incorporating anecdotal tales and folklore, and collect their various experiences together with a view eventually to publication. Diane realised they would need professional help with the final text, and Reginald made a pledge to himself to write the stories he heard in pubs before he forgot them because sometimes rather more gin was drunk than was good for his memory. And a camera? They would discuss that later. The planning sounded good if a little vague, but, with help, it could be firmed up.

Reginald strolled to the stream that coursed between the willow trees and bushes at the end of the long garden. He entered his 'Hide'. This was a wooden construction resembling a garden shed, which in fact was what it was, but with a small, narrow window facing the stream and the opposite bank. He had customised the inside sufficiently for his purposes. Two canvas chairs were positioned in sight of the stream and the bank. There was a ledge before them on which he had placed binoculars, a notepad and usually a glass containing gin and tonic. Behind the chairs and to his right was a small cold store containing the essential bottles of gin and tonic mixer and, in addition, a small plastic box for comforting ice. And finally, directly behind him was a shelf that he had affixed himself to the shed wall. It was to hold books, cups, a transistor radio and any other paraphernalia that he might need.

Unfortunately, he had not listened to the advice of Diane with regards to a spirit level, and as a result, objects tended to slide towards the right, and if not stopped, they would fall off the shelf. He'd overcome such an inconvenience with the judicious use of two heavy volumes of the Encyclopaedia Britannica, which, if placed flat at the end of the shelf, stopped any catastrophes. It was the first time he had ever used the encyclopaedia, and he had found it useful indeed.

The smell in the 'Hide' was quite delicious—a mixture of creosote, wood and earth. On days such as today, the warm sun filtered through the branches of the overhanging willows and warmed the still air within, making the experience of sitting there most agreeable and, towards the end of afternoons such as this, quite soporific. He picked up the binoculars and, having taken a gentle sip from the glass before him, adjusted the focus onto the opposite bank. The canvas chair was comfortable in itself, with his rotund frame fitting nicely. Although by no means seriously overweight, his age and comfortable living had thickened his waist and added a pink complexion to his face already sporting laughter lines and a carefully clipped moustache. White hair trimmed in military style completed the 'jovial gentleman's style he so assiduously promoted.

As reported earlier, Reginald was in his element.

Elbows on the ledge, binoculars to the eyes, he was watching the bushes on the far bank with a concentration not usually associated with him. For the moment, he was ignoring his habitual visitor, the upright, motionless, grey heron on a suppertime fishing expedition, but turned his attention to a couple of pesky little fellers flying in short bursts between the branches of a bush opposite. Brown, grey and flashes of white. Were they hedge sparrows or house sparrows? He was just about to put down his glasses and reach for his *British Birds* book when the shed door opened.

"Group Captain? I apologise for interrupting your afternoon's research, but I have been directed to call upon you."

Reggie Young prided himself on his calm demeanour. *Damn it, sir, difficult to rattle, that's me!* But this had the potential to upset the tranquillity of the afternoon. Without taking his eyes off the bush opposite, he tried to identify the voice. Female certainly. Neither Mrs Braithwaite nor Diane. Apart from the barmaid at the golf club, the teller in the bank and Lorraine, the secretary at his part-time job, he couldn't think of any females he'd spoken to in weeks. He put the glasses on the ledge and turned slowly to look at the visitor. It seemed his afternoon had not been ruined after all, for before him stood an attractive young lady, smiling, if slightly warily, at him. Auburn hair. Very little make-up. She carried a leather shoulder bag.

"Good afternoon," Reginald murmured. "No idea who you are, but you're most welcome. Something puzzles me, however—actually more than one thing—but we'll get to that. How did you find your way into the garden and even to my secret retreat?"

"I apologise once more. I did not intend to startle you, merely to introduce myself and deliver a message. But now you ask, I did find the journey somewhat arduous; not the least difficulty was finding 'Oak Tree Lane' in an avenue of elm trees."

"Yes. Seems like the builder didn't know his trees from Tuesday morning."

A frown flitted across the forehead of the young lady, but she said nothing.

"Never mind that; sit yourself down." Young patted the empty canvas chair next to him. "Like a drink, would you? What's the name?"

The young lady eyed the gin and tonic before the group captain suspiciously and replied, "Lucinda. Lucinda Clayton. Have you any tonic?"

"Freshen it up a little with some gin?"

"Just tonic, thank you." She settled herself into the canvas chair and gazed through the window.

"Ice?"

"Thank you."

Reginald poured the tonic and sampled his own drink before looking at young Lucinda again. In her 20s ,maybe, neat, copper-coloured hair with a fashionable fringe. Cream-coloured linen trouser suit, well-fitted and perfect for a sunny afternoon. "What brings you to Plantagenet House on Saturday afternoon?"

"Odd name. Plantagenet." She let the pause lengthen, and in the end, Reginald was forced to admit that it was his idea of a joke, one that had fallen flat. He smiled. She didn't.

"Ask again. What brings you to sunny Audley End?"

Miss Clayton continued. "When I finally found your lovely home, I parked on the drive, and as I approached the front door with the intention of ringing the bell, it opened as if by magic, and a lady appeared. Unfortunately, I mistook her for your wife. I was quickly disabused of that assumption; her name was Braithwaite. I was then asked bluntly what my business was. After I told her, she escorted me, I must say reluctantly, into your spacious garage and informed me that if I used the door at the back of the garage, I would find myself in the garden. She continued to watch me until I reached this lovely retreat. And what a generous garden as well, if you don't mind me saying so? Long and beautifully manicured lawn! Mrs Braithwaite said you would be found in your 'Hide'. So here I am."

"Right, got you here. Why are you here? That's the next question uppermost in my mind."

"I work for a private firm. We facilitate confidential communication between persons, nothing more. I have to say, very exclusive."

"Got you," Reginald said, although he had no idea what she was talking about.

"I have a message for you from a person with whom you are acquainted, and it was thought necessary for me to relay the message to you personally. And in the strictest confidence. So, here I am."

"Well. Here I am personally, and this is as private as it gets." Reginald was still none the wiser.

"I have a letter for you from the lady I believe you know. Her name is Marcia."

"Yes. Met a Marcia. Letter, you say?"

Ms Clayton opened her bag and withdrew an envelope of discreet, palest blue colour.

"This missive"—she indicated the envelope—"is from Marcia. It is, as you see, unopened and of a most confidential nature. She asked me to draw your attention to the contents and act as you see fit. I have been instructed to take a reply, either written or, if short, verbally."

"Thank you." Reginald opened the envelope and pulled out a sheet of heavy, startling white paper. The letter was handwritten, and as one would expect, the writing was beautifully executed on the copy plate. Ms Clayton sat back and waited for Reginald to read the contents and reply if that was his wish.

Dear Reginald,

Please forgive this intrusion. May I draw the attention of your firm to:

(1) Mr William Oldham, of Bromsgrove and
(2) Mr, which might even be 'Herr', Leon Weber.

Both gentlemen are members of an exclusive golf club near Evesham, Worcestershire, the club where a member of parliament died of a heart attack recently. The addresses of these gentlemen can be obtained from Ms Clayton. I would be grateful for background information and any other particulars you think appropriate on the two, considering the company with whom you now work would be ideal for such an undertaking. I hope sincerely that you have settled into your new position and that your wife continues in excellent health.

Marcia.

Reginald mulled the matter over for a while, refilling his glass automatically but too preoccupied to offer Ms Clayton another drink. This matter must be delicate for Marcia to contact him and the firm for which he was an advisor. On the one hand, he didn't want or need to get involved with the intelligence services again, as once was enough, and on the other, he was intrigued.

"Ms Clayton." Reginald had made up his mind and noticed Ms Clayton's empty glass. "God! Sorry! Another drink?"

"Thank you. No."

"I'll keep this short. Regards to Marcia. I'll engage the firm. Our expenses will be billed. Marcia will deal with that, I'm sure. Believe you have two addresses that you can give me."

The shoulder bag was opened once more, and another sealed envelope was handed over. "I will leave you now. May I call again next Saturday morning for verification that your firm is taking this matter and to explain future communications between Marcia and yourself?"

"Yes. Make myself available. Late morning?"

"Thank you. Morning. There is no need to see me off the premises, I can find my way. Until next Saturday…"

"Ms Clayton, it would be less than gracious not to accompany you to your car. Please allow me…" Reginald stretched past her and opened the door. He went with her through the garden and house and back to her car. She was impressed by the conservatory, dining room and hall, murmuring appreciatively as they walked to the front entrance.

"Thank you for seeing me." She turned and extended her hand. "I will convey your acceptance to the invitation later today."

Reginald closed the door behind her and sighed. The matter was by no means straight forward, and he returned slowly, head bowed to the 'Hide', on this occasion, not to watch the birds and their private lives but to consider his obligations and his own private life. Marcia, he knew, was a senior member of the intelligence services. He had not the faintest idea of how he, an outsider, or the firm could be of use. There was, of course, earlier history between Marcia and him, not always with as much mutual respect as he would have liked. Marcia's interest in these two characters would become clear. But of immediate concern was to persuade his wife, Diane, that he was not going to agree to any programme with which he wasn't comfortable and, importantly, would interfere with plans for their joint future.

As an adviser to the firm, he could leave surveillance to others, but there would come a time, he was sure, that a more personal approach would be needed. Returning slowly to the shed, he poured a stiff gin and added a splash of tonic and ice. Absentmindedly, he noted that the heron was stationary as ever, watching the stream with total concentration. It was strangely soothing.

Diane arrived home at 5:30 and, after pouring herself a generous, dry sherry, walked down the lawn to the stream and Reginald's 'Hide', a much nicer name she thought, than 'shed', and called to him as she opened the door. He twisted around in his chair to welcome her. She immediately saw two glasses on the ledge.

"Visitor, Reginald?" She sat on the vacant canvas chair, sometimes described by her friends as robust, she thought of herself as well-upholstered and fitted, therefore, into the casual chair with the same obvious comfort that Reginald enjoyed in his own.

"Yes. Yes." Reginald looked out of the window. "Young lady from a firm of private communicators—have you ever heard such nonsense—brought a message from Marcia. You remember Marcia?"

"Of course. A lady of seniority and considerable charm and learning. But what of this young messenger?"

"Oh, Lucinda? Nice enough."

"Pretty on the eye?" Diane liked to know of young ladies who visited her husband.

"Yes. Yes." Reginald was deliberately off-handed. Diana was not deceived.

"And what message did this young lady convey?"

"Apparently, Marcia wants me to mention a couple of names to the firm."

"Does she indeed, and to what end, may I inquire?"

"No idea." Reginald finished his drink and poured another. "Want one?" Diane held up her sherry glass, which was still half full. "Probably nothing."

"If I know anything about Marcia, 'nothing' never enters her mind." A thoughtful silence developed between the two, perfectly amiable, but both were deep in thought. They finished the drinks. The understanding between them was such that both knew Reginald would go to London and, more importantly, resist any full-time employment and assiduously avoid any interruption to their plans. Or at least try. If there was to be no escape, he would be mindful of the consequences. There was no need for any discussion.

"Getting chilly?" Reginald felt the coolness of the evening approaching.

"Shall we go up to the house, Reginald? I'll throw something together for our supper. We'll have it in the conservatory. There will still be heat from the afternoon there. Warm and relaxing."

"Absolutely, Diane." Reginald was looking forward to his supper. Mrs Braithwaite had Saturdays off, and Diane, the daughter of a knighted gentleman in a grocery chain store business, was no mean cook. They walked up the lawn hand-in-hand.

*** *** ***

On the same Saturday afternoon, Marcia left her private hotel in Chelsea and drove at a leisurely pace on the M40 to Oxford, then through Godstow Village, past the world-famous Trout Inn, and arrived in the village of Wytham, pronounced Witham. She hardly glanced at the handsome houses and cottages as she drove through and onto a single-track road that snaked its way for a couple of miles through Wytham Woods and ended in a group of houses that surrounded an area of grass. Not enough houses to call it a hamlet, and the community was clearly of substantial means. Marcia's cottage was the smallest house in the group, with only four bedrooms. So secluded was the enclave that only a few locals even knew of its existence, but luckily the local postal worker knew the houses and even their names.

She parked the car on the wide drive, collected her small case and opened the front door. As if by magic, her name had changed to Charlotte Green, her occupation to 'something in the City of London', her status to widow and her address to 'Two Bridges', near Wytham. Her neighbours, with whom she hardly ever conversed, viewed her as a rich, very elegant widow. The most popular rumour was that she worked in a City of London merchant bank and most probably owned it! She did nothing to disabuse them of this belief.

Her evening had been booked weeks ahead; she had been invited by Julian, a retired Mandarin of the Home Office now elevated to the House of Lords, to an experimental theatrical evening in one of Oxford's ancient colleges; a play written by two undergraduates was one that had no stage scenery, no curtain, no props, but hopefully some stimulating dialogues. She arrived at the ancient college at 7:30 for 8:00 pm and accepted a glass of Chateau Chauvin from the bottle Julian had so thoughtfully bought.

"Julian," she murmured, "to what do I owe this enchanted evening?" She looked around the large common room that had been converted into a withdrawing room with leather armchairs, long settees and well-padded upright chairs scattered haphazardly around the room. In the centre, a dining table with four dining chairs took pride of place.

"I thought merely to entertain you differently. You may find it interesting." Julian, white-haired, senior and impeccably dressed, only occasionally visited the seat of government these days but was nonetheless held in the highest esteem by 'those who mattered'.

"I hear you have been elevated to the upper house." Marcia congratulated him.

Julian looked about with undisguised embarrassment, as if Marcia had made a vulgar noise. "Well, one must park oneself where one is told," he muttered hastily.

They settled themselves to hear three and then four undergraduates discuss, around the central table, the importance of philosophy in a society that was multiracial and gender confused and the meaning of common sense! The audience was encouraged to take part in the discussion but seemed reluctant to do so. It was virtually incomprehensible to Marcia or 'Charlotte', depending upon who you were, but she smiled patiently.

After the last few words were uttered by one of the actors, Julian turned to Marcia and asked, "Well?"

Marcia was unsure whether to speak honestly and admit to complete and total boredom or behave as a gentlewoman and compliment the players and, by association, Julian himself. "Interesting," she ventured.

"Rubbish!" was Julian's opinion.

As they savoured the wine, the conversation inevitably drifted to the latest 'cockups' in the government and civil service. Julian, although a raconteur of considerable flair, abruptly changed the subject. He spoke quietly.

"Forsythe? A name to you?"

"Peripherally," she replied enigmatically.

"My hunch, make it central. Slippery customer, he has been stalking the corridors of power to Treasury, Defence, Home Office and Industrial Strategy."

"A busy person."

"Exceedingly."

"Should I know more?"

"We were hoping you might help with that." Julian poured each of them another glass.

No more was said on the topic, and finally 'Charlotte Green' ordered a taxi, returned to her cottage and retired to bed. That was the second time Forsythe's name had cropped up, and that was much more interesting than that wretched play.

*** *** ***

Chapter Five

On Sunday morning, the day after the visit of Ms Clayton, Diane woke early following a sound, dreamless sleep and eased herself from the marital bed without rousing Reginald. Downstairs, she leant against the kitchen table, waiting for the kettle to boil, and watched the sun rise behind the willows into a cloudless sky. A glorious September morning, a joy to be alive, Ms Clayton or not! With water boiling, she made two cups of tea and carried them to the bedroom. Reginald was awake.

"Lovely day." Diane put the cups on the bedside tables.

"Warm afternoon shouldn't be surprised." Reginald stretched.

"Those the papers?" Diane had heard the delivery of the oversized Sunday Telegraph.

"What's not to like?" Reginald got out of bed.

"Reginald! Where on earth do you get these extraordinary expressions?" Diane scolded.

"Here and there. You know how it is." Reginald remembered his erstwhile receptionist, Clarissa, but said nothing.

A perfectly ordinary Sunday at Plantagenet House.

*** *** ***

On the same Sunday morning, a family in one of the new estates that had bubbled up in and around Peterborough was getting ready to enjoy the last day trip of the year to the seaside at Hunstanton. Dad, the middle manager of an electrical engineering firm, commuted to Romford on the outskirts of London daily, thus enabling his young family to live away from the turmoil and expense of the capital. By 9:00 in the morning, they had packed a picnic basket, swimsuits, towels and sun cream into the car.

Dad had settled into the driving seat. His wife, in the front passenger seat, had been a nurse when they had first met but had retired after the birth of the children. Later, she volunteered her services during the pandemic, which mercifully seemed now to be in abeyance. All were looking forward to the day at the sea; the boys, aged 8 and 10, were quietly excited, if not as self-conscious as lads of that age tend to be. They sat in the rear seats. The family was set to go. Dad turned the key in the ignition.

It was reported the following day, both in local and national newspapers, that the explosion was heard more than a mile away at the A1(M) service station. Where the car had stood in the driveway, there was a crater measuring six feet in diameter. The windows of the nearest 10 adjacent houses were blown in. It was a miracle that there were no pedestrians on the street at the time. The fire services, ambulances and police cars arrived within minutes, and the counterterrorist police and forensic experts arrived later. Mother, father and the older boy died instantaneously. The younger brother survived with multiple injuries and was taken to Peterborough City Hospital, where he later died.

Abdul Ahmed, his wife Amna and the boys, Muhammed and Nadeem, had all been born in this country. The family were devout Muslims, and their deaths caused intense sorrow, then later anger, not only at the local mosque but in the surrounding community and the school the boys attended. They had all made innumerable friends in their short lives and were acutely missed. Abdul and Amna's different skills were lost. The following Sunday, from their pulpits, priests in the Diocese of Ely and Peterborough and elsewhere throughout Britain roundly condemned the outrage and re-emphasised that social integration was imperative. The government expressed shock and vowed to stamp out racial intolerance.

*** *** ***

Between Milton Keynes and Buckingham, there is a small village, quaint in its own way, with thatched cottages, orchards and a seventeenth-century pub. But recently, the villagers had become agitated, angry and not a little frightened. The cause of their misgivings was to be found at a site not two miles distant, where a building had been constructed to house a small number of patients suffering the chronic effects of drug and alcohol abuse. Alfred Morris, a local farmer with strong views and a loudmouth, aired his beliefs in the bar of the village public house.

"We'll be having bloody murderers next. Rapists; you wait and see. If you've got daughters, be careful. I'm warning you. Pay attention." This last sentence was shouted and accompanied by his fist banging on the bar, which caused two glasses to jump and a retired postman, asleep in a corner, to wake up in alarm.

Said often enough, Alfred Morris' opinion gained credence, and the daughters of the villagers had begun to resist what they considered unnecessary restraints upon their freedom. Something needed to be done. A meeting was called in the village hall, to which the superintendent of the local police authority and the county medical officer were invited. Both attended. It must be said that anxieties were not alleviated, but what the villagers had no way of knowing was that much worse was to occur within the walls of this new residential clinic, and not before long.

The unit had been built despite strong opposition, not only from the villagers but from within the health and social services. Practitioners expressed little expectation of success for a unit that was experimental; they reminded those who were planning this clinic that addicts were notoriously difficult to treat and complained of the enormous cost. There were to be two nurses to every patient, day and night. One senior, red-faced and short-tempered surgeon remarked, "And post-pandemic as well. Leaves me speechless." Two junior doctors sincerely hoped it did.

On the Sunday that Reginald and Diane planned their leisure activities for the day and Abdul and his family were killed in such atrocious circumstances, within the new unit, a patient collapsed without warning and suffered an epileptic seizure, witnessed by a senior sister on the internal CCTV. The patient was doubly incontinent and died within minutes. Of course, misuse of drugs was suspected, but it was quickly realised that this was no ordinary reaction to illicit drugs; instead, it was something far more serious.

Urgent help was requested from the Regional Health Authority, the police were informed, and finally, the armed forces and Porton Down, the National Research establishment near Salisbury, where specialists in poisons that might threaten national safety were to be notified. Emergency measures were taken at once, and the unit with patients and staff still within it was closed, sealed and guarded by the police and army. If, as was assumed, this was nerve agent poisoning, the consequences could be catastrophic. The body of the dead patient was removed under the tightest anti-contamination measures and taken to a London hospital for a specialist post-mortem examination. The patient was of Asian heritage.

*** *** ***

On the same sunny September Sunday, a third atrocity occurred in Britain, this time in Brighton. If you had been walking on the promenade that evening and turned to saunter into the small, historic streets behind the huge hotels on the front, you might have come across an insignificant public house, surrounded by terraced houses and shops, only 400 yards from the sea. By 9:30 pm on this Sunday evening, the small, friendly bar was crowded, and the atmosphere was jovial and friendly. There was lively chatter and much laughter. If you had gone into this bar, you might have noticed that there were several same-sex couples clearly enjoying a Sunday evening together.

Brighton is known for its acceptance of the LGBTQ+ community, and this bar was no exception and welcomed liberal attitudes. It is to be hoped that you had taken one drink and departed before 9:47 pm, because at that time precisely the clock above the bar was shattered with bullets and stopped at that time; the door opened, and a young man dressed in leathers and a motorbike helmet with the visor still in place entered, carrying a Heckler and Koch submachine gun, emptied 30 to 50 rounds into the crowd, turned and left the bar. Without haste, he climbed onto the pillion seat of a waiting motorbike and was driven away.

He had killed over a dozen customers and injured another ten.

*** *** ***

Again, on that fateful Sunday evening, after supper, Reginald and Diane moved into the withdrawing room, as Diane liked it to be called, settled into cushioned armchairs and picked up their books. Reading for a couple of hours before bed would complete an enjoyable day. The interlude with Ms Clayton, a mere memory, to be dealt with tomorrow. At 9:00 pm. Diane spoke.

"Reginald, switch on the television, will you? We'll see the headlines before bed if you like." Reginald turned on the television. As the headlines on *BBC 24 Hours* came on, they both sat up. There had been a car bomb explosion in Peterborough; a family was killed outright, except an eight-year-old lad, who was seriously injured and in hospital. And then some news of a mysterious death or something associated with a clinic in Buckinghamshire.

"God's teeth!" Reginald exploded. "Had enough of shooting in Cyprus. Saw the aftermath, what?"

"I do wish you would stop using that expression, Reginald. It doesn't mean anything." Diane was reproving.

"Bastards, hell's going on now?" Reginald was not cowed by his wife's disapproval and expressed his anger more forcibly. Diane winced but knew what he meant. "And what's this nonsense in Buckingham?"

"Poor people." Diane was more modest in her language but just as upset.

They turned off the television and went to bed. *And after such a glorious day, as well. Not glorious for that family in Peterborough, that is for sure*, Diane thought.

"Poor blighters!" Reginald said.

*** *** ***

Chapter Six

On Monday morning, Reginald woke to find his wife already out of bed and, by the sound of it, downstairs, listening to the radio. He got up, showered, shaved and dressed. Mrs Braithwaite met him at the foot of the stairs and indicated breakfast was waiting in the conservatory. He went in and stopped abruptly. Diane was sitting with her elbows on the table, head in hands, silent. It was a sight not seen in this household often, but profoundly disturbing. He put his hand on her shoulder; she registered his presence and looked up. "I've just heard on the radio, Reginald, that little child, the one that was injured in Peterborough, has just died."

"Bugger." Diane was too upset to admonish him.

"That's the whole family, Reggie." She had never used the abbreviation before.

He sat down. No words were appropriate. He had come across death before, and it was never easy. But he had never seen Diane like this. He felt responsible, but at the same time, he knew he was not responsible. Ridiculous. Neither of them ate. The silence lengthened, and both heard the newspapers fall through the letterbox. Neither of them moved. After a moment, Reginald stood, went to a window and looked out at the garden. He squared his shoulders, clasped his hands behind his back and stood rigidly upright. It didn't help; there was still bugger all he could do about it. He had a feeling of impotence seeing Diane so desolate. A sound behind him indicated that Mrs Braithwaite had put the papers on the table. No one spoke. The silence dragged on. Finally, Diane took a deep breath. "Reginald, you'd better look at the time. You'll miss your train."

"Not going to London today. I'll phone in and say 'unavoidably' detained. Staying here."

"You are going to London today and for two exceptionally good reasons. Firstly, you have a commitment to that firm, and secondly, you will be far more useful in London than you would be moping about here."

He studied her. Resilient woman, no doubt about it, and there was something in what she said. Guiltily, he felt relief. It made sense to see what was going on.

"If you're sure…"

"I'm sure."

That was it, then. He rang the taxi firm, and they sent Cyril to get him to Audley End Station in good time for the 8:45 am. He took an umbrella, no coat. When the car came, he noticed a new dent behind the rear wheel arch, and Cyril had an egg on his tie. Odd, how something so inconsequential could catch his attention.

"London again, Group Captain?"

"Not going as often as I used to, Cyril, thank God."

Young settled into the back and let Cyril drive him. Strange thing; for some reason, he thought of Gordon Baxter. Old mate from the service. Wife left him. Gordon was dead now, poor sod. COVID? A broken heart? Or both? Blasted thing. Then, unexpectedly, he thought of the phrase 'Of mice and men'. Hemmingway? Steinbeck? Maughan? Couldn't remember. Brighton Rock? That was Graham Greene. Hell had that got to do with anything? Ideas kept running around, coming from nowhere and leading nowhere. Hell was wrong with him?

"You'll need a lift home, will you?"

Young shook himself out of his reverie.

"Let you know from London, Cyril. Probably later this morning. Might be this afternoon."

"Right, Group Captain, put it on the bill?"

"As usual, Cyril." It struck Young that Cyril was about the only person to address him by his rank now. Quite reassuring. He waited no more than 10 minutes for the train, but even so, the platform was gradually becoming crowded. When the train pulled in, there was the usual squash and jostle getting aboard. He was lucky enough to get a seat and perched on the edge next to a large man whose fleshy face was covered with a sheen of sweat. The man's neck rose in a solid column of fat from his broad shoulders.

Reginald noticed some bristles just below the ear that had been missed while saving and some grey hairs protruding from the nose. The man's arms were stretched wide, all the better to read the broadsheet he was holding, but all the less room for Reginald. He gave the impression of being clumsy and slow, making no effort to accommodate Reginald. Opposite, an equally large woman sat with her legs widely parted and a wicker basket balanced on her lap. Not a pretty sight on a Monday morning; any morning comes to that.

Reginald looked around the carriage. The passengers were all talking into a mobile, looking at a laptop, or reading a newspaper. It was a carriage full of commuters who were simultaneously elsewhere. Reginald opened his own Telegraph and similarly lost contact with all those around him. In no time, the train was pulling into Liverpool Street Station, and the pushing and barging through the narrow carriage door began. Reginald was struck twice by backpacks carelessly swung with no thought for fellow travellers. Once quite painfully. He managed to get off the train and join the crowd rushing down the platform. As he neared the barrier at the end of the platform, he had to decide: subway or taxi.

To hell with the expense. He went out of the station to the waiting row of taxis and, at once, felt the heat; there was thunder in the air, and looking up, he saw the blue-black clouds gathering to the south. The noise of traffic and the rushing, pushing urgency of commuters were part of the excitement of London. But it was more than the vibrancy of London. There was an electric feel to the air. Having found a black cab, he climbed in and found the interior large, comfortable and quiet.

"Guv?" The driver twisted to speak.

"I was going to say 'Putney Bridge', but looks like walking's out of the question. Parson's Green; the triangle, please. Let you know when we're there."

"You're right. Here's the rain." Reginald could see sheets of rain sweeping across the sky and hear the chatter of the torrential downpour on the taxi roof and then the clatter of the windscreen wipers at full speed. No time to be walking. After a hazardous journey through central London, they entered Parson's Green, and Reginald called the address through the open partition, and when they arrived, he paid and faced the elements under his umbrella. The central triangle was deserted; trees dripped rainwater continuously, puddles enlarged at an alarming rate, and the few raked leaves were flattened into untidy mounds against the wet earth. Dead leaves lay flat and stuck to shining pavements, making them slippery for unwary pedestrians.

Reginald arrived at the door of 'Mendel Partners', turned around, shook, folded his umbrella quickly and entered. The building, an anonymous pile of bricks, was originally built before the last war as flats had been converted into shops on the ground floor and independent businesses shared the upper five floors. Mendel Partners took up three floors, one above another. The lift was silent, smooth and with padded walls. He stepped out into reception and greeted Lorraine.

"Group Captain. How lovely to see you." The receptionist always greeted him with a surprised expression, one of pleasure. Lorraine, who was known to the clients as Ms Taylor, exuded the confidence of someone on top of her job. From her tightly set hair and horn-rimmed glasses to the tip of her manicured fingernails, she radiated efficiency. Her knowledge of the Internet caused Reginald sleepless nights, and her memory for client details competed with the records kept so assiduously by the registry department.

She was the focal point of the firm, which was divided into several sections: finance and financial stability research; another, investigating the behaviour of individuals, which was once a lucrative divorce section but is now, after overdue legislation, rather more limited; an executive research department, which was more commonly known as head-hunting; and a general research department that responded to individual client needs. Lorraine had knowledge of each division and, most importantly, coordinated their work. The staff had steadily increased in numbers since the launch of the firm, but when needed, more personnel were engaged; this might be one of those times.

"Are we busy, Lorraine?" The group captain was politely seeking conversation rather than asking an important question.

"As always, Group Captain. As always." Lorraine adjusted her glasses and raised her eyebrows—an unspoken query.

"Can I see Mason? Any chance?"

"Mr Mendel is always pleased to see you, Group Captain. Please, take a seat." Reginald sat.

After a quiet consultation on the internal phone, Lorraine looked up. "Will you need a lot of time, Group Captain? Mr Mendel is busy this morning."

"No more than ten minutes or a quarter of an hour."

"Fine. And would you like anyone else in your meeting?"

"I think only from 'Investigations', if anyone is available."

"I know Mr Cotterell is in. I'll let him know he is needed. Will you want my services?"

"Not yet, Lorraine, but maybe not before too long." Reginald stood. He knew the way.

Mason Mendel was a large man with a surprisingly quiet voice. He stood as Reginald entered the spacious office and came around his heavy desk with his hand outstretched.

"Reginald. Good to see you. Not often you get time for me. Everything all right at home? Diane in good spirits? Bird watching not driving you mad? Coffee?" Reginald shook his head. "You've not come about the shootings in Brighton, I suppose? Nor the business in Peterborough? Nasty, both."

"Yes. Yes. No. And no, thank you." Reginald ticked off the answers on his fingers. "And 'no', not those tragedies either."

"Right. So, what can we do for you?"

Mason had started the business some 15 years previously and had gradually enlarged it into a competent investigative company that would research, in detail, individuals, their background, suitability for recruitment, financial standing and so on. Often, he had used staff from an agency in Chelsea, but lately others had joined as advisors or had a special introduction into businesses that would be useful to the company. Reginald was one of these later additions. Word had come from Whitehall that he was an experienced manager, and Mason was promised work from government sources. Also, Reginald had been advised by his own accountant to invest the settlement he had received from Whitehall into the firm. He had joined as a minor investor and part-time advisor.

"Point is, Mason, a tricky one. Bit of a puzzle. But believe me, it'll be well paid."

"Sounds interesting. Go on." At that moment, there was a knock, and Ray Cotterell from 'Investigations' came in.

"You wanted me?" he asked.

"Ray, come in." The three sat in easy chairs before the desk. "Looks like Reginald might have something for us."

Reginald looked from one to the other. He knew them, of course, but the extent of his knowledge was restricted.

"Think I need assurance of confidentiality." He looked at them again.

"Tight, is it?" Mason asked.

"I was in the police before, you know?" Ray murmured. "I know when to keep my mouth shut." Reginald sat for a moment. This was an inquiry that he wanted to follow, but…

"Look, Reginald, everything is within these walls." Mason spoke patiently. "I've already had communication that you might be bringing a delicate matter to us. You have no need to worry."

Ray Cotterell nodded, as if he already knew this was coming. Reginald made up his mind. "Right. This is it." He pulled out the envelope that Lucinda had given him on Saturday and opened it. "On here are two names and addresses. Want background, occupation, dirt, if any, that sort of thing."

"One is in Worcester. The other is in Bromsgrove. You'll need two operatives," Cotterell reasoned. "The two might speak together. It's easy enough to get another investigator. Leave that with me."

"Thing is," Reginald decided to continue, "Donald Muirhead, an MP of little influence that I know of, died while playing golf on a course near Evesham. These two characters are members of the same club. Why Whitehall (he left Marcia's name unsaid) is interested is a mystery to me. But there you are. They want background—and I suppose anything you can dig up."

"Finances?" Mason wanted to know.

"If we can."

"Might have to get the accountancy department involved. I'll talk with them. You better come along, Ray." Mendel had taken over.

"Like I say, don't know what the fuss is about."

"Thank you, Reginald. Shall we meet again in a fortnight. Quick enough?"

"I think so. Fella's been dead for a month at least."

Reginald left and strolled to his office, which was so small that he had room only for a tiny desk large enough to accommodate a laptop and not much else. The room's redeeming quality was a long window, which would have given him a fine view of the 'triangle', but even that was spoilt by a huge tree growing immediately outside that also blocked most natural light. But today, there was not much of that either; sheets of rain continued to pour down. Perhaps in winter, when all the leaves had fallen and it was not raining, he would have a view that would be more exciting. He slumped behind his desk.

No doubt the firm had received commissions from Whitehall as had been promised, but he had no way of knowing. And that made the present assignment urgent, at least in his world. It was the first directly from Marcia, and if she were interested, then it was important. Yet, for the life of him, he could not see why two characters in a golf club in Worcester held any interest in her. Possibly, that would become clear. Anyway, this was his first major contribution to the company's business. Success might bring more, and that would be positive. He would feel useful, and that was an essential part of his nature. This could be a starting point for more valuable contributions. But… and there were a few 'buts'… He contemplated his position in the firm for some time, all the while gazing at his oil painting, a seascape he had taken from his office in Whitehall that Diane would not have in the house. His 'Hide' in the bushes for birdwatching was an alternative place. Yes, he'd take it home.

He felt cautiously optimistic. Enough for today. He looked out at the weather, or as much as he could see of it, and decided on a cab to his club. Why not?

"Thank you." He closed the door of the taxi and turned into the club. Lunch was a secondary consideration; in any case, it was too early. He left the painting at the porter's kiosk. A drink was what was needed. He made for the 'library'. As he entered the large refuge for tired gentle-members of the club, the first thing he noticed was the smell of dust and old leatherbound books. Then the quiet, just a murmur, of muted conversation from the far corner. Only two chaps, looked like civil servants, pin-striped suits, trouser creases you could cut your finger on, bent forward over a small table on which rested their drinks, heads together concocting some intrigue or other, no doubt. The place was otherwise deserted except for the ever-present wine butler. Reginald caught Wilfred's eye, and the butler made his way towards him as he sat in a window recess.

"Group Captain. We have not seen you for ages. A pleasure, indeed."

"Thank you, Wilfrid. Well, are you?" Reginald smiled and looked around. "Club seems empty. Where's the brigadier who was usually over there?"

"Sad, I am afraid, sir. Knocked over by an omnibus, a Number 27A, I believe, as he left the club, just getting dark, must be some four weeks ago."

"Awkward, what? Don't have an accident with a police car or a bus. Too much paperwork."

"Oh, I do not think the brigadier will worry too much about that, sir."

"How's that?"

"He is dead, sir."

"Bugger me. Sorry." Cursing in the club was considered bad manners and required him to contribute to the staff's Christmas fund. He handed Wilfred a fiver. "Makes you think." Again, he looked around the club. "And Clive? Had his fill for the day?"

"Oh, no, sir. He has not been with us for some time."

"Not dead as well, for God's sake, is he?"

"No, sir. Taking a restorative break in the priory, I believe. And before you ask, sir, Mr Pringle is also unwell."

"Old Pringle. Used to call him Pussy Pringle; damned if I know why." Wilfred knew very well 'why' but kept the information to himself. "What's wrong with him?"

"A touch of gout, I believe."

"O-o-oh…painful!" Reginald crossed his legs and settled into the chair. "Think I might manage a G & T; get over the shocking news, Wilfred. Know what I mean? Double gin, me thinks."

"It always was a double, sir." Wilfried wandered off to make the drink. The very engine of the club, old Wilfred. Wouldn't know what to do without him. And his knowledge of the horses was quite remarkable.

Reginald succumbed to the cushions of his armchair and waited for his drink to arrive. The library was quiet, thankfully nearly empty. He used the club for periods of rest, respite times. It allowed him to gather his thoughts and take a more positive approach. Not naturally introverted; nevertheless, he knew he was treading water. Missed more constructive work. His gin and tonic arrived, along with lemon and ice. It was on his account, but he would tip Wilfred on the way out. Usual practise.

Now. Matters in hand. Working part-time was too fragmented. He wanted to be involved in a continuous undertaking. As it was, the job was frustrating. The arrival of Ms Clayton and the messages from Marcia had been a 'Godsend'. The reaction of the firm was positive, and Ray Cotterell et al. were welcome. Marcia must a suspect menace within society that needs finding. Quite how an important but explainable death of an MP on a golf course in Evesham had to do with it remained, for Reginald, an enigma. But he knew Marcia and wasting time was not high on her agenda. Neither he nor his company would be wasting time or effort. Patience was needed; there would be a more hands-on approach.

And at home, he and Diana had to talk seriously about their joint project and, more importantly, start to organise it.

After three-quarters of an hour and, astonishingly, only one drink, Reginald got up to go. He tipped Wilfred handsomely, and as the rain had stopped, he walked to the underground station with a much lighter step.

*** *** ***

In mid-afternoon, the train was almost empty. Reginald was not inconvenienced by a large man on the seat next to him or by the unwelcome sight of a larger lady sitting opposite him. He was able to watch the countryside sliding past and drying out from the morning's downpours in relative comfort. Cyril was waiting for him at Audley End, and he was home before 4:00. Mrs Braithwaite was singing tunelessly in the kitchen. He could relax in the lounge and read the local paper he had picked up at the station. Not for long. He heard the front door, and then Diane appeared in the lounge.

"You're home early, Reginald."

"Yes, Diane. Finished quickly. Went into the club for a snifter."

"Thought you might," she replied knowingly. "I'll get some tea, shall I?"

"Thanks, Diane. And we can catch up. How do you feel anyway? Better than this morning, I hope." He looked at her carefully.

"Oh, yes. Came to terms with it. Everyone is talking about it at the hospital, of course." She had just finished her shift at the London Hospital, where she was a volunteer in the gift shop. "There's no further news, as far as I know. A corpse was sent for special investigation. Word has it, it might be poison."

"Know nothing about that." Reginald was not interested. He had mentioned the bomb and shooting to Mendel, but only in passing. "We had other things to discuss. About Marcia's message, you know."

"I know not to ask questions." She left to organise some tea and, no doubt, chat with Mrs Braithwaite. That suited Reginald. Diane did not take long, and they sat with their cups of tea before Reginald could draw breath.

"And how was Mendel?" Diane had never met the man but had heard about the firm. "Good spirits, was he?"

"You know." Reginald spoke vaguely, looking into the garden and crossing his legs. "You know." Of course, Diane did not 'know' that was the point of the question, but she let it go. Diane, also, did not know of Marcia's curious interest in the late Donald Muirhead, and if asked, she would have confirmed, like 90% of the population, that she had never heard of Donald Muirhead. That would change over the next few months.

*** *** ***

Chapter Seven

Stratton and Mountford arrived together at 'The School' in Streatham for the meeting with Marcia on Tuesday, three days after the tragedies in Brighton and Peterborough and the day following Reginald's visit to Mendel Partners. They had spoken briefly on the way and had agreed that there seemed little if anything in Marcia's preoccupation with Donald Muirhead or his wife but they were prepared to discuss it further with her.

As they walked together through the kitchen, neither Antoine DuPont, who was reading a newspaper and drinking coffee, nor Delphine DuPont, who was busy with the oven, looked up or spoke.

"Brace yourself for an hour's agony on those bloody chairs in there," Hugo murmured as they climbed the stairs.

"And the darkness of the room and the obscurity of Marcia's thinking." Nigel surprised himself with such linguistic agility. Hugo looked at him but said nothing. They knocked and entered.

The room was, as expected, in shadow, and the chairs looked as unforgiving as always. Marcia invited them in, offered a chair each and, without any apparent irony, told them to 'make themselves comfortable'. They sat, and before Marcia could make a start, Stratton said, "Nigel and I have been giving this some thought. We are a long way from being persuaded that this is a fruitful line of inquiry." He was brusque, almost offensive, but Hugo had meant to be challenging or mischievous, not rude.

"Thank you, Hugo; I approve of discourse and"—she paused—"constructive discussion." Marcia sat up straight as if to embark on a lecture.

"Let us start with Reginald. The group captain, I am sure you remember from previous conversations here and your part in the development of his ANCOM committee." She stared at both, but without waiting for a reply, went on, "You may remember him as an eccentric, post-service, lightweight, although robustly built. I remember him, on the other hand, as a thoughtful and perceptive observer and a tenacious seeker of honest purpose."

Mountford, wriggling as usual, running his hands through his hair and tapping his foot continuously, was not prepared to doubt her word. Stratton was. Frowning, he said, "I thought that we put an end to his ANCOM committee."

"And for very good reasons," she exclaimed. "We wanted to focus Reginald's attention elsewhere—Norfolk, as I remember—allay suspicions and lead the miscreants to believe we had lost interest. But of course, in truth, Reginald had reinforced our beliefs. And the closure of that interdepartmental committee was no reflection of my admiration for the man." Then, as a rebuke, she added, "I thought you knew that, Hugo."

"I did," Hugo responded curtly.

"Well then…" Marcia left it there. "Continuing for the moment with the group captain, he is now employed part-time working for a firm of inquiry agents known as Mendel Partners, and I have asked him to involve them in the examination of Leon Weber and William Oldham, two members of the golf club, Nigel, of which you are familiar."

Mountford was indeed familiar with the golf club and the members mentioned.

"Now we await the results of these inquiries, and we will, no doubt, be asking Reginald to join us here sometime in the next few weeks."

Mountford nodded vigorously. Stratton, still trying to come to terms with the 'correction' delivered so openly, remained broodingly silent.

Marcia now moved on. "Let us, for the moment, turn our minds to the dreadful events in Brighton and Peterborough over the weekend. Although the perpetrators have yet not been named, I have noticed that the two events show certain atypical features. Firstly, there was no warning given of either incident, and secondly, no one or no one organisation has claimed responsibility publicly; for the time being, the organisation wants to remain anonymous."

Mountford nodded in agreement that the incidences were atypical.

"However, killing members of a gay community in Brighton and Asian immigrants in Peterborough, in fact, they were wrong about that, is usually the work of extreme political factions. Usually, such factions claim responsibility. This group did not."

Stratton, still smouldering, declared there was no evidence of such an organisation.

"No, Hugo, that is the whole point."

It was Mountford's turn to frown. Disagreements between Marcia and Stratton were infrequent, but there was no doubting the tension that simmered. There was a gentle knock on the door, which at once opened to admit Madame DuPont carrying a tray of coffee and biscuits, distracting them for a moment. "Thank you, Delphine." Marcia smiled, welcoming the intrusion, and Mountford, if not Stratton, relaxed a little. Delphine DuPont left the room and closed the door. Stratton accepted a cup of coffee from Marcia with politeness, added milk and sugar, but without speaking, walked slowly to the window and leant against the frame, gazing out into the street.

Mountford wondered if this was merely to stretch his legs, or with Hugo's back set squarely against the room if this was pique? Marcia also wondered, got up and went to the window. The two contemplated the empty, silent street, not speaking. Hugo realised the stupid position in which he had levered himself and spoke. "Marcia, I'm sorry."

For an instant, Marcia did not reply and then carefully said, "Our aims require our undivided attention, Hugo. I think the inquiry will come together and produce a result well worth waiting for. We need your ability here."

Hugo nodded.

The aroma of coffee had gradually spread through the room and promised warmth and amiability enough to moderate anyone's irritability. Hugo spoke again. "Shall we get on then?"

Behind them, Nigel smiled.

They settled themselves into their chairs as comfortably as possible. Stratton's concerns were well founded, and it was up to Marcia to persuade him, and Mountford, of course, the virtue of her thinking. She suspected the incidents in Brighton and Peterborough were somehow connected, and as well as that, they were also connected to the financial affairs of Donald Muirhead and his wife, Frances. She straightened her skirt, brushed invisible dust from it and clasped her hands on her lap.

Inwardly, she was not as confident as she looked. What she was about to suggest was based on a mixture of facts, such as they were, her intuition and experience. When collated, if she were correct, they would lead to an organisation that might threaten society, at the very least. There was much to be discussed. Hugo Stratton and Nigel Mountford knew they needed to concentrate.

"Let us begin again, but with the facts as we know them." Marcia started. "We have two atrocities, one in Brighton and the other in Peterborough, that have caused many deaths. The victims were either of the gay community in Brighton or a family, British-born, of Asian descent in Peterborough. Following the deaths, there has been no forensic evidence found that identifies the criminals yet. Suffice to say, more than one individual was involved in Brighton; we know that certainly there was a motorcyclist as well as the assassin, and more than one person in Peterborough, although for the time being that is tentative speculation."

Mountford and Stratton nodded their agreement.

"There was no warning of either atrocity or any claim of responsibility."

Again, the two agents agreed.

Now, Marcia moved on to her intuition or supposition. "It would appear to me that these two incidents were carried out by one organisation that doesn't want to be recognised publicly, at least."

Stratton and Mountford agreed that the incidents were unusual in that respect. However, Stratton, having recovered from Marcia's chastisement, was emboldened sufficiently to say, "But I cannot see your connection to a single organisation, secret or not."

"No." Marcia was quick to concur. "But what we can say is that whoever carried out the murders does not seek publicity."

Mountford, sensing Stratton's conflict with Marcia, appealed for composure: "But, as Hugo says, there is no convincing evidence of a new organisation, secret or not."

"No, Nigel, exactly. That is precisely their objective: anonymity." And after a pause she added, "For the time being. Now, I have some extra information that I want to pass on, which may well alter your thinking and dramatically change our conjectures. I am particularly exercised by the rumours that foreign agents offer extremely large sums of money to certain Members of Parliament or prospective members. It is with this in mind that I could not help but wonder what Donald Muirhead was doing, besides playing golf, in the Vale of Evesham with a closet millionaire from Bromsgrove, one by the name of William Oldham, a person of whom you have heard, Nigel.

"I asked a financial adviser in the city to investigate the matters of the late Mr Muirhead's banking arrangements, and it turns out that they are of great interest. He had several accounts, two of which he used for every day, shall we say, overt transactions. However, he had at least two other accounts into which money was, and still is, paid regularly and which is then transferred just as regularly to an offshore bank."

She paused to let that sink in, then continued. "And if the late Mr Muirhead's accounts are complicated, then wait until you hear of Mrs Muirhead's accounts." She looked at Stratton. "You may remember Gerald Simpkin, one in the group that congregated in the cocktail bar of the hotel after the party committee meeting in Cheshire…"

"I do," Hugo said. "Chap on the edge of the group, looking to be included."

"The very same, Hugo." She smiled. "You may also remember the mention of his wife, Avril Simpkin…"

"I do," Hugo said again. "Lepidopterist; wanted to wander on the Muirheads' land; take photographs of butterflies, that sort of thing."

"The very same. You may have wondered what I was doing in Cheshire, where we had that delightful Italian meal. Well, I knew Avril Simpkin, or Reynolds as she was then, as a schoolgirl, a classmate and later working for our agency."

Stratton nodded. This was par for the course, as far as Marcia was concerned. "I talked with her in the morning before our lunchtime date."

"You did?" A question, but in truth, Stratton was not surprised.

"I did, and she told me that Mrs Muirhead is indeed a very officious woman, a lady who does not suffer fools gladly and is of considerable wealth. The supposition for this wealth is based upon three facts: all the children go to extremely expensive boarding schools; the home is decorated to the highest standards; and the furniture is chosen with care, expense not spared; and on the walls, if Gloria is not mistaken, and she rarely is, are several original paintings of some distinction. Finally, Frances Muirhead often travels to London for undisclosed purposes and stays at five-star hotels, often for a week or so. And that does not come cheaply, you believe me."

"On an MP's wage?" Nigel Mountford amplified the inference.

"Precisely, Nigel. I have not yet had the opportunity to investigate Mrs Muirhead's banking arrangements, but soon I will. I confidently predict that they will be as tortuous as her late husband's accounts."

Stratton and Mountford absorbed these new facts. They shed a whole new light on the suspicions Marcia held.

She finished her coffee and sat silently, looking at the two agents from the intelligence services. She knew she had aroused their interest, and her next objective was to put them to work. And that would be much easier to accomplish now.

"It is for us to investigate any mysterious payments to the Muirhead funds and examine the unusual incidents and reasons for the deaths in Brighton and Peterborough. Find if there are any links between the payments and the atrocities. Finally, my thinking here is that maybe there is a syndicate that is acting with financial impropriety."

Mountford was the first to express his understanding. "You mean, that there may be a consortium of some sort that is regularly transferring monies into the Muirhead accounts for purposes yet unknown and, at the same time, financing an action group that commits incidents likely to be mistaken for the activity of extreme groups. Anti-immigrant, homophobic, racist, whatever. Far right groups, in other words."

"Perhaps we have not heard the last of these incidents," Marcia interjected. "The far left may be implicated as well. I will trouble both of you to keep that in mind."

"Both ends of the spectrum," Hugo added.

"Both blaming each other," Nigel continued.

And then together, they said, "To what aim?"

"If both extremes are in direct conflict, who knows what hostility will breakout," Marcia said, "and how much damage will be done to our fragile economy. Look, for example, at the breakdown of relationships in the miners' strikes. The government and the miners' union were poles apart in ideology, and they were not even extremist groups, never mind thoughtless or sociopathic groups. Such a chasm of hatred between groups might become unacceptable in a functioning democracy. I am suggesting that we may well have a syndicate that is prepared to amplify hatred and mistrust between the extremes to produce a society that is unstable and crying out for leadership. That leadership would then be supplied by that syndicate. Eventually, that would put the total resources of the country at the syndicate's disposal. And that is an enormous amount of wealth."

Stratton and Mountford were concentrating. This was a new concept of which they had no experience. It was for Marcia to fill that vacuum.

"I am perfectly prepared to accept, but much of what I have said is merely speculative." She was being modest. "It may be wide off the mark. But at the very least, we must investigate such a proposition."

Stratton and Mountford were ready to trust Marcia's intuitions. It was obviously now up to them to prove, or otherwise, her theory.

"Hugo and Nigel, I have the greatest respect for your abilities in our murky world of espionage, but your abilities will be tested by what I'm going to ask of you. If I may, can I start with you, Hugo? I know you have vast experience in the field and in management with your overseas postings. I must ask you to use your contacts abroad, if appropriate, to unearth any large movements of monies in or out of Britain. It might be useful to talk with border control and their managers to root out any regular movement of people's obscure merchandise or monies across our borders. Northolt is a usual place for private jets to bring in VIPs. Fortuitously, incoming checks over there are vigorous."

"Right." Stratton said no more.

"Now, Nigel. You have worked within our shores for years, and your lines of communication must be well developed. Can you use your relationships to look at your department's records for unusual or irregular changes in employment, finance, communications and so forth? We have all met with Konrad Taylor of GCHQ[*]. It would be judicious to have a word with him."

"Done." Mountford was still for a moment, which made a welcome change.

"And I will ferret away within the city, use my financial acquaintances to trace any abnormal movements of monies. At this stage, it seems to me that exposing assassination groups is unlikely and may even be counterproductive in the overall picture. With sufficiently shared information, we should be able to pinpoint any large consortia whose membership consists of wealthy and suspicious persons. And one other aspect I will be looking at carefully is the staff in Whitehall and the Standards' Committee at the Houses of Parliament."

"And you mentioned Reginald Young." Stratton spoke quietly.

"Yes. He has invited his firm to give us background information on Leon Weber and William Oldham, members of the golf club. If you have no questions, now, can we meet next week, same time, same place? In the meantime, I'll invite the group captain to join us if you are comfortable with that arrangement?"

They were. The three left.

*** *** ***

---

[*] See 'Watching' (First book in this trilogy)

In the backstreet, a lane really, of Lyfen near Cambridge, Reginald found what he was looking for. A tiny shop with small, unwashed windows displaying several new-edition books in bright colours, but of more interest, behind them were old leatherbound books standing like veteran soldiers. This was the second-hand bookshop if he was not mistaken, and it might have secreted on its shelves the sort of book that he was looking for, one describing the British countryside, cities, towns and historical places of interest. The brown woodwork was peeling, but the door opened with a welcoming ring of a small bell attached to the frame above.

"Come in, dear, come in." A large lady in a voluminous, printed kaftan with badly bleached hair and a smoker's cough that rattled satisfyingly deep in her chest leaned on the counter and looked at Reginald. "Just browsing, are you, dear? Or looking for something special?" At the same time, she put out her hand and turned on the lights. "First customer today. You're early." It was 11:00.

Reginald advanced towards the lady warily.

"I've just been catching up with one of the new books that's come in as a house clearance." She indicated an open book before her on the counter. "Not much of a read. This one's on sixteenth-century country practices in agricultural Britain and is just about as exciting as that. I'll stick it away in 'History'. Now looking for something special?" A raised eyebrow.

That's the second time she's said that, Reginald thought, and the way she was leaning forward on the counter made him even more wary. He became aware of the distinctive smell of whisky.

"Yes," he replied. "My wife and I are newly retired, and we're thinking of travelling Britain, listening to local stories, exploring local customs and enjoying ourselves with a view to writing."

"Been done, dearie. Dickie Drey. Behind you, second shelf down, next to the door, the third book along. Last copy I've got."

"Yes. I'll take that copy. But we were thinking of including France as well…across the Dover Straits, you know."

"I know where France is, dear. I've had more men in Calais and Dieppe than you've had cooked dinners. Thought of settling there at one time, but their health service isn't as good as ours or the one we used to have! You've got to be careful. Anyway, never mind all that, not looking for our 'special' section? Mostly Victorian. Unusual, I'll give it that."

"No. Just travel in Britain and France books. As I say, I'll take the Drey." Looking around the shop with more care, Reginald noticed an iron, spiral staircase leading to the floor above. "More books up there?"

"No. That's the meeting room. We have regular get-togethers of various groups. Coffee, biscuits—that sort of thing. Of an evening; useful income, know what I mean?"

"Of course. Any subjects that might interest me or my wife?"

"Shouldn't think so. By the way, call me Aggie, short for Agatha; quite posh, really."

"Thank you, Agatha," Reginald mumbled.

"About these meetings, one is on Greek philosophers; one is on French kings, can you believe? One is discussing modern books thought of as classics of our times. Oh. There's a new one: the politics of post-Nietzsche thinking and pre-war Germany. That's about it. Interested at all?"

"My goodness, your life is varied. Calais to Nietzsche to Greek philosophers, a full life!"

"Suppose I have. Keeps you young, that's what I say, dear."

She wrapped the Drey book and put the money in a drawer under the counter. Aggie did not run to the till! "When's the political meeting? Might be interested. Name's Reginald."

"Reginald what?"

"Young. Actually, group captain." He thought that might add to his chances of admission.

"Really? I'd have to ask the organiser. They don't take anyone," but then she added quickly, "but you should be welcome, I'm sure. Can you come in next week, at all?"

"Wednesday, next week?"

"Fine; I'll find out."

Reginal left the shop, drove into Cambridge and collected Diane. He was well satisfied with his afternoon's work.

*** *** ***

Chapter Eight

If he had not known better, Hugo Stratton would have suspected supernatural intervention. To be granted an interview with Doctor Shawcross, one of Britain's top cyberspace communication experts in Vauxhall Cross, headquarters of the secret information service, and then to arrange a visit to 'The House', a service annex only a mile away, on the same day, seemed almost too good to be true.

And so it was with a light step that he bounded up the steps to the entrance of Vauxhall Cross at 10:00 am on Thursday morning. Big mistake. Stratton had been an efficient and careful agent working abroad for several years and then a case officer of equal diligence for a few more years. His promotion in the service was not a surprise, and again, being chosen as Marcia's assistant in this present enterprise was justifiable. However, the intricacies of cybercity, cybertechnology and the worldwide information network were another matter altogether.

Virtual information technology was different from dead letterboxes, written codes and all the other devices with which he was familiar. Marcia was convinced that a malevolent syndicate or organisation was involved in influencing British politics and society, and it was expected that their communications were electronic. Part of Hugo's task was to trace information transfers, and to do that, he needed the expertise of Dr Shawcross. Then he met Dr Shawcross.

In a windowless room below ground level, a tall, gaunt figure of a man came forward to shake his hand. Unsmiling and of pale complexion, Dr Shawcross said, "Morning," leaving Stratton with the impression that no 'morning' was 'good' or indeed worth mentioning.

Nevertheless, he replied, "Thank you for agreeing to see me." He received no response. Looking at each other in awkward silence for a few seconds, abruptly, Dr Shawcross said, "Let's sit." They did so.

"What's the purpose of your visit?" Dr Shawcross suddenly asked.

Hugo explained his visit, emphasising his interest in tracing the source of electronic mail and recipients.

"Is it possible to identify people sending information on the net and the receiver?"

"Source computers, certainly. Individuals themselves, that is more complicated. It is not simple."

Dr Shawcross lapsed into expressionless silence. From here on in, Hugo Stratton found that asking a question resulted in a single-word answer, and that word was often monosyllabic. The interview became arduous mostly, Stratton assumed, because of Dr Shawcross' limited rapport. Very occasionally, however, he would use a phrase that would provoke a torrent of words and with deft touches of the keyboard, mountains of meaningless numbers, letters and symbols. After two hours, Stratton realised, firstly, he was out of his depth, and secondly, answers to his basic questions would best be found elsewhere. Thanking Dr Shawcross profusely, he escaped, finally descending the steps outside Vauxhall Cross with less bounce than he had mounted them. He wandered slowly across Vauxhall Bridge, making his way to 'The House'. First, a sandwich and coffee in the Tate Britain café.

*** *** ***

Thames House on the embankment in London is the centre of the British Security Service, commonly known as MI5. Nigel Mountford made his way slowly into the building on the same morning that Hugo Stratton had started out with such optimism. Mountford's mood was less buoyant and for two reasons. First, there was no news of an arrest of the Brighton motorcyclists or the criminals who had killed the Ahmed family in Peterborough.

Much more intimidating, however, was the daunting daily task that lay ahead. He had to walk through a room full of computer operators and programmers, mostly young and female, who treated him with profound distrust or completely ignored him. He had no idea how he had gained such disrespect, but he was always hugely embarrassed. As he hurried to his room, which was slightly larger than his mother's pantry, he heard his name being called. He ignored it and, with a sigh of relief, was about to gain sanctuary in his own space when Connie, one of the more mature programmers, appeared at his side.

"You'll like this," she said, with a well-worn innuendo and waved a scrap of paper at him.

"I will?" he managed as he scurried around his desk to the safety of his chair.

"Oh, yes. It's an invitation." She raised an eyebrow.

"It is?" He was now thoroughly alarmed.

"Today. Now, if you want."

Good God, has the woman finally lost touch with reality? Mountford thought amidst rising panic.

"A prison visit, no less," she teased, sitting on the corner of his desk and ignoring the misplacement of the hem of her skirt. Mountford put out a shaking hand, and she gave him the note. The note informed him that 'the police, in the name of Superintendent Malik, wished to advise him that one, Duncan Campbell, had been apprehended at the M23/M25 junction the previous day and had been later remanded to a London prison in order that further inquiries could be pursued. There was a possible connection to the Brighton shootings'.

"Miss Lakeland, give this prison a call, would you? Let them know I'll be there to see Duncan Campbell at 11:30 this morning." This was advance, at last.

"Very good, Nigel," Connie said, and with an adjustment to the length of her skirt, she returned to the computer room. *Called me Nigel*, Mountford realised. Such were the trials of an officer of the Security Service. He sighed.

At 10:45, Mountford stood, took a last look at the note Connie had given him and ventured out into the room full of desks, silent operators and programmers and the syncopated tapping of keyboard typing. He made a dash for the exit. Halfway across the room, a telephone buzzed on a desk somewhere. He could not help it. He stopped. Everyone was looking at the noise, or at least the operator upon whose desk the telephone was situated, all resenting its intrusion but curious to know who could be phoning. Her boyfriend? Her husband? *Please, not my mother*. The mortified girl grabbed the phone in terror. There was a collective sigh of relief from the rest of the room, and Mountford was able to continue with his exit. Computer keyboards started up again.

"Yes, sir?" The poor girl's fright over, and life, such as it was in the computer room, resumed as if nothing had happened. Mountford completed his escape.

The drive to the prison in southeast London took longer than estimated, and as he drove down the tree-lined carriageway near the institution, he looked at his watch. Ten minutes late? Should not matter. As he turned off the main road, he noticed the almost bare trees hardly hid the prison. It was not the old Victorian institution of everyone's imagination, of brutal architecture, but a relatively newly built prison. However, the perimeter fencing, the high walls with small, mean windows and heavy entrance conveyed the purpose of the building.

Inside the gate, once admittance had been granted, and Mountford's Home Office warrant was inspected minutely, he was reminded that he was 10 minutes late and then questioned closely about his visit. The contents of his pockets were scrutinised and stored, his mobile phone similarly. It was almost with regret that the gate officer discovered he was not carrying a laptop. He was asked to wait.

Eventually, he was escorted along a path and into a building that housed those on remand. The prison officer accompanying him knew nothing of Duncan Campbell and seemed to care less. At last, Mountford was shown into a room with a table bolted to the floor in the centre, and the chairs on the opposite side seemed equally immovable. The prison officer asked him to wait and left, closing the door firmly.

Mountford felt the full effect of a maximum-security prison. Accustomed as he was to such places, it still came with its own special threat of hostility. He ran his hands through his hair, crossed his legs and listened for footsteps. He heard nothing, so it was with a start that he heard the door open and a large prison officer enter the room.

"Conway, sir," the prison officer introduced himself. "And you, sir, if I have not been misinformed"—he looked at a piece of paper—"are Mr Nigel Mountford of the Home Office. Am I correct, sir?"

"You are indeed, Mr Conway," Mountford replied.

"Good. And may I ask which branch of the Home Office? Or is it an official secret?"

"Not a secret, no. But something I don't advertise."

"Got your meaning, sir. Shall we say 'spy' then?"

"Not a spy, no. Just an inquirer from the Home Office."

"Right. Got your meaning." Damn it, Conway nearly winked! "We've got a gentleman here that you have come to see, I believe, sir. Our Mr Duncan Campbell has been a bit naughty, has he?"

"You must know what he's charged with."

"Yes," was a long, drawn-out word. "A few right bastards in here, sir, if you'll forgive the expression. Motoring offence. Strange that, and us a Category A prison, don't get a lot of 'driving without due care' here. Yes, strange that." The officer looked at Mountford and waited.

"Yes," Mountford said. In truth, he knew little more himself, but he was not going to say anything further.

"Before I go fetch him, I'm afraid I must tell you that one of the officers must stay in the room while you interview him."

"Sorry. Must be on my own."

Conway frowned at this and gave the problem some consideration, and finally said, "Right, sir. In that case, handcuffs cannot be removed."

"You sure?"

"Absolutely, sir, regulations."

"Okay."

That dismayed Officer Conway, although whether it was because of the easy capitulation or an officer being denied access to the interview was not made clear. In either case, he went on, "There's an emergency button under the desk." He came around and pointed it out to Mountford. "And all around the wall is an emergency strip. Press that anywhere, and the alarm will sound. Oh, yes," he said as an afterthought, "there will be an officer sitting outside the room." With that, he left to fetch Duncan Campbell.

Campbell came into the room a few moments later, and another officer placed the arrest notes on the table in front of Mountford. Before leaving the room, he removed the handcuffs. Perhaps 'regulations' had not filtered down as far as this officer. In any case, Mountford felt much more relaxed. As always, his persona changed when he was interviewing. He sat upright; gone were the twitches, constant movements and crossing and uncrossing of his legs, to be replaced by a professional 'inquiry officer from the Home Office'. That required his full attention; unnecessary movement ceased.

Duncan Campbell, if he was implicated in the shooting of gay customers in a bar in Brighton, was not what Mountford had expected. This young man, in his early 30s, had well-groomed, slightly long hair, was clean-shaven, and even in a prison shirt and trousers, he appeared well turned out.

"Morning. My name is Nigel Mountford. I am from the Home Office," Nigel introduced himself.

"Morning, Duncan Campbell," came the reply, short but not belligerent. The accent was Oxbridge.

Mountford found a clean sheet of paper at the back of the notes and wrote 'Duncan Campbell'. The pen had been grudgingly returned to him at the gate of the prison.

"Your name, you say, is Duncan Campbell. Any verification?"

"If you mean, have I got my birth certificate handy, then the answer is obviously 'No'. If you take my word for it, the answer is 'Yes'."

"Your age, Mr Campbell?"

"Date of birth: 4 July 1991."

"And your address?"

"No comment." This threw Mountford; it was so unexpected. There had been no hint of reticence until now. He looked at Campbell, trying to decide how best to continue.

"Finding your address, if you have given me your correct name and date of birth, is no problem. Just an unnecessary waste of time."

There was no reply. Nor yet any sign of anger. Campbell looked relaxed.

"And your pillion passenger, what has become of him?"

"No comment."

"You had a pillion passenger, though?"

Silence.

"How do you think I know that? Think I guessed? Think I'm a clairvoyant, do you?"

"I have no idea. But in any case, I have no comment to make on that subject."

"Well, there are CCTV cameras everywhere nowadays and are often found in car parks like hotel car parks." No reaction. "There are also automatic number plate recognition cameras around, especially in restricted areas. Brighton, where you were staying, is particularly blessed with such machines."

"Good for Brighton."

"And the service station, Jeremy's Corner on the M23, is also covered comprehensively."

"Very wise. But again, 'No comment'."

Mountford did not want to create an angry reaction. Change direction. "Heard of the shootings in Brighton, have you?" he asked, watching Campbell closely.

"No comment."

"Well, it is a serious business. And if you are implicated, that is serious for you, indeed."

"No comment."

This fellow Campbell needed some understanding. Not your sociopathic, gay basher but an educated, although unforthcoming young man. At first, he had been reasonably pleasant but gradually developed an air of stubbornness, even sarcasm, and Mountford realised Campbell was obviously neither afraid nor willing to cooperate. But that could be that Campbell was protecting the pillion passenger, but there was something more. Arrogance? Knowledge that somehow he was safe? And secure? But he had been arrested, and before long, sufficient evidence would be gathered to send him away for an awfully long time.

But he seemed unperturbed. And he was not stupid. One last attempt.

"You are clearly a person of education, even social standing, and you must surely understand that your present predicament puts you at considerable risk, at least of further investigation. You must also know that if there is any evidence of a connection to the fatal shootings in Brighton to you, it will mean life imprisonment. Cooperation at this stage would be very much to your advantage."

"No comment."

Mountford continued as if Campbell had not spoken. "Tell me, how come you were arrested?"

"It'll be in the notes, I expect."

"Haven't had time to read them yet. Give me your version."

"No comment."

With an audible sigh, Mountford opened the folder on the desk before him and looked at the charge.

"Shoplifting?" Mountford was astonished.

"No comment."

"What did you steal?"

"No comment."

"What did you take then?"

"Take? What do you mean, 'Take'?"

"That's what I asked you."

Campbell had been sitting back in his chair, hands clasped behind his neck, the picture of relaxation. Now, however, the hands came down slowly, and Campbell leant forward, frowning. "You mean took from a shop?"

"That's what shoplifting usually means."

"No comment." But his attitude had changed; he was no longer the relaxed, comfortable prisoner being interviewed at his own convenience, but suddenly he looked angry and ill at ease. "Shoplifting? That's rubbish! And I've no comment."

But Mountford thought gleefully, *You have just said far more than no comment*. Campbell stood abruptly, and Mountford felt suddenly threatened, but the prisoner turned towards the door and spoke. "No comment. Can I go now?" Mountford shrugged and closed the folder, indicating the end of the interview, but as Campbell reached the door, he turned and strode back to the desk. Leaning on it with straight arms and looking down on Mountford, he growled, "Shoplifting! Shit!" He turned and left the room.

*** *** ***

Hugo Stratton left the Tate Café and made his way to 'The House'. The uninspiring name of the Vauxhall Cross annex came, he supposed, from the fact that the establishment in a backstreet behind Tate Britain was nothing to look at. Detached, double-fronted house with a large, wooden door, the whole building looked rundown and in dire need of paint. There were four windows, and each of the two floors faced the street, and anyone giving them a quick glance, even a slow inspection, would have no concept of the anti-surveillance precautions that had been installed. Stratton knew, although any pedestrian walking past would not, that inside, computers were checking incoming and outgoing electrical communications associated with the secret work of the intelligence service and British security. It was, therefore, with considerable surprise, as Stratton climbed the steps, he noticed the heavy wooden door at the entrance was open.

He need not have worried, for once over the threshold, he was faced with a wall of steel into which a small door was fitted. His security badge, together with iris recognition and thumbprint, allowed the door to be opened, and he walked into the entrance hall. A young lady of careful, if casual, appearance looked up, smiled and asked him his business.

"Can I see Mustafa Satti?"

"Yes. Mustafa. Hang on." She dialled an internal number. "He's on his way up."

"Thanks."

Stratton heard the heavy steps of Mustafa coming up from the basement; the door opposite the receptionist opened, and there he was. Overweight. Out of breath. Smiling widely.

"Hugo. Long time since I saw you. You well?"

"Mustafa, how lovely to see you again. Still on a diet, I see." There was a muffled giggle from the receptionist and a raised eyebrow from Mustafa.

"And I hear you are still engaged to the delectable Miss Marcia!"

"Bloody hell, engaged?" Another giggle from the receptionist. "I work with Marcia. Otherwise, I'm married."

"I know that. It only reinforces the old maxim: 'Never bring your wife to work. Unless she is someone else's lover'."

This brought forth an undisguised laugh from the receptionist and a bemused scowl from Hugo.

"Come down to the centre. Let us do some work." Mustafa led the way.

Downstairs, which Mustafa had called 'the centre', was the hub of the agency. The hum of electrical motors was continuous; paper was being turned out at a significant rate, and five or six operands were reading, filing, re-entering and discarding messages constantly. Hugo's first impression was of demanding work; his second was the trust bestowed upon operators by Mustafa. It must mean a comfortable working environment.

"This is where it all happens?" Hugo looked around.

"This is it," Mustafa replied, with a little pride, Hugo noticed. They went into his office, a tiny space built as an afterthought in one corner.

"So, important electrical traffic."

"That's it. We cover e-mails, websites, phones, voicemail, chat rooms, text messages, social networking and so on and so forth."

"What I'm really interested in is this: can you positively identify a person sending or receiving emails?"

Hugo was keen to keep it at a basic level, and that was made easy by Mustafa, who was a jovial fellow, completely on top of his job and happy to keep things simple. He was different from Dr Shawcross altogether. He told Hugo in record time that the frequency and regular correspondence would alert them to take interest, and if sufficiently suspicious, active measures would be taken to identify the source. The identification of equipment used and the actual contents of communications could be monitored. But as for definite identification of the sender or receiver, that was work in progress.

"So, if a known person or organisation began to send regular messages to a receiver or receivers that could be picked out by your department?"

"If the communications were regular and frequent, that would flag up. If the contents of the communications were suspect, we would take a lot of notice."

"If I were to give you possible senders' organisations or names, would you be able to find them electronically?"

"Given time. A little luck. And a little more than a name, then the answer is 'yes'."

"You've been more than helpful. Makes this morning almost worthwhile."

"Weighed under by 'Boffin' Shawcross, were you?"

"Just a little. I'll be in touch, Mustafa. I may come back to you with more specific problems."

"Fine by me."

Hugo Stratton left 'The House' in good spirits. Not a wasted day.

*** *** ***

Chapter Nine

The following day, a crisp, sunny October Saturday morning, Lucinda turned into Oak Tree Lane, miles away from the subterranean computer rooms of the intelligence service and similarly distant from the miserable existence inside a Category A maximum security prison in southeast London. She was about to talk with Reginald Young for the second time. As she drew up on the drive of Plantagenet House and walked to the front door, her steps were more assured and her mood more confident than on her first visit. The doorbell rang with unexpected musical notes, and eventually the door opened to reveal a robust lady of a certain age. The lady sported a charming smile.

Ms Clayton was unsure. "Mrs Braithwaite?" she queried hesitantly. The smile disappeared to be replaced with a lowering of the eyebrows and a pursing of the lips.

"I am Mrs Diane Young, mistress of this house. And you are?"

"Ms Clayton. Lucinda Clayton. I have an appointment with the group captain," Lucinda stammered.

"Lucinda," the well-built lady mused. "A lovely name. Pity about the incorrect identification you have just made. If the group captain and I had been blessed with a daughter, Lucinda may well have been chosen for her given name." There was no mistaking the emphasis on the word 'daughter'. "But we must not stand on ceremony. Please come in." She stood back, and Lucinda, with a temporary suspension of breath, entered.

"Thank you," she managed.

"I think that you will find Reginald in his 'Hide', even on this less than summery morning. You know the way, I think, for last weekend, you enjoyed a drink with my husband while he observed wildlife at the foot of our garden."

She had made it sound like a romantic encounter, which it certainly was not, and frankly, Lucinda found it laughable. They walked through the house to the conservatory, and Diane watched Lucinda walk down the lawn towards the stream and Reginald. *Slim. Beautifully cut linen suit. Finishing school posture and gait,* Diane thought, although perhaps not completely delighted. She closed the door to the garden and returned to her reading, her concentration unsettled.

Arriving at the 'Hide', Lucinda knocked and entered. Reginald was not peering through binoculars today but reading a book. Second-hand, by the look of it. Richard Drey. The purchase from Aggie's.

"Lucinda? You're early." Reginald turned his portly body towards her. "You'll join me? Tonic only if remembered correctly."

"You remember correctly, Group Captain. Thank you."

"Ice?"

"No, thank you."

"Not many people call me group captain these days; name's Reginald."

"Thank you…Reginald." She accepted her tonic in a sparkling, leaded glass.

"And the good Marcia? Well, is she? As serious as ever?"

"'Good'? I think is a given. 'Well'? She certainly is. 'Serious as ever'? Yes." Lucinda joined the banter.

Reginald closed his book, put it on the desk before him and eased himself into a contented position. He picked up his glass, tasted the drink and added a little more gin. He felt pleasantly relaxed. "What have you got for me today?" he asked. "Another billet-doux?"

"Hardly, Reginald. But if you mean a letter, then yes, I have brought a missive from Marcia."

"How commanding."

Reginald held out his hand and took the sealed envelope. "An invitation to the ball? A secret assignation? A message in code?"

"None of those, I fear." Reginald was pleased that the delightful Lucinda was responding to his nonsense. He opened the envelope. "An invitation to meet with Marcia and two colleagues next Tuesday morning in London. No address though." He turned the letter over in case an address had been written on the reverse. It had not. "No address," he complained, "nor, come to think of it, a time. Not like Madam Marcia that."

"All taken care of, Reginald. I will collect you from Liverpool Street Station at 10:00 in the morning next Tuesday, if that's convenient."

"And if it's not?"

"I will still collect you at 10:00 from Liverpool Street Station next Tuesday morning."

Reginald liked that flash of humour. He was beginning to enjoy her company. The door opened.

Diane stood there, smiling. "Now you two, enough birdwatching or discussion of British secrets; there is a chill in the air, and even with your inefficient paraffin heater, Reginald, you must be getting cold. You must both come up to the house and have a coffee, although I notice you are drinking already. A little early for me," she said pointedly.

"Straight tonic," Lucinda defended herself.

"Just the one," Reginald said to no one in particular.

"Well? Have you finished?"

"Oh, yes. I only came to give the group captain a message." Lucinda looked at Reginald.

"Another trip to London. This time, next Tuesday," he said.

"That will be nice." His wife gazed out of the window.

After a short pause, the three walked up the lawn to the conservatory, and when within, Lucinda spoke. "It's time I got on. Plenty to do. I am sorry; I am too rushed to be able to accept your kind invitation to coffee, Mrs Young. I will see you on Tuesday then, Group Captain."

"Yes. And name's Reginald."

The sentence was met with silence, and Diane turned to take Lucinda to the door.

"Lovely to meet you. You must come again," she said, the charming smile back firmly in place.

*** *** ***

As usual, Hugo Stratton was at his desk in Vauxhall Cross on the same Saturday morning and was intrigued to find an email from Border Customs Force marked 'Urgent'. It informed him that a private jet, a Praetor 600, was landing at RAF Northolt. One of the passengers was Brian Boscombe, 'who may be a person of interest to you'. For the moment, the 'interest' eluded him, but he swiftly recalled that Basil Boscombe was the Earl of Kingsworth, brother to the imprisoned Lady Eleanor Keenan.

He noted the estimated time of arrival to be 23:00 hours; the flight was from Jamaica. The biggest decision he had to make now was whether to go home to his wife and children until about 9:00 this evening or remain in the office. He decided home but took the precaution to remind the duty officer of his home number in case of an early landing.

He went home.

*** *** ***

The heat in Montego Bay was bearable, even in the sunshine at midday. The customs' inspection was gentlemanly, even perfunctory; the Earl of Kingsworth passed through quickly and boarded the Praetor 600 transatlantic private jet, where he found there were only four other passengers, none of whom he knew. The take-off was smooth, and soon they were at cruise height in a perfectly blue sky and thousands of feet above the sea; the Caribbean islands slid behind them. He could now settle back, read a book and totally relax until their landing in Britain at approximately 23:00 hours, local time.

Always content to be returning to Britain, recently the earl had become more cautious. His sister, Lady Eleanor Keenan, was in a maximum-security prison, awaiting trial for treason, and a complete division of Whitehall had been closed because of her suspected treachery. He had sold all his lands and assets in Dorset and Yorkshire and moved to the Caribbean with enough wealth that would ensure a secure and affluent future. Subsequently, he had taken advice that led him to invest wisely and extremely profitably, which enabled him to buy into a consortium of hugely wealthy financiers who, as an organisation, were preparing a business partnership that should prove extremely lucrative, if not exactly legitimate.

His recall to Britain was a summons to a consortium meeting when a date was to be set for the start of takeover by 'Action Britain'. For years, much time, energy and money had been donated to intellectual enterprises, mainly university discussion groups; political action committees, both left and right politically; seeds of unrest, dissension and even mutiny had been sown in the higher ranks of the armed services and were well-developed; and special interest groups, a euphemism for violent public disorder and murder sections, were established nation-wide.

These different projects, within 'Action Britain', were set up and were now operative and powerful. The aim, of course, was a debilitating unrest of the populace and the collapse of government, law and order. The vacuum of governance that would follow would be filled with entrepreneurs; the acquisition of the gross domestic product would be enormous. 'Action Britain' was about to take charge. The establishment would be substituted with an oligarchy, the power held by a limited number of people. The earl was aware of a major flaw. Living standards, fairness and public order would have to be re-established and supported. But that would come later, requiring considerable organisation.

Because of the inconvenient detention of his sister, he had decided to travel under his untitled name of Basil Boscombe. This would reduce the risk of inquisition at Border Control in RAF Northolt, which was notoriously strict.

There were two handsomely attired cabin staff who, no sooner had they arrived at cruising height, inquired what drinks or other comforts the passengers needed, gave them the amazingly comprehensive menu and took their orders for the mid-Atlantic meal that would be served later. The drinks were non-stop, if you so requested. He asked for chilled fruit drinks. He was a frequent private air traveller, but even that said, he never ceased to be impressed by how quiet and unhurried everything seemed and the luxury and space within the cabin. In fact, he was so relaxed that he fell asleep after his meal and awoke only when the plane started its descent as they came in to land in Britain.

They landed at RAF Northolt at 11:17 pm. Stratton had arrived at the private terminal building in Northolt Airfield at 10:30 pm. As he got out of his car, he noticed it was a dark, moonless night with a distinct chill in the air that made the warmth of the building welcome. However, inside the building, a major difficulty presented itself; if he were to remain anonymous losing himself among the crowd, it was obvious that such a tactic was a non-starter.

There were no crowds, only two ground staff and one police officer on duty. He needed to sit inconspicuously, somewhere that would give him sight of the exit to the chauffeured taxi service yet remain unnoticed. Not an easy task. He had already discarded the idea of hiding behind a newspaper as being too suspicious or even sinister at this time of night but felt the near universal smartphone would be his prop of choice. He fished it out of his pocket.

"Don't I know you?" A member of the ground staff had stopped and was looking down at him. "Weren't you here last year? Something to do with that delegation from Saudi Arabia, if I remember correctly."

"I don't think so," he replied, although Stratton knew damn well the chap was right. "You must be thinking of someone else."

"Really? Funny, I have a generally good memory for faces. Sure, you weren't one from the Foreign Office?"

"Not me, I'm afraid," Stratton said quickly and with emphasis. He did not want to be rude, and thus remembered, but at the same time, he needed to get rid of this chap. "I'm waiting for an urgent call." He indicated the phone, hoping the person would take the hint.

He was saved, for just at that moment, a couple walked in, and his questioner looked up and cried, "There you are, sir! I've been waiting for you and, of course, your charming companion."

Stratton had no idea who the tall gentleman was or 'his charming companion', but whoever they were had successfully distracted the porter. Stratton looked up at the arrivals' board and realised that the only flight landing before midnight was the Praetor 600 from the Caribbean, which was carrying the Earl of Kingsworth, aka Basil Boscombe. It did not require an 'Einstein moment' to work out who this couple were meeting, but 'why' was a different matter altogether.

They did not give Stratton a glance. The porter who had accosted him earlier was hurrying behind them, carrying one travel bag. He, likewise, did not look at Stratton; carrying a travelling bag required his full attention.

Stratton got up slowly and watched them walk the few yards to the cars. He got in his own and followed them off the airfield, flashing his Home Office Warrant and onto the A40 into Central London and to Park Lane. They pulled up eventually outside a newly built multistorey building and hurried inside. A uniformed door attendant carried the travel bag. Stratton went home to a tired wife and sleeping children.

*** *** ***

Sunday morning found Reginald in his 'Hide' once more. Diane was at church; Mrs Braithwaite was preparing lunch, and the book he had bought from Aggie's village bookshop, 'Around England' by Professor Richard Drey, needed his attention. He would miss golf for a change. He opened the book and reconsidered golf. The title on an inside page was 'Around England'; the subtitle was 'A Brief Social and Economic Description of Post-War England'. The title was not attention-grabbing; the subtitle was uninviting, but never mind. It was wonderfully quiet, with only the occasional plop of a small fish returning to its natural environment after a short exploration of space above the stream or the hoot of a distant pigeon.

Nothing was going on in the 'Hide' or the immediate surroundings or even, as far as Reginald was concerned, the wider world. Isolation. Peace. He opened Chapter One. *Bloody Hell!* He tried Chapter Two. The prose between the multitude of graphs, maps and population tables was so stiff and turgid that he was surprised the book needed hard covers. His mind drifted to bookend use. But for the moment, he ploughed on.

Over the summer, he had transferred some of the objects from his office in the attic to his new 'Room in the Bushes'. A 'room' he knew was fanciful, but it was his own; some books were propped up by three volumes of the *Encyclopaedia Britannica*, positioned flat on the shelf and used as bookends. His seascape hung from a nail. He had given no thought to what the damp or mould would do to his treasured picture, but in any case, few would be upset if it were ruined. Indeed, Diane had been so bold as to say some fungal growth would improve 'the wretched thing'. He had his cooler with bottles of gin, tonic and a tray of ice, and on top of it stood his stuffed peregrine falcon, whose fierce gaze was sufficient to intimidate any interloper. Several glasses stood to attention, or more accurately listed on the shelf next to the books; he had binoculars, a notebook and pen and a newly purchased camera and zoom lens. What more did he need?

For some time, he had been alarmed by Diane's suggestion that they install an intercom in the house. But he had successfully resisted such a device for the present to preserve his sanctuary, and possibly sanity. He loved his wife dearly, but he prized two or three hours of solitude. The downside, of course, was that, from time to time, the door would fly open and Diane would stand there and announce some important command like 'Dinner!' or 'Lunch!' But the worst of all was, 'Guess who's come to see us?' That last verbal explosion was usually presented as a question, but Reginald knew that it was a 'Diane-speak' for 'Come inside and meet…whoever!' Really, it meant some bore had arrived, with boring conversation, a boring voice and no concept of when to leave.

Unfortunately, this Sunday was one of those times. No sooner back from church, refreshed in spirit and vigour, than Diane bounced down the lawn, opened the door with a flourish and declared:

"You will never guess who is here. Come in and see."

Reginald sighed, closed his book thankfully, not that he would admit it, and finished his drink, the third if truth be known, and said, "No, Diane, I can't guess. Tell me."

"Charles and Alice!"

If she had said 'Vladimir Putin' or 'Joe Biden' or even 'Boris Johnson', he would have been surprised, but 'Charles and Alice' were the most fearsome names, for Charles was the local vicar and Alice, his wife.

"Damn me!" Reginal mumbled and followed Diane up to the house.

Charles often spoke in Latin to remind everyone of his classical education and had the misfortune to have chosen the worst dentist in Cambridge. His teeth moved independently in his mouth and occasionally fell out completely even, it was said, by the more critical of his congregation, during that particularly ill-composed sermon in 2018. He was exceptionally tall. His wife Alice, on the other hand, was a person of exceptionally short stature, a mouse-like creature but with the appetite of a horse and the thirst of a refugee from the Sahara Desert. How the two had met was a mystery no one had solved, but again, it was rumoured that the 'flower committee' was working on the problem.

"Charles! Alice! Lovely surprise. Come to refresh yourselves after the rigours of the pulpit?" Reginald was on his best behaviour, mellowed by the morning's gin. "Pre-prandial drink?"

"Oh, a dry sherry would be most welcome," Alice said, a trifle quickly before Reginald could change his mind.

"*Bona dies. Quid agis?*" the vicar boomed. Perhaps he thought he was still in a Latin class.

"Oh, sixty-one, two in November, fair to middling," Reginald responded. The vicar frowned; Alice stopped sipping sherry for a moment, and Diane coughed.

"No, I meant 'How are you?'," the vicar explained.

"Know that," Reginald lied. "I was going on to say, 'sixty-one and still fit'."

Whether Charles believed him or not, Diane knew him too well and tried to cover the ignorance with a clumsy simplification. "Yes, Reginald's as fit as the day we were married."

That sent Alice into a fit of giggles, the exact cause of which was known only to her. Reginald eyed her glass and noticed she had polished off her sherry already. He hurried forward, took her glass and quickly exchanged it for a larger wine glass, filled it with sherry and handed it to her. Diane noted the subterfuge, but the vicar was admiring the garden and missed the incident.

Alice stopped giggling and said, "I remember our wedding day as well. After the guests had gone…"

The vicar's interest in the garden was abruptly concluded, and he swung around and suggested forcefully to Alice that Mrs Young and Group Captain Young might not be interested in their wedding day. *An embarrassment too far?* wondered Reginald. Anyway, he was eager to know the mechanics of the wedding night, given the extraordinary difference in height between the two. Diane could read his mind and quickly changed the subject.

"Your sermon this morning, Charles, was quite thought-provoking," she enthused. "And so instructive."

"Yes, I had given it much consideration." Charles gazed at the ceiling, and for a moment, Reginald thought perhaps Mrs Braithwaite had missed a cobweb but realised quickly that the vicar was looking to an altogether higher world for inspiration. *Bugger me, here we go*, groaned Reginald inwardly. The vicar was now in full flow, and Alice took the opportunity to indicate her empty glass to Reginald. He replenished it with admirable speed. Diane noticed the silent transaction. She disapproved silently.

And so, the happy band enjoyed their drinks and one-sided conversation. Mrs Braithwaite came in and advised the company that lunch was served. It was precisely 1:00. It must be said that Alice needed a little help getting to the dining table, but Reginald, with practiced aplomb, steered her in the right direction. Charles continued his monologue regarding his morning's sermon, as if in a hypnotic state. However, he stopped when he realised that he was at the table and gave forth with a suitable grace in Latin, of course.

"Benedictus, Benedicte..." Charles intoned ceremonially. Reginald was lost. Diane was enthralled. Alice was almost asleep.

"King's College, you know," said the vicar immodestly. "Never forget one's Latin."

No, thought Reginald, *but I bet you don't know why this place is called Plantagenet House.*

How wonderful, thought Diane.

Alice was past thinking, so she smiled instead.

Mrs Braithwaite brought in the ribs of beef and went ahead to carve them on the service table. The vegetable dishes were already present, and after being served their meat, which was in generous portions, they helped themselves. In fact, the portions were so large that Reginald began to wonder if this meal had been arranged. He looked at his wife, who studiously avoided his gaze. He jumped up and, bringing a bottle of red to the table, proceeded to fill everyone's glass. He served Alice first, and by the time he had gone around the table, her glass was empty. With a nod to Mrs Braithwaite, another bottle was brought from the store. Diane was not best pleased. Alice was.

The luncheon before him needed the vicar's undivided attention. Beef was not the easiest meal to consume with his disobedient teeth; it needed to be cut into exceedingly small pieces and then carefully masticated. Even then, there was no guarantee of avoiding a catastrophe. His patience was sorely tried when Diane piped up, "The choir was greatly enhanced by the new tenor," and then suddenly remembering that Alice was a valiant if slightly off-key soprano in the same choir, she therefore added, "in my humble opinion," and unnecessarily, "but what do I know?"

Charles rested his knife and fork, thus allowing him a respite from the toils of cutting meat and said, "Indeed. Diane, we are lucky to have such a chorister in our village. Maurice Marchbanks and his beautiful lady wife have transferred their abode from Cambridge to our village, and at the same time, he has changed allegiance from Trinity College Choir to our own. Quite wonderful!"

Which is more than can be said of your tortured English, Reginald thought, but he did not say so. Instead, desperately trying to show interest in the new tenor, he asked, "What is Maurice Marchbank's surname, just for the record, you understand." He did not make it clear whose record and for what purpose. "Clever sort of chap, is he? What's he reading?"

"Alice!" the vicar replied.

"Alice? That a subject, is it?" Reginald wanted to know. "Something to do with Lewis Carol? Oxford, isn't it? Or is that his surname?" Then it dawned on him. The vicar was trying to awaken his wife from an unseemly repose at the table.

"Yes, dear? Hearing every word." Alice smiled at them all. "Please carry on."

Charles looked down at his plate and courageously tackled the beef again. He risked saying, "Maurice, Maurice Marchbanks, a thoroughly fine fellow." Although if anyone understood what he was on about, they remained silent. After much cutting and chewing, he finally finished his main course without serious mishap and pushed his plate away to prepare himself for the dessert. Ice cream would be a relief. He eyed the blackberry crumble brought in by Mrs Braithwaite with some trepidation. The seeds and his teeth were not compatible.

At various speeds and with assorted dexterity, the group finished the dessert and then returned to the 'withdrawing room', as Diane would have it. Reginald helped Alice to her armchair, and they prepared themselves for an afternoon of quiet restfulness and conversational diversion and, for Reginald, unrelenting tedium. Mrs Braithwaite had prepared after-lunch tea with a light cake. The vicar leant forwards, eyes focused on Reginald and inquired, "And what do you get up to in that 'Hide' of yours, tucked away in the bushes?" He made it sound like a den of iniquity.

"Oh, this and that." Reginald prevaricated vaguely. Then he added, "Taken up birdwatching, but today I started reading a book I bought in the week: 'Around England' by Professor Drey."

At this, Alice sat up, smiling broadly, and said, "Not old Dickie Drey by any chance? My sister and I called him Uncle Dickie."

"Richard Drey is your uncle?" Reginald was incredulous.

"No. Was. He's dead now. Not really an uncle. He was the old chap in the next garden. Had retired from college sometime before. Used to do magic tricks in his shed for me and my sister."

"He did?" they all chorused together.

"He was incredibly good. Retired professor or something, authored a few books, I think. Is it one of those that you are reading, Reginald?"

Before he could answer, the vicar broke in. "I don't think Diane and Reginald want to hear about your childhood, Alice, dear," he said sternly.

But Diane and Reginald did want to hear about Alice's childhood, each for varied reasons.

Diane said, "Reginald, this sounds most entertaining. Let us open a bottle of the excellent dessert wine. I am sure Alice could manage another glass."

Alice's smile broadened even further if that were possible. Reginald was astonished at his wife's proposal. The vicar's frown deepened to a scowl. "Evensong. I am afraid, I will stick to tea if I may." There was another pause and then, "You will be coming to evensong, Alice?"

"No, I don't think so." Alice accepted a glass brimming with dessert wine, and Diane put hers on the coaster placed on the occasional table next to her chair. Reginald poured himself a gin and tonic.

"And where was your childhood spent, Alice?" Diane asked.

"Grantchester. Lovely village."

Diane clapped her hands together. "Reginald and I thought of moving there, but we have made this so comfortable that there seemed no point." She did not mention the eye-watering prices of houses in Grantchester! Then, as a small amusement, she added, "'Stands the clock at ten to three? And is there honey still for tea?' Rupert Brooke. I do love his poetry."

"We lived not far from the vicarage." Diane nearly fell off her seat. The vicar felt badly neglected. Reginald watched with growing enjoyment.

"And Lady Archer?" Diane was breathless.

"After my time there."

There was a short pause while Diane and Reginald recovered from this news. The vicar, of course, knew this already but was not eager to talk about Alice's childhood, for his scowl had become a sulk. He stuck his nose into a cup of tea.

"And Professor Drey...?" Reginald prompted.

"A lovely man," Alice assured them.

"I found his book a little scholarly," Reginald admitted. "And the prose between the maps and tables was not terribly exciting."

"No, he was a very clever man. Few people understood him. Had a little trouble with the police later, but I do not know anything about that. And Mummy would not tell us."

Reginald and Diane exchanged glances but said nothing.

"This evening, when I get a chance and Charles is at Evensong, I am going to fish out some family photographs. I have a couple of albums."

"Alice, how wonderful!" Diane enthused. "If you find a photo of him, we would love to see it, would we not, Reginald?"

"Absolutely," he agreed quickly.

"In any case, you must come around in the week, Alice. One afternoon for tea and cakes."

"I will," said Alice, without a glance at Charles.

"I'm sure you will find time to come," he said with some emphasis and a drop of sarcasm. No one answered him. Alice realised she had taken up much of the afternoon and was aware that her husband was unaccustomed to her enthusiasm and enjoyment of having an attentive audience. She felt a pang of guilt.

Alice tried to repair matters: "Charles has so much more experience of college life and religious studies than I do. Sorry, Charles, you must be bored."

Reginald was not sorry at all. He got up and poured himself another gin.

"Group Captain and Mrs Young, you have been most excellent hosts. Soon perhaps you would be kind enough to accept our invitation to lunch or supper at the vicarage. What do you say, Alice?" The vicar had offered an invitation.

"You will have to take a chance, of course. My cooking is not up to the standard of your excellent meal today, but I will try."

"We would be delighted," Diane responded. "And don't forget to ring in the week."

The vicar and his wife departed. Diane could not believe her luck. Grantchester! Reginald was pleasantly surprised by the afternoon. Uncle Dickie! The mind boggled!

Diane and Reginald spent the rest of the day happily. She forgot to tell him of the message from Mendel Partners.

*** *** ***

Chapter Ten

The offices of Mendel Partners occupied three floors of a brick building, facing the central triangle of Parson's Green, and had been converted from flats to offices in the late 1900s. Reginald made his way via the lift to Lorraine's office, and she met him with the usual: "Good morning, Group Captain! It is lovely to see you again." If her welcome was slightly warmer than usual, the nuance passed by Reginald.

"I think that Mr Mendel is ready for a meeting with you this morning, together with our investigator, Ray Cotterell, and our recruit, Mr Stanley Blake."

"Good, Lorraine; shall we go down? I presume you'll be joining us today."

"Oh, yes." She collected a file, notebook and pencil, and they made their way to Mason Mendel's office. The windowless corridor down which they now hurried was one of the alterations that the builders had designed during the conversion. It connected two of the old flats that were at slightly distinct levels, necessitating a step half-way because the overhead fluorescent lighting was quite visible but was an obstacle for those whose mobility required them to use wheelchairs.

That had not been considered during the conversion.

Lorraine knocked on Mendel's door, and they entered. His office had originally been two rooms, also at distinct levels, and so was naturally divided into 'Mendel Upper' and 'Mendel Lower'. Some of the younger secretarial staff wondered if there was a double entendre to be had from the division.

"Reginald! Lorraine! Come in, please." He came around his desk, hand extended to Reginald, and they all moved up a step to 'Mendel Upper', the conference section with armchairs, a coffee table and three windows all at different heights, giving an all-around vision of the sky either cloudless or, as today, cloudy. They settled into the chairs.

"Coffee will be along in a moment." Reginald was keen to get started, although he was not sure why; he seemed to have all the time in the world. He treated them to a glimpse of home life or at least a weekend of out-and-about life.

"Angela"—he was immensely proud of his pretty, if artless, wife, who he assumed everybody knew by name—"and I went to Malvern over the weekend. Spa, you know. Tearooms. All very genteel. Went walkies on the Malvern Hills and beyond on Saturday afternoon. Stumbled upon Edward Elgar's cottage, quite unpretentious, lovely neck of the wood. My wife loved it."

Reginald thought, *And not far from Evesham*. But he said nothing.

"Went into a pub in the evening; I met a chap whose father's father used to sit with this old boy on a felled tree overlooking a lake—well, a large pond, really—and talk. The old boy was grey-haired, used to sit for hours just looking at the hills; gave the youth boiled sweets. Quite horrible taste," he said.

"And that was Edward Elgar? How fascinating?" Lorraine was breathless.

Reginald was not. He wanted to get on with things, and with luck, this would be it. The door had opened, and Ray Cotterell came in, followed by Mr Stanley Blake.

"Morning, Mason. This is Stan; he is with us for this job."

They sat, and names were exchanged for the recruit. Reginald had met Cotterell before but took a good look at this new chap Stan. Youngish, maybe early 30s, lick of brown hair across his forehead, on his best behaviour. He said nothing for the moment and sat with his hands between his knees.

"Right." Mendel got the discussion underway. "Who wants to start?" He looked expectantly at Ray and Stan.

"You go." Stan's voice was surprisingly low, almost gruff.

"Okay," Ray began. "I've brought my notes." He put his folder in front of Lorraine. "But from memory, here goes. You gave me Leon Weber, captain of the golf club near Worcester. Born Germany; 56; good English. His company expanded to England with the common market, but Weber was left behind after Brexit. He doesn't mind that, believe me!"

"Wait a minute." Mendel put up his hand. "Am I right in assuming that Weber oversaw this offshoot in Britain and when we jumped ship with Brexit, and he was left stranded?"

"That's about it. The German company is a big one. Manufacturers of safety belts or modifications to safety belts. I am not certain of the exact process. Lucrative, though."

"And Weber made a go of it in Britain?"

"That's about it. Developed a specialised market over here. Has made a fortune. Divorced from the parent company now. On his own. Big factory."

"So moneyed!" Mendel stressed.

"Tons of it. His house on the outskirts of Worcester is in the two-million or even three-million-pound range. Two Mercedes, one for the wife. And she's a damn good looker!"

Lorraine moved uncomfortably in her armchair but said nothing. She polished her glasses vigorously.

"And the golf club?" Reginald wanted to know about any connection to the dead MP, Muirhead.

"Captain, this year. Plays off three. Friendly with the other chap you're interested in, but then he's friendly with everybody. No special connection with Muirhead, as far as I could gather."

"Germany doesn't get in the way?" Reginald persisted.

"He's an anglophile right up to his eyeballs. That's the impression I get."

"Seems comprehensive enough to me. What do you think, Reginald?" Mendel asked.

"To be absolutely honest, I'm not sure what Whitehall's after." Reginald did not mention Marcia, although no doubt Mendel knew of her interest. "Their focus was Muirhead and his family, I think."

Stanley Blake had sat forward; he almost raised his hand to get 'teacher's attention'.

"Okay, Stan." Mendel had noticed the movement. "Your turn."

"You asked me for the background on the Bromsgrove golfer, William Oldham." The voice was still gravelly. If Reginald had closed his eyes, he could have been listening to a prize fighter. "Therefore, I found his address, and luckily, he lives in a tiny village between Bromsgrove and Kidderminster, a place called Brakeborough. Typical English village; kids travel mostly to Bromsgrove for school. A fairly isolated place. As I say, the sort of place that you would drive past without a glance except for one thing." Here, he paused theatrically, then added, "There is a huge country mansion and estate."

"Is that right? And can we guess who lives there?" Mendel smiled.

"Got it in one. The local 'bigwig'. One by the name of William Oldham. He's loaded."

"His money?" Mendel wanted to know. "Where did he get it from?"

"That's more difficult. Truthfully, I don't know. But what I did find out from the general stores in the village was that he had arrived here about 10 years ago and bought the huge mansion and land outright, even a small lake. So, brought the money with him. Employs several ladies from the village as cooks, char ladies, that sort of thing. But there was something else I picked up in the village shop." Again, the dramatic pause, which irritated Reginald because of its artificiality, but he said nothing. "Often there's a big 'do' at the mansion, all lit up, music to all hours, food, drink, just possibly other things…" Stanley looked around. "…If you know what I mean."

"We know what you mean. Names?" Mendel asked.

"Not a complete list. One or two names, though. The gentlemen invited to the party on Saturday evenings wear a black tie and the ladies a proper dress. So, it's formal, to begin with, anyway. Sunday is for lazing about, but quite frequently the celebrations continue into Monday, Tuesday…sometimes even longer. And that helps the local community because some of them drop down to the village stores for odds and ends. I've left the names I got in the file." He gave the file to Lorraine. "A couple of names stuck."

"Go on," Reginald interrupted quickly; he was trying to pre-empt any pause, significant or otherwise.

"One was Leon Weber; I think that's the guy Ray is interested in. Another was Watson and another was McIntyre. He came into the shop with a woman. Didn't get her name. I only remember McIntyre because it happens to be the name of one of my teachers at school. But I know it's not him."

"How do you know?" Reginald was sharp.

"He died 15 years ago in a car accident; that's how!" The sharp reply produced a pause theatrical, dramatic, significant, histrionic…take your pick.

There was a general shuffling of backsides, crossing and uncrossing of legs, a cough or two and a sigh from Mendel.

"And still, we don't have coffee," he grumbled. "I'll have to have words."

No one was thinking of coffee. Reginald had made a note of the three names known to be regulars at the parties.

"Anything else?" Mendel asked.

There was nothing else. "Keep tabs on your targets." He looked at Ray and Stanley. "Reginald, I presume you'll be reporting back. Don't worry, Lorraine will be in touch with Whitehall."

"Not exactly Whitehall," Lorraine demurred. "A charming young lady, name of Lucinda, will collect it." That made Reginald sit up, but not for any reason he could put his finger on. He remained silent.

The meeting ended. They got up and went their separate ways.

In his tiny room, Reginald considered the action so far. Firstly, Marcia was no fool; if she thought the presence of the late MP, Donald Muirhead, on a golf course near Evesham was suspicious, then he was prepared to accept it at face value. Secondly, now that he had heard that the two associates or fellow golfers of that club were extremely wealthy and one of them threw weekend parties that sounded immodest at best and immoral at worst, what was he to make of that? Nothing. Nothing new there. Plenty of private golf clubs had members who were wealthy, even extremely wealthy. No doubt many threw parties at weekends that were equally indelicate and rudely improper. He had never been invited to one, but there you go.

Thirdly, Marcia was no prude. Best described as 'receptive'. She would have to be in this line of work, wouldn't she? She would hardly get excited about a party, or especially consider it a matter of national importance. Nothing quite made sense yet, although young Lucinda was taking him to meet Marcia et al. tomorrow. Liverpool Street Station. 10:00 am. And it was convenient.

The phone drew his attention. "Yes?" He spoke calmly. It was Lorraine's, her of the spectacles, memory like a computer and an efficiency to frighten him to death.

"Ah, Lorraine." He was placatory. "And to what, or to whom, do I owe this interlocution?"

"Oh, very good, Group Captain," came the taut reply. "I have your wife on the phone. Are you here?"

"Thank you for your consideration, Lorraine. Yes, I am here. And yes, put her through."

There was a click, and then: "Reginal? Is that you?"

Reginald wondered if a facetious reply would be right. He decided it would not. "Diane. How nice. Just caught me before I went out."

"The club?"

"Home."

"I am in town this afternoon; shift at the hospital. Dining rooms for lunch? I have some interesting news. Shall we say 1:00?"

Immediately, the line cleared and the phone rang again, and picking it up, Reginal heard Lorraine. "Group Captain, how long before you go out to lunch?" Obviously, Lorraine had been listening in. Never mind, but bear it in mind, Reginald noted.

"Half an hour?"

"Excellent. How many copies of the meeting do you want?"

"Four should be ample, thanks, Lorraine." He put the phone down. As he thought, her efficiency frightened him to death. Half an hour later, Reginald left, picking up the copies on his way. He smiled his thanks. Lorraine smiled back.

The 'Dining Rooms', as Diana called them, were a private dining club that was tucked away on the fourth floor of a tall building behind the Tate, not a stone's throw from 'The House', an annex of Vauxhall Cross. Diane did not know of 'The House', and Reginald was determined to keep it that way. They met fortuitously in the lift and were taken up to the dining room. At the door, 'Maxine', the maître d', welcomed them effusively.

"Group Captain and Mrs Young, how delightful to see you again. Window table as usual?"

"Thank you." *Damn it*, thought Reginald, *rather have Wilfred*. Then he mused, *Might make the club after lunch.*

"Thank you." Diane was assisted in sitting and adjusting her dining seat, and then she gazed through the window at the top of the leafless trees bordering the embankment, with the Thames beyond. The view was panoramic from here but uniformly grey. Even the clouds hinted at rain.

Maxine waited to take their orders.

"Plaice would be favourite," Diane considered, and then, "I am working in the bookshop of the London Hospital this afternoon. Voluntary work, of course," to allay any misunderstanding.

"How noble," Maxine murmured. "The plaice is an excellent choice. If I remember correctly, tossed salad but no dressing? And I think a glass of wine, madam. We have a beautifully blended Semillon-Sauvignon Blanc at present."

"Can I have just a glass? Duty calls." Diane was modest.

"And, Group Captain? The fillet steak and vegetable extras, I think. And I think also, the excellent Malbec. A glass?"

"Half a bottle."

Maxine glided off with their orders. Diane opened her napkin and watched a tugboat slowly make its laborious way upstream.

"You have some news?" Reginald brought them back to the putative reason for the visit to the dining club.

"Yes." Diane seemed to be a little reluctant to deliver her news, but bearing in mind that she had enticed Reginald here with this tease, she felt obliged to continue. "We had a letter this morning from my aunt Penelope. You know Aunt Penelope. Lives in Topsham, near to Exeter?" She let the sentence hang for a moment while she prepared herself for the onslaught of disapproval from her husband.

Her mouth fell open, for quite unexpectedly, he said, "How nice. Well, is she?"

So taken aback by his query about her aunt's health that Diane was, for the moment, speechless. She knew extremely well about Reginald's antipathy towards her aunt and that it was both unwarranted and irrational. But antipathy it certainly was!

"And what revelation justifies this communication?" He wanted to know.

"I don't know where you get all these words, Reginald; I really don't." Diane was not only reprimanding but also putting off the moment when she needed to reveal all.

"Well," she said hesitantly. "The truth is that Aunt Penelope would like to see us. It has been such a long time since we visited; it is long overdue."

Gazing steadfastly out of the window but seeing nothing, she waited for the eruption. Instead, she was treated to a long pause, and then Reginald said in what seemed to be a congenial tone of voice, "Well, that does sound agreeable. The estuary of the River Exe is a sanctuary for migratory birds as I remember, and the view from her picture window across the water to the edge of Dartmoor is exceptionally fine."

Diane was doing her best to recover, without giving any evidence of her surprise. She was finding it difficult. Rather than pursue the matter in any detail, she said, "You'll find the letter on the conservatory table when you get home."

"Thank you, Diane. Read it straight away."

It was just as well Diane had ordered a light and delicate fish; anything more substantial would have augmented her bewilderment and precipitated a bout of indigestion. Diane was incredulous. Has he forgotten that he reflexively disliked Aunt Penelope? Was he not listening properly? Has he had a stroke? Their food and drink arrived, mercifully interrupting any need to answer her own questions.

Lunch was enjoyable, and they chatted for an hour or so before Diane looked at her watch and declared she must get to the hospital. They parted at 1:30; she to work and ponder upon the idiosyncrasies of Reginald's mind, and he to wend his way home.

Reginald had contemplated calling in at his Gentlemen's Club but overall decided against it. He was not in the mood for muted atmospheres and discussion about misbehaving members or the list of runners and their chances at Chepstow with Wilfred. He changed direction in Parliament Square and strode along the embankment between the stark plane trees towards the underground and the trains homeward bound. He would be home by 3:00 at the latest. He looked forward to the journey, uncrowded at this time of day.

When he got to Plantagenet House, he called, "Good afternoon," to Mrs Braithwaite, walked through to the conservatory and found the letter as promised lying on the table. He took it to the 'Hide' by the stream, where he eased himself into his chair and read it. Handwriting was a little shaky, but then the old girl was 90 or maybe older, but the message was clear enough. Come down to beautiful Devon and call in. I have not seen you for years; have a rest from the turmoil of London; it would be good to see you both! Both! Well, there you were!

He put the letter on the shelf, poured himself a gin and tonic, lit the oil burner and settled down to think things over. His job with Mendel Partners was unsatisfactory; the dining club was pretentious; there was the feeling of morbidity in his Gentlemen's Club with dying members; Marcia was not as forthcoming as he would have liked, and he was unsure of her interest in a dead Member of Parliament; the meetings at Aggie's Bookshop were unknown and possibly of no consequence; and the book he had bought was unreadable. He was altogether dissatisfied. A short break would help, even if he had to put up with that old bat, Penelope. Birds for him on the estuary; Exmouth and Dartmoor for drives and pubs with Diane; and a bonus of a cathedral city for Diane's profound beliefs and exploration. Ideal. It might be the start of the book they had planned. Why not? He could put up with spinster Penelope and her continuous hypochondriasis and irritability for a few hours.

He made up his mind. They would go.

*** *** ***

The village was poorly lit following sunset; street lighting was dim and not considered a priority in deepest Cambridgeshire. Aggie's Bookshop was shut and shuttered for the night, and a single streetlamp at the end of the road gave little illumination to the entrance. Her premises were in darkness, with no light escaping from the backroom where Agatha sat and waited for her visitor. The armchair was worn to a comfortable contour that fitted her well-padded body, with the table, bottle of whisky and glass within easy reach. Remnants of a meagre supper were evident on a small plate.

At precisely 8:15, she heard the impatient ringing of the doorbell and the arrival of Maurice Marchbanks, the young postgraduate student from the university who was the leader of the study group that met irregularly on the evenings of the week. She finished her drink, wobbled through to the shop and unbolted the door.

"Maurice. Expecting you." She stood back, slightly surprised to see a companion with her visitor.

"Errol," the good-looking young man introduced himself. "I've joined the group."

Agatha closed and bolted the door, and the three of them climbed the spiral staircase into the meeting room above the shop. She turned on the standard lamp, which gave out a weak yellow glow.

"What is it you want? The room is for Thursday evening as usual, isn't it?"

A pause. "Yes. As usual." Maurice had dropped his voice to a whisper, but really there was no necessity for such care; the premises had no other occupants, and even the lane outside was deserted.

"Can we leave something with you?" Errol laid a heavy parcel wrapped in newspaper on the table. "Safe keeping."

Agatha eyed the parcel. She had a fair idea what was in it. She simply said, "Yes."

After the two young men left, Agatha secreted the parcel in the safe, away from the box that intriguing young man called Stefan had asked her to keep last week.

*** *** ***

Part Two: Investigation

Chapter Eleven

Reginald had expected nothing less. There stood Lucinda on Tuesday morning, waiting patiently at the ticket barrier, today in a white blouse and ankle-length black skirt.

"Apologies for being late. Signal failure. Stationary for 15 minutes."

Lucinda looked at her watch but nevertheless smiled. It took truly little time to get to the 'The School' at Streatham and the meeting with Marcia. "Marcia will let me know when you are ready to leave." And with that, the car, a smart Audi, was driven away. Marcia was upstairs in the underlit room that he remembered so well when he came here with Stratton and Mountford months ago.

"Group Captain. A pleasure indeed. You know Hugo and Nigel, of course." Marcia waited for them all to shake hands and Reginald to take the vacant chair. It was as uncomfortable as he remembered from the meeting that ended his short appointment as chairperson of ANCOM, his old, now defunct committee in Whitehall[*]. He still harboured some resentment over that.

He looked at Marcia. She appeared the same: immaculately attired, confident and probably just as forceful. "Diane sends her good wishes to you both." He indicated Marcia and Stratton. He was referring to the occasion when the two had visited Plantagenet House and he had learned of the final demise of his committee and Lady Keenan's arrest.

"How gracious of her! A charming lady and so supportive." Hugo nodded his agreement to Marcia's pronouncement. A silence developed and lingered. No sound from the street outside or within the building. It was a time of introspection, not of anger. All were busy with their own thoughts.

Abruptly, Marcia spoke. "Now then, we have a lot to discuss. Luckily, time is not our enemy today, but who knows about tomorrow?"

---

[*] See the book 'Watching'

Okay, Reginald thought, *and the other way is just to say let's get on with it.* His irritation had not abated altogether.

"Would you like to let us know about the investigations initiated by the Mendel Partners, Reginald?"

Reginald picked up the folder Lorraine had given him, which was lying on the floor beneath his chair. "I've brought enough copies of Mendel's meeting yesterday." He gave one to each person and kept one for himself. They read in silence.

"My goodness, this is comprehensive and so swiftly compiled. We congratulate you, Group Captain." Marcia was fulsome in her praise. Reginald came clean.

"It's the work of Mendel Partners. Super-efficient!"

"Nonetheless, there is plenty to go on here. What do you think, Hugo? Nigel?"

Both agreed silently. Neither held animosity towards Reginald, but both regarded him as an outsider. They did not share Marcia's high regard for his perspicacity.

"Whether it was you or Mendel Partners who drafted this report, it is extremely valuable. It seems to me that Weber and Muirhead were socially friendly, not bosom friends." Marcia spoke slowly. "However, friend Oldham is much more interesting."

All three nodded their agreement.

"But the catch is that Oldham is wealthier and arranges regular house parties where guests are invited to indulge in a surfeit of alcohol and perhaps illicit drugs. Those same guests saunter into the village on Sunday mornings." For a moment, Marcia allowed an interval to develop. The others waited, but their minds were at work.

"Can we make anything out of that?"

Mountford had stopped tapping his feet running, his hands through his hair and twitching, and after some hesitation, he speculated warily, "The exuberant behaviour at the parties might be a smokescreen, concealing something more sinister."

Marcia beamed at Mountford. "Nigel," she congratulated him, "I had much the same thought. It does seem to me that the parties are of such extravagance that a man of Oldham's background would hardly be eager for such public spectacles and take no measures to stop the guests from talking in the village.

Even our friend Leon Weber is reported to have gone into the village stores. So, regular disinhibited parties in the mansion and grounds of a village given by a wealthy individual who takes little or no precautionary measures are surprising. At the very least, worth noting. Unless," she mused, "not all the guests found their way to the village and the gossip in the general stores. Now, let us move on. Nigel?"

Marcia turned to Mountford. "I think you have been visiting a maximum security prison. But before you reveal all"—she smiled briefly—"even if it is a locked establishment, let us entreat Delphine to give us morning coffee." She lifted the phone, and after a short but polite request, Madam Delphine DuPont, with remarkable alacrity, produced coffee and biscuits for all four. "Thank you, Delphine."

The refreshments were distributed, and Marcia asked Nigel to report his findings.

"The prison is secure," he began. "Administration is tight. But I was allowed to interview Duncan Campbell on his own and without hand restraints."

"No handcuffs."

"Exactly." Once Mountford was able to talk about a specific task, he was more confident, and this self-assurance was transferred to the group, who visibly relaxed. While Weber and Oldham had felt like unfinished business, Duncan Campbell had completed his mission, if not to his total satisfaction, having been arrested. But Mountford's announcement was an anti-climax.

"Firstly, according to the police report, his arrest was a perfect combination of curiosity, two slices of luck and straightforward police procedure."

"You have us spellbound," Marcia encouraged him. Was there a touch of sarcasm there?

"The curiosity was that a child had become fascinated with motorbikes and made notes of the make of all bikes parked in the vicinity of his home in Brighton. He noticed this motorbike because it was a Harley-Davidson, and that was his favourite model. And here comes his obsessional curiosity: he made a note of the registration number. That was the first piece of luck. The motorcycle was still there the next morning, but its number plate had been changed. Something had seemed unimportant to a nine-year-old, although he thought it odd; he mentioned this to his father at the tea table, and here's the second piece of luck: his father was a police officer. Police procedure took over and went into overdrive. The child's remarkably lucky interest was reported to the police station, and they immediately looked again at the CCTV recordings in and around Brighton and on the routes north to London. The motorbike had left Brighton but was filled with petrol at Jeremy's Corner Service Station on the A23 to London. Campbell was later detained at the M25-M23 junction. Thence he was remanded in custody."

"And Mr Campbell himself, what of him?" Marcia asked.

Mountford frowned. "A mixture, I would say. He is educated, not a mug or a hooligan. I would think articulate but not in this interview. Most of his answers were 'no comment' except when I pointed out the charge was shoplifting. He became angry, aggressive; in other circumstances, he might have been violent. It was as if he was particularly defensive, maybe about the whole inference of petty crime. Anything else he was keeping to himself. Apparently insulted over a shoplifting charge. I'm not sure. What I am sure of is that his demeanour changed completely, from a relaxed, rather superior, unconcerned and uncommunicative guy to an angry, even aggressive bully. Strange."

"Strange indeed," Marcia agreed. She looked around. "Any thoughts?"

"It did occur to me"—Mountford was dubious—"that he was following a strict code of behaviour that didn't include petty criminality, but that he had a much larger agenda."

The three of them looked at Mountford but had little to add.

"You know, I came across this sort of thing, this sort of model, in the service," Reginald said. "The men were obedient to the discipline that keeps the camp safe and efficient. Any deviation from that discipline or regimentation is frowned upon. But outside that discipline, anything goes, and no one gives a bugger."

"You mean"—Marcia was trying to make sense of Campbell's behaviour—"he was following a code of behaviour that found petty criminality unacceptable."

"Couldn't have put it better myself." Reginald was uncharacteristically humble. Both Stratton and Mountford raised an eyebrow at each other.

Marcia allowed a beat or two and then said, "Hugo. Let us hear of your inquiries."

"With regards to communications between interested parties, both the experts at 'The Cross' and 'The House' agreed that internet tracing was possible, but definitive identification, at present, was complex at best and impossible at worst. We can be sure, however, that they will keep a keen eye, or eyes, open for unusual or repeatedly unusual communications, and if electronic traffic becomes regular, identification may be possible. But…and this is at once important…the second part of my week involved a visit to Northolt RAF Station, where a private jet landed from the Caribbean carrying the Earl of Kingsworth, travelling as Basil Boscombe, Keenan's brother, to be met by a man and woman who were strangers to me but obviously knew the earl. I followed the trio into London, and they entered a new high-rise building in Park Lane. I did not know the building; in fact, it's brand new as far as I could judge from the outside."

There was a pause while they all digested the information so far. At last, Marcia spoke. "Well, well. The plot thickens. Of that, there is no doubt." Three heads nodded. And she could not help but add, "…And all this from my worry over a coronary on a golf course near Evesham!"

Reginald always had a sneaking admiration for Marcia, although on occasion he still resented her highhanded appropriation of his ANCOM inquiry. On the other hand, she had something to do with his recommendation to Mendel Partners and had continued to keep him informed over this situation of Muirhead's death. The jury was still out!

However, he had to admit that she had seen something no one else had, and this was developing into an important investigation. At the centre, and he was certain of this, although he did not know of Marcia's equal conviction, there was a conspiracy, political. If that were the case, mountains of unrelated facts would have to be integrated to reveal the underlying motivation and plotters. The scheme might be the brainchild of a group or an individual with a purpose yet undisclosed. All indications were of malign intent; just how hostile was still to be learned.

Marcia looked at her watch. "This morning has been fascinating, and we have gone much further than I dared hope and in such a brief time. We have not uncovered the fundamental scheme to date, but the indications are that our investigations are becoming urgent. You are all to be congratulated. I hope you can all now see that we are dealing with a complicated conspiracy and one of national importance. As it so happens, I have been called to the presence of Jocelyn Carstairs, a gentleman you will surely remember, Hugo."

"That pompous…" He was either lost for words or felt that his words were too indelicate, for he did not finish the sentence.

"Quite so, Hugo. Quite so. But we must shoulder our misfortunes with fortitude." Marcia was much more diplomatic. "And no doubt, Jocelyn will want to quieten his minister's troubled mind. I must do my best to reassure him, even if he is one of the burdens I must carry!"

The meeting had all but finished; it only remained for Marcia to remind them all that they were to meet again in one week's time and to continue their vigilant inquiries. But a mild obstacle interrupted their withdrawal.

"Excuse me," this was Reginald apologising. "A couple of things. Visited a small bookshop in a village near Cambridge that holds meetings, usually in the evenings, in a room above the shop. One of their meetings concerning pre-war Germany caught my attention, and I'll make further inquiries this evening with a view to becoming a member. Also, Diane and I are ready for a rest, and we would appreciate a short holiday in the southeast for a few days. Be away for the rest of this week."

"A good idea, Reginald," Marcia agreed. "Please rest, away from the worries of our everyday lives. We will welcome you back refreshed and revitalised. I envy you and your wife; Devon and Cornwell are beautiful, even at this time of year."

They all stood, shook hands and left. Reginald was amazed to find Lucinda waiting in the car. Telepathy? Probably prearranged! He did not see Marcia leave in her own car immediately afterwards.

*** *** ***

Jocelyn Carstairs was a man of impressive size, with white hair that was carefully combed and fell in waves onto his collar at an acceptable level. Clean-shaven, heavy-jowled, with cheeks lightly powdered and always dressed in a Saville Row three-piece suit, he was the personification of a senior civil servant. It was said that while at Oxford, he was awarded a blue in rugby and another in boxing and later scraped a third in PPE after asking for directions to the examination buildings from a police officer. It had also been reported that abandoned ladies still wandered The High and The Broad, searching in vain for him. Sometimes, although this may have been only a malicious rumour, a single and forlorn gentleman might be discovered exploring some less than celebrious licenced premises in the hope of finding him.

He was unmarried and lived in a large country house of baroque architecture and the ambience of a mausoleum. The only other resident was a manservant who looked after almost all his needs. His secretaries were accomplished young ladies of impeccable schooling and background and had the irritating habit of leaving after only a few months. Of this sequence of personal assistants, he would say nothing. Others did the talking, but never within earshot.

Marcia had known him for many years and knew that he had a healthy respect, even a fear of her intellect and influence, that was only surpassed by his terror of his minister, at present an irascible parliamentarian who had been promoted well above his intellectual competence. This combination of an angry, defended and incompetent minister and a self-absorbed but under-qualified civil servant made for a volatile situation that required Jocelyn to partake in the soothing balm of strong liquor of an evening. Marcia was aware of these tribulations in Jocelyn's life and therefore felt comfortable in his presence.

The current secretary, Annette, stood up as Marcia entered her office, walked over and opened the door to the presence of Jocelyn Carstairs. She was a tall girl with flawless complexion and carefully cut but fashionable hair. Jocelyn's office was large, of course; his desk was a little smaller than a tennis court, of course; his swivel chair moved without sound but quickly through 360 degrees; he was reliability informed that 400 degrees was not possible! The secretary's office, filled with impressive electrical communication machines and other devices of which he knew extraordinarily little, was the domain of the above-mentioned personal assistant, who knew all his moves and prevented a sizeable number of them.

She treated him with superior indifference; he would treat her to expensive dinners if the preliminary signs changed and she showed some enthusiasm. Marcia was aware of this as well.

"Marcia, my dear, come in. Come in." Jocelyn's greeting was so antiquated that she was not provoked, instead accepting it as part of Jocelyn's attempt at jocularity.

"Jocelyn, this is so pleasant." She looked around the spacious room and noted the dust that had accumulated on the reference books placed ostentatiously upon the shelves that covered one wall completely. "How are you?" She sank into one of the voluminous armchairs, and Jocelyn took the other. The secretary awaited his instructions.

"Annette, so kind of you to be there. We could have some tea. Marcia, China, Indian, herbal, Taiwan, green…?" The sentence was not finished. Jocelyn must have realised that he had made enough impression with the choice of beverages.

"Just Typhoo, please, Annette, if you have it." The smile that was exchanged between the two ladies had no need for words. Jocelyn, if he had noticed, would not have understood their shared amusement.

"Typhoo it is, Marcia." Annette skipped from the room, and Jocelyn's eyes followed her, but in Marcia's formidable presence, he felt it wise not to comment.

"And to what do I owe this audience?" Marcia asked with the faintest of disdain. If there was any such inference in her question, Jocelyn did not notice.

"So good of you to interrupt your assignations to join me. How are your investigations? Uncovered any suspicious activities, have we?" This was a question Marcia was not prepared to answer at present, and therefore, she deftly sidestepped and answered another question. "Our efforts have been rewarded to such a degree that we have all agreed to redouble our endeavours."

While Jocelyn was trying to make sense of this tangential answer, Annette re-entered and placed a tray, upon which were a teapot, cup and saucer, jug of milk and biscuits, on the occasional table next to Marcia's chair.

"The best Typhoo," she breathed.

"The best," Marcia responded.

"Jocelyn, I will bring your herbal tea directly." Annette disappeared again.

"Marcia, please carry on. Do not wait for me." Jocelyn was magnanimous. He reclined into the cushions of his chair, placed his elbows on the arms of the chair, folded his fingers together and stared at the ceiling. Marcia waited.

"My minister is a worried man at present," he began. "He worries about most things most of the time, but now his anxieties have reached a crescendo. Quite frankly, Marcia, I fret about the possibility of ulceration of his tummy, and I recommend that he take antacids. Sound advice, is it not?"

"Indeed, it is." Marcia wished the senior civil servant would condescend to tell her the nature of these overwhelming worries of his minister.

"And what brings about this unease?"

"You may well ask."

"I just have." Jocelyn's focus came down from the ceiling, and he looked at Marcia. Was this woman being impertinent? She sat demurely and at ease, not obviously discourteous. But you could never tell!

Jocelyn pulled himself together and started again. "My minister has several matters weighing heavily on him. And of course, he comes in here to share them with me and gather what advice I can offer." Jocelyn now focused on the carpet in modesty. *Is this really the state of government?* Marcia wondered. *Surely not.*

"I understand," she soothed. "It must be a burden. Perhaps if the case were broken down into basic elements, each could be dealt with separately."

"Marcia, you are a marvel! As I am sure I have told you before. Simplification. That is our goal!" Marcia sighed. She waited. Jocelyn appeared to have some difficulty organising his priorities for his minister. She decided that a helpful prompt would be to everyone's advantage.

"Your tea." Annette drifted in silently and gave Jocelyn his herbal tea.

"You're an angel!" He never missed an opportunity. Marcia continued as if there had been no interruption. "Is your minister being pressed on political matters?"

"It is difficult to know where to begin. There are so many imponderables now."

"Let's make a start," she said.

Jocelyn launched into an exploratory, if speculative, address. "I am uncertain where to begin, but here goes. Primarily, there seems to be a general unease in the electorate, the cause of which is hard to put one's finger on. Brexit might be one source of complaint, although of course my minister would want to play this down. We are about recovered from the pandemic, and although again, my minister would like to take some credit for that, the economic repercussions are just beginning to be felt and may escalate next year. Again, there are growing numbers of illegal immigrants that might be causing unrest, and in certain towns and cities, there is resentment towards legal immigrants, even of persons of different faiths that have been born and brought up in this country; look, for example, at the bomb in Peterborough and outrages elsewhere. And the continuing laissez-faire attitude of some communities towards public morals.

"The Brighton shooting may be a reaction to that. Although, of course, I certainly do not condone such disgraceful behaviour. Never let it be said, 'Jocelyn's homophobic'; well, not aloud! And the decreasing influence of the church. The list is almost endless."

Marcia interrupted. "Jocelyn, here I think we can simplify as you have so beautifully put it. That may lead us to a central adversity."

"Go on." Jocelyn concentrated.

"If there are indications of rebellious discontent, to which you have so succinctly drawn attention, this might have the hallmarks of reactionary or right-wing politics. If the lethal explosions in Peterborough and elsewhere are symptomatic of racial intolerance, again, this might signify a reactionary mindset. Either way, we can assume that if the two types of outrage are connected, then we may be dealing with an underlying malign conspiracy aimed at destabilising public security."

For a full 10 seconds, Jocelyn was speechless. He wished Annette was taking notes, or he was recording all this. At last, he managed: "Are there any warnings of such a conspiracy?"

"That is what my group is working on. And with some success. You may assure your minister; we work together."

The relief was tangible. Jocelyn had something solid to offer his minister, and that would show how carefully he had listened to his master's voice. They might all relax a little.

"My thoughts precisely," he said obsequiously. Marcia smiled.

"Your group has my full support, and of course that means the support of the minister. In fact, I have even started an acronym for you. 3C4!"

"Good heavens! Why an acronym, and what does '3C4' mean?"

"Originally, there were three of you, approved by my department; now there are four." Jocelyn folded his hands below his chin and smiled in a self-congratulatory way. "And it is concise, self-explanatory and secure." Marcia did not point out that the last two words were contradictory; she merely nodded. "There we have it! I will report to my minister that I have the situation under constant review and am expecting results imminently." It was Marcia's turn to be speechless. But she had a long memory!

"Incidentally, when can I expect the results of your endeavours? Proof of a conspiracy? Names of those involved? That sort of thing. Soon I hope, before the balloon goes up?"

It took Marcia quite a while to calm herself and then, she said, "I will let you know of the conspiracy and the names of those involved as soon as I have them."

"I knew I could rely on you, Marcia. We make an extraordinary team, don't we?"

"Extraordinary."

*** *** ***

Reginald arrived home to a warm welcome from Diane and a generous gin and tonic. He was pleased with his day and looked forward to proposing that they should take a break. She would be delighted.

"Saw the lady Marcia today. Told her that we had been invited to Devon for a few days, and I was taking the rest of the week off, away as it were."

"Reginald!" She nearly ran across the room and kissed him, but thought better of it. "I am so glad. And you showed your authority!" Reginald looked down modestly.

Diane spoke. "Have another G and T, and I will ring Auntie Penny immediately." She bustled off. Reginald looked at the bottle of gin longingly but decided against another. He intended to go to Aggie's Bookshop this evening and discover whether he had been admitted to the group of historians, or whatever they were. *There's dedication*, he thought to himself, and when Diane returned, she gave no sign of dismay when he told her that he was going out again for a while after dinner. She had packing to attend to anyway.

Reginald parked his car on the rough road when he got to the village that same evening and walked down the darkening lane to Aggie's Bookshop. As he approached, two men dressed in motorbike leather were putting on their helmets and mounting high-powered machines that were parked outside the shop. They drove off.

Odd that, he thought, *motorbikes are everywhere. Brighton, then the arrest, then Mountford's prison visit, now at Aggie's.* It seemed odd—in fact, so odd that he made a note of the fact that he saw that one of the drivers had a ginger beard before it disappeared under his voluminous helmet, and one of the number plates was WVO, or it might have been VWO, or maybe WWO. The numbers eluded him. Curious, he should even notice. But…

Agatha opened the door for him after some heavy and persistent knocking, and looking at him, she did not recognise him for a moment in the shadowy doorway.

"Aggie," he reminded her of his voice.

"Of course, the group captain." Then she hesitated. "Will you come in?"

"No, thanks. Flying visit so won't come in. The meeting this Thursday. Can't make it. Going away for a few days."

She was relieved, for the chairperson of the group had shown reluctance to invite an unknown group captain, and after the parcels she had been asked to look after, she was not surprised.

"Don't worry, Group Captain. I hadn't asked him yet in any case." She had grabbed at the first excuse that came to mind.

"Okay. Back next week. I'll drop by."

"Certainly, Group Captain," she said with relief.

"Incidentally, you stay open late. Noticed couple of chaps leaving as I came down the lane. Motorbikes?" Again, she hesitated but quickly recovered.

"Oh, nothing really. They just heard of a book that I might have in." Again, she had grabbed the first excuse that came to mind.

"Right." Reginald turned away. "Drop by next week."

"Very good, Group Captain. Very good." And with relief, she shut the door, locked and bolted it. As he walked back to his car, he was not altogether satisfied. There was something, maybe nothing, about this shadowy bookshop. Or was it his imagination?

He turned his thoughts to Devon as he climbed into his car and drove away.

*** *** ***

Chapter Twelve

Wednesday, 20 October and Thursday, 21 October

Diane woke from a deep sleep, climbing out of a complicated dream that was rapidly evaporating as she became aware of her surroundings. She slowly felt a surge of pleasure. It was Wednesday; she and Reginald could relax for a few days. Out of bed, she opened the curtains and looked at a cloudy sky. The light woke Reginald, and he smiled immediately.

The previous evening, they had discussed the journey. West, then southwest via Oxford and the Cotswolds, staying a night or two in Broadstairs; or by rail via London, then to Exeter. The train was a favourite, winning because no driving was involved and getting them to Exeter in one day. Diane had telephoned to arrange the tickets and hotel accommodation and to let Penelope know to expect them.

"Aunt Penelope is looking forward to our visit, even if it is for only a few hours. She is probably lonely. The tickets for the trains await us; it is just getting there now," Diana exclaimed. They were both looking forward to the break, and Reginald was particularly relieved to escape from the investigation that was not progressing as quickly as he would have wished, although that might have been because he was unable to see the whole picture. He was also determined not to sabotage their mood by expressing his reservations over the elderly aunt.

"We might make a start on the book; what d'you say?"

"Yes…" Diane's thoughts were on taking it easy, not drafting books, but she said nothing. They were ready and waiting impatiently for Cyril and the start of the expedition. Only 8:30 in the morning, the train to Liverpool Street was almost empty, and after crossing London, at Paddington, Reginald was delighted to discover Diane had booked the high-speed train with first-class seats.

"Diane," he congratulated her. "Luxury all the way." She merely smiled. On occasions, a holiday is needed by both partners, and there was a mutual expectation of contentment even though Topsham was not one of the wonders of the world. They were going to enjoy themselves. Play truant!

At St David's Station, Exeter, they came out on the concourse to find a young man holding a card upon which was written: 'GROUP CAPTAIN YOUNG'.

"That's me!" Reginald declared, as if suddenly discovering his name, and then at once wondering how Marcia knew he would be there.

"You are the group captain, sir?" A young man approached. "Your car awaits, sir."

"Happy Birthday, Reginald," Diane congratulated him.

"God! Forgotten all about it. Wait a minute. Not till Saturday, surely."

"Close enough," she said rather smugly.

The hire car was a smart, four-door Toyota, and Reginald was relieved to find it had a conventional gear shift. He switched on the windscreen wipers, then nonchalantly switched them off, after which he indicated left and pulled away from the station forecourt as if nothing untoward had happened. Diane said nothing. The young man stood on the pavement and waved tentatively.

Reginald was quickly reminded that his wife was the personification of organisation. She told him the route to the hotel in detail, and he had more problems fighting the controls of the car and once finding them, supervising the bloody thing, than finding the hotel. Once there, they found the view of the surrounding countryside spectacular.

The golf course fell away from the main building into a shallow and attractive, wooded valley, which in October was a riot of autumn colours; the fairways were cleared of fallen leaves and the rough at a reasonable height. Inside the hotel, the receptionist welcomed them and briefly outlined the facilities that were on offer, which included unlimited golf and swimming; there were two indoor swimming pools. The gym was open to them as was the steam room and the 'massage suite and sun beds'.

"Where's the bar?" Reginald received a disapproving glance from Diane and a wide laugh, together with instructions from the receptionist. Their room was spacious, en suite and with views over the golf course and surrounding countryside. Later in the evening, they found the dining room maintained the excellent standards of the hotel, and they retired well satisfied with their choice of travel and accommodation, and with themselves!

*** *** ***

Mountford had little to go on except that he had noticed in the police file on Duncan Campbell that there was a brother whose address was recorded. Marcia had given him no instructions for this week, and as a follow-up to his prison visit, he decided to look at the brother's address, which was in Shepherd's Bush, not the easiest place to get to. It is a busy area, thick with traffic, but eventually he found the house in a side street near the local underground and the famous Shepherd's Bush market and White City Stadium. The street was quiet after the constant noise of the area. Late Victorian terraced houses built on both sides.

At the end of the road, there was a newsagent and, opposite, a small café. The two-storey houses were substantial and well-built, made into ideal, middle-income family homes. Many had been converted into flats, although the particular house he was interested in showed no evidence of such a conversion. A search of the land registry had revealed that it was owned by a Mr Andrew Stewartson, whose occupation was not difficult to find. He was an architect. Driving slowly past, Mountford could discern no sign of life, but to be on the safe side, he stopped, walked back to the front door and rang the bell. It was answered at once. Had the occupant been watching his approach?

"I'm sorry to disturb you," Mountford said with professional confidence. "I am looking for accommodation in the area and was told by the newsagent along the road that you rented a flat." He thought this was plausible.

"I'm sorry, it's been taken." That was pure luck! "It's true that I was renting the upstairs as a flat, but that tenant left suddenly, and a new tenancy has already been agreed. There are several other flats on the road. Your best bet would be to go to a local estate agent and make inquiries. Incidentally, I don't advertise the flat; how did the newsagent know?"

"Local gossip," Mountford answered with remarkable mental agility.

"Yes." There was a note of uncertainty in the voice.

"Thank you." Mountford made to move away, but not too quickly, lest it caused lingering speculation.

The door closed behind him, and there was nothing for it except to sit and wait, and the tiny café had a full view of the house. He waited an hour or so, drinking a couple of cups of tea, before giving up and driving home. He had achieved little, other than making himself known to Mr Andrew Stewartson. Not his best afternoon's work.

*** *** ***

The envelope was pale blue and contained a short typewritten note on heavyweight white paper. Marcia found it in her secure letterbox on the morning of 21 October 2021. It had been hand-delivered.

Dear Marcia,

1. Contact with Aggie's Bookshop, inconclusive. We can discuss this more fully later, if you wish.
2. Mr Errol Campbell is the brother of Duncan Campbell, who is, at present, residing at Her Majesty's Pleasure. I have the address of Errol Campbell.
3. A suspicious death, possibly poisoning with a nerve gas, is reported from a London hospital. Inconclusive yet.
4. There have been several racial and homophobic attacks throughout England. At present, I can find no single organisation claiming responsibility, nor a geographical pattern.

—Lucinda

Having read the note, Marcia burnt it along with the envelope and afterwards rang Lucinda on their private, secure line and asked her to contact Avril Simpkin and collect her from the train at King's Cross for lunch at their usual country club the following day, Thursday.

*** *** ***

Thursday, 21 October dawned cold, grey and with a persistent drizzle. Marcia took no notice; she had much to do. She was dressed and lightly breakfasted by 9:00 and set off in her car to 'The School' in Streatham. There, she was to meet Stratton and Mountford at half past nine. They met in the murky and uncomfortable room of 'The School', where coffee awaited them.

"Does that coffee have a distinctive French smell?" Marcia wondered idly, sipping it with obvious satisfaction. Mountford was not sufficiently sophisticated to give an opinion, but Stratton, who had been across the channel more times than he cared to remember, opined that coffee smelt the same everywhere. He was re-awarded with a raised eyebrow from Marcia.

"There's a lot to get through," she began. "So, let's make a start. Nigel?"

Mountford produced his notebook, found the place and got down to business.

"I decided to look at the address of Duncan Campbell's brother, Errol, that was given in the police file at the prison. It's in Shepherd's Bush, and after a bit of searching, I found that the house was owned by an architect, Mr Andrew Stewartson. I visited. He was in but told me that though he did have a flat for rent, he had recently re-let it, the previous occupant having left suddenly."

"He was not suspicious of your visit?" Marcia wanted to know.

"Said I needed a flat for work, and the newsagent had mentioned the address."

"Satisfied, was he?"

"I think so. I left quickly, saying I'd talk to an estate agent."

"Did not ask your name? What your work was? Took the number of your car?" Marcia continued to probe.

"No. No. And I don't think so, although it's possible."

"You mean he might have noted your registration number?"

"Like I say, possibly." Mountford closed his notebook.

Marcia reflected on what she had heard. If she had any doubts, questions or objections to Mountford's activities, she did not voice them. The three sampled their coffees again. It became noticeable how quiet the area was. Listening, Stratton could make out the traffic on the main road about a quarter of a mile away, but nothing in the vicinity. It made him uneasy, but he had no idea why it should.

"So," Marcia broke the silence. "We know that Errol Campbell has digs in Shepherd's Bush, but we have no connection with him to the atrocity in Brighton—"

"Apart from the fact that he is Duncan's brother and the assassin was a pillion passenger on a motorbike, but not on it when Duncan was arrested on the M23." Stratton interjected.

"Very true." Marcia tapped the table absentmindedly with her knuckles. "Very true."

Silence. Mountford was uncomfortable with quietude. He started to ease himself into the uncomfortable chair, run his hands through his hair, all the obsessional meaningless movements of marking time.

"Do we keep a watch on the Shepherd's Bush address or what?" he asked.

"Not yet," Marcia murmured. "Let Mr Stewartson settle down again." But then as if that had made her mind up for her, she said, "And, Hugo? Anything to report?" Stratton outlined inquiries he had made at Whitehall on Sir Brendan Forsythe. He could find no connection between Lord Kingsworth and Basil Boscombe, or whatever he wanted to call himself. As well as that, he had found that the earl had not contacted his sister, Eleanor Keenan, or the prison in which she was being detained.

"And her co-conspirator, Ms Stacey Donato?"

"Not a cheap."

Marcia, on this occasion, did not allow a silence to develop; instead, she said, "So far, so good. We have four distinct lines of inquiries; firstly, the connection of the brothers Campbell; secondly, the meeting of Kingsworth and Forsythe; thirdly, the questionable parties at Oldham's estate near Bromsgrove; and finally, just possibly a suspicious, graduate clique that meets at Aggie's Bookshop. I will let you investigate whatever you feel is important, and can we meet again next Tuesday, the 26th?"

This invitation to 'investigate whatever you feel is important' was typical of Marcia's method of allowing innovative approaches to be made by others and fresh directions to be explored and taken, and on no account was it to be confused with the paucity of her own theories. Both Stratton and Mountford were aware of that. They left the house in separate cars, which gave the motorcyclist momentary indecision. He decided today to follow Stratton. It transpired that this was a crucial mistake.

*** *** ***

Chapter Thirteen

The country club where Marcia met Lucinda Clayton and Avril Simpkin was near Kingston-upon-Thames, an exclusive club. But this was not the only reason Marcia had joined; the other was the challenging golf course and the outstanding tuition of the golf professionals. She played off 'one', and in her younger days had been tempted by the Ladies' Professional Circuit, but the intellectual demands of the Secret Service had been too tempting to ignore. Her favourite table, next to one of the huge, plate glass windows, had been reserved for her and her guests, and as Lucinda Clayton and Avril Simpkin arrived, they found her sitting there, admiring the splendid expanse of the countryside and the eighteenth green with obvious satisfaction, even in the October weather.

"Please join me," she welcomed them. "We must eat, and then a little business." Over lunch, which was delicious as would be expected of such a club, they talked about many aspects of their lives but never touched upon their years in the service. When they had finished their desserts and coffee and a dish of light chocolates had been served, Marcia quietly drew their attention to a couple of matters in which she needed their help. She required surveillance and infiltration into two groups. Both Lucinda Clayton and Avril Simpkin understood they had been chosen for two reasons: that they were unknown to the groups and that they were both highly trained. They arranged secure lines of communication, and Marcia stressed the need for speed; the matter, in her view, had become compelling. Emergency action was designed, which added to emphasise Marcia's premonition of impending criminality or even national insurrection.

Without haste, Marcia rose from the table, signed the tab while thanking the staff generously and left. The other two followed ten minutes later. Neither harboured any doubts about the importance of their mission.

No one had followed any of them to their rendezvous.

*** *** ***

On the same Thursday morning of October 21, Diane and Reginald woke later than normal, whether that was because of the comfort in the king-size bed, or tiredness from journeying the previous day or newfound relaxation, was something they were not prepared to consider. They were on holiday for a few days. Reginald struggled out of bed and pulled the curtains wide. He was expecting nine holes of golf and a couple of drinks in the 'nineteenth' before lunch. After his eyes focused on the heavy, dark clouds and the persistent drizzle, he changed his plans.

"Perhaps we could go to the cathedral?" he asked.

"Have a bite to eat at lunchtime and visit Aunt Penelope this afternoon," Diane responded with enthusiasm. "Or perhaps you would rather prefer a round of golf?"

"No, I think Exeter this morning and after lunch, Penelope."

Diana could hardly believe her ears; she had not yet seen the drizzle that would have given her a clue to Reginald's unexpected magnanimity. And to emphasise his determination, he added, "When duty calls…"

Luckily, she did not reply because after she climbed out of bed, pushed her feet into her slippers and joined him at the window, she took a glimpse of the rain, and without further ado, said, "Exeter. Aunt Penelope. Agreed," and went to get ready.

Later in the car, Reginald declared, "That breakfast was superabundant."

"Where on earth do you get these words? In fact, I think that is one you made up," Diane responded.

"Quite probably."

After correctly finding the ignition, the engine purred into life, and Young began searching for the windscreen wipers. "Where the hell are the windscreen wipers?" he asked, rather abruptly.

"On the windscreen, I should think." Diana was less than helpful.

"No, I mean, how do you turn the bloody things on?"

"Like you did yesterday." Diana looked out of her side window. Reginald said nothing. No point in making things more difficult. He successfully indicated right, then left, turned on the lights and turned them off, and then quite miraculously touched another lever and the windscreen wipers leaped into action.

"Seems like they have several speeds," he grumbled while experimenting with the lever that had started their movement.

"Yes," Diana said.

Diane navigated them to the centre of Exeter, where they had been assured there were numerous carparks but finding one with space still available was more difficult, even in October. However, they managed to park within five minutes walking distance of Cathedral Green. Sheltering under their umbrellas, they found the cathedral, and their spirits lifted—in Diane's case, quite literally.

The cathedral, not as large as some they had seen, was characterised by two solid towers; it sat majestically, surrounded by well-maintained grassed areas and wide paths. The west door and window above were beautifully designed, and the invitation into the House of God was unmistakable. They accepted the invitation to enter, at once finding the nave cool, even chilly, impressively high and with magnificent fan vaulting. They heard the organist practising, and the echoing notes and an accompanying vibration of the bass pipes, together with the murmur and prayers from the few seated were captivating. They wandered along both sides of the nave quietly, looking at the tapestries. Diane was mesmerised.

Diane decided to take one of the seats furthest away from the altar with a full view of the eastern window to take some time for contemplation. Reginald left having arranged to meet her later in the traditional pub they had seen on the edge of the green as they walked to the cathedral. On the way out, he bought a glossy cathedral booklet to read while he waited for Diane and then strolled to 'The Ship', still huddled beneath his umbrella. The outside had looked ancient, and the inside reinforced the impression.

Low oak beams, wooden flooring, a long, polished bar with a wide selection of real ales on tap and separate tables for those having a meal. It was early, but even so, a few customers were leaning on the bar, putting the world to rights, as was their habit. There were five of them, indistinguishable from each other at a casual glance, apart from one, an uncommonly tall man, dressed in a worn sports jacket with patched elbows, a shirt with no collar and an aggressive turn of phrase. His hands were leathery, revealing physical outdoor labour.

"And yourself?" The young lady behind the bar smiled warmly at Reginald as he approached the bar.

"Half of draught, please. Which of the ales would you recommend for a lunchtime drink?"

"This one." The bartender indicated the pump handle. "It's only three point five. Just a half?"

"Just half. A long day ahead. And driving."

The group at the bar took no notice of him, continuing their heated discussion. Reginald could feel the frustration in their words—an undercurrent of anger. He sipped his ale, intending to take his booklet to a table and read while waiting, but their voices were insistent and the topic obviously of immediate importance to them, their voices becoming querulous. Reginald's attention was drawn towards them. He listened.

The tall man spoke, his voice monotonous but antagonistic. "The wife's mother is in an old people's home; that's the problem." He took a swallow of beer, then carried on with a long condemnation of social care in the community. "They discharge them from the hospital, not a bit better, straight into a home probably with COVID, if you ask me. Then the whole place gets quarantined; must speak through a window when you see her."

"Bet your wife doesn't like that!" This was a small man on the outskirts of the group, struggling to be included.

"Not bloody likely. Then I get it in the neck! No beds in the hospitals; that's the problem. So, they have no choice, know what I mean?" And without waiting for an answer, he continued, "And the ambulance service is overworked. You're best off getting a taxi if you need to get to the hospital."

"Then you have to wait for a couple of days in a corridor," the little man said. This time the group turned to him, nodding in agreement.

"If you're lucky."

There was a pause while the group considered the imminent collapse of the National Health Service.

"And half the nurses are from overseas," another said.

"That's right. Same everywhere. Immigrants coming over here, half illegals. God knows what ideas they bring with them."

"Look at the prices; going up everywhere; we're having to cut back, the missus and me. Only just got enough for a pint now. Know what I mean?"

Reginald heard defeat and bitterness in their voices. There was a generalised dissatisfaction with society, all aspects uncritically lumped together.

"My boy can't get a job anywhere," another complained. "There's no work to be had around here. Same everywhere I'm told."

"It's them coming over from France. That's what it is." The little man contended. There was a suggestion of racism.

"There you are," the tall man agreed, although quite what he was agreeing to was unclear.

"You're right, 'Sky'." This threw Reginald. Short for 'Sky high'? 'Skyscraper'? A reference to the man's height, anyway.

"It's all this woke business. That's what it is for starters." 'Sky' changed direction. "Let me ask you, what's a woman?"

That brought sly smiles.

"What? I'll tell you what," he went on, without waiting for an answer. "It's not what they're born with nowadays, it's what they want to believe. You can't have men running around in frocks inside women's prisons, changing rooms, hostels for the battered. I ask you! And you can't say nothing, or it's 'antiphobic', or some such bloody nonsense."

"It's still us blokes that get a battering, that's for sure," was the opinion of the little man, to accompanying nods.

'Sky' hadn't finished. "And what's more, wages are not rising. Next year, there'll be a rise in the cost of living, houses, petrol, food. You name it. Nurses will want more, railways, teachers. What's more, what about us? What about us? Unless somebody does something, there will be a revolution. For sure. Anyway, we need one. Even more, what about the unions? Strikes all over the bloody place. That'll make matters worse."

Reginald retired from the bar and found a table where he could see the 'Green' and Diane as she arrived. The discussion had been muddled and traditional; he found it difficult to take the implied racism and transphobia, that was for sure. There were many non sequiturs, misconceptions, misunderstandings, plenty of errors, but one thing was clear: in that group, certainly, there was deep dissatisfaction. Whether that was widespread and to what degree, he was soon to find out.

Diane came in, refreshed from her quiet time at the cathedral. Reginald did not mention the eavesdropping, and Diane was busy with the menu, so talk was suspended for a moment. She asked for white wine, and they shared a platter of English cheeses, meats, breads and dips before returning to the car and heading for Topsham. Diane was strengthened, and Reginald a little chastened. Any complacency about the current state of society or the prospects for the economy that he held had been severely tested by that group. The comfort of his middle-class circumstances might not be universal; undoubtedly, it was not. He wondered if others sensed danger as he did.

It was not the best day to motor along the estuary road to Topsham, although the clouds were getting higher and the drizzle was easing. The 'satnav' showed four to five miles and estimated their journey to take 15 minutes. Exeter spread outwards never-endingly towards Topsham; the road was bordered on both sides by detached houses set back behind leafless trees and severely pruned hedges. To the right, the River Exe was hidden behind hedgerows, trees and fields, with only a glimpse now and again of sailing boats at anchor on calm water. Far in the distance, on the opposite side, a gentle hill was just visible, which Reginald knew was the edge of Dartmoor.

Topsham, as they expected, was a small town, a main road with side streets off to the left and right and tall houses clustered and hiding the estuary. They had no difficulty finding Aunt Penelope's building, which looked as if it were originally two narrow houses now converted into a building with separate apartments, each bought and maintained by wealthy owners. Reginald felt the high façade and tall, steeply, stepped gable ends bore a marked resemblance to houses bordering the canals in Amsterdam. They pulled onto the inadequate drive with room for his car only—one more at a squeeze. Diane rang the bell to reception and waited. Eventually, the door opened, and a skeletal, tired-looking woman of late middle age asked for their names.

Diane answered a little brusquely, "I am the niece of Miss Penelope Castle, one of your residents, and this is my husband, Group Captain Young."

"Good afternoon," the weary lady replied. "We have been expecting you. Please come in." She opened the door further and stepped back to allow them in.

"What a pleasure to meet you. I knew, of course, of your visit to dear Penelope, and she will be overjoyed to see you." She smiled at Diane. "She is such a refined elderly lady." Reginald took stock. This woman was a snob; he could live with that; the flat must have cost a fortune; that was none of his business. It remained to be seen how capable Aunt Penelope was. They were taken into the manager's office. The tired lady sat behind her seriously polished desk, upon which a leather desk blotter was absolutely central, two pens, one red, the other black, perfectly aligned at the side and two telephones, again one red, the other black, exactly an arm's length away from her. There were ledgers, hard-backed books and diaries in a small bookcase. There was not a speck of dust to be seen. Reginald added 'obsessionalism' to his growing list of dislikes.

"We have carers on call 24 hours a day, and our kitchens supply meals if so required. But I'm pleased to inform you that Penelope needs neither of these services…yet. And in any case, they are expensive. She is self-sufficient, but her activities are a trifle inflexible."

"You mean she's not sociable?" Diane remembered the remote spinster of her childhood!

"Perhaps not exactly antisocial…However, as I have indicated, she is perfectly capable of looking after herself." The manager was anxious not to emphasise any tensions that Penelope's demeanour caused. Reginald now added 'provincial', 'insensitive' and 'mercenary' to the growing list of personality traits he most disliked. The manager, whose name was displayed on her desk, 'Mrs Marriott', unnecessarily rearranged the pens before her.

"Do you have any trouble recruiting carers?" Reginald asked nonchalantly.

"Goodness, no, our residents have ample means to cover such inconvenient costs." Reginald thought that group in the pub would know that only too well.

"Will I come up in the lift with you?" she asked uncertainly.

"We can manage perfectly well, thank you," Reginald interposed quickly. Mrs Marriott's relief was almost hidden but not quite.

The lift was large, presumably to take end-of-life containers; he didn't mention that to Diane. It quietly ascended to the top floor. Aunt Penelope took a proper time to answer the doorbell, as was her habit they came to learn. At last, she opened the heavy, wooden door and gazed at them with a quizzical expression. "Is that you, Diane?" she demanded.

"Hello, Aunt Penelope. You were expecting us?"

"Next week," came the short reply. There was a prolonged and uncomfortable silence. "But now that you're here, you might as well come in."

"I rang you yesterday. You remember?"

"Of course, I remember; not away with the fairies yet. Although, I don't know…" She either fell asleep or had become bored with the sentence. Either way, she gave up and didn't finish it.

"I said to you yesterday, we were coming today." Diana had raised her voice, as one often does to the elderly.

"No need to shout. You said next week. Never mind, come in. You're here now. Is that you, Reginald? Good of you to come and see an old trout like me." At least, she had spoken to him. Made a change.

She turned and strode back into the lounge; they followed; her back was upright, straight and firm, her posture would have been the envy of a much younger woman. She had pure white hair that was cut carefully, and she wore a light beige twin set. As she turned to indicate where they should sit, Reginald could have sworn he saw a twinkle in her eye.

A complete change, and very much for the better. Gone was the hypochondriacal old woman, welcome the rejuvenated Aunt Penelope. The lounge overlooked the estuary, which from up here was clearly visible, and Reginald remembered the picture window and admiring a glorious sunset beyond. His eye fell upon a new acquisition: an expensive-looking telescope pointing directly at the river or at the bank on the far side.

"My! Penelope, magnificent instrument here." He walked towards it.

"Don't touch!" The command was emphatic.

Reginald stopped instantly. He remembered a drill sergeant with much the same voice.

"I have it trained upon a certain post on the opposite bank. I count the number of birds that perch on a post there in a given hour, throughout the year."

Really? wondered Reginald. *Hell for?*

As if reading his thoughts, Aunt Penelope said, "I'm assisting the local ornithological society by counting birds that perch on it throughout the year. The society is studying bird migration and summer nesting along the estuary."

"Others in the study?" Reginald was impressed with the old girl.

"Oh, yes. We meet regularly to collate our results. We might publish them at some time in the future."

Penelope excused herself and vanished into the kitchen. A few minutes later, she reappeared with a tray laden with a pot of tea, milk, cups and saucers, plates and some small cream cakes.

"Goodness, Aunt. What a feast!" Diana exclaimed. Reginald thought, *Expecting us, after all!* But he said nothing. He picked up a paper and retreated behind it. The conversation between Diane and Penelope was vigorous with lots of information traded, and even occasionally a little laughter. Reginald had reached 'The Obituaries' before Diane called for his attention. "I was thinking, Reginald, perhaps the three of us could go out for supper. I think that you would like that; would you not, Aunt Penelope?"

"Certainly," was the eager reply.

"Where do you recommend?"

"There's a family business overlooking the green here in Topsham. Tables are politely separated, the cutlery is of the first order, and the service is excellent."

"Food?" Reginald wanted to know.

"Traditional home cooking. Local produce," came the swift reply.

"Let's go." Diane was enthusiastic.

"Good idea." So was Reginald.

By the time they had left the house and were in the car, the rain had stopped, and if Diane was not mistaken, there was a hint of sunshine or setting sun in the sky. The restaurant was two or three minutes away by car; the meal was appetising and the conversation lively. Reginald enjoyed himself, and that was a considerable bonus considering his previous antipathy to the old girl. They drove her back to her apartment, went with her inside and where Diane said she would call the following day. They drove back to their hotel in Exeter, and on the way, there was much discussion about what had happened to Aunt Penelope; she was a changed woman. The ornithological society? The apartment? Was there an elderly man in residence?

"Don't be ridiculous, Reginald," Diane scolded. She presumed he was joking.

At the hotel, Diane decided to put her feet up for the rest of the day; Reginald decided he would go down and book half a round for tomorrow. "Hell with the weather!" Diane smiled.

"Don't have too many gins and tonic, Reginald," she admonished. When he'd gone, she got into bed with a book, but before reading, she considered how much better Penelope was and how much easier it had been with Reginald. He might even have enjoyed himself.

Reception pointed Reginald the way to the 'Golf Bar' where he could book around for tomorrow. He walked through the hotel and at last found himself leaning on a wide, welcoming bar and enjoying the first of a couple of gins and tonic or so! Finding a couple of chaps for nine holes tomorrow was no problem, and he enjoyed their company for the rest of the evening. Bed called about 10:00.

"I'm going up now. 9:00?"

"Promptly," came the command.

He retired for the night.

*** *** ***

Chapter Fourteen

Lucinda had been employed as Donald Muirhead's junior research assistant for several years before his sudden death on the golf course in Worcestershire. Having been awarded a respectable degree in modern languages from an established university, after acceptance into the civil service and a successful apprenticeship with MI6, she had become Marcia's close colleague. She was placed in Westminster and specifically in Muirhead's office. Her ease with languages was useful, and she worked closely with the Member of Parliament. It was not long before she was invited to his lodgings in Shepherd's Bush, where she had met Andrew Stewartson, brother of Mrs Muirhead and owner of the house. It was during one of these visits that she noticed two or three letters addressed to the 'Muirhead Association', which were read and filed by Andrew Stewartson and never taken to Donald's Westminster office. It made her wonder, nothing more. She assumed they concerned his business interests in the north, but her curiosity was aroused.

She was a young lady who had enjoyed the intellectual challenges of university life and had socialised freely in her spare time. There had been several romantic liaisons, none that had been sufficiently rewarding to become permanent. Her relationship with Donald never became anything other than professional; they were comfortable with their working relationship. This friendship extended to 25 Carpel Street and included Andrew Stewartson and Mrs Muirhead.

After Duncan's death, Lucinda continued to visit occasionally, collecting the post or messages for the office; there was no mysterious post addressed to the 'Muirhead Association', and she assumed that if there was any, it had been removed to be filed by Andrew. Although she knew that there was a new lodger, she never met him. However, when Lucinda mentioned the name to Marcia, it created great interest. His name was Duncan Campbell.

As time passed, Duncan Campbell no longer visited, and she learned later from Marcia of his incarceration in one of Her Majesty's prisons and his possible connection with the Brighton shootings. It was evident that this address in Shepherd's Bush was of more than passing interest to the police and Secret Services. Now, Lucinda was more careful in her chatter and any behaviour that might be construed as intrusive. Her change in attitude, minimal though it may have been, was not missed; Andrew Stewartson became more watchful and less affable. But that might just have been Lucinda's impression; she was not sure.

In any case, she had reported the change in atmosphere to Marcia. Eventually, through guarded conversations, she learned the 'Association', whatever it was, had other centres operating throughout the country. Finally, after some time, she was trusted enough to be invited to meet others in one such centre. The invitation was so important to her purpose that refusal was not an option; she was told of the planned trip on a Saturday morning, and although she had immediately telephoned Marcia, she could not contact her but had to leave a message.

When she arrived at Carpel Street, Mountford happened to be watching from the café. He did not immediately recognise her but knew that he had met the young lady before, or someone extremely like her. He could not place her but checked the registration number of the Audi. Now he remembered; Lucinda Clayton! Late school acquaintance and university fellow graduate. Damn odd. What was she doing here? He had no idea but would report to Marcia first thing on Monday.

On the fateful Saturday, Lucinda was met inside 25 Carpel Street by Andrew Stewartson, who did his best to allay any fears she might have about the journey. She had been told that she would be introduced to another working party of the 'Muirhead Association', and for this, she would make the journey of a couple of hours on the back of a motorbike. This mode of transport, unusual as it was, she accepted.

Unusually, there were three ladies present in Carpel Street, and they went with her to a bedroom where she was asked to change into jeans and a sweater and then handed motorbike leathers and a crash helmet. Her own clothes and her mobile, she was told, were to be looked after there. It was the last request; the relinquishing of her mobile that came was an added warning. Hiding her reluctance, she complied. Finally, she left the house with Errol Campbell, climbed onto his motorbike and was driven away. Mountford saw the departure but could not definitely identify Lucinda. He found the incident puzzling. However, if it was Lucinda, it indicated her agreement; certainly, there was no coercion. Something to be discussed on Monday morning with the help of CCTV and ANPR information.

Riding as a pillion passenger on a powerful motorbike was not a comfortable experience even when well protected with leathers, a visor and a helmet. For the first part of the journey, the intercom to the driver remained obstinately silent, but there was some relief in that the motorcyclist was competent, and the speed remained modest. She had been told that the journey would take about two hours and the possibility of staying overnight had been mentioned but quickly explained as 'the tying up of some odds and ends', which sounded too trifling to be true. Each small element of preparation amplified the possibility of danger. In the conventional sense, Lucinda was without adequate protection, without no mobile and unarmed. She felt more isolated than ever before; in the jargon of her training school, she was 'naked'.

The last anxiety, and a major one, was her awareness that the motorcycle guard was Errol Campbell, the brother of the imprisoned Duncan and a possible perpetrator of the shootings in Brighton. If she held her cool, she had the advantage of this knowledge, which Errol Campbell did not know she possessed and which she might use later. In the training, she had been complimented on her resourcefulness; now was the time to test it. By the time the motorcycle had left the suburbs of London and they were travelling north, Campbell had increased the speed but remained well below the legal limit. At last, he spoke into the headphones.

"Comfortable?"

"Just about. Getting used to it."

"There's a bar behind your seat that you can hold if you prefer that to hanging on to me." He implied that he would prefer her to hold the bar.

"Where are we going?"

Without answering the question, he replied, "We'll be about two hours." And that was all. Still, she did not know the destination or the purpose of the journey. They headed north in silence. She started to read the road signs obsessively to memorise the route if she ever needed to retrace her journey and to keep her mind active. She counted off Borehamwood and a stop for petrol at Apple Green Service Station. "We don't need anything from the shop," she was told quickly as she climbed down from the pillion passenger to stretch her legs. Then they continued north on the A1(M) and passed Hatfield and Knebworth. All the motorway signs were marked to the NORTH. It had taken over an hour, but at Junction 9, they turned left towards Letchworth, and after a couple of miles, Campbell stopped in a layby where he changed the number plates. She resisted asking the obvious question but was alerted even further to the dangerous nature of the journey. Having restarted without a word, they executed a U-turn and travelled back along the A505, over the A1(M) and towards Cambridge. And so, she noted onto the A10.

In Cambridge, she seriously began to consider escape. As they slowed in heavy traffic? At red lights? But on the other hand, Marcia's instructions were to gather as much information as she could of the suspected nationwide organisation of insurrectionists from 25 Carpel Street, and that would include Cambridge if that were part of the 'Muirhead Association', she presumed. They continued around shiny streets and down narrow cobbled lanes until out of the city and north again, if she were not mistaken. After a few miles, they came to a village, signed Lyfen, entered the village and turned into a side street parking outside a bookshop. The proprietor appeared to be called 'Aggie'.

No explanations came from the front, but Campbell got off and rang the bell. The door was answered by a middle-aged lady, probably Aggie. They entered, and Lucinda was invited to use the toilet and 'change out of those leathers'. She appeared in the sweater and jeans she had been given on Carpel Street. They climbed up metal spiral stairs to a reading room that doubled as a coffee shop. There were six persons sat in a rough circle, all drinking coffee except Aggie, who picked up a glass half filled with an amber fluid liquid, which she sipped slowly.

Judging by her complexion, it was not the first of the day. The room was well lit; there was a four-bulb chandelier. A counter was placed along one side of the room, upon which a coffee-making machine stood gurgling and giving off a smell that was vaguely reminiscent of coffee. She politely turned down a cup of liquid that was dispensed from this machine. Around the edge of the room were small desks with accompanying chairs, no doubt to provide encouragement for reading or browsing books from the shop below.

"Oh, come in." A man of about 30, dressed smartly in a jacket and flannels and sporting a college tie, pointed at two vacant chairs. "So, you will be Lucinda, no doubt. And of course, we know your escort." He smiled at Lucinda, the smile not reaching his eyes. "This is your first meeting with us, and welcome. You both have motored some distance to be here, and I am grateful. We know, Lucinda, that you were the personal secretary to Donald, and you are therefore most welcome to join our working party. My name is Maurice Marchbanks."

He raised himself a few inches from his seat; it was a gesture of convention rather than a genuine courtesy. Lucinda pushed her chair back a fraction, and this suggested deference. Marchbanks acknowledged the movement with a condescending inclination of his head. The group relaxed. The chairperson had shown approval.

"I feel that I must introduce myself again and clarify the situation here." Marchbanks was eager to convey his importance. "As I have said, my name is Maurice, and I am privileged to have been chosen to chair this small working party." Lucinda noted the false modesty and the omission of who had appointed this self-important prig. "It would be tedious of me to introduce our other members who you see, but you'll get to know them over time." It was as if he could not be bothered to introduce them, they were much lesser mortals. He paused ostentatiously and adjusted the sleeves of his sweater.

This gave Campbell the opportunity to stand, walk across the room and hand Marchbanks a sealed envelope. For the first time, Lucinda noticed the ginger beard. "That's for you," he said. No smile, no eye contact, no expression in his voice. Lucinda realised quite suddenly that Errol Campbell was not very bright. Marchbanks took the envelope, tore it open and read the brief note inside. Lucinda took the opportunity to survey the assembled company; a young lady who had little makeup but was smartly dressed smiled at Lucinda; the two young men casually dressed did not smile; a tall, slender man wearing glasses and a serious expression was considering his own thoughts and took no notice of Lucinda. An intellectual? Perhaps a mind to challenge Einstein? Perhaps not.

A large, broad-shouldered and rather handsome man, with a severe crewcut muttered, "Brad." But no more. American? Canadian?

"I see," chairperson Marchbanks said after he had read the note with studied concentration. He raised his eyes slowly and looked at Lucinda, but said nothing. Then: "Being Donald's personal assistant must have given you some insight into his long-term hopes for our future prosperity and our exciting ideas." The sentence sounded like a question, and Lucinda felt herself on thin ice.

She had no idea what his plans were or indeed if he had any. But this self-important 'leader' was obviously probing. She wondered what was in the note from Carpel Street and who had written it. Meanwhile, the room held its breath.

Lucinda thought of the training college in the remote Highlands of Scotland, north of Inverness, and the class waiting until Mr Dryden, 'Call me Stan—and if you did, that was your first mistake!', took them through the psychological interrogation techniques and defence against the same. The thought was useful. She could not remember the details, but the memory alone prepared her for what might be coming.

"We're all in this together." Marchbanks stretched and examined the ceiling with exaggerated care. If she went along with that, that would be the second mistake!

"We are removed from Donald's busy life here in Cambridge, but your presence takes us to the centre of things."

"My personal transactions with Donald certainly covered a wide variety of topics, some more urgent or important than others, but always pertinent to his position as a backbench Member of Parliament." She considered that vague enough to cover most eventualities.

"Of course. Of course." Marchbanks slowly turned and focused on her face. "His work must have been arduous. He had a large, rural constituency, did he not?"

"One of the largest in Parliament, but not densely populated."

"Yes…and his surgeries; I believe the term is borrowed from the medical profession." He smiled at his attentive audience. "Did you attend those necessary but tedious meetings?"

"No. On no occasion did I travel out of London with him."

"Did he report back any matters of special concern?"

This gave her an excuse to become less cooperative without causing offence. "Constituency matters were strictly confidential, but at the heart of his passion for fairness." *Be careful*, she warned herself. *Mistake here. Do not engage in unnecessary cordiality.*

"Of course. Ever mention the name of Weber or Oldham, did he?"

"Not that I remember," came the slow answer.

"Kingsworth? Forsythe? Mean anything to you?" *An interesting mispronunciation there. Don't correct it!*

"The last name rings a bell. Civil servant in Westminster, is that the one?"

"That's the one."

She felt the time had come to show some disquiet. "I am not sure what I am doing here. And I am not sure of this questioning." She looked at each in turn, very deliberately.

One of the young men leant over and whispered something to Siobhan, who giggled quietly.

"Something I should know?" Marchbanks quickly looked at the pair, punching out the words with impatience.

"Oh, nothing, Maurice, nothing." Flustered, Siobhan blushed furiously and apologised. The young man did not blush.

"I see," Marchbanks said and left it there. He then continued. "The reason we invited you here, Lucinda, is because we would like to express our sincere concern over Donald's death. It must have come as much of a shock to you as it did to us, but more, we now feel isolated. Sometimes we feel that we plough a lonely furrow…"

He looked around again for approval of his choice of words. He was unrewarded by any response.

"Do you mean you are not sure of your place or purpose in the association?" It was a risk, but one worth taking, Lucinda felt.

"Not exactly, my dear." The condescending 'my dear', she had expected for some time.

A pause stretched over the next few moments and then a few minutes. The young men became restless.

"I think we can clarify matters a little further tomorrow." Marchbanks sat back. "I will make a few phone calls this evening, and we could meet again tomorrow. Is that acceptable to you, my dear? Agatha," he spoke across Aggie, "will make you very comfortable tonight; have no fear."

Was that a threat?

"I hadn't planned on staying overnight," Lucinda replied by way of mild resistance.

"Please, my dear. We are friends here, are we not?" Marchbanks looked around the group; this time, they smiled complacently. "Very good. Let us adjourn and meet again tomorrow."

Everyone stood. The group, apart from Brad and Lucinda, departed without another word.

Downstairs, the door was closed and bolted, and Aggie, with much puffing and blowing, appeared at the top of the stairs. She filled her glass again. Lucinda was not offered a drink, and Brad refused one. She waited for the next move, but nothing happened. Then:

"Lucy? You don't mind me calling you Lucy? Less of a mouthful."

"No, I am fine with that. And Aggie…it is Agatha?"

"It is, but no one has called me that in years—not here, not Dover, not Dieppe, not Calais, nor any other anchorage I've pulled up at in my travels. Look, let's stop buggering about; come into my flat; we can sit in the kitchen."

With that, she walked to a door that Lucinda had not noticed before. Brad was close behind Lucinda. The flat was not large but independent of the bookshop and meeting room. It was part of an extension built on as Aggie's private residence. Aggie shut the door and adjusted a digital lock. As they sat in the kitchen, Aggie refreshed her whisky yet again from another bottle.

"Hungry?" Aggie asked. "We can get you something…" But this sounded like an obligation, not a genuine offer.

"I am fine. I do not want anything now. Perhaps a warm drink?"

"Brad, make some tea. Okay, Lucy?"

"Thanks." Lucinda fished for an explanation. "I was not expecting this. Feels like I have been kidnapped. Uncomfortable, that is for sure."

"Don't worry. We'll look after you, won't we, Brad?" Brad merely nodded. A man of few words and Lucinda wondered if his thought processes were any more active.

Tea was made, and they sat at the table in silence. Eventually, Aggie pulled herself together and encouraged Lucinda to 'make herself comfortable and then turn in for the night'. She was escorted by Brad to a substantial-looking door, which when opened revealed a small, rudimentary and uncarpeted room. It was sparsely furnished with a single bed, a bedside locker and lamp and a wooden chair. She noticed at once there was no window. It was more of a converted storage room than anything else.

"Basic," she commented.

"Enough for you," Brad replied. "I'll call you in the morning." He turned his back and went out, closing the door behind him. Lucinda heard the key turn in the lock, and for the first time, apprehension gave way to a start of fear in her throat. That was no good! She resolved to search for a defensive implement.

They had taught that anything could be useful. She had expected control, even restraint, but not confinement. This was final!

It was beyond doubt that she was going nowhere in a hurry, maybe never.

*** *** ***

Chapter Fifteen

On Saturday, Lucinda was taken to Lyfen by motorcycle. Mountford sat by the plate glass window of the café in Carpel Street, trying to make sense of what he had seen. An Audi had pulled up outside 25 earlier; he had checked the number plate on his smartphone: Lucinda Clayton! Late of school and fellow student at Oxford; what was she doing here? Half an hour later, two motorcyclists had emerged, mounted the Yamaha, one as a pillion passenger, parked outside and driven off. Was Lucinda one of those cyclists? No way of recognising her in those leathers, helmet and visor. Trying to follow a motorcycle in London traffic was out of the question. He would have to rely on police CCTV tomorrow to get the general direction. For the moment, there were questions and no answers.

By lunchtime, Mountford was filling up mostly with shoppers from the local market. Some families and some couples. A few children were testing their parents' patience. He had tackled the huge cottage pie and chips and was on his third mug of tea and second daily paper but was becoming uncomfortable. The café was crowded, and he was occupying a seat. The noise level had risen. The large daughter of the proprietor approached and leant over him to wipe condensation from the window; she peered into the street; her bosom overwhelmed him.

"Plenty of people from the market," she murmured and bending down even further collected his plate. "Not busy then? Killing time?"

She looked out of the window again, then guessed, "Number 49? It's dodgy there. Parties until the early morning; they say, not specifying who, a couple of them have been inside."

"Right." A useful misunderstanding. "Right." He folded his papers and prepared to leave.

"Going to the market? If you know what you're looking for, you can get a bargain. Go early, though. Morning's best. This crowd will have been there this morning. Bags everywhere. Can't move."

"Yes, might go." She took his money, smiled and returned to the counter. *No good coming here again*, he thought. He collected his change and left. Forget the receipt; enough damage had been done. Leaving, he glanced down the road and caught sight of Lucinda's Audi still parked outside Number 25.

Later that evening, after the café had closed, Sophie, the buxom daughter of the establishment, squinted through the drops of condensation and between adverts at the deserted Carpel Street. Quiet now; the crowds from the market had left. No pedestrians. What was that fellow looking for—the one who had been in earlier? Sat for two hours, ate a plate of food, left half of it, had some tea and read a couple of newspapers. Spoke to no one. Was watching or waiting. Like she said. Those at 49 needed watching, but he had not seemed interested.

There had been some work done on 25—two houses made into one—but it was not a listed building or anything, and no one had complained as far as she knew. It would not be that. On this side of the street, the chap in 14 was said to be overfriendly with the bartender in the local. But that was just tittle-tattle; in any case, he had been in a couple of times, and he was nothing to write home about. The street was just like any other. To hell with it, she dismissed him from her mind. It was time to put her feet up. Watch television.

'That fellow' who had sat watching the street was now back in his bungalow in Ruislip. His requests to the police for CCTV coverage might give him some indication of the direction of the motorbike. All he could do was wait till tomorrow for the reports.

He tried a telephone number he had been advised to use once, and once only, and then only in a matter of urgency.

"Good evening." The man's voice was totally neutral.

"I'm calling for Marcia. Can I have a number?"

"Afraid not, sir. If you give me your number, I will ring you back directly." Mountford did so, and twenty seconds later, the phone rang.

"I have the person you require. If you stay at that number, that person will call you shortly." The line was disconnected. Five minutes later, the phone rang.

"Hello," he said.

"You called? Urgent?"

"I think so."

"We will meet tomorrow; usual place; 10:00 in the morning. Soon enough?"

"It is." The phone went dead. Mountford was left with his thoughts all night; some of the time, he managed to sleep. Had he turned on the television before he went to bed, he would not have slept at all, for that same evening, there had been a 'serious incident' reported on the news. Scores of passengers had been killed or injured, the result of the detonation of a bomb in the first carriage of a London underground train carrying thousands of supporters from a soccer match.

There was televised footage of passengers running in panic on a station platform and mangled coaches sliding towards the station platform. Further images were of police and ambulance crews running into the subway entrance, bodies being lifted out of the coaches, or what was left of them, bandaged and disorientated casualties being led away and the newsreaders clearly distressed at the images of carnage before them.

Next day. Sunday morning, 24th

Unaware of the explosion on the subway, Mountford nevertheless could not sleep. He tried to account for the appearance of Lucinda in Carpel Street in the bigger picture. Trouble was he did not know what the bigger picture was or even if she were part of it or had stumbled into it by chance. He catnapped throughout the night and only fell asleep fully as the dawn light inched its way around the curtains. It must have been about 4:00. He did not know what woke him later, but looking at the clock, he found it was 7:30 already. His first coherent thoughts were of the disappearance of Clayton, if disappearance was what it was. He got up as the Sunday papers landed with their usual thump in the hallway. He got ready for the Marcia meeting.

At the breakfast table, he opened the papers as he dipped his spoon into the cereal bowl. The spoon never reached his mouth. The front pages of both papers were covered in photographs of casualties, ambulances, police and general mayhem. The headlines reinforced the images. More than 60 had been injured, and at present, the number of deaths was 21. A major incident in the capital had been declared; police throughout the country had been put on full alert. He knew very well that SO15 and Special Branch would be out on the streets, Vauxhall Cross and Thames House, actively analysing what evidence had been collected, even at this early stage. He was only surprised that his own emergency signal had not been activated. The meeting with Marcia had become suddenly very urgent.

Mountford put his spoon down without taking a mouthful of cereal. He walked across the kitchen, turned on the small television on the Welsh dresser and returned to the table. The picture came into focus: rows of injured people sitting on the ground, wrapped in blankets, clutching mugs of tea. It was amazing how tea materialises in emergencies. A reporter was bending over and talking. The time given at the bottom of the picture was 18.31. Must be a recording of yesterday evening.

"We were in the second carriage," the injured man said, "…coming into the station…then this almighty explosion in the carriage in front…and everyone started yelling…a little kid was hysterical…is that the word?…I could see through the door…the front carriage was blown apart…I couldn't hear for the noise…the metal on the sides…people screaming…blood everywhere…on my new jacket…and the smell…burning, but more…like I've never smelt before…and the train still screeching into the lights of the station…that's right, the lights in the train had gone out…and everybody was screaming…" The reporter moved on. The cameras panned back, and viewers could see lines of ambulances and paramedics, doctors and nurses hurrying back and forth. The commentator wondered how the hospital emergency services were going to cope with all this, particularly after the pandemic and the backlog of admissions to hospital beds.

The screen was now showing images from the platform. The bombed train had ground to a halt, with three carriages protruding from the black tunnel. The driver's cabin had been obliterated completely, and the driver was clearly dead, and the many injured and dead were being carried from the carriages onto the platform. A reporter spoke to a witness. "Were you here when the accident happened?"

She replied between sobs, "This was no accident; it was an explosion, if you ask me. Bloody murder—that's what it was. An old lady got pushed over. Don't know what's happened to her; it's chaos down here. If I got hold of the…" The scene was cut abruptly.

The camera swept across the station, and viewers could see a woman collapsed against one of the walls, screaming in agony, surrounded by paramedics and several passengers. The newscaster told the viewers that the circumstances were too horrific to be reported. Mountford later learnt that her eight-year-old was standing in front of her, watching for the train to appear from the tunnel, when the explosion occurred. Shattered glass and sheets of metal were expelled from the tunnel with the force of the explosion, and one of them had decapitated her child in front of her.

Mountford could barely believe his eyes or ears, even though he was accustomed to the carnage that he had seen since joining the service. He left his breakfast untouched, made for the car and drove towards Streatham.

Taking a circuitous route to Streatham and 'The School', avoiding central London and inevitable congestion, Mountford made reasonable time. Even in the suburbs, however, and south of the Thames, the increased police presence was obvious. Pulling up in the lane behind 'The School' and next to Marcia's car, he was not surprised to see Stratton's 4x4, but there was also another car he could not identify. The back door to the house was open, and he rushed through the kitchen. Delphine and Antoine were busy with coffee and did not look at him. Upstairs, the room was the same: shadowed and comfortless. Marcia, Stratton, and the owner of the third parked car, Reginald Young, turned their heads and peered through the gloom towards him as he entered.

"Sit down, Nigel, why don't you?" Marcia was in her usual dignified self. At first glance, calm and self-possessed; at second glance, controlled. "Coffee will be up shortly."

Mountford sat and nodded at Stratton and Young. Young? That was unexpected. What was he doing here?

"You have heard, of course," Marcia started without preamble. There was hardly any necessity for the question. Stratton and Young had seen the news last night, and all three had heard or read the later reports this morning. None of them had been surprised to be called in now; they were aware of the urgency of the situation. Diane had been woken by the insistent ringing of the telephone at about 5:30 am and realised immediately the seriousness of the call; she had expected Reginald to head off. And that was the case.

He had decided to drive; she wondered about the wisdom of the decision, but he had left in a hurry. He found the M11 less busy than usual at this hour, but for the M25 drive through London was much more difficult. There were police everywhere and some roads were closed; perseverance got him to Streatham, a trifle flustered.

"I think it is true to say our Special Services are now fully active. The joint intelligence committee has been called to emergency session, and Cabinet Secretaries have had their weekends interrupted, to say nothing of cabinet ministers. Communications will not be as smooth as those few words would imply, but the whole emergency machine will be operational as from now," Marcia informed them.

She sighed, paused for a moment, then spoke carefully. "We are separate or, at least for the time being, separated from the constraints of the government or service. We have the advantage of not having to answer to parliamentary secretaries or a cabinet or ministers or their advisory committees." Again, the pause. "But we will need to keep abreast of the developments. And I will take that task upon myself. You will all continue your individual and, for the moment, independent investigations if you would."

"You mean we won't have to appease Jocelyn Carstairs, or anyone like him?" Hugo muttered.

"I would not put it that strongly, Hugo. But yes, we will in the immediate future be undeterred by diplomatic or governmental supervision." She looked expectantly at the door; she had heard Delphine mounting the stairs, no doubt carrying reviving coffee. "I believe, and I think with justification, that this dreadful occurrence will not be the last. I believe this is the latest in a series of atrocities that will affect the whole country. The Brighton shootings and the Peterborough explosion may appear to be separate incidents. Now, they are the beginning of a nationwide wave of destruction."

Nobody commented for some time. "If that is indeed the case, it is also my belief that there will be a nucleus, centre or committee that will be organising widespread disorder or even anarchy."

"But your evidence is thin." Stratton wanted to add 'intuition only', but he merely looked at the others instead. Then experimentally, he added, "We know of no such conspiracy, and even if there is one, what is the purpose behind it?"

"Let us leave that for now; we can come back to it later. For the moment, we are uninhibited by the constraints of bureaucratic government influences. For how long is another matter!"

The door opened, and there was Delphine with coffee and biscuits.

"Delphine! What timing!" Marcia beamed her thanks to Madame DuPont, who withdrew at once without a word.

The three men stood to help themselves to coffee, leaving Marcia sitting alone, looking silently at the door and quietly nibbling at a biscuit. Stratton and Young stood by the window, studying the empty street and listening to the noise of traffic on the main road some distance away.

"You're here because of the military?" Nigel asked.

"No idea. Certainly not military; nothing to do with me now; no contact. Was phoned this morning. Attend. Prompt 10:00. That's as much as I know."

Group Captain Young was candid. "Damn thing's a mess, for sure. A bigger plot? God knows. Not me!"

"Not your usual line; this, I mean." Stratton waved his hand about the room. "Unless you're learning a new trick or two at Mendel Partners. That is what they call themselves?"

"No tricks. Old or new. More a holding brief. Yes, Mendel Partners."

"Odd title." Stratton looked at Young. "Does that mean you're a partner?"

"Something like that. Nothing to do with this business…or not that I've been told."

"But you've had some bloke sniffing around the golf course at Worcester and that place in Bromsgrove."

"Asked to report on specific targets. Nothing to do with this, apparently."

"Mm." Mountford was noncommittal; he knew Marcia too well to swallow that. But he left it there for the moment. "Well, whatever's behind all this, it's diabolical, and that's for sure."

"Damn sight more than that." Young added, nodded and continued to study the empty street. Mountford heard the distinctive sound of a motorbike pulling up somewhere out of sight. Stratton joined them at the window. The street remained free of traffic or pedestrians.

Marcia coughed discreetly, and they turned in unison and walked back to their chairs.

"Gentlemen. I think that the coffee break can be considered finished. We need to cast our minds to business. Let us start with you, Nigel. You have been watching Carpel Street, I believe." Marcia sat back and waited. It was her usual form of inquiry, merely to mention the area of interest and let the agent develop his or her own narrative.

"Saturday…God, that was only yesterday…I parked myself in the café on Carpel Street and watched 25." Mountford started hesitantly, having hardly recovered from the visions on television this morning. "Just after lunchtime, an Audi pulled up; I've checked with the police, belongs to a Lucinda Clayton, whom, quite by chance, I know."

"Lucinda Clayton, you say?" Marcia interrupted.

"That's what the police told me. No idea what she was doing there. Anyway, knew her at school and at university; would you believe? Bright though. Anyway, about an hour later or something like that, two characters came out and drove off on a Yamaha motorbike that was parked outside. Helmets, visors, the whole works. Not able to name them. One might have been Clayton, but I can't be sure."

He looked around. No one was particularly excited about this piece of information, but of course, with Marcia, you could never tell.

"I couldn't tail the motorbike in a car, so I had to let them go…"

"But you alerted the police?" This was Stratton.

"Certainly, and they watched them on CCTV onto the A1 and a petrol station, Apple Green Service Station, where the pillion passenger stretched his or her legs but didn't take the helmet off, nor go into the shop. The driver, now without his helmet, was seen to sport a ginger beard."

"Good." Marcia sighed. "Good work, Nigel."

"But then, Marcia, not so good. We have them to Junction 9, then they seem to turn left onto A505 towards Letchworth."

"What d'you mean, 'seem to turn left'?" Stratton was showing his seniority.

"Well. They go off the radar."

"Off the radar? What do you mean?" Stratton was short.

"What I say. No sighting after the turn-off."

Marcia leant forward and spoke softly. "I think you mean, Nigel, there is no sighting of the number plate again. The motorbike itself will hardly have vanished."

"Yes, it's what I mean," Mountford replied diffidently.

"So, it is perfectly possible that the number plates were changed?"

"That's true." Mountford perked up. "We had thought of that. The police checked the A505 in both directions. Towards Letchworth, there were two other bikes seen, one with a pillion passenger. But neither were Yamahas. Going back to the other way along the A505, over the motorway and towards Cambridge, in the next hour, there were six motorbikes, three pillion passengers and two Yamahas."

"What about continuing on A1(M) north or, for that matter, going back to London?" Stratton was quick to ask.

"Still checking. Nothing yet."

"The police and you, Nigel, have been very efficient. It is possible; therefore, is it not that the pair were going towards Cambridge?"

"That's what we thought."

"Very good. What do you think, Reginald?" Marcia asked quietly.

"You're talking about Aggie and the bookshop in Lyfen?" Reginald asked.

"I am."

"That's an interesting thought," Reginald agreed, staring at the ceiling and at the lightbulb attached to it without a shade.

"And your thoughts?" Marcia would not let it go.

"Perfectly possible, I suppose. Can't see a connection yet. Aggie spoke of a Thursday evening meeting, but I've not followed it up."

"Perhaps you should?" Marcia gently prodded.

The group fell silent, each with individual considerations of the facts as known personally. Stratton was the first to speak.

"Marcia, there appear to be several issues of immediate concern to us all. It would be helpful, correct me if I jump the gun, but it would be helpful if we were first to separate matters that occupy our group's attention before, with your overall view, placing them within the context of a conspiracy. That is if there is one."

Marcia took some time before answering. "Hugo, your well-organised mind leads us to the essence of our labours. Your suggestion is an excellent one and a suggestion that is constructive." *Okay, got your drift*, Reginald thought.

"First of all, we have the death of Muirhead on a golf course in Worcester. Apparently unrelated to anything except atheroma of his coronary arteries. But lo!" *Okay, so now she's a conjuror!* Reginald thought. "He was known to two, if not more, extremely wealthy golfers, at least one who is a rather special millionaire."

She paused. The group waited. *Nothing new!* Reginald thought.

"The millionaire, of whom I speak, William, or Bill, let us be friendly, Oldham holds regular and uninhibited parties on his estate, to which, among others, Mrs Frances Muirhead has been invited."

Another brief rest. This time, Marcia stood, hands behind her. *A lecture?* Reginald hoped not. She sat down again. Reginald relaxed.

"From our point of view, those parties are interesting. On one occasion at least, Frances Muirhead attended such a party and met, would you believe, Brendan Forsythe of all people?"

Stratton sat forward. "*The Brendan Forsythe?*"

"The same." Marcia smiled. "I know because Frances told an ex-agent of ours, Avril Reynolds, who you know, Hugo, as Mrs Simpkin, the lepidopterist wife of Gerald Simpkin of Chester, and someone who has befriended Frances Muirhead."

"Damn me!" Stratton was shaken. "I'm beginning to understand…" *Wish to God I did*, Reginald thought impiously.

"So, there we have the first link." Marcia seemed satisfied with herself. "Brendan Forsythe meets Bill Oldham, the millionaire who meets Mrs Frances Muirhead."

"A connection or series of connections is established," Mountford mused. "But that's all."

"So far." Marcia smiled again. "So far, Nigel. But here, your investigation is proving crucial."

"It is?"

"Certainly."

"How?"

"Like this." Marcia when folded her hands together, Reginald groaned inwardly. *This gets more like Hercules Poirot by the second. Better listen, though.*

"You went to Her Majesty's prison and interviewed one, Duncan Campbell. And was he forthcoming?"

"He was. Not."

"Except in one special respect. He was insulted when you suggested he might be charged with shoplifting."

"That's true."

"Why is it true, I wonder?" Marcia contemplated this curious reaction. "Thoughts?" she asked the group.

Mountford was considered by many at Thames House to be a relative youngster showing exceptional promise, combining attention to detail, which was an essential part of his work, with keen observation. Yet he had not developed into a fully rounded agent, but hopes were high. Not so with Hugo; his years of service, a degree of scepticism and his resolute determination to reach his objective had made him an excellent agent. He was already marked for gradual promotion. His methodical mind made him ideal for the present situation.

"I think we can agree," he said carefully, "that the number or series of contacts between these people puts it beyond doubt that it is not haphazard. For Frances to meet, even socially, with Oldham, who was acquainted with her husband, cannot be a chance. And further, she denied knowing of the golf matches in Worcestershire."

"Quite so." Marcia waited. "Go on, Hugo."

"If the encounters were pre-arranged, what is the purpose behind them? And are we likely to discover that purpose?"

"I agree with you, Hugo, wholeheartedly. Trying to intrude into these transactions is bound to be challenged. No. We must move in another direction."

"And that is?" Mountford asked.

"You're halfway there yourself, Nigel. What was Campbell's brother Duncan doing at 25 Carpel Street, and the very fair Lucinda? Who seem to have disappeared?"

"We don't know, this Lucinda." Stratton was quick to respond.

"But the group captain does." She looked at Reginald.

"Oh, yes. Came to see me one afternoon with messages from you, Marcia."

"Quite so. She has been known to me and the service since leaving university. A lady with an uncommonly inquisitive mind. And so, the final link. Lucinda worked for me as Muirhead's personal researcher in Westminster, visited Carpel Street and has disappeared on a motorbike heading towards Cambridge, we think."

"Well, bugger me!" Reginald exclaimed. "And I know the place."

"Absolutely."

*** *** ***

Chapter Sixteen

"Absolutely."

This was not Marcia repeating herself at 'The School' in Streatham but the Reverend Charles Fowler gently congratulating his band of 'flower ladies' who had surrounded him after morning service in the village church. He was about to enlarge upon this theme, but quite suddenly, he screwed up his face into a confusion of grimace and panic, and his body became contorted as his hand desperately searched below his cassock and within his trousers. The whole spectacle was most alarming. The ladies of the flower-arranging group waited anxiously. At last, his hand reappeared from the ecclesiastical folds together with a voluminous handkerchief, which he clamped to his mouth and nose, thus not only avoiding the spread of noxious viruses with the explosion of a sneeze but also capturing his errant teeth before they escaped his mouth.

The flower ladies sighed with relief.

The vicar's wife, Alice Fowler, made a note in the flower-arranging diary to ring the dentist. This peculiar note was the topic of some puzzled discussions over the next few weeks. Was the dentist a florist as well?

Immediate crisis over, Charles Fowler reassured the ladies around him that he was quite well, thank you; the flowers today were quite magnificent, thank you, and he and dear Alice could rest assured that all was well in the parish. Some members of the choir were passing the group while this was all going on, and the younger members wondered wildly what 'old Fowler' was doing below his cassock. Such impure thoughts and words were quickly nipped in the bud by the choirmaster, who, together with his leading tenor, one Maurice Marchbanks, frowned upon such flippancy.

Diane had recovered from Reginald's hasty departure at first light this morning and had attended church as usual. The congregation was bigger than it had been for some time, with the flock slowly recovering from the shock of the COVID pandemic. Rules had been relaxed, and the populace was slowly returning, if not to normal, then stoically to tradition. Their attention, quite naturally, had turned to the slaughter in London; the prayers were for the victims, the injured and the relatives. First the lockdown, now bombs! The vicar implored those present to donate monies for the families thrown into financial difficulties over the atrocity.

Diane knew that would not be ignored; some members of the congregation were from the gentleman farming community, others from the new housing estates that were springing up houses, which were certainly not 'affordable' as the government had promised, and villagers who were generous to a fault. The overall sentiment was of sympathy, closely followed by incomprehension. What was the meaning of this outrage? Was it nationalists of one country or another? Racial? Hardly, on a busy rail line. Interreligious? Again, hardly. As an afterthought, some considered it an expression of popular dissatisfaction with society. Had anyone claimed responsibility? Not as far as anyone was aware.

The congregation drifted towards the church hall for tea and cakes, all prepared individually, thus avoiding the spread of any COVID infection lurking in the church, which was something most people had forgotten anyway. A quick survey of the church hall revealed that no one sported a mask. The church wardens had organised the refreshments with their usual efficiency, and this was as it should be, Diane, a senior lady in the congregation, opined.

Although she would modestly disavow such an accolade, she was regarded as an important person in the church hierarchy. It was rumoured that even the vicar treated her with special deference. She sat one chair away from Ivor Davies, the choirmaster, a man she secretly could not stand. She had found through unpleasant experience that this was the minimal safe distance from his appalling halitosis and far enough removed to diminish the sound of his adenoidal whine. Maurice Marchbanks, on the other hand, was a young man she secretly believed was of immense potential. He sat next to her.

"How are you, my dear?" The choirmaster leant forward and addressed her across Maurice, who instinctively sat back in his chair. This term of affection Diane found objectionable; she said nothing but smiled benignly. "Your choir is a credit to the church," she said rather pointedly.

"Thank you. We work hard, do we not, Maurice?"

"Undoubtedly. The treble descants can be quite exhilarating, and our organist, Mr Deacon, is excellent. That is always a bonus." The young man was fulsome. "In some ways, I think we are beginning to compare favourably with my old college choir, Kings. If only the church was larger, the ceiling vaulted. Perhaps with the addition of larger organ pipes, who knows what might be possible?"

"You sang in Kings College Choir?" Diane was impressed. "How long ago?"

"Oh, several years ago. I had finished my degree in modern history and was drafting a dissertation for my thesis. Got involved in the choir, but then at the completion of my master's degree, I got married and moved out to this lovely village. I am incredibly happy. Expecting an addition to the family soon."

"How absolutely marvellous!" Diane exclaimed while noticing that he got married, moved to the village and was happy. That to the one side for the moment, this story – incomplete, as far as she was concerned was at least romantic. It lacked only any mention of his wife or even her name. Nevertheless, he was an ambitious young man, full of love and hope for the future, she felt sure.

"I did not know Sarah was expecting…" I choirmaster looked around and, at the same time, supplied the name so far missing from the narrative. "I do not believe I have seen her here today. I must congratulate her."

"No, absent today; a slight indisposition, nothing to worry over. Merely a little morning sickness."

Marcia again noticed the minimal reference to his wife, and 'morning sickness was a slight indisposition', was it?

"And your work?" Diane explored tentatively.

"I write," was the short and seemingly definitive answer.

"Fascinating. And with your education, you must be so knowledgeable. Your writing is scholarly, is it?" Diane was genuinely interested in this young man and was wondering whether an invitation to dinner was in order, with his wife, of course! But the conversation was cut short by the arrival of Alice Fowler, the vicar's wife. Smiling, chattering and giggling, the usual bundle of nerves. Maurice got up to leave.

Diane called him, "You must come and dine with us one evening. You and your wife. An exciting time! In fact, tomorrow evening, if you are free. Would that be suitable?"

"Thank you. I would like that." He hurried away. Diane noted with some disquiet that the invitation had been accepted without reference to his wife yet again. But so be it.

Alice took the now-vacated chair, much to Diane's relief. The vicar settled himself into a chair opposite, dabbing his mouth discreetly, ensuring a firm location for his teeth before he tackled an iced bun served to him. Having successfully taken a small bite of the cake and feeling sufficiently reassured, he spoke to those around him. "A gratifyingly full house this morning." He beamed. "Although scarcely a time for celebration."

There was a murmur of consent. "I thought your sermon so appropriate, Charles, in these troubled times." Alice made her contribution and then added, "We all labour under the effects of that dreadful pandemic and its lingering after-effects. And your references to the seven plagues of Egypt and God's wrath are so pertinent to our failing society. It is so easy for us to look for a scapegoat when such troubles overwhelm us. And, of course, your helpful references to biblical teachings in times of stress and misfortune will strengthen our resolve."

Alice was not known to be a conversation stopper, but that was the effect of her expressed opinion. Everyone looked at her, eyebrows raised, and she blushed crimson. The silence was lengthening, and yet no one came to her aid. Finally, Charles said, "How very true." And to emphasise the point, he repeated, "How true, Alice. I gave much thought to suffering and its alleviation." The relief around the table was profound. There was a mutual sigh of relaxation. Alice recovered.

Members of the congregation started to leave. "I will take my leave of you, my dear," whined the choirmaster, giving Diane one last blast of his breath. "I look forward to seeing you again next week."

"Oh, certainly," Diane replied bravely, "look forward to the choir, Mr Davies."

The hall was suddenly empty, the only sounds that of washing up from the regular volunteers. *Salt of the earth, those kitchen ladies*, Diane thought. But then her mind drifted to the sermon and Alice's comments about it. It was exceptionally unusual for Alice to venture an opinion, especially in front of her husband. Normally quiet, even subservient, today she had spoken almost forcibly. She must feel strongly about the subject. Her parish work must have called to her attention to the suffering among the flock that was becoming unbearable.

Diane resolved to talk with Reginald when she got home. And Alice as well, later, to discover the degree of resentment and unrest smouldered under the apparently placid surface of the village and population at large. She had a feeling it was far more than she suspected. Sometimes, she realised how insular her life had become.

But for the moment, her mind turned to the kitchen. She must hurry in and thank the 'kitchen ladies'.

*** *** ***

Marcia stood, walked across the room and turned to face the others. She leant back against the door. Whether this was an unconscious gesture of closing the room to intruders or not, it certainly had that effect on the three men who were sitting and watching in the gloomy, comfortless room.

"As I see it," Marcia began thoughtfully, "we need to act promptly. I have been advised that there is incontrovertible evidence of illicit bomb-making factories in Liverpool, Birmingham, Stockport, London and, curiously, Felixstowe. The bombmakers most probably are seriously disaffected members of the populace. If we can prove a conspiracy involving William Oldham, the late Donald Muirhead and his wife, Frances, Brendan Forsythe and a consortium of wealthy backers, it will strengthen my hand when I make the final petition for a national joint action. I will seek cabinet approval. It is that serious.

"Following the unfortunate death of Duncan Muirhead in Worcestershire, there are several questions that need answering. Firstly, Muirhead was friendly with millionaire William Oldham and, surreptitiously, so was his wife, Frances. My erstwhile colleague Avril Reynolds, Simpkin to you, Nigel, has also told me that Forsythe has visited William Oldham at his mansion. This is evidence of a direct connection between Muirhead, Oldham and Brendan Forsythe. Is there any evidence that shows the millionaire William Oldham was putting undue pressure on Muirhead as a Member of Parliament? And if there was, what was the nature of that pressure? Secondly, soon after the apparently unrelated outrages in Brighton and Peterborough, Duncan Campbell was arrested as a suspect. Then his brother, Errol, visits Muirhead's lodgings in Carpel Street. Are the brothers Campbell part of the Carpel Street faction, which, do not forget, also included Donald Muirhead?

"While you wrestle with those problems, I will ensure that MI5, MI6 and the Home Office know of our profound belief that a powerful group plans to overthrow our democratic society, and I will strongly suggest an interdepartmental body is set up with powers of arrest and investigation and has full backing of proper ministers, even cabinet. I can adequately represent our views on such a conspiracy.

"That will allow you, Hugo and Reginald, to investigate the disappearance of Lucinda. I will ensure you have all the necessary assistance you require from the police." She continued in a quiet voice but with an intense feeling, "That is of primary concern to me and the department. I believe she is in grave danger."

They appreciated the urgency in her voice.

At last, Hugo Stratton recognised and fully concurred with Marcia's original hypothesis. There was a widespread conspiracy operating in Britain, although its exact intention was still a mystery. The highest offices had to be involved and as soon as possible.

Marcia remained against the door, hands behind her on the old-fashioned ceramic doorknob. Looking at each in turn, she waited, as was her custom, for contributions. Stratton was the first and, as it turned out, the only speaker.

"I am persuaded; no, that is not strong enough. I am convinced there must be an underlying conspiracy. But what is the purpose?"

"Exactly, Hugo." Marcia had not moved. "Anyone else?" Nigel and Reginald sat and waited, quite silent.

"Let me put it this way, gentlemen." Marcia returned to her seat. "We require only for the consortium to show itself. In the meantime, the more inter-related connections we make, the surer we can be that all this is not just random activities of individuals that have nothing better to do with themselves."

"And that's bloody unlikely." Reginald had contributed it last.

"Quite." Marcia gazed at him.

She let the silence lengthen and then said quietly, "Brighton, Peterborough, London Underground; where next? And still no declaration of intent. It can only mean more carnage is planned. I hope my endeavours with the government will be successful."

The three men had no doubt about the seriousness of the situation.

"And if you blame the establishment, you blame the first in line. The police, then the government," Mountford mumbled, almost to himself.

"There may be protests?" Reginald murmured.

"Much more," Marcia emphasised. "Much more. Civil unrest, disorder, rebellion, anarchy."

"I'm now worried," Stratton declared. "This is urgent! Good God, to save lives, if nothing else."

"It is! I will speak with Vauxhall Cross today as a matter of top priority. Ministers and the government must be alerted to the threat and must act. And I will demand the immediate formation of a joint crisis group of members, consisting of branches of our law enforcement agencies, secret services and all the auxiliary services. The secret services, police, counterterrorism, GCHQ, all need to be involved. This must be a nation-wide response. We have no time to lose. In the meantime, Hugo and Reginald, exert your best efforts to find Lucinda, and Nigel, if you would work with Avril Simpkin to watch Carpel Street, that will be of immense help."

This is a Marcia I've not seen before, Reginald thought on the way to his car. *And one I like.*

*** **** ***

Diane arrived home, spiritually revived, if unfortunately, troubled by the outburst from the diminutive Alice. She looked forward to the excellent Sunday lunch that Mrs Braithwaite would have prepared and, of course, sharing it with Reginald, although she abruptly realised that that was unlikely. Reginald would certainly not be home yet. He had departed in a rush this morning; Marcia had called.

Walking into Plantagenet House, Diane smelled the roast beef that awaited her for lunch. Mrs Braithwaite had been advised of the absence of the group captain and had laid out only one plate at the table. It was to be a solitary meal, but two or three glasses of Bordeaux would help. Reginald would make for the gin as soon as he walked in.

It was 4:00 before Diane, who had almost finished the supplements from one of the heavier Sunday papers, heard the front door open and greetings exchanged with Mrs Braithwaite.

"That you?" she called unnecessarily.

The door to the lounge opened, and Reginald came in and, all in one swift movement, moved towards the gin. She had been correct!

"Stopped by the club?" she asked, putting down the paper.

"No, as it happens. Meeting went on. Roads were busy. Middle of London is impossible. Taken nearly three hours to get back."

"Tired? Put your feet up; there is no rush. Mrs Braithwaite is making up something cold. Healthy salad and cold beef, the works."

"Just a snifter first." His nose disappeared into the glass, and with a satisfied release of breath, he sank back into the cushions. "Long drive that."

"You are quite safe?" Diane had been married to a group captain in the RAF with responsibility for lawfulness; she knew of dangers but was still worried.

"Thank you, yes."

There was an unspoken concern between the two; however, both, in their ways, depended on that.

Mrs Braithwaite brought in and laid out on the table a cold buffet of several dishes for Reginald to help himself. He thanked her profusely, and when she left the room, he refilled his glass.

"Don't spoil your meal," Diane admonished. He merely looked at her.

"All in good time." He sat down to his meal, and Diane joined him, although she was not eating. She would have never countenanced allowing him to sit to eat on his own in their house. She was, after all, his wife.

Eventually, they relaxed back into their armchairs and enjoyed coffee together. Diane knew that Reginald would not discuss any details of the meeting with Marcia but nevertheless was keen to understand, in general terms, the nature of this emergency on a Sunday morning. She waited.

"How was church?" Reginald inquired finally, which took her by surprise. Always solicitous, he had however much on his mind, she was sure.

"I think there was an increase in the members."

"Excellent."

"And more for refreshments after."

"Excellent." Again, the one-word answer.

"I managed to keep reasonably separated from that dreadful choirmaster…"

"That's not like you, Diane, to be critical."

"…It is his breath. Not so much him. I got a chair between us; that helped. Maurice Marchbanks sat on it."

"Who's Maurice Marchbanks?"

"I knew you would say that. He is a tenor in the choir, was in Kings College Choir, now lives in the village. Wife expecting a baby. I invited him to supper. Tomorrow actually. He is very presentable."

"Kings?"

"Yes. Very polite, well-mannered, a writer."

"A writer? What's he writing?"

"No idea, really. Took a degree in modern history. So, history, I imagine."

"Fictional?"

"I do not think so, Reginald. Why all the questions?"

"Oh, no reason."

"Anyway, you will find out tomorrow evening; I have invited him and his wife for supper." Fait accompli!

"Right." The mumbled reply could have meant anything. Diane did not inquire further.

Sometimes Reginald could be so irritating! Diane thought to herself. *Change the subject.* She said, "Alice was odd today. You know Alice? The vicar's wife."

"Yes, yes." As if he knew everyone in the church! "How odd?"

"She voiced her opinion quite forcefully. Odd enough for you?"

"Well, yes, that sounds odd for Alice."

"Not only the trouble in London that you rushed off to this morning, but a growing unease in the parish. She meant the villages, I think."

"Unease? What unease?"

"She thought people were fed up. Unhappy. Thing is, Reginald, I took note of what she said; she visits the villages, hears all the gripes, I suppose. And from what little I know, the economy is a bit shaky after the pandemic. Perhaps more than that. Prices going up, food, energy. They're on about carbon neutral before you can turn around. Awfully expensive. Petrol beginning to cost a fortune. No buses soon. People will strike for more money."

"Not noticed."

"No, Reginald, we would not notice. We are quite privileged. Not sure we know all that goes on."

"Finger not on the pulse?"

"Something like that. Alice gave me quite a jolt today. Woke me up. Not all is well, Reginald, I tell you."

"You mean not only the bomb but over and above that?"

"Alice was talking about something else. People do not know what is coming next. Worry about feeding themselves. Heating themselves. Health issues."

"She didn't say all that, surely?"

"No, but it's what she meant."

"Perhaps we better watch the news; what d'you say?"

"Good idea. Then bed?"

"Then bed."

*** *** ***

Lights in Whitehall burned late into the evening. Jocelyn Carstairs was not in a good mood. He had been called away from his snooker game with the local retired general in a military man's country house. That did not go down well with the general; cussed old sod when he wanted to be. Mind you, Jocelyn…

"Bring yourself in, Forsythe," barked Carstairs as Brendan put his head around the door.

"There's a chair there." Carstairs pointed to a chair on the opposite side of his desk. *Got to keep them in their place. Hell did he get a knighthood for? Buggered if he knew.*

"You called me in?" Forsythe took a chair.

"Balloon's gone up. Minister's been on the phone shouting at me. Damned if I know why. I didn't let off the bomb."

"Neither did I." Forsythe tried a joke. It did not come off.

"No one said you did."

They sat in silence for a moment. Two emergency vehicles sped along Whitehall.

"Must be some other hiccough. Too long after the bomb."

"Probably." Forsythe was more circumspect.

"Now, listen to me, Forsythe. Got to do something about this mess, or make noises that we're doing something."

"Taken care of." Forsythe sat back with a superior crossing of the legs.

"Taken care of? What d'you mean?"

"Interdepartmental meeting tomorrow. All the big heads will be there. Counterterrorism, SO15, Home Office, Foreign Office, Secret Services, GCHQ; you name it, they'll be there."

"Ministers?"

"At their discretion. Certainly, their private secretaries."

"You?"

"Oh, yes."

"Me?"

"Of course."

"Well, that's something. I'll let the minister know."

"I would if I were you." Carstairs frowned at Forsythe, who hurried from the room.

*** *** ***

Chapter Seventeen

Often, Marcia asked her agents to work independently, and now was such a time. The interdepartmental meeting, which she was due to advise, was booked for 11:00 this morning, Monday, 21 October; it would be in a subterranean room near Whitehall. She needed all her energies to encourage a blanket programme of observation, investigation and, if possible, arrests within the movement that she suspected, no, knew, was attempting to organise a breakdown of society in Britain. That movement would grow out of general unrest and dissatisfaction. It would spread to vital services such as the NHS, ambulance service, social care and even government. The void left would be filled with a coalition of extreme right and left factions. In order that everyone would appear to be satisfied, or at least placated.

A tall order to persuade all those services, something that required 100% of her concentration. Any distraction, personal and painful though it may be, could not be allowed to impede that goal. She was going to direct Hugo and Reginald, who, at first sight, were an unlikely duo, to direct their combined energies and abilities into the release of Lucinda, without raising speculation within the Lyfen group that this was part of a bigger operation. She suspected that this was not a unique group but one of many at various universities around the country. She had called the meeting for 10:00; the interdepartmental meeting was at 11:00.

It was to emphasise the gravity of the situation that she had called the agents together one last time before the demanding work began. The three agents, Hugo, Nigel and Reginald, arrived early, helped themselves to coffee and waited for Marcia in the depressing gloom of 'The School'. The door opened, and she strode in purposefully at precisely 10:00.

"Gentlemen," she began. "Today marks the end of our preliminary inquiries. It would be too crass to call it the end of the beginning, but you understand my meaning."

They nodded.

"As I said yesterday, your investigations have been crucial. We have been able to construct, from your important work, the definitive thesis of subterfuge, which if allowed to flourish, would threaten the complete way of life in Britain."

They listened.

"We have already seen atrocities that are apparently unrelated. Certainly not claimed, or alleged even, to have come from any known faction of society, which leaves us with a situation best dealt with by our huge professional services, of which you are a part, but for the moment, seconded to me. It is my intention to recommend that the services widen their investigations from seeking and arresting the perpetrators of these last three incidents but also to include the examination of political and university groups around the country, trade unions, racial and homophobic cabals and even inflammatory orators or lecturers.

"I am sure that such investigations are already under way, but I must impress the urgent need to draw together the various components of the overall composition. It is my belief that such a wide-ranging investigation will eventually bring to light a significant pattern of behaviour, even name the principal conspirators." I would not want to impede your operation in Cambridge or"—she nodded to Nigel—"Carpel Street. There are some very perceptive people coming to the interdepartmental meeting, and I want to be completely unaware of your actions. Unconscious knowledge can be recognised too easily these days. I want to go in without any knowledge of your activities."

The three nodded. It made perfectly good sense. Their task would be to concentrate on the release of Lucinda and, secondarily, the apprehension of the members of the group at the bookshop, which had to be accomplished without Marcia's knowledge. That way, she could not refer to their activities, consciously or unconsciously. If successful, they may follow the leads back to Carpel Street and hopefully further.

"Gentlemen, I will leave you to get on with it." And with that, she left the room and drove to Whitehall.

*** *** ***

MORE THAN A YEAR EARLIER, to be precise, in July 2020, Siobhan Behan took her first tentative steps to broaden her knowledge of genetical science. She made up her mind to attend a little-known group of 'theorists' who, so she had been told, were exploring modern society, philosophy and inheritance.

On the night in question, Siobhan looked in the full-length mirror in her tiny bedroom and did not like what she saw. Standing naked after her bath, it was true that she could see her skin had taken on a healthy glow; the major trouble was with the proportions of her body; nothing was quite balanced. What was also obvious, however, was that she had dyed her hair red.

Brought up on the west of Ireland in County Mayo, where her father and mother were always busy on the cattle farm, she had a lonely childhood; her secondary school was some distance away in Castlebar, which meant her friends were not within walking distance. Fortuitously, she had an elder sister who had provided companionship at least through her adolescence. The family, as everyone in the village and around, were Catholics and ministered by Father Vincente, an absolutist but happy in his work. As she grew into her teens, Siobhan's mother had remarked that her chest had developed 'womanly curves'. Siobhan's was the closest her mother ever came to discussing 'womanly' matters.

She, of course, had learned all about a woman's reproductive capabilities at school, but she could not but help thinking the other girls went into unnecessary detail. It all sounded like a pretty dreadful business whichever way you looked at it. But in conversation with her mother or with Father Vincente, even in the confessional, she found questions concerning sexual matters impossible to articulate. She did notice, however, the good father talked more to her sweater than to her face as she grew older.

She had always been bright, and at an early stage in school, she had been described by one of the teachers as 'borderline gifted'. It was therefore unsurprising that she won a bursary to Cambridge, the first from the local area to do so. She read philosophy at Newman College and was now a first-year, postgraduate member of St Edmund's College, which was the only college in Oxford or Cambridge with a chapel worshipping the Catholic faith. Standing naked before her mirror, she realised that her mother's dire warnings that young men with immoral intentions would pester her into immodest activities were unnecessary.

The sight of her body reassured her that she was safe from such conduct, but rather than become dispirited with her inability to attract young men, she had applied herself to her studies with commendable vigour and taken a 'First'. Her choice of subject for her postgraduate thesis was daring for a student burdened with the misguided perception of 'a good, Catholic girl from County Mayo'. It was the influence of Darwin's Theory of Evolution, upon the nineteenth- and twentieth-century philosophy. This interest in biological functioning might have been a Freudian reaction to the inhibitions of her sheltered adolescence. She had become fascinated with evolution and how it had been almost universally accepted as fact, except perhaps by the fundamentalists within the church.

She had read some of Galton's, who was Darwin's cousin, work on 'Selective Breeding' and knew her father, and farmers in general, had used selective breeding for generations. The selection of grasses had started in Mesopotamia before Christ was born. She realised that Nazi misinterpretation of that work led to the horrific slaughter in Europe during the Second World War and the discrediting of 'eugenics' thereafter, but her interest had been re-ignited when she attended a lecture entitled 'Genetic Modification, Embryo Selection and Human Enhancement' given by a King's junior fellow, who had now left the university; it was rumoured under a cloud. His name was Maurice Marchbanks.

And, without doubt, he was handsome.

The lecture had been delivered at a private residence on the outskirts of Cambridge, in a room that was large but could not be described as a lecture theatre. The attendance was modest, perhaps seven. They sat as far away from each other as possible because of COVID restrictions introduced by the government. This encouraged an open discussion to develop. Siobhan welcomed this participation with the lecturer and was determined to make at least his acquaintanceship.

How to do that was another matter, but for once in her short life, she was lucky. She just happened to be thanking another member of the group for passing her coat when Marchbanks approached the two of them. It was clear he knew the man and suggested they pop into a local for 'a quick half'. "Bernard, my throat's dry after all that talking. What do you say?"

"Good idea, Maurice," Bernard replied. "Care to join us, Miss…Miss…sorry, don't seem to have caught your name?"

"Siobhan." She smiled.

"Right. Siobhan."

"Yes, I'd love to join you." She had never said anything like that before. She was proud of her courage.

The pub selected by Maurice and his friend Bernard was not one of the large, celebrated and popular hostelries in the centre of Cambridge but a small local seventeenth-century ale house, whose clients seemed to have been there since opening night. The layout was simple: four small rooms around the central bar area. It reminded Siobhan of the prison systems made popular by Jeremy Bentham in the nineteenth century.

From a central position, the bar, the wings of the institution and the four small rooms could be viewed, and beer was served with a minimal amount of effort. Winchester, Pentonville or Wandsworth, all those institutions had been built on the same plan, and the drinkers were similarly dressed uniformly in grey, and the atmosphere was just as subdued. The publican and his wife, however, seemed much more amiable than warders from a prison that she had seen act on television, although the lack of activity, loud conversation or laughter in the rooms were comparable.

They chose a room that was panelled in the darkest, varnished wood, with a bench around the walls and a central table, marked by spilled beer and cigarette burns. A reminder of past times. Maurice bought three pints of beer without asking what either Bernard or Siobhan wanted. They sat around the table. They considered they were within the laws of COVID restrictions, and the proprietor raised no objections. Possibly, he had not heard of the restrictions!

"Bernard, we're due to meet on Thursday, are we not?" Maurice took a mouthful of beer. He exhaled through his nose with evident satisfaction.

"That's it. Usual time. Usual place. I'll be there."

"Good."

That exhausted that topic of conversation. As Siobhan waited for more, she sipped her bitter; unaccustomed to either the size of the glass or the taste of its content, she returned it quickly to the table. Bernard looked at her. "More accustomed to Guinness, I would imagine."

Both men were looking at her, and she became flustered. "Not really. No. I don't drink a lot as a rule. Never really got used to it."

"Lovely freckles," Maurice murmured, "especially when you blush." And of course, that made matters a good deal worse.

"When did you come up?" Bernard was by far the gentler of the two. "I assume you are at the university."

"Yes. Yes, I am." She took a sip of her beer to give herself an opportunity to gather herself and then said, "I came up in 2018, and I'm just starting my postgraduate thesis."

"College?" Maurice asked.

"St Edmund's."

"Good Catholic Chapel there," he declared. "Catholic girl, are you?"

"Yes, I'm a member of the Catholic community but not particularly religious in the formal sense. No. I'm much more interested in modern thinkers and just, possibly, comparative philosophies and religions. My postgraduate work will be on nineteenth and twentieth century philosophy and how much Darwinism and evolution may have influenced modern thinking."

"Right." Again, Marchbanks said no more. Silence.

Bernard had finished his drink. "Maurice? Siobhan? Can I get you anything?" They replied in unison.

"Yes, please."

"No, thank you."

Bernard worked it out.

At that moment, one of the doors opened, and a man with a cloth cap came in. "This where the crib match is?"

In unison, they replied, "No."

He went out of the other door without a word, trying to find the match in another room, no doubt. They were on their own again.

Bernard returned with two pints and a bag of crisps. Settling at the table again, he asked Maurice how he was keeping. "Comfortable," came the reply. "I view the political landscape with some trepidation, however."

"Trepidation? Strong word, isn't it?"

"I think not. Keep my ear to the ground; there seems to be trouble brewing. Not sure which way the country is lurching."

"That's always the case, isn't it?" Bernard fished in his pocket to retrieve his mobile. He gave it a cursory look and put it back again. "I mean, everyone moans about the establishment, don't they?"

"To a certain extent, but there are one or two issues that are beginning to get critical." Marchbanks ticked them off on the fingers of his left hand. "One, the NHS, waiting lists, GPs—or lack of them. Two, the economy. Three, massive government debt, which is about to get much, much bigger. Four, leadership, and I think that is the one of paramount importance."

"Oh, yes," Bernard agreed. "We need a strong director and direction."

The two lapsed into thoughtful silence. Siobhan was bothered by the anger, which was unspoken but clearly fundamental. Particularly in Maurice Marchbanks' outburst.

Quite suddenly, Siobhan felt out of her depth. These two had moved away from her area of interest, evolution, onto something political. She was rapidly losing interest in the topic, if not Marchbanks himself.

"I think I'll get back," she said quietly.

"Need a lift?" This was Marchbanks. Tempting though the offer might once have been, she had her bicycle at the house. "Thanks, but no. I'll take my bike."

"Okay." Bernard smiled at her. She blushed and left. The two men sipped their beers. She was not mentioned.

The COVID pandemic brought havoc to the hospitality facilities of the country. The draconian first lockdown, its relaxation, the second lockdown in November 2020, the tiered system and then the third lockdown in January 2021 left many bemused, some angry and several establishments bankrupt. She was working in solitary concentration on her thesis and had become friendly with another postgraduate, Rebecca, whose social life was as limited as Siobhan's.

When the third relaxation of restrictions lengthened and the pubs were safe to enter in July, inside as well as outside, she plucked up courage and asked Rebecca to come with her for a drink in the ale house she had visited with Maurice Marchbanks and his friend, whose name she had forgotten. When they arrived, she was reminded how basic the premises were, and Rebecca was not slow to show her. Siobhan saw the pub through her friend's eyes; the dark, panelled snug now appeared to her to be what it was: a tired, small space that needed re-decorating; the old-fashioned benches were just old and uncomfortable. The central table—well needed replacing!

"This is where you came?" Rebecca asked incredulously.

Siobhan was suitably mortified. She had forgotten how unexciting the place was.

"Sorry, I forgot," she mumbled.

"This Marchbanks must be pretty exciting, is all I can say." Rebecca shrugged.

They left after one glass of wine, and that was a Spanish Chardonnay.

Two weeks later, it must have been somewhere at the start of August, when Siobhan received a letter in her pigeonhole at college. It was fortuitous that she had stayed on through the summer break, or she would have missed it.

Siobhan,

I chair a group that meets on Thursday evening. We are a group of like-minded postgraduates and occasionally other guests, and we discuss the state of society and the British community today.

I would think your contributions to such discussions might add a new dimension to our thinking. If you would care to join us, I will pick you up at the Porter's Lodge at 7:30 pm on Thursday, 11th.

This week.

Maurice Marchbanks.

She folded the letter back into the envelop and considered the invitation. No address. No date, except the coming Thursday. Typed, but not by a secretary. No signature. Certainly, to the point. And others would be there. Safe enough. But after the experience with Rebecca and that miserable pub, she had to wonder what sort of place they'd be going to. She'd be safe, she reassured herself. And in any case, she would leave the letter with Rebecca, just as a precaution. She would go.

Siobhan was picked up by Marchbanks at 7:30 pm precisely on Thursday and taken by car, an old Citroen C4, to her first meeting of a group he called 'Shared Action'.

"Have you heard of us?" he asked as they sped through Cambridge and seemed unsurprised when she said that she had not. They drove north towards Milton, but after that, she was lost. It was now dark; the signposts went past too quickly to be read, but eventually they slowed down through the village about another four miles further on, where she managed to read the village sign: 'LYFEN'.

On a dark side street, Marchbanks pulled up outside a bookshop advertised as Aggie's Bookshop. The premises were in darkness, but a light shone from an upstairs window, so clearly someone was in. Marchbanks rang the bell, and after about 10 seconds, a light came on and the door opened. A middle-aged woman, slightly out of breath and a little flushed, stood back, and without words being exchanged, they were waved in.

The light was good enough for Siobhan to make out bookshelves around the walls and a long, central table with books placed in such a way that the titles were uppermost. Another light from upstairs illuminated what looked like a metal spiral staircase, and there was a murmur of voices from above. She followed Marchbanks up the steps, the woman, the owner, behind. At the top, she found herself in a room with chairs in a circle. Four men looked at her from their chairs; for Siobhan, it was an unsettling experience.

"As you see, we have a new member here for her first meeting," Marchbanks introduced Siobhan offhandedly.

"Come on in. Join us." This was with a touch of impatience, whilst he took a seat in the circle. "She is a postgraduate at St Edmund's, studying the effects of the theory of evolution and modern philosophies. I think it is a suitable adjunct to our studies of the present-day politics and political movements."

Siobhan took a seat. She had bridled at the word 'theory'; evolution was surely a proven matter.

"Hello," she said diffidently. She was greatly relieved to see Bernard there, the other person in 'that' pub.

He smiled at her encouragingly. "Pleased to meet you again," he said.

And Siobhan's first meeting got underway. Bernard introduced her to his friend, Ralph. That left only two whose names she did not know. Then, belatedly, one of them, a tall chap with unruly hair and glasses, sighed, "Lawrence," as if the business of mentioning his name was unnecessary. The last to admit his name was a large man with a severe crewcut, who muttered, almost inaudibly, "Brad." The woman who opened the door initially settled with a glass of what looked like whisky, and Siobhan realised if she were not mistaken, and by the flushed complexion, this was not the lady's first today. Quite what she was doing here was a mystery because she remained silent throughout the whole meeting.

Siobhan can now remember little of the meeting, which was as dynamic as it was. There seemed to be talk of the disproportionate number of privileged undergraduates, but that was a matter of some congratulation, not recrimination as she had so often heard before. There was some talk of a joint meeting with another 'branch' in Newcastle, or some such remote northern university, but overall, the meeting was low-key, unexciting and purposeless. She got a cup of coffee. Or at least that was what she thought it was.

Around 9:30, Marchbanks looked at his watch, a signal that the meeting was at an end. The other members got slowly to their feet and returned their cups to the counter that held a coffeemaker and started to put their coats on.

"I hope that was instructive," Marchbanks said. "We'll see you next week?" And without waiting for a reply, he spoke over her shoulder to Bernard, who was about to leave. "Bernard, going to Cambridge? Be a good chap, run Siobhan back, will you? I can bypass the bloody place on my way home then."

"Sure," Bernard replied. "We'll drop Ralph off on the way. Okay?"

"Okay with me," was Marchbanks' short reply.

After they had dropped Ralph at Milton, she felt more comfortable, if the truth be told first time all evening. The bookshop had been uninspiring and the meeting boring to the point of somnolence. Marchbanks was not the attractive young man she had originally thought. Bernard was a much more easy-going individual, much more friendly and a more sensitive young man altogether. Pity his hair was so long.

"What did you make of us?" he asked.

She even gave herself a chance to consider before replying. "I have to say, it wasn't what I expected. In fact, I'm not sure what it was all about. I suppose I had imagined some discussion about various political and philosophical movements and how they had developed. I suppose with reference to my own work."

She finished lamely, gazing out of the window in excruciating embarrassment and convincing herself she had made one of the most ignorant statements of her life. Her mother would have called it 'vapid', a novel word in her mother's vocabulary, not always appropriately used. It was one of those moments when she was overcome by humiliation and mortification and when she knew positively that she had made a fool of herself. She was out of her depth and didn't even know it!

"Rubbish," came the astonishing reply. "What you saw tonight was the typical Marchbanks. Huge ideas, huge theories, plenty of imagination. Deficient in application and, most unfortunately, rapport. I have immense respect for the feller. Clever, chess champion, if that's anything to do with anything, founder of the universities' action groups."

"Sorry."

"Don't be sorry, happens to lots of people when they first meet him. If you ask me, and no one has yet, I will say he has a one-track, obsessional mind. Know what I mean?"

"I think so."

The atmosphere in the car had relaxed again. Bernard talked about other things, dropped her off at St Edmund's and said he would chauffeur her next week.

"Okay?"

"Okay." He drove off.

That was the middle of August, and it was not until nearly a year later that she first saw Lucinda. By that time, she had become a regular member of the 'Club' but had made few contributions and was beginning to lose interest; the arrival of another young woman escorted by a man in motorcycle leathers was strange. At the end of the meeting, she saw that the new woman, Brad and Aggie remained behind. She felt a chill of unease. Nothing she could be certain of, just unease. In any case, she had become dissatisfied with the meetings. Siobhan decided not to attend any more.

And that was one of the best decisions of her life, but she didn't know that for some time.

*** *** ***

Chapter Eighteen

After Marcia left Stratton, Mountford and Young in the academy at Streatham, the three of them turned towards each other. At first, all seemed straight forward; what she wanted was the activities at 25 Carpel Street and any leads from there unearthed. But damn it, it was a lot more complicated than that.

They pooled their knowledge. The 25 and 27 had been knocked into a single establishment, so it must now be quite extensive. It was known to have been Donald Muirhead's lodgings whilst in London, and it was thought that the property was owned by Frances Muirhead's brother, Andrew Stewartson, who still lived there. Mountford had spent a nervous lunchtime in the local café and had seen, as was later confirmed, Errol Campbell pick up Lucinda Clayton from the same address.

It was assumed, although there is no certainty, that the destination of the motorcycle pair was Lyfen, a village near Cambridge, the home of Aggie and her bookshop. Was Mountford to keep an eye on Carpel Street for developments? Was Stratton to investigate Frances Muirhead? Was Young to maintain interest through Mendel Partners in Weber in Worcester and Oldham in Bromsgrove? If that were the case, no one would be following up in Lyfen.

Stratton, by no means the oldest in years, had nevertheless served many years in the Secret Service and was the natural leader. But he looked to Reginald and raised an eyebrow.

"Thoughts?"

Reginald had plenty of those; the uppermost in his mind was a gin and tonic, but that did not seem like a useful topic and to pursue at the moment. Instead, he said, "Simple. Think we must keep things simple. Concentrate on one aspect only. What Marcia asked, wasn't it?"

"We can't afford to drop any leads." Mountford was troubled. "We'll meet again Wednesday; what do you think?"

It was agreed, and they left.

In the taxi on the way back to Liverpool Street Station, Reginald decided to give the club a miss. He would wait until tomorrow after he had visited Mendel Partners and caught up with the latest news on Worcester and Bromsgrove. Then he would leave that side of things to Mendel's agents. And this evening, Diane had invited the star tenor from the church choir, together with his wife for dinner—or was it supper? Liverpool Street Station was thankfully quiet. He had the carriage almost to himself, so he could look out through the window and lose himself in his own with his own thoughts.

He had no idea how others thought, but he assumed that they thought actively; in other words, they put their minds into gear, called upon their reserves of memory and constructed logical ideas from what resulted. That would be an active thought, wouldn't it? Well, his was more passive thought. He looked out at the scenery without seeing it as they travelled and thoughts, whatever they were, just popped up. Sometimes they made sense. Often, they did not. By the time he was climbing into Clive's taxi at Audley End Station, he was still preoccupied. He told Clive to 'put it on the bill', opened the door into Plantagenet House, made for the lounge, exchanged welcomes with his wife, who was reading the newspaper, poured himself a large gin and tonic and sat in his favourite armchair. He watched a pair of squirrels hunting for winter fuel, no doubt, and, on occasions, rushing across the lawn in pretend fights. He continued to gaze at the garden. He supposed he was in a pensive mood. *Don't be daft; I don't do pensive.* He sighed.

There was a rustle of newspaper, and his wife spoke. "You're in a pensive mood this afternoon." Just went to show, he knew nothing, not even about himself.

"What d'you mean?" He was startled.

"What I say," came the unhelpful reply.

"Right," he murmured and continued to gaze at the garden.

"Something on your mind? Marcia in good form, was she?"

"Yes. Good form," he answered absently.

"You haven't forgotten Maurice is coming to dinner tonight."

"No, course not. Looking forward to it. Isn't his wife, or something, coming as well?"

"Yes. His wife. Not 'something'."

"What's the girl's name?"

"Please, Reginald, not 'girl', and it's Sally, I think. Or is it Sandra? Or Stella? For the life of me, I cannot remember. Do not call her anything until we are sure."

"Right, Sally, we think. Or Sandra. Or Stella. But don't say it. Not like you to forget a name, Diane." Reginald lost interest and studied the behaviour of the two squirrels again. Diane gave up.

The Marchbanks were due for drinks at 7:30 and dinner at 8:00. Both Diane and Reginald changed into informal outfits that were acceptable for receiving their guests. Diane went fussing in the kitchen until she was told to leave by Mrs Braithwaite, who was not only proud of her own cooking but liked to prepare all meals alone. Suitably chastened, Diane returned to the lounge.

"Have a wine, Diane?" Reginald was still a little preoccupied.

"I think I will." Diane poured herself a large glass of Bordeaux. "Not drinking too much?" She looked at Reginald's glass of gin.

"Never, Diane, never."

She said nothing but sipped her wine, and they waited. The doorbell sounded at precisely 7:30 by Diana's ever-right wristwatch, and she hurried out to welcome the guests. Reginald took the opportunity to replenish his glass quickly, while welcoming sounds came from the hall and the 'oohs' and 'aahs' indicated the gift of flowers and coats were taken. Diane was to be heard reassuring her guests that they were exactly on time and that Reginald and she were not time-watchers.

"Come in and meet Reginald. Reginald, I do not believe you have met Maurice and his lovely wife."

Reginald stood, walked two paces forward and extended his hand to 'the wife' and Maurice, and strictly obeying the command not to call the 'girl' by any name until they were sure of it, he said, "Evening. Lovely that you could join us for dinner. Get you a drink?" He waved to the settee, and the guests sat.

"I'm afraid, for the time being, I'm denied alcohol," 'the wife' said. Then, diffidently, she added, "A little one is expected."

"How wonderful!" Reginald gushed. "Can I get you tonic water? Squash? Tap water?"

"Not tap water." Maurice spoke hurriedly. "I believe the water is fluoridated in this area."

"It is?" Reginald wondered what the hell that had to do with anything. Diane frowned; she knew very well that Reginald was aware of the fluoride in the water. He was playing one of his games. Not a good sign, so early in the evening.

"Oh, yes. Scientifically unsound."

"It is?"

"So, I have read. We play it safe, don't we?" He addressed 'the wife'.

"Oh, yes, Maurice. Take no chances," she agreed.

Reginald was getting desperate. How long would this go on? Would they leave without Reginald ever knowing the girl's name?

"What can I get you, then?" Reginald spoke directly to the girl.

"Could I trouble you for a freshly squeezed orange juice?" Maurice answered.

"You want orange juice?" Reginald was shaken.

Before another word could be uttered, Diane broke into the exchange. "Your wife will have fresh orange juice? And what will you have, Maurice?"

"Thank you. A glass of white wine, just a small glass, please."

As Diane went past Reginald on the way to the kitchen to fetch an orange, if they had one, she gave Reginald a look with which he was remarkably familiar. 'Behave yourself', was said without being said.

"Now then, you two," Reginald took the hint and started again, "I believe you've moved into the village. Lovely place?"

"Yes, delightful. Small, thatched cottage. Been here for about six months, and I love it."

Reginald was now at the drinks table and was filling half a glass with dry white wine, chilled, of course, which he handed to Maurice. "And you write, I believe?"

"Yes, left college behind and decided to write. I have two articles awaiting publication in a couple of the better papers. And I have started on a book."

"Fascinating. Diane and I were considering a joint venture ourselves. Nothing academic, you understand? What are your particular interests?"

At that moment, Diane reappeared triumphantly, carrying fresh orange juice. "Trust my wife to find your every need!" Reginald beamed at the girl, still waiting for her name.

"Thank you," she said to Diane. "I'm sorry to have put you in all that trouble."

"Please, it was no trouble…" he said, waiting for the name, which was not forthcoming. "It was no trouble. Our lady, Mrs Braithwaite, has everything in that kitchen of hers." And again, at that moment, the good lady appeared from the kitchen and announced dinner was ready.

"Mrs Braithwaite." Reginald was determined to brighten the atmosphere. "Thank you. You are wonderful."

"I thought it was such a lovely evening, you would be comfortable in the conservatory," Mrs Braithwaite announced. "I have turned up the heating, and there is still some warmth left from this afternoon. I hope that is satisfactory."

"Absolutely," Reginald assured her. "I love eating in the conservatory, as I am sure our guests will." He left no room for disagreement.

They moved into the conservatory, which was indeed warm, as Mrs Braithwaite had pronounced. They sat at the table.

Having supper in the conservatory in the late evening was one of Reginald's secret pleasures, particularly when they had visitors. He loved looking out into the garden as the evening darkened and the trees around the stream and his 'Hide' gradually dimmed and finally disappeared into the dusk. As the light faded, the windows turned into mirrors, and the table became the centre of their world. Diane knew he felt like that, even if it had never been expressed openly.

"How cosy," 'the wife' said.

Reginald had had enough. "Terribly sorry, please forgive me," he said in his most subservient manner. "Diane told me your name before you arrived, but it quite escapes me."

"Sarah," Maurice Marchbanks said before his wife could answer.

"Of course. Of course." Reginald looked at Diane but said nothing. Mrs Braithwaite, saving the situation quite unintentionally, came in carrying a large bowl of avocado salad starter.

"Excellent." Marchbanks was enthusiastic. He smiled at Sarah. Reginald smiled at Sarah. Diane smiled. They helped themselves and began to eat.

"You were in the Royal Air Force as a group captain, I believe," Marchbanks said, sprinkling a small amount of pepper on his salad and leaning towards Reginald. *Thank God, Mrs Braithwaite was back into the kitchen.* Reginald blessed whichever lucky deity was passing. "A rank of some distinction. Presumably had some flying hours under your belt."

What an extraordinary expression, Reginald thought but said. "Yes, flew a bit. Not as a pilot, you know."

"Ground crew?"

"Sort of. Didn't see any action; nothing like that."

"Oh." Marchbanks sounded almost disappointed.

Reginald munched the crisp leaves of lettuce. *Cos?* He was relieved that Marchbanks had started the personal questions, but he was reluctant to mention his role in the force. Time to move on. "I think Diane was telling me that you sang with King's before joining our local church?"

"I had that privilege, yes." Marchbanks 'preened' himself.

"What a marvellous experience! I envy you; quite tone deaf myself."

"Oh, come now." Marchbanks smirked. "Nothing a little training wouldn't rectify, I'm sure."

Reginald looked at him. The more he watched the exaggerated mannerisms of Marchbanks' eating, the more uncertain he became that the whole behaviour was acting, and worse, Marchbanks did not know he was acting. Reginald wondered if this bloke cared about anything.

"You were at Cambridge?"

"Yes." The affirmative was drawn out to emphasise such an achievement.

"I didn't have the advantage of such an advanced education. I'm sure it was a valuable period of your life."

"Oh, yes." A self-satisfied answer. "Modern languages. A first." *Well, it would be, wouldn't it!* There followed a monologue of Marchbanks' academic studies in the German language, both literary and philosophical. Before he had really got into his stride, Reginald had lost interest. Names such as Walter Benjamin, Rainer Rilke or Margaret Bohne meant nothing to him, and as for the contemplations of Ernst Bloch or Nicolai Hartmann, he was uninterested. Such well-known names as Nietzsche or Marx (he was German, wasn't he?) or, God forbid, Hitler were not mentioned.

Reginald's attention drifted, and he gazed at the mirrored images of his guests in the black windows and was startled to see that at the presentation of each name, Marchbanks pulled a different face! And at the same time, he flourished his fork in theatrical movements. Whether the faces and gestures were appropriate or not, Reginald had no idea. But what an astonishing performance! He was fascinated until he noticed all was quiet, and Marchbanks had stopped speaking and was looking at him.

"Wouldn't you agree?"

Damn it, Marchbanks wants a reply. "Well." Reginald ran for cover—metaphorically, of course. "Much of what you said is above my pay grade…sorry, understanding." He smiled.

"Yes, it would be."

What a shit! thought Reginald, but smiled.

"Mrs Braithwaite brought in the pork roast and all the accompaniments, and they settled into the main course. Reginald noticed Diane talking animatedly to Sarah, and the young girl was listening attentively."

"Sarah, don't bore Mrs Young with the trivialities of village life, such as it is."

"Oh, please, Sarah and I are having the most entertaining gossip." Diana was reassuring Sarah rather pointedly.

"No doubt." Marchbanks applied himself to the food before him, burying his fork under a mound of apple sauce and leaving little for anyone else. That last remark from Marchbanks rather dampened further conversation, and they finished the main course in virtual silence. Mrs Braithwaite reappeared and began to clear away the plates when Marchbanks acted in a quite remarkable way. He jumped up, looked at Mrs Braithwaite and said, "Mrs Braithwaite, you are a treasure. Such a wonderful meal and so expertly cooked. Truly cordon bleu!" And then, of all things, he took her hand and kissed it.

Mrs Braithwaite's mouth opened, but no words came out. Her whole body froze. Reginald realised her embarrassment at once and moved to relieve the situation.

"We all agree, of course, Mrs Braithwaite. Coffee in the lounge?"

"Yes," she managed and fled to the kitchen.

"Shall we go in?" Diane was equally nonplussed by the behaviour. They adjourned to the lounge, where coffee, chocolates and soft fruit awaited them.

Reginald drank some coffee, listening to the noise of conversation around him. He had become disinterested in the air and pretentiousness of Marchbanks. But it was more than that; there was a self-interest that was unpleasant. And yet, the extraordinary performance with Mrs Braithwaite signified something even more. The whole episode was put on because Marchbanks had thought it was expected of him, or, more ominously, he had no idea this was not expected of him. Reginald saw the behaviour as a pretence—complete play acting. Whichever way he looked at it, it was without meaning, except possibly self-promotion of Marchbanks' 'unique' importance. He wondered what Diane had made of it.

"Tempus fugit," Marchbanks proclaimed, and Sarah stood up at once.

"Anxious to go?" Diane spoke quietly.

"The lady needs her sleep." Marchbanks seemed to be reproving his wife, insinuating that he would have been happy to talk long into the night. Reginald would not have been happy to talk long into the night. He jumped up.

"Of course, Sarah, you must take care of yourself," he said in his most compassionate voice. "We have enjoyed your company this evening, and speaking personally, I can't wait for Diane to tell me all the village gossip."

Small titter. Disapproving expression from Marchbanks.

"Of course," Diane was quick to add her concerns to that of her husband. "We hope we will see a lot more of you"—she paused shortly—"both over the next few months. And then we can welcome the baby."

Smiles all around. Coats fetched and polite noises made. After the front door closed, Reginald made for the lounge, the gin and his armchair. Following him, Diane quickly poured herself a large glass of red wine and sat. Most unusual for her to take such a large glass, and so quickly. They remained silent for several minutes, both remembering and examining the evening in their own minds. Reginald was at pains to raise Diane's spirits; he knew she must have been surprised and disappointed at Marchbanks' behaviour.

"Much gossip?" He started on neutral ground.

"Sarah is quite interesting. A bit too mouse-like for me, but interesting enough. She watches her neighbours quite closely, and I think she is moderately amused by some of their behaviour. You know, there are one or two in the village who set themselves apart, even disparage some of the fellow villagers. But she has made friends with the shopkeeper's wife and…" She was having difficulty trying to remember any other friends.

"Anyone else?"

"I'm not sure Marchbanks approves of her socialising."

"Why on earth not?" Reginald wanted to know.

"Perhaps he's jealous. Or conceited."

"You can say that all right!" Reginald finished his gin and poured another; Diane did not object.

She said, "A disappointing evening?"

"Yes. Not just disappointment but astonishment."

"I know what you mean. And I am sure Mrs Braithwaite feels that as well. I must go into the kitchen and pour a little oil and what may be troubled waters."

"You know, Diane, I caught him making faces in the reflections of the window. God knows what he was doing. And he seemed to me to treat his wife as an appendage and an inconsequential one at that. What do you think?"

"Disappointed, Reginald. Surprised."

"You know, he reminds me of the description I was given by a psychologist early in training. 'A man takes walks to the shops, and on the way back, he sees a child being run over and watches the appalled and frightened reaction of the child's mother. The man is not affected at all by the tragedy, but when he gets home, he practises the look of shock on the mother's face. It is as if he is learning how to react to the accident but is unable to feel it. That man is a psychopath'."

"Whatever are you on about, Reginald?" It was too late to start talking in riddles; Diane was not amused.

"He meant the man could not feel the pain, but he was trying to find out how to show the pain."

"Is that right? I have got more important things to worry about." And Diane hurried off to placate Mrs Braithwaite. Reginald gazed at his glass of G and T and realised how he had seen Marchbanks' behaviour mirrored in the exaggerated delivery of speeches by some politicians. They have expressions to illustrate 'concern'! To illustrate 'confidence'! And so on. But they mean nothing. Worth remembering.

*** *** ***

Almost 160 miles north of Plantagenet House and the unusual dinner party held there, and at virtually the same time, word reached the Greater Manchester Police Force from the Home Office that there was a general and serious threat to life from subversive groups acting in unison throughout the country. Manchester was one of such area at risk. The counterterrorism unit and the firearms unit were mobilised, and inter-departmental discussions were initiated.

*** *** ***

Chapter Nineteen

On Tuesday morning, 26 October, Hugo Stratton stirred and roused himself slowly; he felt the warmth of his wife Krystyna next to him. He afforded himself a few moments of leisure before making a start to the day. For more than 10 years, he had been posted abroad, leading a double life of an 'economic adviser', 'cultural attaché', 'industrial consultant' and other meaningless occupations while controlling numerous agents spying in hostile nations. Such a duplicitous life, after a time, had become second nature to him.

The constant danger and responsibility had made him ever-vigilant, even distrustful. It was a relief to be stationed back in Britain with his wife and ready-made family where relationships could be open and uncomplicated, even if it took some time to adjust. The constant caution remained. Having given himself those few self-indulgent moments, he got out of bed and prepared for the day ahead.

As he washed and dressed, he heard Krystyna calling Jan and Natalia to get themselves ready for school. Stratton had met his wife and two children in snowbound Krakow after he had completed an urgent repatriation of an agent from the city. Krystyna, a divorced woman, was working in the British Embassy, and although she speculated on Stratton's mysterious past, she tolerated his professional reticence. After considerable official complications and resistance, the four flew back to Britain, set up home and are now settled in Finsbury Park, north London.

Krystyna was a lecturer in modern Russian history at the LSE. Stratton had continued to work for prolonged periods abroad while his family made a home for themselves. Now that he had returned permanently to this country, adjustments in living had to be made. Chairs were reallocated; table manners had changed; and various trifling household routines were altered. But gradually, the family had established satisfactory compromises.

Stratton left for work in the city at 8:00 am, reassuring his family he would be home in the evening. At that time, he was not to know that today, Tuesday, 26 October, was to become the first day of intense counterterrorism in action throughout Britain. At Vauxhall Cross, he found a message from Mountford, coded and secure, of course, informing him that Nigel would continue to watch Carpel Street but would remain in direct communication if required. The other message was of a different order of importance altogether.

A 'scrambled' voicemail awaited, advising him that one Siobhan Behan of St Edmund's College had walked into a Cambridge police station and declared that she suspected a kidnapping. This unlikely story from a young lady who had perhaps been studying too hard nevertheless had been passed on to Vauxhall Cross, hence, via the descrambler, to Hugo Stratton, a person known to be interested in the disappearance of a young lady, possibly in the Cambridge area. Stratton opened the small cupboard on his desk and withdrew a briefcase. In it, he had overnight clothes.

This was a matter of top priority. Marcia had suspected that Lucinda Clayton, who had been the parliamentary assistant of Donald Muirhead and was distrustful of the relationships and motives of those sharing Muirhead's digs at 25 Carpel Street, had gone missing. Mountford had seen Lucinda Clayton's arrival and possible departure as a pillion passenger from the premises; road traffic cameras had followed a motorbike towards the A1(M); possibly changing number plates and making for Cambridge, although there was no certainty about the destination. That had been three days previously, and the disappearance had become sinister.

The voicemail required urgent action, and Stratton prepared to travel to Cambridge forthwith. It just might be that this was the first sighting of evidence of her whereabouts. And it came as a welcome relief, even though possibly fraught with difficulties. He left a message for Mountford to keep surveillance on Carpel Street and rang Group Captain Young at home at Plantagenet House. That was near Cambridge, wasn't it?

"Diane Young. Good morning." The pleasing, mature and confident voice of Mrs Young reassured him that he dialled correctly.

"Mrs Young. Good morning. Hugo Stratton. Something a little untoward may have occurred, and I wondered if the group captain had yet left for London and the usual meeting with Mendel Partners?"

"Mr Stratton, how lovely to hear from you. Are you well—"

But before Diane could go on, Stratton said curtly, "Is the group captain still at home?"

"Indeed, he is. I will call him on the phone immediately." The receiver was placed on a table, and Hugo heard footsteps retreat and heavy ones approaching at an infuriatingly leisurely pace.

"Reginald Young."

"Reginald? Hugo Stratton."

"Hugo. Something urgent?"

"Yes." Hugo's voice was calm, but the phrasing shortened to almost terse. "Young lady by the name of Siobhan Behan has walked into a police station in Cambridge and reported a possible kidnapping in the area…"

"Behan? Behan? Means nothing to me."

"No, but we want to know of Lucinda Clayton's whereabouts after the motorbike trip to, possibly, Cambridge."

"Yes, but what's that got to do with this Behan girl? Seen Lucinda, has she?"

"At present, I do not know. But I take it seriously."

"So, this Behan person is at the Cambridge police station?"

"No. That's the point. I have spoken to a chief super, and he authorised her return to college with two plainclothes police officers acting as chaperones. I'm not sure he took the story that seriously, so we need to move quickly. Meet me at St Edmund's College Lodge at noon, can you?"

"No 'can you?' about it. Course I'll be there."

Reginald returned the phone to the cradle and deliberately sauntered back to the conservatory, and his wife. She raised an eyebrow but said nothing. Reginald admired her patience. He sipped his coffee.

"Can't go to London. Needed in Cambridge," was all he said.

"I see," she replied, but asked no question.

"Not sure about times today." He gazed out of the conservatory window at the chilly morning and wondered if his heron was standing in the stream. He had got the feeling that he would not be in his 'Hide' for some days, if then. "May not be back tonight. Not sure."

Diane rose without comment. He had heard her mount the stairs, and in 10 minutes, she reappeared. "Small case by the front door, Reginald," was all she said.

What a woman! It was as if nothing exceptional had happened. Interdependency was the basis of their marriage.

"Thank you. No need to go much before quarter past eleven. Better ring Mendel's; let them know I won't be in."

*** *** ***

Stanley Burbridge arrived at his place of work at 8:00 am promptly. He opened the door to the porter's lodge and inspected his domain. Looked shipshape; no unsightly litter; wastepaper basket emptied. Only Thomas, the apprentice porter, made the place look untidy sitting at the back, slurping from a mug of tea and reading an insufferably common tabloid newspaper.

"Thomas!" Burbridge spoke forcefully. "Please lay that awful rag on the desk before you in order that no one can see that you're reading such tripe!" Everyone who knew Thomas, including his mum and dad, called him Tom. It was only the pompous Mr Burbridge who would use his full name. The college had standards to maintain, and they should start right here at the porter's lodge!

"Certainly, Mr Burbridge." Tom sighed inwardly.

"In any case, what are you doing, sitting there reading? Isn't there work to be done?"

"I've taken the dailies to the common rooms and delivered the Times and the Guardian to the vice president and the dean."

"Good." Burbridge was satisfied that the working day had begun smoothly.

"I'm waiting for the post to be put into the pigeonholes, then I've got to go to the senior tutor's rooms and move some furniture." It seemed to Tom to be a full morning's work, and to Mr Burbridge, adequate. He could relax and therefore divested himself of his jacket of his suit and took his usual position, leaning on the counter looking out into the entrance of the college and watching the procession of graduates, tourists and visitors. Without his jacket, he was able to show off his gold-plated, adjustable sleeve holders that his wife had given him as a present some years ago. He put his pipe in his mouth, unlit, of course, but it added gravitas to his presence, and he looked over his half-glasses with satisfaction. Another day. He did not know it yet, but it would be a day unlike those he had so far experienced at St Edmund's College.

At noon, two men approached the porter's lodge.

"Good morning, gentlemen. How may I help?" Burbridge straightened up.

The younger one showed Burbridge a card, upon which he noted, with some surprise and not a little misgiving, the crest of the civil service of the government.

"I am Mr Stratton. My companion here is Group Captain Reginald Young."

At the mention of the gentleman's rank, Mr Burbridge removed his pipe (still unlit) from his mouth and squared his shoulders.

"At your service, gentlemen," he said with due diffidence.

"If you could direct us to Ms Behan's rooms."

"Thomas!" Mr Burbridge was at his most officious. "Accompany these gentlemen to Ms Behan's rooms, please." Tom jumped up. He had heard the conversation at the window of the office and realised this was a matter of some seriousness. *But rooms? Bit of an exaggeration, if you ask me!* But he knew better than to voice his opinion. "If you follow me," he said to the two gentlemen as he walked into the first quadrangle. They disappeared.

Mr Burbridge was not idle in his speculation. *Oh,* he thought, *she returned to college yesterday evening with two persons—police if I am not mistaken, even though they were in plain clothes—and now a government officer and a group captain to see her.* Much to discuss with Christine over tea tonight.

Tom took them across several quadrangles to an older building, where they climbed a staircase. Ms Behan's room was on the top floor. On arriving at their destination, Tom withdrew, and Stratton knocked. The door was opened by Siobhan; behind her were two young ladies in plainclothes, clutching their handbags before them, clearly the police. Reginald was struck by her small, neat stature.

"Hello?" She smiled, perhaps with relief.

"I'm Hugo Stratton." He showed her his card. "And this is Group Captain Young. You are expecting us?"

"I am indeed." Her accent was Irish. The smile was now frozen. One of the two police officers behind her held out a hand and inspected Stratton's card cautiously before passing it to the other. Apparently reassured, the three stood back and invited the pair in.

Reginald was immediately reminded of his study at Plantagenet House, although this room was much smaller and the ceiling much lower. There was, however, a dormer window that let in a slither of daylight, but he guessed that the electric light above was permanently switched on. The room was cramped; a single bed, a wardrobe and a bedside cupboard were the key features, but a desk and chair below the window offered a working area, and someone, unlikely to have been this young lady, had put up a shelf along which were displayed books and box files. Five persons in the room made it uncomfortably crowded.

"We'll sit on the bed," one of the police officers said. Siobhan took one of the two chairs, and Stratton the other. Reginald stood with his back to the room, looking out of the window. He could see the cold October sky but without clambering on the desk and looking down, nothing else.

"My name, as you know, is Hugo Stratton, and my colleague is Group Captain Reginald Young. Could we know your names?" he addressed the police officers.

The taller of the two with short blond hair replied, "We are both Kate. When we work together, I am 'Kate', and my friend is 'K'."

"As in K-A-Y?"

"No, the letter K."

Reginald was pleased it that had been explained to their satisfaction, if not his. Nevertheless, when he turned and looked at them, he saw that the one speaking, 'Kate', had helpfully held her hand up, and the brown-haired police officer, 'K', nodded her head. He turned back to the window, none the wiser.

Stratton started. "Ms Behan, it has been reported to my department (he did not say which department) that you have knowledge of a kidnapping. Perhaps you can tell us about it."

"Well, I'm not sure it was a kidnapping." Siobhan was apprehensive, if not downright embarrassed.

Great, thought Reginald. *Two Kates and I can't tell one from the other unless she holds her arm in the air. And this girl Siobhan isn't sure if all this really happened. Wasn't Alice in Wonderland written in Oxford?*

Stratton was made of more long-suffering stuff. "Tell us about your suspicions, right from the beginning."

Falteringly at first but with growing confidence, Siobhan developed her narrative.

"It must have started about a year ago when I went to an extra-mural lecture on modern ideas on the influence of Darwinism."

"Extramural?" Stratton asked.

"Outside the university."

"I see. Sorry, carry on."

"Anyway, the lecture was a bit of a disappointment, but I went for a drink afterwards with the lecturer and his friend. That is how it started."

She told Stratton and Young of her invitation to evening seminars or group discussions in a village near Cambridge and had attended them regularly ever since. She initially went with the lecturer, who was the leader of the group, but this arrangement was changed, and his friend—a chap called Bernard, who had been in the pub earlier—gave her a lift regularly thereafter, and the meetings were in a bookshop.

"Wouldn't have been 'Aggie's Bookshop', by any chance?" Reginald asked nonchalantly, still gazing at the sky. Behind him, Siobhan looked startled, as if she were amazed that anyone would know the place.

"Yes," she said. "In a tiny village called Lyfen."

"Know the place. Second-hand books, mostly. Down a side street. Owner's an old soak. That the one?"

"Aggie. Yes, but I don't know if I'd call her an 'old soak'."

Reginald braced his shoulders, studied the sky, all the while considering Siobhan's statement and finally responded. "I would," he said.

Stratton looked from one to the other. He had been caught unawares. But so be it. "Please, Siobhan, carry on with your story," he managed.

Siobhan recovered from her surprise and 'carried on'. She told them that she had been attending the meetings for about a year and had become bored with political debate; the meetings were not helpful to her or her thesis, and she was considering leaving the group.

"However, there was an extra meeting called on Saturday, only a couple of days ago, come to think of it. There were two extra chairs put out for visitors. Usually, there were only five members: the leader, Bernard my friend and his friend Ralph and a big, crewcut American or Canadian called Brad. And a young man called Lawrence; he was different. Noticeably quiet. Hardly spoke. Well-dressed, glasses and thoughtful."

She continued: "Back to last Saturday, just after the meeting had started, two new members arrived. Now this really made me wonder because they were both in motorbike leathers head to foot with helmets and visors. They sat down, took off their helmets, and it turned out that one was a man and the other a woman—an attractive young lady with raven-black hair. To have motorbike members was odd enough, but that one young lady was quite extraordinary. That really set me thinking."

Siobhan stopped, mildly breathless. Stratton said nothing for some time but was prompted by Reginald, who turned from the window and addressed Siobhan directly.

"New members; bikers turn up; one of them is a girl. All unusual?"

"Well, it had never happened before, not while I was there, anyway."

Reginald turned back to the window. Stratton took over again. "Any names were there? Any names?"

Siobhan was modest. "You'll have to forgive me; I am not sure I've remembered all the names accurately, but here goes: the male motor biker was Elliot, the girl Lucinda. I'm fairly sure of those two. Aggie gave her full name, but I've forgotten it. Maybe Agatha, maybe Anthea. Not sure."

"No mention of Weber?...Oldham?...Kingsworth?...Forsythe?"

"I don't think so. Wait a minute, Muirhead and Muirhead Associations, whatever they are."

"That's particularly good." Stratton smiled, this time reassuringly. "And what happened at this meeting?"

"Well, this chap Elliot gave the leader an envelope with a note inside, which was read, but nothing was said. There was a bit of a discussion, and the leader said he would make a few phone calls and speak to Lucinda again on Monday, that would be yesterday. He told Lucinda she would be staying there. That is when I thought this was getting out of hand and became thoroughly suspicious. And yesterday, I went to the police."

"Excellent," Stratton gushed encouragingly. Reginald was not smiling when he turned from the window and spoke directly.

"Notice you have a good memory. For most things. But one thing: you keep calling the leader 'the leader'. No name, has he? Or is there another reason?"

Siobhan was too embarrassed to admit an earlier infatuation, but no doubt that was why.

"Marchbanks," she mumbled.

"Would that be as in 'Maurice Marchbanks'?"

"Yes."

"Well, damn me!" Reginald returned to serious contemplation of the sky. Stratton was lost.

There was a lengthy silence. Stratton was trying to understand the interjections by the group captain, and Reginald was trying to come to terms with how small the world was.

"I think, Siobhan, we have had an exhaustive and fruitful discussion. The group captain and I will talk this over and decide the best way forward." He looked at Reginald's back. Reginald nodded.

"Perhaps, if you were to stay here for the time being, it would be for the best. These young ladies"—he smiled at Kate and 'K'—"will remain here or make appropriate arrangements." As an afterthought, he said to the police officers, "Please don't use your mobiles."

They nodded. They were quite aware of that particular restriction.

"Group Captain, I think we should retire. All right with you?"

Reginald made no reply, but it was clear that he acquiesced.

In the porter's lodge, Mr Burbridge contemplated Thomas with a jaundiced eye.

"I suppose you're watching the time."

"Yes, Mr Burbridge. Nearly time for home."

"But not quite, Thomas, not quite." Burbridge raised himself up onto his toes and took the pipe, which was still unlit, from his mouth. Regaining his normal posture, he continued gleefully, "One of the essentials for a successful porter, Thomas, is a keen sense of anticipation. It is obvious to me that Mr Stratton and the group captain have been with Ms Behan for some time, and many require the services of our guest rooms. Anticipating such a requirement, I want you to alert the housekeepers to make up two beds."

"Very good, Mr Burbridge. I'll deal with that." And Thomas disappeared from the lodge in search of the housekeepers.

Mr Burbridge smiled to himself with satisfaction. Unfortunately, Thomas reported back to Mr Burbridge that there was only one guest room available, but before the head porter could vent his displeasure upon the innocent youth, Tom added, "But with twin beds." Mr Burbridge relaxed, and when Stratton and Reginald reappeared, they informed them of his arrangements for them. "Should they so desire."

Stratton and Reginald desired nothing more. It was safe; it saved them hunting for accommodation; it was central to Cambridge and any action first thing tomorrow morning. "Thank you, Mr Burbridge." Stratton smiled. "We will make use of your excellent suggestion."

Stratton and the group captain retired to the guest room immediately. When they got there, Reginald explained that he had been in Aggie's Bookshop some weeks earlier and volunteered to join the 'Study group' but was still awaiting an invitation, and Marchbanks he had met as one of Diane's church acquaintances. Shortly after the explanations, Stratton walked to the Cambridge police station to learn of tomorrow's activities, and Reginald, remembering the embargo on mobile phones, went in search of a public telephone. He rang Plantagenet House.

"Diane Young."

"Won't be home tonight. Lock the doors." Reginald put the phone down. Diane did not ask where he intended to stay or why he was not coming home.

Stratton did not get back to the guest room until nearly 10:00. He told Reginald that he had been briefed on several subjects; the most important for them was that they accompany the kidnapping negotiator and the armed police of the counterterrorist force at 4:00 am in the morning to facilitate the release of Lucinda Clayton, if she was in fact in Aggie's Bookshop in Lyfen.

As well as that, there was nationwide action arranged for tomorrow morning, when all forced entries, arrests and investigations were to be synchronised at precisely 5:00 am. There were two kinds of groups to be formally arrested and examined: the first, the major, violent and most difficult arrests were to be made in Stockport, Liverpool, Birmingham, South London and Felixstowe, where militants were planning a coordinated bombing campaign that would cause civilian disruption, death and destruction; the second group of units were smaller, each situated in or near a university, primarily as intelligence gathering and political cells, in Cambridge, Lyfen at Aggie's Bookshop, Oxford, Warwick and Newcastle.

Stratton and Reginald had to be at the Cambridge police station at 3:00 am promptly. They climbed into their respective beds, set the alarm clocks, three of them to be on the safe side, and attempted to sleep.

*** *** ***

Chapter Twenty

Wednesday, 27th

Awake by 3:30 am, Stratton dressed and peered out of the window, waiting for Reginald to catch up. He loved this time of day, watching for the merest glimmer of grey light on the horizon and then cautiously spreading up across the sky in the virtual silence. He was roused from his preoccupations by Reginald behind him.

"Ready?"

Stratton refrained from the obvious riposte, and they set out for the Cambridge police station in Parkside. Entering a room at the back of the police station, they listened to the briefing given to the armed response officers and a few words from the National Kidnap Negotiator, who was there merely to help if the abductors at this late stage wanted to negotiate, although that seemed unlikely. They would not accompany the police in forced entry to Aggie's Bookshop but wait here for reports and arrests, if any.

In the village of Lyfen, Mrs Florence Wellacre, known to everyone as Florrie, of course, had the dubious privilege of living next door to Aggie's Bookshop. She was at the window of the back bedroom as usual by 4:30. She had had trouble sleeping since the death of her treasured Labrador 'Wilkins' and was watching, disturbed by some activity that she thought she saw in the back lane. She woke her husband. "Come and look at this, Bert, quick!"

Albert was not well pleased. *Bugger me, it is only 4:00.* Nevertheless, he got up, dragged himself to the window and peered into the darkness of the back lane. Sure enough, he could just make out six or seven figures bent double, slowly edging their way along the next door's fence.

"Bugger me!" he exclaimed, which his wife felt was not a great deal of help.

"What do you make of that?" she inquired in an agitated whisper.

"Buggered if I know." Albert was a man of few words.

"Well, what are we going to do?"

"Bugger all, if you ask me. Stay here, seems safest." Albert was also a man of limited vocabulary and courage.

They both goggled at the scene and listened intently. They heard not a sound.

"Quiet buggers, I'll say that for them," Alfred opined in a whisper.

Then quite suddenly, with terrifying shouts and yells and a blaze of floodlights, the rear door of Aggie's Bookshop, or at least Aggie's two-storey extension at the back of the bookshop, was forced open, and all the mysterious figures disappeared inside. Florence, now thoroughly frightened, demanded, "Go and get the phone, Bert."

"Not bloody likely; it's downstairs." Albert's vocabulary had broadened, probably because he could not understand what was going on and by sheer fright. Both stood at the window and peered at the unbelievable activity.

Enhanced by the silence and darkness of the night, the sounds emanating from Aggie's Bookshop were amplified enough to make one's hair curl, unless you were like Albert, totally bald. Florrie crept to the front bedroom and found that the street was crammed with police cars and sinister, dark, unmarked vans. Then, headlights were turned on. It seemed slightly less congested than the centre of Cambridge. But only just.

"Come and look at this lot," she called to her husband.

He arrived, looked out of the window and declared: "Bugger me!"

*** *** ***

There is a particular stillness in the canteens of large organisations at night; it is as if no one wants to disturb the quietness of the small hours. The staff go about their duties softly, and the few customers taking a break pick up their trays and place them on tables with exaggerated care. The conversation is hushed.

In the police canteen, Stratton and Young inspected their sausage, eggs and beans with little enthusiasm. The tea was sweet. No question there; two heaped spoonsful of sugar, and that was that! Neither spoke, but both were thinking earnestly. They knew that Marcia held Lucinda in special regard, and further, they acknowledged that Lucinda had been conscientious in her investigation of Muirhead's lodgings in Carpel Street. Her transport to Lyfen from London had been unusual on a motorbike but that indicated a certain acquiescence and her desire to explore the Muirhead Association, whatever that was, further; in fact, explore it as far as Lyfen in Cambridgeshire.

According to Siobhan, Lucinda had attended only one meeting and that, unusually, was on a Saturday. It seemed probable that she had been held against her will after that meeting.

Her release was a priority, hopefully before she was harmed. However, Reginald could not help troubling himself with his extraordinary connection to Maurice Marchbanks. But that was something else altogether.

Stratton and Reginald, for different reasons, waited impatiently on the return of the rescuers. The canteen clock mounted on the wall behind the service counter ticked loudly and metronomically. Occasionally, a dropped spoon or fork sounded like a rifle shot, or maybe Stratton and Young were on edge. About 5:30 am, a number of vehicles could be heard drawing up in the parking space behind the station, and doors began opening and closing; there were sounds of footsteps and conversation in the corridors outside the canteen. The noise increased significantly, and Stratton and Young had just stood to investigate further when a chief inspector entered the canteen and beckoned them to follow him. They walked along a corridor painted 'government cream', passed several doors until the inspector knocked and entered a door marked 'Chief Superintendent'.

"Come in." The chief super was behind a huge desk and held a phone to his ear, the other hand across the mouthpiece. "Be with you in a second. Take a seat." He continued his conversation, speaking in short sentences, and finally putting the receiver down and giving his full attention to the inspector, Stratton and Young.

"As the inspector knows," he said, "this morning's operation has been 100% successful. We have released Ms Clayton from the confinement to which she was subjected and have arrested"—he looked down at his notes—"Agatha McRae and an American, Bradley Adams. Being an American may present us with problems should we come to lay charges against him, but we will cross that bridge when we come to it. Ms Clayton is in the 'R and R suite' being looked after, undergoing a preliminary debriefing."

"Thank you!" Stratton and Young spoke simultaneously, equally relieved.

"When can we see her?" Stratton asked.

"This afternoon. There's no rush, is there?"

Stratton was considering Marcia's coordinated raids across the country; Reginald was considering Lucinda's state of mind. Both came to the same conclusion; there was no rush.

The house in which 'the R and R suite' was situated was approximately a quarter of a mile from the police station, nestling in a row of houses, and from the outside, it was in no way outstanding or special. The inside was completely different; armed officers were in every room, and no one was allowed in without thorough checks. On this extremely busy day, Wednesday, 27 October, police and secret services, together with counterterrorism and tactical armed officers, were raiding premises in Liverpool, Stockport, Felixstowe, Birmingham and London, where militant terrorist factions were planning major nationwide disruptions and murders.

Elsewhere, smaller university groups, such as those in Lyfen in Cambridgeshire, Oxford, Newcastle, Birmingham and London were to be closed. The coordination, timing and degree of force used were all controlled by a coalition of senior officers. These included Marcia, whose original brainchild this had been, the heads of MI5 and MI6, senior officers from the various forces involved, the head of counterterrorism and a high-ranking officer with administrative powers in armed response units. The action taken was reported through Jocelyn Carstairs to the appropriate ministers, to the cabinet and eventually Parliament. But here in this Cambridge house, all attention was on Lucinda Clayton and her safety.

Stratton was to concentrate on the connection between Carpel Street and the abduction of Lucinda in the village of Lyfen. It was certainly one of his major preoccupations as he entered the house containing the 'R and R suite'. Reginald was concerned with that episode but was more worried about Lucinda's wellbeing.

The typical central, urban house in Cambridge, as stated above, was unremarkable from the outside. Inside, they were met by profoundly serious police officers. Each officer carried firearms but not smiles, and the search for weapons even included a security body scanner. Having satisfied these overenthusiastic officers that they carried nothing that might possibly be construed as dangerous or subversive, they were ushered into an office and confronted by a sergeant. It was at this stage that Stratton stressed his position as an agent of the government and laid his identity card on the desk in the front office.

"We've seen that already." The sergeant was dismissive.

"Quite so," Stratton replied with barely concealed impatience. "Perhaps now you would like to ring the number on the card."

Reluctantly, the officer did so. "So, an agent of the government." He sighed, having called the number and spoken briefly. "A spy?"

Stratton looked at him in silence. It was clear he was not about to answer such an inane question. They were allowed in to see Lucinda.

The room into which they were shown was large, decorated in pastel colours and comfortably, if modestly, furnished. Lucinda sat in an occasional chair at a desk, upon which were writing paper and a variety of pens. There was no phone. On another chair, a WPC in uniform and armed sat quietly watching their entry. Lucinda leant on the desk, propping her head up with her hand; her auburn hair, luxurious and obviously recently washed and brushed, fell across her neck onto her shoulders. She was wearing a fashionable dress and low-heeled shoes. She smiled.

"Group Captain, what a pleasant surprise! How are you?"

"We're supposed to say that to you," he replied, but he was relieved she was her usual, independent self.

Lucinda ran a hand through her hair and took a deep breath. "Much better after a shower." She nodded at the door that presumably led to a bathroom. "And a change of clothes from those dreadful ones given to me on Carpel Street. Gave Daphne"—she smiled at the WPC—"the exact details of my measurements, and as you see, she has an excellent eye for cut and colour."

At that, 'WPC Daphne' looked down demurely.

Reginald wanted to know the full name of the shy WPC.

"Daphne Kendricks," she supplied.

"But tell me," Lucinda resumed, "who is your silent companion? At a guess, I would say a gentleman is employed purposely by our government."

"I think that describes my position adequately," Stratton replied stiffly, and slowly turning to look at WPC Daphne Kendricks, he said, "I think the matters we need to discuss with Ms Clayton are confidential."

Before he could go on, she said, "I understand."

"To put your mind at rest, we have been thoroughly searched and our identification verified." Which was not strictly true, of course. "We'd like to talk with Ms Clayton alone."

Daphne rose, walked to the door and turned. "Lucy, I'll be just outside."

"Thanks, D."

"Now, gentlemen, we are on our own, and you need answers, I am sure. Two things: firstly, it has been a long day, and although I am in much better spirits, I am physically tired, so can we keep this short, for today at least? And secondly, I assume that Marcia knows of my release," Lucinda began.

Stratton and Young had seated themselves on a sofa, which was comfortable enough but much lower than the chair on which Lucinda sat. They felt strangely at a disadvantage. Stratton was nevertheless determined to collect the basic facts. He gathered his senses together and spoke.

"Marcia is helping to coordinate a nationwide investigation into a suspected insurrection today," he said rather evasively. "However, I'm sure that she has been informed of your safe return."

"I wouldn't like her to worry unnecessarily, but I understand that this whole matter is considerably larger than a dawn raid in a tiny Cambridgeshire village," was Lucinda's considered opinion.

"If we might concentrate on your predicament over the last two or three days, that would be extremely helpful," Stratton started. "I'm sure the police have dealt with the mechanics of your abduction and incarceration, but I think we would like some details of the connection between London and Cambridge."

"It would be best if I start with what I know of Carpel Street, and then the journey to Lyfen will become more comprehensible." Lucinda had commandeered the interview again. "I was always suspicious of the visitors to Carpel Street when Donald was alive. I went there quite often with him; the other occupants of the house, apart from Andrew Stewartson, Donald's brother-in-law who owned the property, seemed oddly peripatetic, as if they only visited the place occasionally to discuss matters covertly and together as a group. The one hint I had of that was that there was a loose coalition that went under the name of 'Muirhead Associates', to which they all referred. I could not find any reference in writing to this organisation but came to realise that it had at least one branch in Cambridgeshire. As it turned out, a bookshop in Lyfen!"

"So, when it was suggested that you go to this other place connected with 'Muirhead Associates', you readily agreed," Stratton interrupted. "Even on a motorcycle that was driven by a guy called Elliot, I later discovered his name was Elliot Campbell."

"Even on a motorcycle, as you say, but not 'readily'! I went with the express purpose of finding out more about this mysterious 'Muirhead Association'."

"And did you?"

"Not directly. What I did find was a group of people discussing vague topics, nothing that I could really describe as seditious or revolutionary. It was therefore a surprise when, at the end of the meeting, it was made clear that I was to remain there without my consent."

"Do you suppose that in Carpel Street the 'Association', for want of a better word, had become suspicious of you?" Stratton gently probed.

"Without a doubt," was the short reply.

"Can you remember who was present?"

"Certainly." Lucinda now proved her training. "You know that Elliott Campbell took me as a pillion passenger to Lyfen Village. We drew up in a dark side street, and we were let into a second-hand bookshop called 'Aggie's Bookshop' by the proprietor, Aggie, or Agatha. I overheard her call him 'Mr Campbell'. We went up a metal, spiral staircase to a meeting or coffee room where there was a circle of chairs. Two seats had been reserved for us."

She then concentrated as she mentally pictured the room and the occupants. "The chairperson was called Maurice Marchbanks. He was definitely a man in charge and did not tolerate frivolity. Then, two young men with longish hair, casual jackets, and a young lady, named Siobhan, smiled at me. A serious, spectacled gentleman who did not speak and an oversized American called Brad, or Bradley. Oh, sorry, and the proprietor Aggie, who sat drinking whiskey and saying nothing. That's the lot."

"I congratulate you on your memory, especially after the difficult circumstances in which you found yourself. So, if I heard you correctly, there was a man named Marchbanks, four chaps, including our American friend, one girl and Aggie."

Reginald coughed politely. "Sorry to interrupt. You said Marchbanks?"

"Yes. Marchbanks. Maurice, if I remember correctly."

"You remember correctly! Thought so. When we spoke to Siobhan earlier, she mentioned him as well. Know the feller."

"You do?" Lucinda and Hugo turned to look at Reginald. He smiled loftily. "Had him and his wife for dinner only last week. Thoroughly unpleasant—him, not his wife." For a moment, no one spoke, and then Lucinda resumed.

"That's it. I can't remember anyone else being there."

"Not a large gathering."

"No."

"And after the meeting, what happened?"

"Marchbanks wanted to make some phone calls, and I was taken forcibly into Aggie's living quarters, which is an extension added on to the bookshop. At the back there, can you believe it? I was locked in a room!"

"There is no need for us to ask you about how well, or otherwise, you were treated. We're sure the police have dealt with that. For the time being, considering your fatigue, I think we can leave it there and let you have some rest. Thank you, Lucinda. Can I congratulate you on your stamina?" Stratton sat back, apparently satisfied. Reginald thought he detected just the faintest tremor of fatigue, possibly relief mixed with prolonged anxiety. Either way, the young lady certainly needed 'R and R'.

"Is there anything we can get you?" he asked. "Any shopping? Chocolate, or something to drink?"

"When I first met you at Plantagenet House, I sensed your kindness," Lucinda responded. "But no, thank you. A good night's sleep is what I really need!"

On the way out, Stratton and Young thanked WPC Hendricks and left. She smiled in reply and hurried back into the room to keep company with Lucinda.

*** *** ***

There are several subterranean chambers below the ministry buildings that dominate Whitehall. It was in one of these huge rooms that Marcia kept an attentive eye on the success or otherwise of the dawn raids on centres of supposed revolutionary activities nationwide. The quiet conversations, urgency and activity of those present resembled a Churchillian bunker from World War II, but with added banks of television screens, an abundance of smart phones, and electronic gadgetry undreamt of in the 1940s.

A person of some discernment would have realised that the room was roughly divided into six areas of activity, each recording the outcome of the surprise raids in Liverpool, Stockport, Felixstowe, Birmingham, London and the group of smaller university cells. At the end of the room, a trestle table had six open wire baskets, in which data, photographs, evidence and statements were collected. All the evidence was being collated with more intelligence added from G.C.H.Q. Simultaneously, computers were being fed the data for cross-referencing and analysis.

When Marcia was present, she sat at a desk surrounded by, but separate from the hectic activity in the room. She had made a considerable investment into this nationwide operation, persuading several ministers and private secretaries, even her own department, of the threat to society. On the one hand, she was gratified, if that is a suitable word, that her forecast of multiple factions of insurrection across the country was proving correct. On the other hand, she realised she had yet to find a pattern, and from that, she would be able to state with more authority than she felt at present that there was an underlying organisation intent on insurrection.

Preliminary reports arriving revealed each location was equipped with sophisticated bomb-making facilities and additionally, timing devices that suggested delayed detonations. There was a postscript to every report that most ignored. Not Marcia, though, who noticed a certain similarity in these brief supplements. Although the exact wording differed between them, each postscript mentioned a covered lorry parked near the locations, and in each lorry were more devices and explosives that could be used in bombs. Whether these were additional supplies that had just been delivered or were supplies being removed from the sites, it was not clear. It was a fact that Marcia tucked away in her memory to be used in figuring out the structure of the overall scheme when that became manifest later.

It was her guess, and it was a guess that this organisation was made up of a multinational panel of entrepreneurs set on disrupting British society and replacing it with an oligarchy that would control the Gross National Income, a sum of money standing for the total wealth of the nation, and these widespread 'factories' of destruction were all part of one organisation.

If her theory were correct, she would have to concentrate her attention and the attention of her small circle of professionals, namely Stratton, Mountford, Lucinda and Avril in Bromsgrove, on how such a multinational organisation was able to garner such wide support; how it had been coordinated; and, of course, who had financed it.

A great deal of investigation and identification of collaborators, even within the government, was going to be needed. With the successful completion of the present nation-wide operation, they would need all their energy to expose off those involved in such enormous treachery.

She could understand now why it had been so wise to include Reginald Young. It was becoming clear to her at least that Mendel Partners of Parson's Green were extraordinarily useful.

*** *** ***

Chapter Twenty-One

Wednesday, October 27th

The smell of the custody suite in the police station was difficult to describe, and Aggie was in no fit state to attempt such a complex task. She knew she had been arrested and brought here in the early hours of Wednesday morning, and for the first few hours, she was able to consider her situation. She knew it was not good. She had been in plenty of police cells before, mostly abroad, but there, they were for minor offences—nothing to get excited about. This was different. This was serious. They had insinuated, no, that was wrong, they had charged her with 'false imprisonment'.

As time drifted by, her world started to shrink. Increasingly, her own body and its reactions preoccupied her completely, her surroundings becoming strangely blurred and unimportant. By food time at midday, she guessed that as they had taken her watch, she had begun to get uncommonly agitated; there was a knot in her stomach, and she found her hands shaking so much she could not hold the spoon they had given her. In the afternoon, she began to feel sick, really sick, but she had not eaten anything. Waves of anxiety and nausea were slowly replaced by excruciatingly painful cramps in her abdomen. On the bed, she rolled into a ball, her legs drawn up, and she moaned in agony and wrapped her arms around her knees. When an officer brought her a cup of tea, she could not speak to him; in fact, she was hardly aware of him. His words were distant, 'out of focus' and then suddenly loud, as if his voice were spasmodically suppressed and then released. When they dimmed the overhead light for the night, she was so agitated, she could not sleep and gradually lost touch with reality. By Thursday morning, she did not know where she was, but she knew she was dying of thirst. Sounds made no sense to her; shouts made her jump as if a bomb had gone off, and then, if she looked carefully, she could see tiny creatures crawling out of the floor and under the cell door and even climbing onto her body. She began to panic and scream, and by the time the custody officer got to her cell, she was fitting.

They called a locum doctor; he came three hours later. "Bit of a drinker?" he asked. An injection, some tranquillisers given to the duty sergeant with earnest instructions about dose, 'give her plenty to drink', and an exhortation to be watchful of her person. Should there be any significant deterioration, call him again.

Now Aggie had completely withdrawn within herself, frightened by the tiny creatures all around her, continually retching, unable to understand why she could not vomit and past caring. More serious treatment was becoming necessary. But Aggie did not know that.

Three cells away, Bradley Adams was saying nothing. That was nothing until a representative of the American Embassy arrived to advise him. However, requesting the presence of such a representative was proving difficult. So far, the police could not obtain proof that Bradley Adams was his name, and his passport looked suspiciously like a forgery, his driving licence notable only by its absence. Worse still, the American Embassy denied any knowledge of him and would not attend. The duty inspector was informed, a man slow of intellect but quick to temper, especially if faced with a prisoner as uncooperative as Adams.

"Now, listen to me!" the inspector hollered. "I've had enough of your games. You're no more an American than my bloody cat! Let's be having some sense out of you. What's your name? And I don't mean 'Donald Duck'!"

"That's okay then, because that ain't my name."

"I didn't think it was!"

"Why mention it then?" Adams wanted to know fairly reasonably.

"Mention what?"

"Donald Duck."

The inspector gave up. He looked at his watch. *Only an hour and I can go home*, he reasoned. *Let someone else talk to this madman.*

*** *** ***

At the porter's lodge in St Edmund's College, Mr Burbridge took a surreptitious glance at his watch. Tom noticed.

"Only three quarters of an hour now, Mr Burbridge," he said with a mischievous grin.

Mr Burbridge hid his irritation. He had suffered Thomas long enough today. Having some time to himself seemed like a clever idea. "Thomas, if you have completed your onerous labour for the day," he said with gentle sarcasm, "you can run along home early for once. But do not think you can make a habit of it."

"Thank you, Mr Burbridge." Tom had missed the sarcasm and, in any case, did not care, so long as he got off early. "I'll clutter on, then." He put his coat on and left. Mr Burbridge could relax. He leant on the counter, and his thoughts wondered to Ms Behan. Not one to take cognisance of rumour, Mr Burbridge could not ignore the 'whisper' that Ms Behan was returning to Ireland sooner than expected. And the lady officers were to accompany her. He wondered what that was all about; the mind boggled. Perhaps a topic of conversation with Christine over tea this evening.

*** *** ***

Saturday, 30 October, three days after the raid on 'Aggie's Bookshop', two plainclothes officers called on Albert and Florrie. They were fortunate to catch them both at home. Albert had been given a sick note by his doctor. His varicose veins were playing up again.

Florrie, inspecting their warrant cards without being sure what she was looking at, invited them in. "Cup of tea?" she offered. They both accepted.

"We are sorry to interrupt you at home," the taller of the two officers apologised as he sat at the kitchen table. "We are from CID and have come to offer our apologies for the disruption the other night and give you some explanation."

"I should think so." Albert was truculent. "Frightened the life something awful out of the wife, all that row and police." Florrie looked at him, remembering his reluctance to go downstairs for the phone but said nothing.

"We apologise," the officer repeated.

Albert, gaining confidence, continued: "Well, what was it all about? That's what we want to know."

"I'm not in a position to give you full details of our activities, but suffice to say we have been successful in releasing a young lady from the premises and arresting two other occupants."

"Like that, was it?" Albert's thoughts always strayed from the course of interpretation.

"We thought as much," Florrie added darkly, adding two pence worth of inuendo.

Neither officer responded, but they sipped their tea gravely. All this raised Albert's fevered imagination.

"Always thought that Aggie was up to no good. Said to you, Florrie, didn't I? 'She's up to no good,' I said. But didn't think she'd have gone that far with a young girl." The officers looked at each other again. The conversation had strayed far from its intended objective. "We believe it is a bookshop."

"Not much of one," was Florrie's opinion. "A few daytime customers, suspicious-looking," she added with a 'knowing look'.

"And in the evenings?" The other officer tried to steer the discussion towards more useful information.

"She shut about 6:00, but some evenings, there were groups of students, I think, from the university." Albert had lost interest; now there was no smut being talked about.

"Seems a long way to come for a meeting," the taller officer mused. "Any regular meetings that you noticed?"

"Yes, Thursday evening was regular as clockwork." Florrie was sure. "Usually, four or five turned up. Once or twice, a motorbike. Bit unusual that."

"Would you recognise any of them?"

"No, I don't think so. Never got a good look, really." Florrie almost apologised.

"The shop's shut, is it?" Albert wanted to know.

"For the time being," was the noncommittal answer. The officers stood. Nothing more to be gained here, for now. "Thank you, both, and again, sorry for the disturbance and our intrusion."

Florrie saw them out and returned to the kitchen and Albert. "I'll put the kettle on for some more tea. What do you think of that lot then, Bert?"

"Quiet buggers, I'll say that for them. Didn't tell us a lot, did they?" was the bored reply. "What's for tea?"

On Monday, 1 November, five days after the rescue of Lucinda, Stratton, Mountford and Young arrived at 'The School' in Streatham at 10:00 am. They acknowledged one another, and Reginald said, "Three-line whip, is it?"

"Feels like it," Mountford mumbled.

Hugo Stratton and Reginald Young entered the back door and walked into the kitchen. Monsieur and Madame DuPont looked up, and Antoine said clearly, "Good morning, gentlemen. And on time!"

Stratton came to an abrupt halt; never had anyone looked at them as they entered, let alone spoken. This was quite unexpected. They climbed the stairs, slightly puzzled, and on arriving at the first floor, Reginald opened the door to the meeting room. It was his turn to come to an abrupt halt. The room was brightly lit; a Venetian blind hung at the window, and a new fluorescent light shone from the ceiling; the uncomfortable wooden chairs had been replaced with six armchairs; the tiny table was replaced with a long, oak, highly polished side table; the standard lamp had gone, and a large rug covered the floor.

"Good God!" It was the best Reginald could manage.

In reply, Marcia walked forward, as always immaculately dressed, and invited them in, indicating the armchairs. Already present, Lucinda, elegantly attired in a two-piece suit, smiled. Another lady, in a pleated skirt and high-neck sweater, was introduced as Avril Reynolds, or Simpkin, take your pick. She was the wife of Gerald Simpkin, a party volunteer in Cheshire and herself was a part-time lepidopterist and friend of Frances Muirhead, Donald Muirhead's wife. She was also an earlier colleague of Marcia. The impressive table was laden with plates of cream cakes and assorted biscuits, and coffee was percolating gently at one end. The smell was fragrant and warm.

"I would have worn a bowtie had I known we were having a party." Reginald was still amazed.

Without a glimmer of a smile, Marcia said, "You should have done."

The three men chose a chair each and looked on in astonishment as Marcia circled her guests, offering coffee and cakes, before she sat down and sipped her own coffee with obvious enjoyment. Stratton was the first to recover. "To what do we owe our new meeting room and the very welcome refreshments?"

Marcia thought for a moment and spoke slowly. "We have completed an important objective; the nationwide raids on suspected centres of insurrection has been successful and many arrests, and much evidence has been collected. I thought these deserved some form of recognition, hence the relaxed atmosphere. It remains for us to discern a pattern or underlying scheme to confirm my original thesis that these atrocities are not random acts of needless vandalism, unconnected and without purpose. Of course, and equally important, Lucinda has been rescued from her incarceration."

Lucinda smiled. Stratton said, "If I remember correctly, Marcia, you postulated some weeks ago that there was a group of multinational entrepreneurs who were conspiring to overthrow our establishment, or governance, and replace it with an oligarchy that would have control of the gross national income and thus access to an enormous amount of money."

"Hugo, you are correct. Those were not my exact words, but a fair summary of my belief."

"So, we can take a break." Mountford bit into a cake, smearing his top lip with cream.

"Not exactly, Nigel," Marcia said carefully. "We cannot afford time to rest. I prefer to think of this interlude a time for composure, assessment and hopefully a plan to identify the criminals and apprehend any traitors in our society.

"Finally, is the country ready and waiting to embrace a change of establishment? I think that it is, or very soon it will be. The COVID pandemic was devastating; some say 15 million lives were lost worldwide. But more than that, the fight and precautions taken against it were extremely expensive. It left our government, and many others, economically drained. I am convinced that the war threatening on the borders of Russia and Ukraine will almost certainly start shortly and worsen the pressure on citizens' finances. This war will mean a shortage of oil from Russia and grain from Ukraine. These two factors will increase prices around the world, not just in the West. Fuel will be in short supply and more expensive, which will of course affect transport and then commodities in the shops.

"Add to that, the increase in price and availability of grain for us and around the world, and we will suffer enormous damage economically. My forecast is that these problems will begin early next year and increase throughout the year. Remember what happened in Russia during the early part of the twentieth century and disastrously in Nazi Germany after defeat in World War I? Revolution from the far left in Russia and the far right in Germany was the result.

"We will suffer in the next year or so from the same financial problems. Poverty will drive anger and unrest. This in turn will cause demands for increased wages, and if those demands are not met, strikes will be inevitable. If industrial action spreads to public services, as I am sure it will, the emergency services will need help, and as usual, it will be the police that we will turn to in social crises. This in turn again will deplete resources to combat crime, and deprivation will mushroom.

"On the brighter side, the British character is not susceptible to extreme views. The far right and the far left are unlikely to persuade people on the street to join radical groups. If the present establishment breaks down, as I believe it will, our citizens are much more likely to accept the moderate, balanced governance, which is precisely what this group of entrepreneurs will offer."

"That is a very pessimistic outlook," Reginald suggested, his thoughts directed to images of a society he had never encountered, certainly not in this country.

"Precisely. A nationwide breakdown of society to be replaced by an unelected bunch of sociopaths." Strong language indeed from Marcia. "Let us take as a given that our communities will react in the way I have just described. It is beholden on our government to intervene. However, it is also essential that this group of invaders be identified and their activity stopped."

This seemed like a natural break, and Stratton stood, walked over to the table to refill his cup.

"An excellent idea, Hugo," Marcia agreed. "Let us all take a breather."

As Marcia stood at the table waiting patiently to refill her cup, Nigel Mountford spoke to her quietly. "I have this constant worry. What was the purpose behind the abduction of Lucinda, and what was to become of her?"

"A pertinent question, Nigel," Marcia replied in conversational tones. "Lucinda and I have already discussed this. Lucinda was aware of the danger in which she found herself. The Carpel Street group had already become suspicious of her, and her introduction to Lyfen was a calculated risk. In fact, in the Lyfen meeting, Marchbanks told her he had some phone calls to make and would see her the following day, Monday. That meeting never took place, and we must assume that his suspicions had been reinforced. Both Lucinda and I think it highly improbable there was an intention to release her alive. In fact, during her incarceration, she was devising means of escape. She is resourceful and well trained."

"That is reassuring and, at the same time, frightening," Mountford responded. "But the matter is academic now, thank goodness." Marcia nodded in agreement.

Reginald helped himself to another coffee and, turning his back to shield his cup from the company, added a little whisky from his hip flask. "Enhancing the flavour?" Lucinda spoke quietly over his shoulder. Like a schoolchild caught smoking behind the bicycle shed, Reginald hurried to his seat and sat, blushing. Having waited five minutes or so, Marcia resumed her discourse.

"Now we come to the elements of this sorry business that concern us directly." She had the full attention of them all. "As is obvious from her presence here today, Lucinda has been released from her inconvenient confinement. The exact motive behind her detention is yet obscure, but we can assume with some degree of certainty that the occupants of Carpel Street had become suspicious of her motives. I have thought all along that this conspiracy relies upon widespread centres of activity. It is possible, no probable, Carpel Street, and by extension, Aggie's Bookshop in Lyfen, is one of the branches of this widespread organisation. And we have inside information of Carpel Street and its visitors from Lucinda; then information from Lucinda, and a young lady Hugo and Reginald met in St Edmund's College, Cambridge, called Siobhan Behan, about the curious meetings in Aggie's Bookshop in Lyfen must be another branch of this organisation or possibly an extension of Carpel Street centre.

"Coincidentally, we are in the happy position of knowing something about another possible branch of the organisation. Reginald is a member of 'Mendel Partners', a company that has made inquiries into a wealthy gentleman called William Oldham, who befriended Donald Muirhead before his death. You may consider that the friendship between a Member of Parliament and a wealthy industrialist is not unusual, or even noteworthy. However, when we learn that Oldham knows Frances Muirhead, the deceased Donald's wife, even when she denied such knowledge to Stratton, we can become justifiably suspicious."

Marcia paused; she wanted to emphasise her belief that Muirhead's death on a golf course was geographically odd, to say the least. She continued, "Frances Muirhead has attended 'parties' at Oldham's estate near Bromsgrove. And again, we are in the happy position of having inside information. Avril Simpkin"—she turned to the other young lady present, with a bow of the head—"or Ms Avril Reynolds, as I once knew her, if you prefer, is a friend of Frances Muirhead and has been a guest at Oldham's estate. Avril, who retired from our service some years ago, is now in a position to let us have news from inside the Oldham Estate. This mansion and grounds, I am sure, are another branch of the syndicate, and even better, Oldham, being extremely rich, may well be a member of the inner ruling group within the organisation.

"You will remember some time ago I drew attention to Muirhead's death in Worcestershire, and from it, we have traced a connection to William Oldham of Bromsgrove, a wealthy gentleman of unconventional parties, and then we find Frances Muirhead, Donald's wife, has visited Oldham's estate near Bromsgrove, possibly attended his parties, even though she claims to have no knowledge of Donald's golfing excursions to Worcestershire. We are lucky enough to have Avril here, an experienced agent and a long-standing friend of mine"—she gestured to Avril—"who has befriended Frances and has been to the 'Bromsgrove' estate. We are therefore ideally placed to have inside knowledge of two branches of this organisation: one in Carpel Street and the other in Bromsgrove.

"It is an excellent start to our investigations. We must now finish the task of establishing the central conspirators behind this criminal organisation or consortium, call it what you like. Firstly, let us confirm that Carpel Street and Oldham's estate are two branches of the organisation; secondly, we must try to discover if Oldham is an important link between Parliament, the late Donald Muirhead MP, and the businesspeople who control the widespread organisation. And thirdly, I must uncover the network of active factions that make up the widespread political agitators."

Marcia was tired, but she had set up her thesis and had named three areas of investigation that still required work. Her determination and enthusiasm to conclude the investigation were infectious.

Stratton prepared himself; the next few days and weeks were to be crucial. "Another thought here," he said hesitantly. "With the countrywide raids and the safe release of Lucinda, will not the members of the central organisation realise that the conspiracy has been recognised?"

There was a pause. Everyone appreciated the logic supporting the question. The answer came from Lucinda. "It is very possible that the Muirhead Association and the organisation will realise the danger of detection. But that does not mean they will stop their efforts. They must have had an extensive network across the country and, at the very least, some information from, or influence in, government circles. There is yet much to be done if we are to put an end to this threat."

"I totally agree," Marcia added.

Mountford was so anxious to get started, he had stopped fidgeting.

Young was captivated. His experience in the RAF police division was one thing, this was a whole new ballgame, but he felt that he had been welcomed into the murky world of espionage.

"We await your instructions." Stratton was all business. Marcia looked around the group, decided they were ready to begin and gathered her thoughts.

"Because Lucinda is known to the Muirhead Associates and Avril to William Oakham in Bromsgrove, I think Avril would best investigate the abode of Andrew Stewartson in Carpel Street with Nigel; try and ascertain whether there is any continuing link with Parliament. Reginald, if you would continue your working relationship with Mendel Partners, introduce Lucinda and you might be able to take a closer look at William Oldham and his relationship, if any, with the central group of entrepreneurs. Those two branches are then fully covered. Importantly, we want to ascertain whether there is a connection to Parliament on the one hand and the central organisation on the other. Hugo, I have a challenging task for you. I want you to concentrate your efforts and mind on Brendan Forsythe in Whitehall and any close 'friends'."

The instructions were clear. Those present were keen to get started. Marcia smiled at them, and they left at proper intervals. This is where the real work for them started, and Marcia knew it. She had every confidence in them.

Reginald gave Lucinda the address of Mendel Partners in Parson's Green, Fulham, and she drove off with the intention of meeting him there. He called a taxi. He had remembered advice given to him many months previously by his erstwhile friend Mikhail Stephanopoulos. "It is easier to watch someone if there are three of you. It's less suspicious." And the investigator from Mendel's, Stan Blake, would make an ideal third person. He hadn't felt so determined since…well, whenever.

*** *** ***

Reginald's taxi dropped him outside Mendel Partners, where he caught up with Lucinda.

"Been through the wringer, young lady," Reginald commiserated. "I'm sorry."

"It was not your fault. It is all part of life's rich pattern!"

"It is?" *I'm glad it's not part of my life's rich pattern!* Reginald thought. "Right, this is Mendel's, an inquiry agency. I work here part time, but things are hotting up."

"Yes, I gathered that."

"You did? Good. Let's start. Feeling this is the crucial and final part of our inquiries."

*** *** ***

Chapter Twenty-Two

Afternoon, Monday, 1 November

Lorraine looked up, and on seeing Reginald, she awarded him her usual, sparkling smile. As Lucinda followed the group captain into the office, her smile froze.

"Let me introduce you, Lorraine. This is Lucinda. She will be helping me while I work here at Mendel over the next few days, maybe weeks. Who knows?"

"Good morning." The welcome was less than enthusiastic. "If I remember, we met before."

"Yes, I called in briefly some weeks ago. A message from Whitehall, I think."

"I seem to remember." Lorraine remembered all right, but she was less than content with the memory. Reginald noticed nothing amiss.

"Boss in?" he inquired.

"Mr Mendel is in his office as usual."

"Give him a buzz; let him know we're here, will you?"

"Both of you?" Lorraine inspected Lucinda with a critical eye.

"Yes, both of us." Reginald did not know what was going on.

Lorraine spoke briefly on the intercom. "He will see both of you directly." She made it sound like a ludicrous concession.

As they walked to Mendel's office, Reginald, bemused as always with young ladies' behaviour, consulted Lucinda, "What's wrong with her today?"

"You do not know?"

"No, I don't; that's why I asked."

"She fancies you!"

Reginald stopped in his tracks. "Wait a minute! She's middle-aged!"

"So? All I know is that she fancies you. Nothing to worry about."

"That's all right, then." Reginald was speechless for all of ten seconds. They continued to Mendel's office, Reginald shaking his head.

Mason Mendel sat behind his desk but stood as soon as Lucinda entered the room. Notwithstanding his continuing devotion to Angela, his rather unworldly wife, he scrutinised Lucinda with an experienced gaze.

"Good morning." It was an earnest welcome. "Please, take a seat...both of you." At last, he remembered Reginald! Slowly, Mendel retreated behind his desk, and using the intercom, he asked Lorraine to rustle up some coffee. Her answer was short.

"Now then, Reginald, you bring with you a charming assistant, I have to say. But that to one side, our investigations are satisfactory, I hope?"

"Sure. Sure, Mason. No criticism there. Seems we are upping our interest in Mr William Oldham—Bromsgrove feller, you remember—and we want to take another look. Stan Blake about, by any chance? That was the name of your chap taking a look at William Oldham, wasn't it?"

"Yes, that was him. I'll see if Lorraine knows where he is." The conversation with Lorraine was short, but the outcome was satisfactory. "Yes. Appears he's with Ray Cotterell now. But he'll be with us shortly. Good chap. Reliable. Thorough."

"By the way, don't worry about finances, Mason. It's Whitehall."

"I'll send the bill when all this is finished."

Within a minute or so, there was a knock at the door, and Stan Blake entered and took a chair.

"Reginald here, and his lovely assistant, Lucinda, need your help again, Stan," Mendel declared.

Blake inclined his head towards them but remained silent.

"We don't want to take up too much of your time, Mason, but is it okay if we ask Stan to elaborate on Oldham's background? My office will be okay," Reginald said.

"Fine with me," Mendel replied. "But your office? Bit small, isn't it?"

"We'll squeeze in."

"Never. Use the room here where we interview prospective clients. It's much bigger."

Mendel's suggestion was accepted. He was correct; it was a much bigger room with two windows and comfortable chairs, much more conducive to relaxation. Although Reginald was a small partner in Mendel Partners and he had supplied the names of Leon Weber and William Oldham for investigation, it was Lucinda who managed the interview. "Mr Blake, or can I call you Stan?"

"Stan is good." Reginald winced.

"Okay, Stan, I have read your report on our friend William Oldham. Can we explore it a little further?"

"Certainly, I'll try to help."

"Good. Your excellent and detailed report makes it clear that Oldham is decidedly rich, and he made money from selling his small aluminium processing plant in Black Country. Given even that he was at the forefront of energy conservation and low carbon emissions, the profits from such a sale in no way covered the expense of buying his mansion and estate in Brakeborough. We surmise that there was an injection of a substantial amount of money at some stage. We wonder where that money came from and why."

"The same thought crossed my mind, but I have no means of accessing his bank accounts. So, I'm not able to tell you where the extra money came from."

"That confirms our own belief that extra funds were paid to him. Why...That is the question we must address."

"Parents were not rich?" Reginald chipped in. "No moneyed relatives left him a fortune?"

"Not to my knowledge."

"Okay." This was Lucinda. "We are left with a puzzle. Extra funds. Where from? Why?"

"Something to chew over." Reginald rubbed his chin. "Shall we leave it there for now?"

"One other thing before we call it a day," Lucinda said. "Any dirt?"

"You mean something we could use?"

"Exactly."

"Well." Stan Blake considered the question carefully. "Nothing from his earlier history that I know of, but...The parties he gives at the estate are known in the village for their excess. There are whispers of drunkenness and perhaps the misuse of drugs. Noise late at night, causing some mutterings."

"We've heard those rumours." Lucinda and Reginald concurred. "Right, plenty to go on. That will do for starters." Lucinda wrapped it up. "Can we meet here tomorrow, ten sharp, and visit Brakeborough? We may need to stay a few days."

"My car?" Blake asked.

"Your car." Reginald had the last word.

*** *** ***

As Lucinda talked with Stan Blake and Reginald in the Mendel Partners' interview room, Avril Reynolds (Simpkin) and Nigel Mountford were searching estate agents in Shepherd's Bush for rented accommodation. They were seeking basic accommodation to rent in Carpel Street but were anxious not to draw attention to that street or, of course, their purpose. This had led to several unfortunate misunderstandings; in fact, this inquiry at this next estate agency was typically misinterpreted.

They trudged into the agency, quite tired and glanced around. The usual advertisements of houses and flats to buy or rent were displayed around an open-plan office, which in fact was a large room; each desk was distanced from its neighbour, each near-identical. A young lady sat frowning at a computer screen. They chose one such lady at random.

"Excuse me. May we interrupt you briefly?" Avril was quietly spoken and polite.

"Can I help?" The monotone answer was curt, without enthusiasm.

"We're looking for a small flat to rent for a few weeks," Avril continued, outwardly unperturbed. Mountford stood behind her, gaze cast down, shy.

"Oh, yes." The assistant examined them slowly. "How many bedrooms?"

"It does not matter. One? Two?"

"I thought so." Her response could have meant anything, but her scrutiny made the meaning obvious. "Let me see." She returned to her preferred medium: the computer screen. "…Two-bed…large, ground floor…space for parking…Holland Park. Any good?"

"A little far from our work." Avril sounded disappointed.

"Just a minute. We have two that specify short-term leases preferred…one overlooking Brook Green…bit too far?"

"The other…Carpel Street…one bedroom flat…first floor…parking permit needed."

The expression on Avril's face did not change. Nigel remained with his eyes cast down.

Sounds a trifle basic. "What do you think, Roger?" This was Nigel's assumed name.

"I suppose we could take a look." He appeared to be disinterested.

"What length of rental are we talking about? The minimum is six months." The young lady was already busy typing. "I can arrange a viewing this afternoon."

"Time?"

"Two o'clock."

Avril and Nigel met the owner at the address at the stipulated time; they noticed at once the polygonal bay windows, one above the other. This would afford them an excellent view of Number 25 for their camera. They arranged for references, were given a key to the front door, one for the flat and agreed to move in on Wednesday, 3 November.

The young lady at the estate agency did not give them another thought except, perhaps, hoping they would enjoy their temporary love nest.

*** *** ***

On the same day, Monday, 1 November, Hugo Stratton set his mind to entering the corridors of power in Whitehall, and he knew one of the undersecretaries in the Foreign Office, a man of discretion yet with his ear to the ground. He decided that was as good a place as anywhere to start. He rang him.

"Fancy a drink at lunchtime, Wesley?"

"That you, Hugo? How are you? Long time no see. What do you want?"

"Fancy a pint, lunchtime?"

"I see…right. The Clarence?"

"One o'clock?"

"Fine."

Hugo arrived at The Clarence early. Two Chelsea pensioners, resplendent in their scarlet uniforms, sat with pints before them, having taken a longer stroll from the hospital than was usual. They accepted his offer of refills with smiles and the dignity always associated with those veterans.

Settling at the bar, Hugo ordered a half and waited. Wesley was a young man with a bright smile and an air of learning about him, a likeable companion. He knew how to avoid bureaucratic intrigue yet kept abreast of office scheming. Marcia would have liked him. His university was Oxford; his politics, as far as Hugo knew, were liberal; and he was without significant baggage. In short, a civil servant destined for an exalted position…eventually.

"Hugo. Damn it, how are you? What are you up to these days apart, of course, from being hired out to Marcia and her merry band?"

"How did you know that?"

"Oh, here and there." Wesley was his customary discreet self. "Mine's an orange juice."

"What!"

"Office policy now. Lunchtime goodies are off the agenda."

"Puritanical?"

"Efficiency." Wesley smiled.

They installed themselves at a window table, conveniently apart from the other drinkers. The pub was not overcrowded, but a substantial noise of chattering rendered their conversation virtually inaudible to others.

"What is it that you're really after?" Wesley was straight to the point.

"Nothing serious." Hugo's voice did not sound as nonchalant as he would have preferred. "Can I ask you for your discretion?"

Wesley merely looked at him; the answer was clear. "Have I ever been careless?"

"Of course not. That's not exactly what I meant. I wondered whether there had been any unusual requests or inquiries—inquiries that might have been ambiguous or not quite straight forward."

"What aspect of our work in particular?"

Here, Hugo had to tread carefully; if no word had reached Wesley of a possible nationwide conspiracy, he might be leaking information without justification. But that seemed highly improbable. However, his dilemma was solved for him.

"You mean, had I heard of the police raids in Liverpool, Birmingham and elsewhere? Of course, I had. The whole of Whitehall has heard. Nothing secret there."

"I thought so, but further than that, have you had any reason to believe anyone has been inquiring specifically or without good cause, or exceptionally, about these raids?"

"If I had, it would not be made by direct request, and as far as I know, no one is on our radar who is undesirable. Well, no more than the usual ones we know about!"

"Any liaisons outside marriage or any causing more than a raised eyebrow?"

"Probably plenty of that, but nothing to unduly worry the headmaster!"

"If anything does crop up, can you let me know?"

Wesley turned his head sharply. "Absolutely not. I'm not paid to be an informer for MI6, or anyone else, and I'm surprised you asked me for a drink just for that!" This was voiced unusually loudly, but before Hugo could respond, Wesley continued sotto voce, "But I'd keep an eye on Bernard Forsythe if I were you." Without another word, Wesley stood, turned and left the pub.

*** *** ***

Not more than a mile from where Hugo and Wesley spoke, Marcia was in deep conversation with Jocelyn Carstairs. Jocelyn was a worried man because his minister was a worried man. And Jocelyn's sleep was disturbed by this fractious minister. That was an inconvenience he suffered with difficulty. Marcia was asking for more time, and that was yet another inconvenience. She needed to apprehend the central members of this conspiracy, not just the activists who did the bombing or the dirty work. Jocelyn reluctantly agreed. He would put it to his minister. Goodness knows how his minister would react.

As soon as Marcia had left, Jocelyn called his secretary. "Would dinner tonight be welcomed, Annette?"

"Very much so, Jocelyn." His secretary knew that dinner would consist of many courses, not all of them in that discreet restaurant in Bloomsbury.

*** *** ***

The excitement surrounding the storming of Aggie's Books by the police, later the release of Lucinda and the arrest of Aggie and another man unknown to the villagers, had subsided. Albert, the next-door neighbour, was still suffering with his varicose veins, which kept him at home, but gradually his interest in watching from the window at the forensic officers in white overalls and white caps diminished. He had hoped for some books or magazines to have been discarded in Aggie's dustbins, but it appeared that the complete contents of the bookshop were taken away for examination elsewhere.

Florrie, his wife, had a rather more stimulating time. She had a part-time job as a cleaner at the local post office and corner shop, and her stories of the early morning police raid were related to spellbound listeners. The stories slowly became exaggerated, all the better for the audience.

Inside 'Aggie's Bookshop', the forensic officers went about their business systematically. All books, magazines and papers from the counter were packed and dispatched to a Cambridge police station. None were of immediate interest, except possibly those from Aggie's 'Victorian Section' at the back, which had illustrations that challenged the credulity of some of the officers. But that was mild titillation. They found nothing serious or of a more serious significance, except for an old safe. There was some debate as to whether it should be opened at once on the premises or in Cambridge. Wise heads prevailed. It went to Cambridge.

Then came a close examination of the extension. This was Aggie's independent flat, in which Lucinda was held prisoner. They examined the room in minute detail, taking away many samples. At the weekend, there was a lull in the investigation, only for it to recommence with added activity on Monday, when officers from MI5 and the counterterrorist police arrived.

"Those buggers are giving it a good going over; I'll say that for them," was Albert's summation of the proceedings.

Florrie agreed, apart from the language.

"I always said she was up to no good, didn't I? But I didn't know it was this serious." That was Albert's last word aside from inquiring, "What's for tea?"

In Cambridge, hours were spent on scouring all books and papers for possible evidence concerning either the widespread conspiracy or details of the 'Muirhead Association'. Nothing was found amongst the confiscated books and papers, but when they eventually opened the safe, they struck gold.

*** *** ***

As Reginald travelled to Plantagenet House, he realised with growing certainty that he had a delicate evening ahead of him. Cyril, the taxi driver who picked him up at Audley End Railway Station, was uncommunicative this evening, and that suited Reginald fine. He was in a pensive mood until he remembered he did not do 'pensive mood'. He opened the door to Plantagenet House and at once felt the warmth fold around him like a blanket. It was good to be home.

"Is that you, Reginald?" The routine inquiry from Diane in the lounge.

"It is I." Reginald considered it best not to try a jest this evening. He joined his wife in the lounge, poured himself a large gin and tonic and sat opposite her, wondering when it would be an opportune time to broach the subject of Brakeborough. He need not have worried.

"I have packed a small case." Diane smiled, sat back and folded her arms with obvious satisfaction.

"Packed a case?" Reginald desperately tried to recall if they were due to go somewhere. Having searched his somewhat erratic memory, he decided they had not arranged a trip, and therefore he asked again with more confidence, "Packed a case?"

"I have." Diane was almost enjoying the look of confusion her husband tried to hide. "You will need it tomorrow, surely."

"Tomorrow?"

"Marcia rang. Told me she had asked you to venture on an expedition with Lucinda."

"Good God!" Reginald's relief was profound. But he quickly added, "Going in Stan Blake's four by four. Three of us are checking on a chap." He stood to refresh his glass. "Like a drink?"

"No, thanks, not just yet."

He regained his armchair and some of his composure. "Have to work away for a few days, Marcia's orders." He relaxed a little and took another therapeutic swallow of gin. Any easing of tension was premature, however.

"Stop press news from the village; Maurice Marchbanks has disappeared. Sarah is devastated."

"Disappeared?" *Although, come to think of it, it's hardly surprising,* Reginald thought to himself.

"And there is more! The police have closed a bookshop in a village, on the other side of Cambridge, place called Lyfen. Is that the bookshop in which you found that book by Professor Drew?"

"Certainly, went to Lyfen. And a bookshop? Don't know if it's the same place."

That was enough excitement for one evening. "What's for dinner, do you know?"

"Chicken, I believe. Mrs Braithwaite will let us know when it is ready. No rush is there, Reginald?"

"No rush."

The evening passed in relative calm, following the earlier misunderstanding. After a satisfying dinner, they retired before 10:00. "You have an early start tomorrow, Reginald," Diane reminded him a little unnecessarily.

*** *** ***

Chapter Twenty-Three

Tuesday, 2 November

Mr Frank and Mrs Marjorie Armitage owned the village stores in the tiny village of Brakeborough, near Bromsgrove, Worcestershire. Marjorie was also in charge of the sub post office on the same premises. Her salary, together with the profits made in the store, afforded them a comfortable living—nothing extravagant. At 6:00 on the chilly morning of Tuesday, 2 November, Frank opened the shop promptly, as was his custom. Having sorted out the dailies for the young paperboy to deliver when he got around to showing himself, Frank had time to reflect on the disturbances of the previous night.

He was not in the best of humours. There had been a party at Oldham's mansion, but the music, drunken laughter and shouting were louder than was often the case and had kept him and Marjorie awake half the night. And to make matters worse, just as they were getting to sleep in the early hours, there were sounds of police cars arriving, sirens wailing, floodlights everywhere, escalating screams, yells and what sounded like unbounded panic. The police had been called many times before by irate villagers, but this was different. There were many more police cars than were necessary for a simple disturbance. This was a serious business.

Frank was decidedly tetchy. One thing was a little sleep, but in addition, there seemed to be an unwelcome profusion of police officers. And incidentally, where was his breakfast?

Marjorie came into the shop, thus relieving Frank of his duties, and encouraged him to retire to the 'back' to eat his cornflakes. The paperboy came in, collected the papers and rode off on his bicycle. Not a word out of him. Nothing new there. But the village was stirring. Mrs Taylor came in together with a dressing gown, slippers, a chronic cough, but no teeth; she bought twenty fags and a scratch card. Not a word out of her. Nothing new there. Then the crowd! Gertie, Doug and Kelly all arrived in a bunch, questioning and 'simply dying to know what had gone off at the mansion'. Marjorie did not 'rightly know' and therefore was unable to satisfy their curiosity, but it did not stop them from guessing. They were still at this exciting pastime when two constables came into the store. Now they would get the details. The older of the two police officers asked for the Daily Mail; the younger took guilty glances at the 'Men's Magazines' on the top shelf.

"Trouble last night?" Marjorie spoke quietly, encouraging confidentiality. Gertie, Doug and Kelly crowded around, ensuring confidentiality was the last thing on anyone's mind. Holding his copy of the Daily Mail, Officer Birtwistle straightened his back and coughed discreetly into his fist. He surveyed the ring of expectant faces; it was not often that he had such an audience, and he took a moment to savour their suspense.

"You understand I am not at liberty to divulge details of our investigations at this stage." He paused for a second to ensure that the younger constable, Raymond, was listening, for Birtwistle had a duty to educate his young partner on the correct method of addressing 'the masses' in such circumstances and avoiding unseemly panic. "All I can tell you is that a serious incident has occurred within the precincts of the Oldham Estate last night. An official statement will be issued at noon. That is all I can say at present."

At the end of this pretentious monologue, he turned on his heel, collected Raymond and the pair exited the store. As they walked back to the estate, Raymond wondered if there were any words in the English language that were more likely to cause unfounded rumour than those just spoken by his senior partner. In the village stores, Raymond's best predictions were just beginning.

Marjorie contented herself with the knowledge that she, as the village store proprietor, would be the fountain of all village gossip. Gertie, in her unofficial role as spokesperson for the ladies' darts team in a nearby public house, was ideally placed to spread the news outside the village. Doug was a regular at the neighbouring social club, and Kelly, a much younger person, managed the village playgroup. The three listeners in the stores were ideally placed to guarantee the 'incident' would be circulated widely. Of course, it would be exaggerated as it circulated.

Constable Birtwistle remained oblivious to the alarm he had started.

By the time Stan, whom Reginald insisted on calling Stanley, Blake drove into Brakeborough in his four-by-four with Lucinda and Reginald as passengers, tension within the village was palpable. A police officer on traffic duty officiously asked the purpose of their visit and was only placated when Lucinda showed him her official government pass. But even then, before they were allowed to go ahead, he needed to 'confer with his superior'. An abrupt conversation was conducted on his mobile phone, and he stepped back, thought about saluting, but decided against it.

They drew up at the gates of the estate, where they were questioned again, but word had been broadcast in the estate rapidly, and Lucinda was allowed through almost at once. Stan and Reginald were denied entry.

"Let's go to Bromsgrove, get some digs. We may be here a few days," Stan groaned.

"Bugger lodgings!" Reginald replied. "Know any decent hotels near here, do you?"

"There's a four- or five-star hotel on the outskirts of Bromsgrove. I've never been there."

"Well, Stan, today's your lucky day. Make haste, my good man."

The hotel was as comfortable as its stars predicted. They took three single rooms. Reginald signed the hotel register for the others, as it would come out of Mendel's budget, which in turn would be reimbursed. He decided to inform Lucinda of the arrangements by mobile later, and she could join them, assuming she could cadge a lift. Reginald had the feeling she would have no trouble there.

Stan and Reginald met in the bar half an hour later. They had a long wait.

Lucinda had been met on the estate by Chief Inspector Gideon. They shook hands, and instantly Gideon was mindful of her attachment to the intelligence services. He had earlier experience of dealing with that lot, and the memories were not pleasurable. Cagey bunch; gave nothing away; had other goals. He resolved to make the best of it.

"Government service?" he asked with assumed indifference.

"Yes," came the unhelpful reply.

"Interested in one of the guests? Mr Oldham himself? That sort of thing?"

"That sort of thing," came the brusque reply.

Unenlightened, Chief Inspector Gideon resigned himself to minding his own business. He had quite enough on his plate without having to deal with secret agents and their secret programmes. But better be polite.

"How can I help?" he implored, mostly in hope and with little expectation of an unambiguous response.

"For a start, who has died?"

"Pass."

"What do you mean 'pass'?" Lucinda regarded him keenly. *Was he being impertinent?* she wondered. Apparently not.

"No idea who he was, for the moment."

"You mean you have a man who is dead but has no identification? No wallet? No Bankcards? Fingerprints unknown to us or Interpol?"

"Negative to all of those. And what is more, his death is suspicious."

"Before we get to that, William Oldham knew him, did he?"

"Oldham says not."

"So, a guest at the party or a gate crasher?"

"Doubt if he was a gate crasher. Private security is tight."

"Oldham not being as open as he might be."

"Exactly."

Lucinda frowned. Time to move on to the cause of death.

"Okay. How did our unknown man come to die, as far as you can tell?"

"We will have to wait for the official post-mortem results, but as far as I can see, he appears to have been strangled. Found in the lake. Face down. Fully clothed."

"Gone for a drunken swim?"

"Not with those marks on his neck."

"Marks on his neck?"

"Looks like thumbprints to me. Strangulation is my guess. Then pushed into the lake."

The chief inspector viewed Lucinda's puzzled countenance with mild satisfaction. It was a strange one, no two ways about it. Let's see what that lot of 'special agents' make of it, if they ever deign to tell us, that is.

Lucinda arrived at the hotel.

*** *** ***

Whilst Lucinda was talking with Chief Inspector Gideon in Brakeborough and Stan and Reginald were booking into the hotel in Bromsgrove, Diane had a duty to perform at home in Plantagenet House. But this particular duty was not straightforward.

Exceptionally, Mrs Braithwaite had been asked for advice. What did she think was right for afternoon tea with Sarah Marchbanks, the deserted wife of

Maurice Marchbanks? Diane had prepared the question with two motives in mind. Primarily, what do you offer a pregnant, deserted wife as comfort food? And secondly, to prepare Mrs Braithwaite for the visit of Mrs Marchbanks. The memories of Maurice Marchbanks' assault on her person remained troublesome.

"Poor girl," Mrs Braithwaite sympathised. "And expecting too. I'm afraid I did not take kindly to her now-absent husband. But what can we offer for afternoon tea? Do we know if she has any cravings now that she is pregnant? In any case, would you leave it with me, Mrs Young?"

Diane was relieved.

The awkward situation had arisen only because Diane felt it was her duty to offer support to the girl. She had invited her for afternoon tea while Reginald was away in Birmingham or wherever Marcia had sent him with that young lady, Lucinda.

Sarah Marchbanks arrived at 3:00, and Diane welcomed her at the front door and invited her to sit in the conservatory, where they would have tea. Sarah was quiet, as expected, but surprisingly composed, or at least appeared to be composed.

"Sarah, how are you?" A question Diane regretted asking as soon as she had formed it.

"I'm well in myself. The worst of the morning sickness has passed, thank God, and I am thrilled to be expecting my first child." Diane noted the 'my', not 'our'! "With regards to Maurice, I'm beginning to adjust, but in all honesty, it is an effort."

"I am sure it is; I am so sorry."

Mrs Braithwaite bustled in, all smiles. "Are there any particular foods you enjoy at present?" A careful question.

"Bananas. Eat them all day if I could. Stupid, I know."

"Not stupid. Bananas—full of potassium." Mrs Braithwaite retired to the kitchen intent on making banana sandwiches and adding extra bananas to the fruit salad.

Diane knew that Mrs Braithwaite would get the knowledge needed.

"Tea will not be long. In the meantime, I can hear all about your preparations for the baby." This seemed safe, but privately, it gave Sarah an opportunity to vent her anger.

"I've all the essentials, I'm sure. Mother has seen to that! And now he saw fit to go absent…you heard about the disappearance of Maurice, have you?"

A direct question. It needed a direct answer.

"Yes. I have heard."

"In a way, I suppose it's my own fault. At the beginning, it was fine; living in Cambridge near where I grew up, knew lots of people. But suddenly, without explanation, we moved out here. Knew no one; encouraged not to make friends; outside the house lonely; inside the house, I had to know my place; it got that I was looking forward to the baby for the wrong reasons."

"The wrong reasons?"

"To have company."

"That is awful."

"To be honest with you, Diane, I'm at the end of my tether." The age difference had endowed Diane with matriarchal characteristics, at least in Sarah's mind, which allowed anger and frustration to burst out. "He's always said that he's much cleverer than me. Why he chose me, I can't understand. More than that, I've suspected there's another woman for ages. Sealed envelopes I'm not allowed to touch; phone calls at all hours, short and secretive; his own room—study, I suppose you would call it—is out of bounds to me; goes off to a village on the other side of Cambridge every Thursday, sometimes more often; goes away to conference weekends all the time. I've suspected another woman for ages. Diane, honestly, I'm bloody fed up with it…oh, sorry. Sorry."

The explosive curse surprised Sarah as much as Diane. "I'm sorry. It's all caught up with me. If I ever see him again, he's going to meet a new Sarah!"

Before Diane could reply to this outburst of anger and frustration, Mrs Braithwaite reappeared with the tea. "Banana sandwiches," she enthused happily and was disappointed not to receive an acknowledgement.

"Thank you." Diane saved the situation. "Sarah and I are discussing her unhappiness. You understand."

"Of course."

"I'm sorry. I was deep in thought. Thank you for the banana sandwiches; it's just what I need." Sarah spoke shyly. Mrs Braithwaite smiled and returned to the kitchen. Diane believed she now had Sarah's trust and felt confident enough to ask, as gently as possible, when Marchbanks left.

"That's the amazing thing. We had such a lovely supper with you on that Monday, and he seemed in really good form going home. He thought I ought to go to bed, so I did, even though I wasn't very tired. However, I fell asleep. It wasn't until I woke on Tuesday morning, and he wasn't in bed or in the house that I realised he had gone. No word, no note, just gone."

"In the night?"

"In the night."

"Did he take any luggage?"

"No, I don't think so. But most of his files have gone from the study; his mobile is gone, and he took the car."

"He said nothing about leaving?"

"Nothing." Diana decided to leave it there. Sarah was obviously still confused, and goodness knows what the future holds for her. And where Marchbanks had gone was anyone's guess.

The afternoon was darkening, and the silences were becoming embarrassing. Sarah was obviously preoccupied, and Diane needed to speak to Reginald urgently. Their own agendas became important.

After a long silence, Sarah said quietly, "I'll walk back."

"Let me take you in the car."

"No, I'll walk. It'll do me good. Tire me and I'll find it easier to get to sleep."

Sarah took her leave, expressing her gratitude for Diane's understanding. Now Diane needed to talk to Reginald—and quickly.

*** *** ***

Lucinda arrived at the hotel at 8:00, just as Stan and Reginald were finishing their dinner. She joined them.

"Well?" Reginald queried.

"It looks like it may have been murder. But no one knows who the victim is, or perhaps more accurately, is not saying who the victim is."

"Post-mortem?"

"Tomorrow. I will ask for photos of the face, any body art or conspicuous physical defects. We might get lucky."

"So, a party last night, bit raucous, got out of hand, then what?" Reginald wanted more.

"The chief inspector told me the corpse was found in the lake about 3:00 in the morning; a couple who had too much to drink and maybe smoked some wacky-baccey panicked. Screamed their heads off, so everyone came running. Dragged the body out. The inspector, an observant sort of chap, noticed marks on the neck. Possibly strangulation. Post-mortem tomorrow will hopefully tell us the cause of death. Incidentally, the inspector's name is Gideon, same as the Bible people."

"But why in the lake?" Stan asked.

"Why indeed!"

"Can I please finish my supper now? We'll meet first thing tomorrow morning."

Stan and Reginald took their leave. Stan to the bar; Reginald, surprisingly, to the public telephone in the foyer.

He had enough change.

"Diane, that you?"

"Reginald—"

"Speaking from the public telephone, but you're on our landline. So brief. Few days more."

"Reginald, person we ate with on Monday then took the car. Registration should help."

Reginald replaced the receiver.

The three met again over breakfast on 3 November. Lucinda was expecting a police car at 10:00 to take her to the post-mortem. They would gather again in the afternoon.

Stan and Reginald drove to Brakeborough and straight into the village without the hindrance of officious police officers or, in fact, any police officers. The main street was surprisingly wide and edged with grass banks. It descended through the village and ended at the far end with the six-foot ornate gates of Oldham's estate. Two police cars were stationed at the gates.

Brakeborough today appeared calm after yesterday's excitement. It was a typical Middle England, tidy village, with bungalows set back from the road, long front gardens and semi-detached houses with front doors opening directly onto the pavement behind the grass banks. There were several newly built, box-type houses, the bricks still bright tan-coloured, and the windows were machine-made and regimentally spaced. They had small spaces behind a low fence, which seemed to be an apology for a front garden, most with a square of grass but little imagination. There were a few villagers gossiping, but more interestingly, four police officers with clipboards were conducting doorstep interviews. Routine in such cases.

"Stanley." Reginald awarded his companion the full name as was his wont. 'Stan' did not fit Reginald's mood! "Pull up at the village stores. Fund of information, I'll be bound."

Stanley obeyed.

They entered the store. "Morning." Stanley was bright. "Do you happen to have a copy of the local paper?"

"Comes out on Saturday." Frank did not look up.

"Telegraph?"

"National on the rack by the door. Local comes out on Saturday." Clearly a different approach was needed. Reginald moved over to the grill that protected the safe, monies, stamps and whatever the sub post office sold. Marjorie watched him approach.

"Thank goodness for you." Reginald positively radiated amiability. "Desperate need of a dozen first-class stamps. And a post office in such a tiny village. Wonderful!"

"They haven't closed us yet," Marjorie replied. "But maybe soon."

"Damn nuisance, ask me. And no pub either."

"No. Closed last year. It was struggling anyway; COVID finished it off."

"It would. Dragging life out of these old villages in my opinion."

"You're right. New around here, are you?"

"Yes. Never been here before. My friend and I are touring the area. Just came look-see."

"Thought I hadn't seen you in this neighbourhood before."

"Quiet. We like quiet. Saw some police on the main street. Like buses that lot; never see one, then you see four all together." The bait was taken.

"Had a bit of trouble yesterday up at the mansion, Oldham's place," Marjorie replied.

"Oh, yes?"

By now, Frank had noticed his wife in conversation with one of the strangers. And it sounded as if they were chatting about the death. He wandered across. This might get interesting, and he did not know who the stranger was. Stanley decided to read 'The Telegraph' and keep his ears open.

"Trouble? What trouble?" Reginald muttered.

"To be honest, we're not exactly sure. Two police came in yesterday and said there had been trouble in the estate and there'd be an official statement today, but we've heard nothing"—she caught sight of her husband eavesdropping, and so in a louder voice—"have we, Frank?"

"No," muttered Frank.

"Noisy party?" Reginald wanted to know, off-hand, of course.

"More than that. Someone said there'd been a drowning. They're always having drunken parties up there; it's not a surprise, really."

"Well, well. Anyone from the village involved?"

"No. None of us are invited to the shindigs, are we, Frank?"

"No," Frank mumbled so quietly that Reginald hardly heard him. Anyway, Frank had suffered enough, nothing going on. He'd be better off taking the money for 'The Telegraph'. He retired behind his counter.

"Plenty of gossip, though, I bet." Reginald persisted.

"Oh, yes. Oldham's jamborees, flashy cars, lots of money. I knew something like this would happen one day; said so, didn't I, Frank?" But her husband took no notice.

"Anyone ever call in after a party?" Reginald tried cautiously.

"Oh, yes. One or two. One lady, I remember, not posh but okay for money is my guess. I think her husband was an MP. Can't be sure, though. Name…name…?"

Reginald knew the name but kept his mouth shut.

"Can't remember the name." Marjorie was ferreting about her memory without success.

"Frances Muirhead," Frank called emphatically across the shop. "That was her name." And he quickly concentrated on the sports page of 'The Mirror'. His wife would be irritated; she liked to know all the important gossip.

"Stanley!" Reginald cried out. "Time to hit the road."

"Okay, boss."

"Thanks for the stamps. I hope for your sake and the village, the authorities keep your post office open."

"That's nice. See you again, maybe." Marjorie had taken a shine to the gentleman with a grey moustache, posh accent and 'man-of-the-world' look. Reginald would have been pleased to have heard those words.

They drove back to meet Lucinda after her assignation with the mortician and the pathologist this morning.

The meeting at the hotel was brief. Lucinda had suffered a long day, some of it distressingly at the mortuary and was in no mood to linger before bed. Suffice to say, the unknown male was approximately 35 years of age, white, well-built, with no distinguishing deformities or tattoos. He had been strangled then deposited in the lake. There was no excessive water or aquatic material in the lungs to suggest drowning. The hyoid bone was fractured, an almost certain sign of strangulation.

Time of death: approximately 2:00 am on Tuesday morning; the exact time is uncertain. After Lucinda had read her summary of the findings, Reginald spoke.

"Party went on till Monday night, Tuesday morning?"

"Yes, unusual. Police have recorded the names of the guests still at the mansion and from previous records were able to say there were far more people there than ever before."

"Anyone we're interested in?"

"I have only glanced quickly at the list; I will tell you more tomorrow morning."

They were about to leave on their separate ways, eventually to their beds, when Reginald turned and said, "Incidentally, Frances Muirhead has definitely been here, even been into the local stores. Remembered only because her husband was a Member of Parliament, though. God knows how anyone knew that."

"Very good, Reginald," Lucinda said, and finally the group broke up. Enough for one day.

*** *** ***

Chapter Twenty-Four

Wednesday, 3 November

A group of four or five houses occupied a sheltered position behind Wytham Woods, near Oxford. The door of 'Two Bridges' opened, and Charlotte Green stepped forth, turned her face up to the sunshine and sniffed the country air appreciatively. She closed the door, checked if it was locked with a gentle nudge of her hip, turned and walked briskly towards the woods and Wytham Village.

Mrs Kendall of 'Fern View Villa' watched this mundane activity with a startled expression. For Ms Green to be at home on a Wednesday was unheard of. Immediately, Mrs Kendall began to speculate the cause of such irregular behaviour. Sacked from a city merchant bank? But Ms Green owned it, did she not? She could hardly sack herself! Taking a holiday at home? Midweek? It was a conundrum and no mistake. Mr Kendall would know. She would have to wait until he returned from the newspaper offices.

None of these wild guesses came even close to the reason for Ms Green's presence at home this Wednesday. But then, she was not the most communicative of neighbours, and to be honest, Mrs Kendall did not know with certainty that Ms Green was a merchant banker.

Ms Charlotte Green was the most taciturn of neighbours. In London, Vauxhall Cross and Whitehall, she was known as Marcia, a senior agent of the state who was not given to broadcasting details of her personal life. Living behind Wytham Wood, known as Charlotte Green, was merely an extension of that clandestine lifestyle.

She walked briskly into the wood, looking up occasionally to catch sight of the blue sky between the leafless branches; there were, however, a few ominous clouds scattered across the sky. Was rain forecast? She was dressed appropriately for trekking, with corduroy trousers tucked into woollen socks above uncommonly heavy boots. She held a remarkably heavy walking cane. Her stride was firm, back straight and head held up, with a hint of past military training, softened now with maturity. Wytham Woods was one of her favourite walks; she enjoyed the sudden open grassy clearings and marvelled at the smooth trunks of beeches, the sturdy elms and the rough, grooved bark on the trunks of oaks; even the huge roots at the end of an old tree blown over in earlier winds suggested former strength.

Her path was unmade; the silence was broken only by secretive rustlings in the ground cover, mysterious, and that suited her indecision, for she had to decide whether to pursue those who schemed to encourage the awful actions of the would-be bombers and murderers or channel her energies and those of her team in exposing traitors within the government. There was a third question yet unanswered. What was the underlying motive?

She appeared from the wood, no closer to solving her problems than she had been when setting out. She walked along the road to the White Hart Inn, hardly noticing the ancient, stone-built cottages, but just as the inn came into view, a sudden burst of rain quickened her step, and with relief, she entered the bar. If the village of Wytham was quintessentially 'Historic England', so was the pub with its flagstone floor, open fires and heavy wooden beams. A fox-red Labrador came to investigate her, decided she was friendly and graciously allowed her to fondle an ear. She asked for a gin and tonic with no ice and carried it to a convenient table. The Labrador followed her and settled at her feet. She waited.

Julian made his entrance, shaking his umbrella and placing it carefully, still unfurled, behind his chair.

"My dear, Charlotte!" he exclaimed, as if meeting her for the first time in 'simply years'. "How the devil are you? Missed the rain, have you? I have always had a notion you lived in Wytham." She inclined her head but said nothing. "And now it is confirmed," he finished, twinkle in the eye.

"And how are you, Julian? Busy? Bored? Fed up with undergraduates? Or are you thriving?"

"Oh, thriving, of that there is no doubt. Life is now so much easier. Can I tempt you to another of those things"—he pointed at her glass of gin—"or shall we have a drink with our luncheon?"

"If you are driving, it would be safer."

"Indeed."

They went through to lunch. As they ate, the rain and clouds disappeared as quickly as they had come. Whatever breeze there was had been dropped, and a cold, grey November afternoon enveloped the village. The open fires in the pub radiated comfort, and the Labrador forsook the attention of Marcia and lay before the burning logs.

By the time they left, Julian needed the headlights of the Citroen Berlingo.

"The Morris traveller has gone?" Marcia asked.

"The woodwork finally gave up the ghost. It was damn nearly fifty years old. Nearly broke my heart. But I've got used to this."

"Your traveller had a certain distinction, especially in London."

They pulled up on Long Wall Street, close to the side entrance of Julian's college and walked around Deer Park towards his rooms. A stag raised its heavy head and watched them suspiciously. It snorted loudly, and vapour blasted from its nostrils as it shook its antlers ominously. It had its harem to protect. The mist had thickened, drifting up from the Cherwell, and the trees on the far side of the park were only just visible. The colonnade stretched across the first floor. They turned onto a staircase, climbed to the first floor and entered Julian's rooms.

It was incredibly quiet and invitingly warm—a comfortable room. Books lined the shelves on all four walls, as high as the lofty ceiling. What was left of the afternoon light came through two tall Georgian windows. The college tower was just visible through one of the windows, almost hidden in the mist.

"The days of lapsang souchong and crumpets toasted before gas fires are well past me now. Gin?"

"With some tonic, Julian, if you please."

They settled into cracked leather armchairs on either side of a low coffee table, apparently at peace with each other and the world. However, both knew the rarefied atmosphere of academia differed markedly from the practicalities of everyday living. Both had worked for the government, and they understood extremely well the chasm between political theory and its practical application. There were material questions that needed answers quickly if disaster were to be averted in Britain.

"Word has it, you have been instrumental in encouraging the forces of law and order to thwart a series of outrages planned across the country." Julian steepled his fingers and gazed out of the window.

"The word that has reached you has been somewhat distorted," Marcia murmured. "I merely suggested urgent action was needed. Others agreed."

Julian nodded but continued to gaze at the grey afternoon through the window. He was not deceived by her modesty; at last, he spoke.

"And what was it that drove you to ask for, no demand, a joint meeting with heads of senior security services and ministers or their representatives? Surely, it was more than an intuition?"

"Oh, yes. My small working party has been gathering information on three fronts: we managed to infiltrate a secretive group that met regularly in a small village, Lyfen, near Cambridge, but with rather mixed results; we have been able to come close to a wealthy businessman called Oldham who lives near Bromsgrove; and after your suggestion, I have initiated an investigation on Brendan Forsythe."

Julian made no response; instead, he stood, refilled their glasses and resumed his seat.

"That stag in Deer Park reminded me of basic animal instincts to protect their own territory, their own family, own interests." He was gazing through the window again, ensuring he used the correct words.

"And you believe we are similar."

"Undoubtedly. We naturally protect our own families, then neighbours rather than strangers, then communities rather than intruders."

"Hence natural nationalism?"

"Well, it is being taken to extremes in some countries; Le Pen in France; Alternative for Germany (AfG); Swedish Democrats that are vociferously anti-immigration; Spain, Italy, Brazil, Argentina, Bolivia…it is endless. Even America, in the name of Trump, wants to keep Mexicans in Mexico!" Julian was frowning in concentration or anger.

"But that primal urge of self-protection is surely modified by civilisation. That is the fundamental characteristic that makes us human. I think many would be persuaded to defend their own, but it is the extreme exaggeration of those instincts that is so pernicious. And the Nazi movement in the last century is an example of that 'par excellence'.

"Exactly. We must be constantly vigilant, ensure no such fanaticism emerges here as a practical alliance. The country is recovering from the pandemic, and it will not be long before the huge expense of our defence against that dreadful viral infection will impinge on the lives of us all. The population that will become increasingly impoverished will seek solutions, and it may well be that one of those solutions will be far-right madness.

"Financial difficulties and consequential dissatisfaction are fertile breeding grounds for extreme politics. With due respect to you, Charlotte, shall we use that name here? The movement you have been investigating goes far beyond politics. It is my view that although the far-right politics may seem like a speedy resolution to the general turmoil, there is behind this quasi-political movement a sinister criminal intent. I believe this organisation is even more dangerous than neo-Naziism, if that is possible."

"Thank you, Julian. That is my belief as well. And it is big! It has an agent, or agents, in government circles and aims to replace democracy with an illegal authoritarianism, bleeding Britain of its national income. It is not a political party, more a criminal junta."

Julian stopped gazing out of the window; he turned and studied 'Charlotte' slowly as if gauging yet again her ability to complete the evaluation of such an organisation. They sipped their drinks and withdrew into themselves to ponder the issues. A gentle tap at the door disturbed their concentration.

Julian called out to the visitor, "Ah, Lucas, come in." An undergraduate, complete with a commoners' gown, entered and took a seat deferentially.

"'Charlotte, meet Lucas, one of my more enterprising young bloods. Destined for a first, if I'm not mistaken, Lucas?"

"Hardly, Doctor Brooke."

It had been a long time since Marcia had heard Julian's title.

"Such modesty, Lucas, is almost unbecoming. Nevertheless, I am pleased that you were able to drop in this afternoon as arranged." *As arranged?* wondered Marcia.

"Drink, Lucas? Gin?"

"Goodness me, no, thank you, sir. Perhaps a small beer if one is to hand."

"I think I can manage that."

Julian turned to Marcia. "I have asked that Lucas call him this afternoon as I knew you would be here. He has an invitation for you."

Marcia looked at Julian and then at the young undergraduate, Lucas. She was at a loss. "An invitation?" she asked incredulously.

"Yes. To a society that meets in north Oxford fortnightly. This society, like your club in Lyfen, does not advertise its own existence. In this ultra-sensitive climate, the university would hardly condone the convictions expressed in this club; it is as secretive as your 'book club' or whatever it is in Lyfen. A brother, or sister, organisation."

"Lucas, who I am sure will grace the corridors of Whitehall and eventually, no doubt, the rooms of your service, has managed, by dint of his apparently genial and compliant personality, to gain membership in this secretive gathering of right-wing academia. He has told them about the guest he intends to bring tonight. You have just been transformed into a far-right devotee, employed as a civil servant within the precincts of Whitehall."

"You mean, Lucas here is to introduce me to this society as a potential mole within Whitehall?"

"Exactly that."

Julian sat back, smiling benevolently. Lucas found immense interest in the carpet and sat thoughtfully silent. Marcia sat. A stag barked intimidatingly. Outside, the afternoon was wrapped in mist.

During the same afternoon in London, hardly any residents of Carpel Street saw the young couple move into Number 42. In fact, those who did, paid little attention. Number 42 had the reputation of a short-stay lodging house; the tenants were transient and insignificant. Had Avril and Nigel known this, they would have been well pleased, for insignificance was a welcome attribute of their service. They arrived in a small van, plainly advertising 'REMOVALS', and with a telephone number that, if any dared to phone, would inform the caller the firm had moved but had forgotten to leave a forwarding address. The driver, dressed appropriately in a brown overall, carried in some crockery, a box of cleansing materials and, with Nigel's help, a divan. After that came a box of substantial dimensions, upon which, in bold lettering, was stencilled 'TELEVISION—HANDLE WITH CARE'.

The residents of the street would have been surprised, and perhaps perturbed, had they seen the box unloaded because it held not only a television set but a highly sophisticated camera with continuous recording capabilities. The removal van driver obviously possessed many skills, for he set about tuning the arial of the television to produce a picture and then set up the camera, camouflaged with a curtain, trained upon 25 Carpel Street, their objective.

He left, and the removal van was driven away. Avril and Nigel were left to their own devices.

Later, after a college dinner in Oxford, Marcia met Lucas in the porter's lodge and took a taxi to Summertown, North Oxford. In a side street, not a million miles from Saint Edward's School, they arrived at a new building of four floors, surrounded by trees and a limited gravel car park. Lights shone from the windows on all floors. As they closed the doors of the taxi and Marcia paid the driver, the evening chill caught them unexpectedly.

"It will be warm inside; trust me, 'Charlotte'," Lucas assured her.

"What is this place?" Marcia asked when the taxi had driven off into the fog.

"It's billed as student accommodation, which in part it is. However, the ground floor is just one room, which I believe is soundproofed and has heavy drapes on the windows. It is in effect a small lecture room, where the meeting will be held this evening."

Marcia drew her coat about her; it was not only the cold fog that sent a dash of apprehension down her body but it had been a long time since she had enacted a primary role in counterintelligence.

They pushed through the double doors and walked across the foyer to the small lecture room. Rows of chairs, about thirty in total, were arranged facing a low platform on which a lectern stood unattended at present. There were about fifteen persons present, young and of both genders. Marcia would have guessed them to be undergraduates or young graduates. A tall, serious-looking young man, his jacket draped across his shoulders like a cloak and his face marked by severe acne, approached Lucas, and they shook hands. Lucas called him, "Brian." Spelt B-R-Y-A-N.

"Lucas," murmured Bryan, surveying Marcia closely. "Is this the lady from Whitehall you said might attend tonight?"

"Indeed, it is." Lucas smiled cheerfully. "I think it would be useful for you to suggest a name for her; she can hardly use her own." *What thinking; I might well have done the same thing, dropped the ball in this Bryan's court.* Marcia silently approved Lucas' tactic.

Bryan, if indeed that was his real name, smiled. "No, it is best not to use given names. University authorities are so dreadfully boring, don't you find?" This was said almost in a parody of an upper-class, Eton drawl.

"There is no need for further subterfuge; I come ready with a pseudonym."

"Charlotte is not your real name?" Bryan's languid diction was even more irritating to Charlotte's sensitive ear.

"You would not expect me to chance identification, surely?" 'Charlotte' fell into her earlier professional character easily.

"Of course not." 1–0 to Charlotte.

"That to one side for now; I believe our speaker for tonight has just arrived, and I must go and welcome him. Perhaps you will inform us before our lecture of your intentions, especially within the government, to help our small association." Bryan beamed at her meaninglessly.

"Certainly not." 'Charlotte' took him by surprise; he almost took a step back but controlled himself quickly. "I will do no such thing." She displayed an air of confidence and radiated authority. "My role within the civil service is private, and further, I have yet to assess your association, as you call it or even if it is legitimate."

'Charlotte' wondered for a moment whether she had gone too far, perhaps precluding her from either membership or attendance, but her tone of voice must have reassured this Bryan character.

"Of course, you are absolutely correct," he drawled slowly. "We would never encroach upon your personal life. Sufficient that you share our views."

'Charlotte' nodded without answering. Bryan pranced off through the doors to greet 'his guest', and a little while later, he returned with a tall, broad-shouldered and handsome young man. Under a well-ironed white shirt, he wore a black t-shirt, trousers with a crease to cut your finger and ankle-high boots with fashionably elasticated sides. To the observant 'Charlotte', only his red hands, hard-skinned palms and broken nails were at odds with his upmarket appearance. Bryan called the meeting to order 'ever so politely', but before he could introduce the speaker, 'Charlotte' was on her feet.

"Good evening, everyone." She looked around at the startled, upturned faces. "You may not have been informed of my invitation to your meeting, but I would like to thank you for entertaining me. I am here merely to listen. My work is within the government, and my exact concerns are not for general dissemination, enough to say that many of my principles are shared with your beliefs. Lucas, here, my sponsor, will be happy to talk with you if you have any reservations about my presence. Bryan, I apologise for the interruption; I will not speak again." 2–0 to 'Charlotte'. She had pre-empted Bryan's attempt to get her to disclose more than she wanted.

Bryan, still trying to come to terms with this forceful woman, addressed the meeting again. "Thank you, 'Charlotte'; Lucas has guaranteed your 'bona fide' credentials."

The room settled down to listen to their speaker. Bryan introduced him as 'Ralph, an invaluable asset to our growing influence in this country' and took a seat on the front row. Ralph stood at the lectern and glowered at his audience. When he spoke, his voice was surprisingly soft, but with erudition, education, even politeness. It would soon become clear that the essential virtue of tolerance was missing. The question of the hands soon was solved. He was a member of the 'Newcastle Branch' but had recently taken employment in the construction industry, working as a general labourer. This gave him access to the workers of all trades and, importantly, the 'General Labourers Union'.

After briefly describing his infiltration into that workforce, he described how this was yet another successful invasion of the 'great unwashed'! In passing, he mentioned equally successful inroads into the military, emergency, transport, energy and engineering occupations. "And only this evening, it had been reported to me, even into the heart of government." He looked at 'Charlotte'.

There followed far-right propaganda. Nationalism and the right to our own country; homophobia and the preservation of moral fibre; Islamophobia and the right to have our own religion; the benefits of strong cooperation within our own society but the exclusion of outsiders. And so the ranting started. The speaker's voice became a shout and then a shriek of outrage, as if he were trying to convince himself as well as the listeners. The words changed to pure vitriol and hatred and became meaningless; the emotion was almost hysterical. 'Charlotte' had heard all this nonsense many times before. It was always difficult to sit complacently through it and not respond. But her role tonight had to be passive. She sat and listened.

At long last, the meeting ended.

'Ralph' came to shake 'Charlotte's hand, a proceeding that she managed with spurious grace.

"So delighted to make the acquaintance of a member willing to spread our truths as I am." His obsequious words contrasted with the steely-blue, unemotional eyes.

'Charlotte' inclined her head. "How long have you laboured in the construction industry?"

"Too long, my dear, too long." The thin lips smiled without mirth. He turned and sauntered away to talk with Bryan. Lucas and 'Charlotte' made good on their getaway.

At the end of a long day, 'Charlotte' climbed from the taxi and was watched carefully by Mrs Kendall at Fern View Villa, who made note of the time. She opened the door to 'Two Bridges' and sighed with relief as she came to rest in her cushioned settee. It had been a long day, although satisfactory in some ways. If Hugo had managed to gather some information on Forsythe and Avril with Nigel could observe the 'Muirhead faction' at 25 Carpel Street, their efforts would begin to connect the various branches of this criminal organisation.

What she did not know yet was that Lucinda had watched the post-mortem in Worcestershire that very day, and although the dead man found in Oldham's Lake had not yet been named, photographs of the body were due to be circulated the next day, Thursday, 4 November, and this would change the investigation from a political intrigue to, as she had previously thought, a criminal conspiracy of urgency.

*** *** ***

Chapter Twenty-Five

On Monday, 1 November, as soon as Marcia had indicated the areas of interest that needed immediate scrutiny, the team had set about their tasks with vigour. The same day, Reginald, Lucinda and Stanley Blake, from Mendel Partners, had prepared to visit Brakeborough Village near Bromsgrove; Nigel Mountford and Avril Reynolds agreed to rent the flat at 42 Carpel Street; and Hugo Stratton contacted his erstwhile friend Wesley, who worked inside government and who had mentioned Forsythe and later in the week had trailed Forsythe to Brakeborough. The members of her 'company' were spread widely, although it appeared initially that Brakeborough was the centre of activity. It would become obvious later that this was a misconception.

Having arrived in Brakeborough on Tuesday to find a murder had been committed on Oldham's estate early that very morning, Reginald, Stanley and Lucida had eventually taken rooms at a starred hotel near Bromsgrove and had provoked some serious reflection amongst the staff. The receptionist supposed they might be from the press 'about that dreadful murder in Brakeborough', word travels quickly in rural mid-England; the maître d' and chef worried the guests 'might be from the Michelin Guide'; the concierge studied the paucity of their luggage and opined they were 'peculiar or dubious, but definitely outré, don't you know?' And the wild imaginings of 'Boots' were best not discussed with persons of a delicate disposition.

After breakfast, the following day, unaware of the staff's keen interest in them, Reginald and Stanley met Lucinda in her room. She opened her laptop, and they pulled up chairs, crowding around the screen. The mortuary technician had promised to email photographs of the deceased and the pathologist's preliminary findings. As the image of the dead man's face appeared, Lucinda exclaimed, "I thought so! I was not allowed near the mortuary table, but from where I stood, I was almost certain. Now, I am sure. That is the motorcyclist who took me from Carpel Street to Lyfen and the meeting with Marchbanks! It's Elliot Campbell."

The name meant nothing to Stanley Blake, but Reginald remembered Siobhan mentioning the name.

"What was Elliot Campbell doing at Oldham's party?" Reginald wanted to know. "And is he connected to Duncan Campbell, who was seen in prison by Mountford? Are the pair of them connected to the Brighton shootings? Complicated, know what I mean?"

Stanley Blake did not. Lucinda Clayton did. They paused to think.

"Right." Reginald needed to articulate his thoughts. "The Campbells are implicated in the Brighton shootings, maybe. Elliot Campbell takes Lucinda, here, from Muirhead's rooms in Carpel Street to Lyfen. Marchbanks is there, and he has disappeared. You're not allowed to leave"—he nods at Lucinda—"while 'Marchbanks makes some inquiries'. Hell's going on?"

Lucida followed this with difficulty. "But why kill Campbell here? And where is Marchbanks?"

"Seems to me, nothing useful here. Let's get back to Marcia. She might see the bigger picture," Reginald persuaded them. They dispersed to pack, pay and leave. After they had left, the staff of the hotel were none the wiser. But rumours continued to circulate, ever more outrageous as time passed.

In Brakeborough, the mood had calmed somewhat. There were fewer police officers stalking the street, but the gates to Oldham's mansion remained stubbornly closed. The village store and post office returned to a more normal routine; the papers were delivered by the surly youth; Frank stayed irritable; Mrs Taylor won £2 on a scratch card and immediately converted her winnings into another card; she lost her money but said nothing; Gertie, Doug and Kelly congregated every day, as usual, for a chat at the store's counter.

Only Marjorie suffered. She had become marginally detached, as if her mind were elsewhere, which, in fact, it was. Twice she miscounted someone's change, something no customer had ever experienced in her post office before. She had no idea where that handsome gentleman with the moustache had gone and had started daydreaming; it was all very trying, especially for Frank.

*** *** ***

On 42 Carpel Street was an ordinary terraced house that had been converted into two flats for mostly transient tenants. Avril Reynolds, or Simpkin if you prefer, and Nigel Mountford had rented the first-floor flat, which was self-contained with its own kitchen, bathroom and toilet. Two young ladies shared a ground floor flat.

The camera and recording equipment allowed them some free time. They did not have to sit morning and night peering at Number 25, thank God! Nevertheless, they studied the street. It was not a place of excitement.

Nothing happened of great note. The young ladies on the ground floor engaged themselves in a row on the first night that Avril and Nigel were in residence, and at one stage, crockery could be heard crashing either to the floor or against a wall. But it soon calmed down. As well as that, the house was not exactly malodorous but merely damp.

Nothing happened of great note. This was the life of two agents engaged in observation. But after four days of this existence, on Monday, 8 November and when boredom had become distressing, early that afternoon, 25 Carpel Street burst into activity. Everything is, of course, relative. This flurry of activity would not be considered worth mentioning in most circumstances, but to the agents, in uneventful Carpel Street, this was activity at last and, therefore, noteworthy. A removal van had arrived with a pantechnicon, a driver and his mate attired in working overalls, trolleys and canvas straps aplenty; this was obviously serious business. Andrew Stewartson came out and talked with them. They disappeared inside.

"Check the camera," Avril commanded.

"And the recorder." Nigel was equally excited.

Nothing happened for half an hour, and during that time, Avril and Nigel left the house, separated by several minutes, to sit in their own cars. They were prepared to follow more than one vehicle if necessary. They waited for a further thirty minutes, and then the door of 25 opened, and the removals began. Neither agent took photographs, lest anyone notice, but the recorder was still functioning in the room. The street would be under constant observation.

It took more than an hour to empty the house. Avril, who was closer to the action by 50 yards, noticed a large padlock and bar securing the filing cabinet being carried into the pantechnicon; otherwise, the furniture that was commonplace might be removed from any residence. The van, now filled with the contents of Number 25, drove away, followed closely by Andrew Stewartson in his Toyota. If the Muirhead Association was prospering, Stewartson was not spending it on fancy cars. Avril and Nigel followed the van and car, but at Western Avenue, the van turned left and the car right. Avril followed the car.

Settling in four or five vehicles behind the van, Nigel accompanied the pantechnicon onto the M40, past Oxford and onto Birmingham, then the A38 to Bromsgrove and finally into the village of Brakeborough. It had taken almost three and a half hours; they had driven nonstop. Nigel pulled up outside the village stores and watched the van go through the gates of Oldham's estate and disappear along the tree-lined drive.

He got out of the car and walked slowly into the store in order to stretch his legs as much as anything else. Frank, his elbows supported by the counter, was reading a newspaper. He looked up, pushed his glasses up into his hair and stared at Nigel without speaking.

"Good afternoon." It seemed like an innocent enough greeting but elicited only the slightest of nods. "Have you a local paper?"

"This week's Gazette?"

"If that's what it's called."

The newsagent gave a theatrical sigh, walked to the end of the counter and picked up a paper. He made his way back and placed the paper in front of Nigel with exaggerated care.

The headline read:

MURDER IN BRAKEBOROUGH.

"You've had some excitement then." Nigel glanced at the headline.

"I wouldn't call it excitement, more like a killing." Frank returned to his reading.

"Sorry." The conversation, if that is what you could call it, was going nowhere, and Nigel was looking for much more. But where to try? Being a newsagent was demanding work with no mistakes. But rescue materialised in the form of Marjorie, who deserted her post office cubicle to talk to the stranger. It was not often they got more than one stranger in here in a single week, and you could hardly call the reporter from the 'Gazette' a stranger, and even if this one had not the mature allure of the military gentleman, at least he was new.

"Yes. Quite a to-do." She gazed at the paper.

"Police?"

"Goodness me, yes. Hundreds of them."

"Don't exaggerate, Marjorie." Her husband, if he was her husband, sighed again. It was obvious she could not put up with much more of this and rolled her eyes upwards. Nigel had some sympathy for her; it was his unfortunate manner that was so difficult to cope with.

"Do you know any details?" Nigel asked.

"It's all in the paper. You can read it." The husband had pre-empted a long narrative from his wife. She was not best pleased and returned to the post office. Supper would be an egg and boiled if you were lucky tonight.

In a curious way, her retreat behind the Perspex was a blessing in disguise. Dour though the husband might have been, he summarised the events of Tuesday night and morning surprisingly well and without the unnecessary embellishments that his wife would have added.

"Seems like a bloke, no name yet, was killed, maybe strangled in the grounds of Oldham's estate. Police pretty tight-lipped." At this, he gave his wife a meaningful look. "Anyway, no one is sure what went off."

"Not from the village, then?" Nigel queried.

"Not as I know." Then, quite suddenly, he straightened up. "Not a reporter from a London daily, are you? If you are, there's nothing more we can add."

Nigel received the message loud and clear. "No, not a reporter, just an interested outsider." It was on the tip of the husband's tongue to tell him to keep on the outside then, but that was perhaps even too rude for the newsagent.

"Thanks for the paper." Nigel put the money on the counter and left. Really, this was nothing new. Villages were well known to be insular, and Brakeborough was no exception. Undecided whether to stay in the neighbourhood or not, he drove into Birmingham and booked into a modest hotel. Another long drive was not what he wanted, and, in any case, by morning, he might have sorted out priorities.

*** *** ***

During the same week that Lucinda, Reginald and Stan visited Brakeborough, Hugo Stratton was uncertain of his next move, a novel frame of mind for someone of such a well-ordered disposition. Wesley, of the Foreign Office, had made purposeful mention of Forsythe but simultaneously made it abundantly clear that he wanted no part of any ongoing investigation. Hugo did not want to jeopardise his friend's prospects of promotion, and in any case, direct questions within Whitehall would inevitably lead to unwanted conjecture and even back to Forsythe himself. He was keen to avoid both. Finally, he decided to focus on Forsythe's activities away from government offices. He started with Sir Brendan's residence.

The address was easily obtained, but Stratton was surprised it was Redbridge, not the exclusive or excessively priced area as some in London. However, the street was near Wanstead Park, which was another glorious green space nestling in the capital. Stratton decided to stroll within the park where he might be inconspicuous and which should take him to the sight of Forsythe's street. The trees, tall against the black sky, towered above him, and the bushes dripped earlier rain onto the grass.

Towards the centre of London, he could see the glow of streetlights and rockets zig-zagging upwards before splintering their cascading, multicoloured sparks above the rooftops. His path was shadowed in early evening darkness, and he trod carefully; the path took him along the edge of the park, and at last, he saw the street in which Forsythe lived, at least when he was in London. Night vision binoculars allowed him to find the address, which proved to be a brick-built apartment block and, according to the nameplates, contained four apartments.

Stratton waited patiently. The ground floor lights were on; somebody was in, but he had no way of knowing which apartment Forsythe occupied. A man, wrapped in a heavy overcoat with the collar turned up, approached the black-painted door, so varnished as to act as a mirror and pressed one of the doorbells. A brief muttered exchange followed, and the door was opened from the inside. Stratton had seen enough; it was time to return home and join Krystina, Jan and Natalia around the bonfire.

There was much work still to do on Sir Brendan Forsythe.

*Saturday, 6 November

Just before 1:00 the following afternoon, Stratton trailed Forsythe's Mercedes from Whitehall north through London, presumably to Redbridge or his country house, which Hugo had found was in a village called Astwelling, but no, Forsythe veered northeast, then onto the M40. He stopped at the first service station and then continued to Birmingham and Bromsgrove. Hugo had heard of Brakeborough, of course; now he was going to see it! And sure enough, Forsythe drove through the open gates of Oldham's estate and, like all before him, disappeared into the avenue of trees.

The village stores beckoned, as they had to those before. Frank was reading a newspaper on the counter. Marjorie had closed the post office at noon and stood by the door, gazing purposelessly at the main street. There were few customers on a Saturday. Stratton did not want to disturb the peace, but he paused to speak to Marjorie.

"Beautiful village. Quiet. Calm." Stratton looked up and down the main street appreciatively.

"Not much going on today; just a furniture van driving into the estate. It wasn't quiet at the weekend, I can tell you. Police everywhere, police cars all over the place; quite a frenzy on Oldham's estate."

"A party?"

"After the party, apparently, someone was killed there. We've not had an official statement yet, but I saw the mortuary van taking the body away, and the gates of the estate have been closed ever since. Police are still at the mansion, though."

"Whose estate is it?" Nigel affected ignorance.

"Oldham. But he's long gone. Saw his Bentley drive away yesterday."

"Name doesn't mean anything to me, but the size of the estate looks impressive."

"Oh, it is. Not that we've ever been in there. One or two from the village are working the grounds, and they say it's massive. And the house itself—it's more of a mansion, really."

"So, worth a bob or two?"

"I'd say."

"And you tell me that the owner has left…where to?"

"No idea. Never actually spoke to him, but some of the partygoers at the house have been in. One of them was the wife of an MP. The lady with her was quite nice, bought some chocolate I remember."

"Odd what we remember, isn't it?" Nigel kept the chatter going.

"Yes," Marjorie replied vacantly. "Odd what you remember."

Nigel pushed his hands into his trouser pockets, showing his intent to stand and gossip.

Frank called irritably from within the store, "Nearly time to shut up shop. I'm going out the back to get changed and make some tea. Okay, Marjorie?"

That's that, then, thought Nigel, *best laid plans o' mice and men. Gang aft agley. Where the devil did that come from?*

Marjorie did not respond to her husband's announcement, merely shrugged, turned and entered the shop. Nigel gave up. He debated with himself whether to drive back to London and, he supposed, Carpel Street. There was not a lot he could accomplish here.

*** *** ***

Therefore, it was whilst the members of Marcia's team were thus fully occupied that had she decided to take a short break at her home in Wytham and meet Julian Brooke in the village inn, The White Hart. Her visit afterwards to Oxford had come as something of a shock; she had been accompanied by the young man Lucas and had been unceremoniously introduced to a far right meeting, which she felt, no, knew was in some way connected to the Oldham-Muirhead association.

Following this sobering encounter, every day she had walked through Wytham Woods, savouring the smell of grass and bushes, and tried to analyse the diverse elements of this subversive and widespread syndicate. These woods had held many memories for her, happy if not exactly carefree, and she had now been plunged into yet another national emergency. Unlike the intimidation from the Cold War and Russian menaces from outside our shores, this was a danger that was being orchestrated within our society.

Mrs Kendall watched the daily strolls with growing impatience. Her husband had been unable to throw any light upon the gainful employment of 'Charlotte Green', which had not helped Mrs Kendall solve the problem of 'Charlotte at home' week. Her husband had finally told her 'to mind her own business', which had, in its turn, led to a deterioration of interpersonal relationships within 'Fern View Villa'.

Marcia had decided to finally shed her real name on Sunday; she would return to London as Marcia. It was a bright morning as she closed the door behind her, and after ensuring security with a nudge of her hip, she looked over to 'Fern View Villa' and waved a cheerful goodbye to Mrs Kendall. She had known of the watchful neighbour since she had seen the curtain twitch on her first day. Mrs Kendall was the least of her worries.

Oxford was busy, but she knew her way around and drove past the University Athletic Stadium, the old Iffley Road track where Bannister became world-famous by running around a cinder track four times in less than four minutes, and further out of Oxford until she pulled up at the Iffley Church, ancient and peaceful. She walked between the gravestones and trees until she stood before a headstone, and standing perfectly still for a moment or two, she allowed herself some deep thought with her head bowed. Then abruptly, she turned away, climbed into her car and made for London.

Chelsea was a welcome sight, the private hotel even more so. The concierge was his usual pleasant and official self, and her room was immaculate, awaiting her return. Her few days away had not been the total relaxation she was seeking. She had looked forward to Julian's easy companionship and his scholarly and discerning mind. He had been held in the highest esteem in the Home Office, hence his elevation to the Lords, but now he had retired and had resumed his first love, that of research and tutoring modern history.

She had been looking forward to lively discussions, and there had been plenty of that, but to introduce her to Lucas, whose surname she did not even know, a young man Julian was obviously preparing for a career in her service was disconcerting, and it clearly illustrated that Julian was still very much involved with government service.

Julian had made it clear that one underlying criminal enterprise by using simplistic, far-right philosophy, could influence an already dissatisfied populace and act in a variety of ways that could substantially disrupt society. He had added another dimension to the organisation.

She needed now, firstly, to arrange in her mind the extent of the criminality, and for that, she needed a quiet period of reflection; secondly to confirm her suspicions with reports of her small force of professionals; and thirdly, to tie up loose ends, such as the whereabouts of Marchbanks and the exact structure of command behind the plot. They would have to move quickly if their endeavours were to produce the immense benefits to the nation.

*** *** ***

Part 3: Connections

Chapter Twenty-Six

Marcia had lost touch. She had been in Wytham and Oxford for almost a week, and although she had allocated tasks to each of the groups, she had not received any observations or analyses in return, not that she had asked for any. Yet.

Time had come to bring the structure of this criminal enterprise into the open and put together the various leads her team had uncovered. She sent a coded message to Hugo Stratton at Vauxhall Cross to instruct him to arrange a full meeting at 'The School', Streatham, on Friday, 12 November.

For the time being, she needed to put the Summertown meeting in Oxford into perspective. Donald Muirhead's death on the Worcestershire golf course had made her suspect of dishonesty, or at the very least, irregular behaviour. This had led her to uncover sinister activities throughout the country, all linked and possibly masquerading as a quasi-political movement. Now she realised how diverse and ominous it had become.

Marcia left her very private hotel in Chelsea, intent on walking towards Westminster, but as she entered Victoria Street, she was drawn towards the brick and stone edifice of Westminster Cathedral. She could not remember the last time she had visited a cathedral, a church or, indeed, a Christian service. Certainly, at school, she had been introduced to Christian philosophy via the Church of England culture; at university, she had occasionally attended College Chapel—more to listen to the superb choir than to worship God.

But after…her faith, which had not been strong initially, had gradually evaporated in the chaos of life, love and finally secret service. Therefore, it was surprising that after such a long spell of abstinence from Godly thoughts, she was drawn to the building, but she did not enter its portals to seek forgiveness or proffer supplication but for a period of quiet contemplation.

At the other end of the same street, Westminster Abbey was in the shadow of Parliament and much better known. Marcia had no wish to join the crowds, even in November, who would be admiring the architecture and royal grandeur of the Abbey; instead, she was attracted to this ornate and relatively peaceful cathedral. As she had supposed, the huge place of worship was quiet, the murals and statues shimmering in the candlelight; murmured prayers were the only sound; and the fragrance of incense had a clean, forest smell. It was not quite the same as the scent of Wytham Wood, but she was at once reminded of her walks there. A printed notice announced the chapel beside her as the Chapel of the Blessed Sacrament. As luck would have it, the chapel was vacant, and she took the opportunity to sit undisturbed.

Marcia sat and composed herself. She relished the sounds, sights and aroma of this inspirational building, and like many before her, she felt insubstantial in such a vast space. Gradually, however, her thoughts came into focus as she pieced together the various elements of her investigations, from the explosion in Peterborough to the shootings in Brighton to the underground bombing in London and the planned atrocities in large cities.

If it were one large criminal scheme, there would have to be an organisational centre, and where better than Carpel Street, an address of insignificance but with connections within Parliament and with at least one university group? Such a large criminal scheme would require a financial framework, and this seemed to her best arranged at Oldham's estate near Bromsgrove. Whether there was a link to foreign monies, remained to be discovered.

There were irritating questions yet to be answered, and to facilitate that, she needed a team meeting and, possibly, additional scrutiny by the members. Having clarified her thoughts, Marcia stood, returned to the nave and, on her way out, left a substantial donation. She emerged with a spring in her step and made her way along Victoria Street to Whitehall and an unplanned but urgent discussion with Jocelyn Carstairs, he of the coiffured hair, the obliging secretary and limited perception.

Victoria Street was longer than Marcia had remembered, and by the time she had crossed Parliament Square and walked around Whitehall to the offices of the government, her step was less sprightly but her intent was just as bright. She wished the armed police officer 'good day', showed her pass, entered the building and ascended the stairs to the offices of Jocelyn Carstairs. His secretary, Annette, a charming, if pestered young lady, looked up from her desktop computer and smiled.

"Marcia. How lovely!" She sounded as if she took pleasure in the greeting; perhaps she did. "Can I be of any assistance to you?"

"Annette." Marcia's memory for names was prodigious. "Is he in?"

"Jocelyn is busy at present. He has a visitor."

"Is one at liberty to ask the name of this visitor?"

"Sir Brendan Forsythe," Annette replied with significant emphasis.

"How fortunate! I wish to meet with Sir Brendan as well. I can kill two birds with one stone, if the metaphor is not too malevolent or unseemly." And before Annette could manufacture a hindrance to delay any interruption, Marcia had swept past and was in Jocelyn's office.

Carstairs and Forsythe crouched opposite one another across a knee-high table, upon which a coffee jug, cups and accoutrements were placed. They appeared to be engaged in a congenial, if intense, conversation, and her abrupt entry was an intrusion. Forsythe, upon seeing her, was initially the less ruffled and managed to smile a welcome. Marcia was followed by the flustered Annette, who was apologising for the sudden interruption.

"Please, Annette." Jocelyn beamed at Annette. "Marcia is a time-honoured friend and esteemed colleague. She is welcome. Marcia, please come in, take a seat, help yourself to coffee. Another cup if you would be so kind." He smiled at Annette yet again.

Annette withdrew with a furrowed brow. It was now Forsythe's turn to look uncomfortable.

Quickly another cup, saucer and spoon were supplied, and the door finally closed as Annette left. Marcia helped herself to coffee and cream, and the three settled. Did Marcia feel a crackle of anxiety now emanating from Forsythe? Or was it her imagination?

"Jocelyn, I am thrilled to have found you in. I have come to offer my congratulations to yourself, your minister, the anti-terrorist police, MI5 and GCHQ. In the apprehension of those engaged in bomb-making activities nationwide." Marcia was complementary.

"Thank you." Jocelyn lowered his gaze with befitting modesty. "Our intelligence and police services acted swiftly and efficiently. It was no more than was to be expected of them. In reality, I did little other than oil the wheels." If he was fishing for compliments, he was wasting his time since Marcia knew very well that he had done nothing but inform his minister and, possibly, not even that.

"But an achievement of formidable importance." Marcia looked at Forsythe, who sat motionless. "And you would agree, Sir Brendan?" she prompted.

There was a moment of hesitation. Or was it her imagination again? Then Forsythe replied, "Absolutely, extremely accomplished exercise."

A satisfied silence descended on the trio, each with their own thoughts. They sipped their coffees, and Jocelyn put down his cup and carefully stroked his hair. Marcia allowed some time to pass for self-congratulation. It was Forsythe who finally found it necessary to speak. "Your department was not involved?" He could not help himself.

"Hardly. That is not our remit." Marcia waited for a response. But waited in vain. Stillness returned, this time unmistakably accompanied by unease. Jocelyn Carstairs started to wonder if there was some unexplained agenda here; he had years of experience watching groups and knew unspoken awkwardness when it was present. Often, he had no idea what the trouble was; Annette usually sorted that out for him, but the lovely girl was not here. Damn it! But Sir Brendan spoke.

"Jocelyn, it's time I moved on. We have finished the business that brought me here, and I am sure you and Marcia have much to discuss. I'll take my leave."

"What a pity. But if needs must…" It was almost as if Jocelyn was losing an ally.

Sir Brendan stood, shook hands formally with Marcia and, very congenially, with Jocelyn. In a moment, he was gone. As soon as the door had closed behind him, it opened again, and Annette asked, "Do you need me for anything, Jocelyn?" Fortuitously, Carstairs, remembering the presence of Marcia, quickly repressed the prurient reply that sprang to mind. "If not, I have plenty to do before lunch." Annette withdrew smartly, and Jocelyn was left to his own devices, something he was not good at.

"Well now, Marcia, is there anything more?" he asked, hoping there was not. But unfortunately, Marcia gave no sign she was about to leave; in fact, it was the opposite.

"I have two subjects I need to bring to your attention."

Carstairs sighed inwardly. Any idea of an early lunch disappeared with those words, and more ominously, he had a premonition that Marcia was about to rummage through relationships within Whitehall. There were one or two stones he preferred to leave undisturbed and not reveal what lay below. He was not sure whether she had authority to view all personal files but rather feared she did.

He asked unenthusiastically, "How may I help you?"

"The first subject touches upon the putative conclusions that might be drawn from the investigations of my small team of researchers. At this stage, I believe it would be counter-productive to disclose details of our findings."

"How, counter-productive?" Jocelyn Carstairs was now thoroughly suspicious. Nothing new there. He was punching well above his weight, and he knew it. *Where the hell is Annette?* he wondered frantically.

"It would be easy to create misconceptions, even cause needless anxieties. But now, above all, calm must prevail if we are now to prevent insurrection."

"Insurrection, you say?" Carstairs was profoundly disturbed. "You mean the government might fall? The whole establishment dismantled? God forbid! Where will that leave us?" Carstairs had at last got to the most important part of his worries: his own welfare.

"My ambition is to prevent such a catastrophe." Marcia spoke quietly. And then the bombshell. "And you can help."

"Help? Help? What do you mean to help?" Jocelyn was thoroughly troubled. He might be seriously inconvenienced.

"You can be of assistance in many ways," Marcia answered enigmatically.

"I can?"

"Certainly. And I will ensure that the aid you supply will be duly recorded. Do I make myself clear?" Carstairs was crystal clear on the last point. He was so relieved that he poured himself another coffee, even if it would make his pulse race.

"Shall I call Annette?" he proposed optimistically.

"I think not. It is a little premature yet. We will certainly need her and her appointment book later."

"So be it," he murmured obligingly.

"You are a senior member of the civil service (the first compliment) and familiar, I have no doubt, with Julian Brooke, who has been elevated to the upper house (the second compliment). I have had the opportunity to speak with Julian (the first name did not go unnoticed by Jocelyn) recently, and he has shown great interest in our endeavours, even going as far as to introduce me to a local group that has connections to our work. He is sure unrest within the country will lead to an attempt to change our constitution."

"Rebellion?"

"In a word." Marcia paused in her presentation to let Carstairs absorb the full gravity of the situation.

Whether Forsythe understood the full implication or not, the situation was left unanswered; in any case, Marcia wanted only to entice him into her scheme. Preferably with as little understanding as possible, hence her reluctance to reintroduce Annette into the meeting for the moment. Later, she would become indispensable and not just to arrange the diary.

"Marcia, I am all ears," Forsythe breathed. He was so excited at being included in such clandestine guarding of the status quo that he had lost sight of security—and his own security at that!

"Ears? Jocelyn, that is exactly what I want you to use and as near to the ground as you can! Anything that strikes you as unusual: gossip, sudden change of plan, sudden termination of a plan…there is no need for me to lecture you on the recognition of duplicity." This was the third and final compliment. Carstairs inwardly preened himself but outwardly limited himself to a casual caress of his hair. This was a recognition of his professionalism! But wait a minute, what was she getting at exactly?

"Duplicity? Surely not in government offices!" he managed.

"Precisely that. And in government offices." Marcia gazed at him thoughtfully. Silence. Carstairs' thoughts were frenetic. *Is this woman suggesting I am somehow involved with insurrection?* he asked himself. *She is powerful, no doubt about that; her words carry some weight. Undeniably, I need to be watchful.*

"You cannot believe that I would have anything to do with treason?"

"My dear Jocelyn, of course not. In fact, the reason I am here is quite the reverse. I am here to persuade you to continue your guardianship of good administration."

"My guardianship?" The relief in Carstairs' voice was manifest. He hoped it was not obvious. To Marcia, it was, and that was exactly what she wanted.

"You see," she continued, "certain actions within the government have led me to wonder about our security. The leak from Lady Keenan's department (see book: 'Watching') was luckily nipped in the bud or at least before any real damage ensued. But I have my suspicions that that was not the end of that particular saga. And we don't want any recurrence, do we?"

"Absolutely not, my goodness, absolutely not." Carstairs was nodding his head so vigorously that several strokes in his hair became a necessity.

"You see, Jocelyn." Marcia persisted a trifle heavily. "There may be concerted efforts to overthrow democracy."

"Overthrow...democracy...?" Carstairs could hardly believe such a monstrous suggestion. "I will do anything in my power to stop this abomination!" He was momentarily carried away by national fervour.

"I am so glad to hear that." Marcia sat back. "Perhaps you can, as I have already said, keep an ear to the ground; be aware; be judicious to whom you speak and what you say." Marcia thought, *If this does not get back to Forsythe, I do not know what would.* "Perhaps we could call on the good services of Annette to pencil in a meeting for later this week?"

No sooner said than the intercom was pressed, and Annette appeared promptly and with the appointment book.

"Come in and make yourself comfortable," Carstairs effused. "We have been in an important discussion." He spoke gravely, as befitted movers and shakers of the civil service!

Annette sat between them, diary and notebook at the ready. Marcia admitted to herself that this young lady was attractive, unquestionably efficient and, best of all, shrewd. It was this last attribute that drew Marcia's favour more than any other.

"If we could pencil in a meeting, perhaps Friday this week? Noon? On 12 November. Can you arrange that? And of course, be there yourself?" Marcia's request was more of a gentle command, and this did not go unnoticed by Annette or by her boss, and her proposed meeting in 'The School' would be over by then.

"Of course." Annette opened her diary. "Would that be convenient?"

"Perfectly." Now for one last thrust. "I hope I did not interrupt an important discussion with Sir Brendan, one of the cornerstones upon which our establishment has been built."

"No. Of course not." Carstairs was quick to reassure her, and in Marcia's mind, the proximity of Forsythe and the establishment should be enough to encourage Carstairs' tongue.

"And thank you for listening to me today." Marcia looked at Carstairs and smiled; then she turned to Annette and said, "Of course. I will see you on Thursday?"

"Of course," they replied in unison.

*** *** ***

Marcia descended the stairs, and as she stepped out onto Whitehall, Reginald was walking vigorously into his Gentlemen's Club, not more than one hundred yards away. They did not see one another. The reception area of the club was patrolled as usual by the concierge; Reginald acknowledged him with a smile but without breaking stride made for the euphemistically named library, in search of reviving liquid sustenance. Taking his usual seat by the window, Wilfred, the aged and knowledgeable wine butler, put down his paper and walked across the room.

"Your usual, sir?"

"Wilfred, top of the world! How are you?" And being reassured as to the health of Wilfred, he felt sufficiently adventurous to ask after Wilfred's wife.

"I am not exactly sure, sir."

"Not sure? Devil d'you mean?"

"Not speaking to me at present, sir."

"Sorry about that. Time will heal, don't you know?"

"I suppose so, sir." Wilfred did not sound bothered either way. Reginald gave up.

"Slight modification to my G and T today. Slice of lime, please."

"Lime, sir?" Wilfred could barely believe his ears. "Are you sure?"

"Absolutely, old chap. My wife read it in a Sunday supplement. All the rage these days, don't you know?"

"All the rage? Goodness me. Whatever will they think of next?"

"I know, Wilfrid. Told the little lady I would try it out the next time I was in the club. Might add a little to the taste, d'you think?"

"Doubtful, sir."

Wilfred wandered away, gently shaking his head. *Might ask the wife tonight. Damn, I can't, not speaking to me. Wonder if Chef's got any limes?*

Reginald surveyed the room. Brigadier wasn't here, dead, under an omnibus. Clive had escaped from 'the priory' and was on red wine as usual. Reginald waved to him, but the response was vague, even disorganised. Must be on his second bottle. His 'rest' had done little to diminish his thirst. Three gentlemen, attired in pin-striped suits of varying shades of grey, the 'uniform' of the civil service, heads together deep in conversation, were no doubt considering the perilous current situation in Britain and how they were going to advise their respective ministers that would, in turn, enhance their positions.

But in the far corner and, coincidentally, the darkest part of the 'library' sat two strangers talking in hushed voices to old 'Pussy' Pringle. *Hell's going on there? Wilfred would know.* And so, with this puzzle irritating his consciousness, Reginald waited patiently for his experiment with gin and tonic plus lime.

At last, Wilfred reappeared together with a glass of gin and tonic, on which floated a slice of lime. The look on Wilfred's face mirrored the G and T: sour.

"Your drink, sir."

"Thank you, Wilfred." Reginald took a sip and said nothing.

"It is to your liking, sir?" Wilfred had lingered to gauge the reaction.

"Next one with lemon, don't you think?"

"Undoubtedly, sir." Wilfred was relieved.

"Now, a word in your shell-like." Reginald leant forward. "Know old 'Pussy' Pringle? Without looking around, who's with him? Sure, I know the face of one of them. Can't place him, though."

"No need to turn around, sir; he has with him two guests. One goes by the name of Mr William Oldham. The other is not known to me, but I can glance at the visitors' book if you so wish."

"No rush. When it's convenient. Thanks."

Wilfred walked away with the refinement expected in this club. A few moments later, he left his desk and with a measured step made his way to the reception area. Almost ten minutes elapsed before Reginald called for another drink. "With lemon, Wilfred."

"Very good, sir," And as the butler served the drink, he quietly said, "Andrew Stewartson, sir," before slowly returning to his desk. Quite what Reginald thought of this nugget of information is not recorded. But he relayed this to Marcia when he next met her.

Hugo Stratton had been instructed by Marcia to call a meeting at 'The School' on Friday of the same week, 12 November, but circumstances had overtaken the group. Nigel Mountford remained in Birmingham, continuing his investigation of Oldham Estate, although Lucinda Clayton and Avril Simpkin were free, but Hugo and Reginald were flying to Düsseldorf, a city of the Northern Rhine. It was a long time since Reginald had set foot in Germany.

*** *** ***

Chapter Twenty-Seven

Friday, 12 November, dawned cold and grey over London. Hugo Stratton, in a heavy coat, was waiting for Reginald outside Liverpool Street Station at 8:00 am. *An ungodly hour by anyone's standards,* Reginald felt. They drove at once to Heathrow Airport, with Stratton explaining that Border Force had reported their quarry's flight to Germany in October and how he, Stratton, had been liaising with the police for an extradition warrant. At Heathrow, after some searching, they found Inspector Mayweather, the police officer who had been collaborating with the CPS and district judge to obtain the warrant.

"Damn thing's much more complicated since Brexit," he complained.

"But you have it?" Stratton experienced a spasm of anxiety.

"I have. And the relevant documents. And copies faxed to Germany." The nervousness passed. "We'll be met by the German Federal Police; should be straightforward. Same crime in both countries, good prospects of conviction. Like I say, should be straightforward."

They were escorted, without the tediousness of customs and passport scrutiny, to a Bae 146, where seats had been reserved for them. Aboard the plane, Sandra, which was short for Cassandra, and Robyn were the cabin crew for today's short-haul flight and were waiting for them. Having stowed away their jackets, the crew displayed pristine white blouses and business-like scarves. Skirts were knee-length. The sensible three-inch-heeled shoes completed the smart uniform. Their smiles were equally sophisticated.

"Should be an easy trip. Hour and a half, half full with only 73 passengers and no drunk holidaymakers." Robyn waved her clipboard. "One thing: we've got seats reserved for three police."

"Police?"

"Bringing someone back, apparently. Escaper, criminal of some sort, I suppose."

"Dangerous?"

"Shouldn't think so. Wouldn't use us otherwise."

Stratton, Reginald and Mayweather walked along the jet bridge.

"Morning, gentlemen," Robyn and Cassandra said in unison.

Robyn continued, "Have a pleasant flight."

"Thanks," Stratton retorted. The three sat in the reserved seats, and the other passengers came aboard and settled down. Doors locked, safety instructions given, belts secured, the lights dimmed, and they were off. The plane bounced its way to the take-off runway, and the brakes applied. They heard the roar of the engines, the release of the brakes, and they were careering down the runway and finally tilting up into the air, lifting away from London into the clouds on their way to Düsseldorf.

At cruising height, Reginald relaxed; the combination of monotonous engine noise and the chatter of the other two about their respective offspring, together with a disagreeably early start to the day, must have been soporific, for it seemed to him that they had hardly left the ground when a reduction of engine noise woke him abruptly from a comfortable doze. The plane's slow descent to their destination had begun. Turbulence through the opaque grey cloud was minimal, water streaking the windows; then, suddenly, the geometric patterns of the fields and roads could be seen far below and finally airport buildings flashed by. A jolt as the plane landed, the taxiing, after that an abrupt halt and silence as the engines were turned off. They had arrived.

As Inspector Mayweather had promised, a federal police officer collected them as they emerged from the plane and hastened their transit through the reception area. The welcome was not as fulsome as Reginald had expected, which he attributed to Brexit rather than German restraint, if such a thing even existed. A car whisked them along the A25, and they were within the city limits of Viersen within 30 minutes.

It was a small city, and Reginald was immediately impressed with the litter-free streets and an apparently relaxed atmosphere. They drove through Viersen without stopping, but Reginald caught a glimpse of an open park in which trees surrounded graceful sculptures; most of the streets were tree-lined, and the main square was wide, litter-free and bordered by shops and restaurants. As Reginald had experienced in his time with the RAF, there was an orderliness that was striking.

At the police station, the driver escorted the three Englishmen into an inner office, where they were introduced very formally to a member of the

Bundespolizei, who had the administrative papers on his desk. Reginald learned later that this was a captain in the federal police. He had the distinct impression that this was one of the captain's more pleasant tasks.

"Good morning, gentlemen. May I offer you coffee before we deal with this matter?" His English was virtually accent-free.

"That would be most kind, Herr Lehmann," Stratton replied in accent-free German! Reginald had a dreadful feeling that this was going to develop into a contest of languages.

Coffee arrived with startling alacrity, and the relevant warrant from the German court was produced. No sooner had that been glanced at and agreed upon than the prisoner was ushered in, handcuffed. He looked steadfastly at the carpet.

"I am afraid that Herr Marchbanks refuses to speak," the captain growled. "He would not even ask for legal representation at the court. He was followed from the airport at the request of the British police and has been staying with a Herr Muller here in Viersen. We arrested him at the flat. He has not spoken since. Of course, his legal rights were presented to the court, but the order was granted. He is all yours." He sounded relieved.

"Morning, Maurice. Remember me?" Reginald tried good-natured banter. He received silence, although Marchbanks looked up at him and quickly back at the carpet. The captain sighed. Stratton was busy autographing various documents. Inspector Mayweather looked as if he couldn't wait to get Marchbanks on his own. All this was cut short by Herr Lehmann, who ordered a constable to return him to his cell.

At last, the origin of the captain's ill-humour became obvious.

"We have suffered enough because of the criminality of the Nazi Party. Since 1945 (he interestingly did not say the 'Defeat of 1945'), there have been attempts to revive far-right idiocies of the Hitler regime. You may have heard of this; we must contend with growing anti-immigration, Islamophobic, holocaust-denying, racial supremacy groups. In 2012, it was estimated that there were 26,000 far-right sympathisers in Germany. And this is particularly difficult for me, but it has also been reported there are 200–300 police officers who have far-right allegiance. Can you believe it? You have similar groups in your country, I think. The BNP, the National Front, no? And now I believe you are investigating a new right-wing threat, one that this Marchbanks is involved with. Virtually every country in the world suffers from this contagion! I will be extremely pleased when you remove this prisoner from our country."

That leaves me in no doubt about your feelings, Herr Lehmann! Surprising though, that after nearly ninety years, you should still be ashamed and obviously embarrassed, Reginald thought.

"If you would be kind enough to escort Mr Marchbanks to the airport, we will accompany him very closely back to Britain." Stratton wrapped up the proceedings.

"A pleasure, Herr Stratton." And Lehmann certainly sounded as if he meant it!

*** *** ***

As Reginald, Stratton and Mayweather were over the channel returning to Britain with their prisoner safely handcuffed to Inspector Mayweather, at Plantagenet House, Diane rested her hip against the kitchen table and watched Mrs Braithwaite write a shopping list for her next foray into 'one of the more discerning shops' of Cambridge. Diane was frowning. A blackbird was pecking at the kitchen window. Mrs Braithwaite must have forgotten to put out the crumbs, but that was not the reason for Diane's unease. She had invited Sarah Marchbanks for afternoon tea, and yet there was no sign of the absent husband, Maurice. On top of that, Reginald had flown to Germany on some secret business, or at least business he was not allowed to discuss with Diane.

"Mrs Braithwaite, Sarah is due at 3:00. I'm sorry to inconvenience you with yet another chore, but can you rustle up some light afternoon tea? Cake, tea and biscuits. That should be ample. I doubt if the poor girl has much appetite."

"Of course, Mrs Young. You had already asked me."

"I had? I quite forgot. A lot on my mind."

"I'm not surprised." Mrs Braithwaite was sympathetic. "The group captain away in Germany…it was Germany?"

"Yes, Germany. But he should be home this evening, and that's what I'm worried about…"

"The group captain coming home?"

"No. It is who he is bringing back to Britain."

"Really?"

"A trifle awkward, I'm afraid, in the present circumstances."

This left Mrs Braithwaite bemused. It was not like the group captain to worry his wife unnecessarily. It must be important or sensitive, but then it was none of her business.

"Chocolate cake? Some biscuits?" Mrs Braithwaite suggested.

"Excellent, Mrs Braithwaite. Thank you."

Diane ambled back to the lounge. Not her usual firm stride at all.

Sarah arrived, as expected, exactly at 3:00, and Mrs Braithwaite ushered her into the lounge, asking as to her health and inquiring if the 'baby was kicking'. The answers were: 'fit as a fiddle' and 'quite a lot at night'.

"Mrs Young." Sarah beamed. "Thank you for asking me here this afternoon."

"Not at all. A pleasure." Diane looked at her carefully. Certainly, she seemed to be thriving during her pregnancy. Sarah smiled readily. Her eyes were bright, and her hair was freshly washed. Overall, a picture of health. Diane was greatly relieved. This was a vast improvement from Sarah's previous visit. She would try social chatter and gauge the response.

"Sarah, you look well. I'm so pleased."

"I feel well. I think being pregnant is good for me."

"Yes." Diane gazed past her guest. Perhaps she was saddened that Reginald and she had no children.

"For the first time since I married him," Sarah continued, bringing Diane back from her reverie, "I feel fulfilled. That's not the right word…like…competent…important…proud of myself. That's it! Do you know what I mean?"

"Not exactly. We have no children, as you know, but I think I can imagine your delight." Again, Diane looked past Sarah blindly at the wall.

"Yes," resumed Sarah, oblivious to Diane's sadness. "If I ever see him again, and sometimes I hope I never will, he'll meet a completely different person."

Mrs Braithwaite arrived with tea, cake and biscuits and retired just as quickly.

"Help yourself, Sarah." Diane waved at the tea before them on a low table. "Nothing there that you should not eat, I think." A conspiratorial smile.

"No. Now that he's gone, I eat everything." Sarah giggled. Diane noticed her visitor had not used the name of her husband Maurice once since she had arrived. The two ladies helped themselves. The quietness was therapeutic.

"Your husband Maurice," Diane began rather more boldly than she would have predicted before meeting the new, confident Sarah, "has left. Permanently?...Or?..." The sentence was left unfinished.

"Mrs Young...sorry, Diane...personally, I don't care whether it's permanent or not. In any case, if he does return, I'm not putting up with anymore of his nonsense."

Well, there! thought Diane. She asked, "Where has he gone? Do you know?"

"The police found his car in Heathrow. Ticket control tells us he took a flight to Germany. God knows why."

"Does he know anyone there?"

"I don't know. There have been one or two letters with German postmarks, but I was not allowed to read them. And now they have gone with him."

The conversation turned to more prosaic subjects: the village, the choir without Maurice, shopping in Cambridge, Sarah's mother...and so on. A pleasant afternoon. Sarah went home about 4:00, and Diane was left with the distinct impression that whilst Maurice Marchbanks was away, Sarah Marchbanks flourished. What would happen when, or more likely if, he returned? It might be another matter. Mrs Braithwaite opened the front door and wished Sarah well. She drove back to the village. Diane returned to the lounge, thinking, *Reginald? Marchbanks? Germany? If that was the big secret, she had cracked it!*

She smiled.

*** *** ***

Because Hugo Stratton and Reginald Young were in Germany attending to the extradition of Maurice Marchbanks and Nigel Mountford was still in Birmingham trying to make sense of Oldham's estate and the antics within, the meeting at the 'The School' in which Marcia had hoped to gather the last strands of this conspiracy together had been relegated almost to a disappointment.

But not quite.

Avril reported to Marcia that 25 Carpel Street had been closed since Monday, four days ago, and Andrew Stewartson had driven to a newly built, high-rise block in Park Lane, where he had parked and entered. He had stayed there overnight. Her co-worker, Nigel Mountford, had followed the pantechnicon away from Carpel Street to Brakeborough and Oldham's estate. Carpel Street house was deserted, and with the aid of local police, Avril confirmed that all the furniture and fittings had been removed, and unfortunately no written material had been left behind.

Next, Lucinda described Reginald and Stanley's visit to Brakeborough and her interview with Inspector Gideon regarding the murder that had occurred on the estate on Tuesday morning, some 10 days ago. The body belonged to one Errol Campbell, the brother of the incarcerated Duncan Campbell, and he had died due to strangulation, not drowning; he had been found in Oldham's Lake. Lucinda's impression of Brakeborough was that it was a quiet mid-England village, disturbed only by the regular raucous parties on the estate. The murder was the most extraordinary happening in living memory. The police presence was resented but tolerated given the circumstances.

Oldham had disappeared. Nigel was still investigating the situation.

Marcia thanked them and hurried on to her meeting with Jocelyn Carstairs.

Annette's office was deserted. Marcia looked at her watch. Noon. *Curious.* She stepped to Jocelyn's door and gently tapped. Not a sound. *Curious, noon precisely.* After a few moments, she took a seat and waited. She didn't have to wait long, as in burst Annette, out of breath and apologetic.

"Jocelyn will be here in a second. We were with the minister. Difficult to cut that short."

"I agree." Marcia was prepared to wait. "Tell me, how are you and your revered principal getting on?"

"You mean together?" Annette blushed.

"Well, not exactly, Annette." Marcia, for a moment, was unsure of herself, a condition to which she was unaccustomed. "I mean, rather, how do you find the work here? Busy? Boring? Stimulating? Demanding?"

"Certainly not boring," Annette replied stoutly. "It varies. Some days are busier than others, but I suppose that is true of most jobs."

"So, you see this as a job, not a vocation?"

"Well, it is more than just a 'job'. Jocelyn has considerable influence in governmental affairs. And that rubs off."

"I am sure it does." Marcia smiled and sat back. Annette busied herself on her typewriter, a little unsettled but unsure of the exact reason. This Marcia 'no surname' had a strangely unsettling effect on one. The door opened, and Carstairs bustled in, looking at his watch and apologising to Marcia for his tardiness.

"Ministers," he moaned, "think you have nothing better to do than listen to their incessant complaints." It was on the tip of Marcia's tongue to ask what else he did with his time but thought better of it. Carstairs unlocked his door, and Marcia and he entered his office. At the last moment, Marcia turned and asked Annette to join them. Had she been asked at that very second, 'Why did you invite Annette in?', she would have had difficulty answering. A hunch? Intuition? Suspicion? Afterwards, she decided it was no more than politeness. But with what consequences!

"Okay. Let's all sit." Carstairs was jovial and superficially unperturbed; his feelings might have been quite something else. "Now then, Marcia, you wanted to continue the chat from two days ago."

"That's right, Jocelyn. One or two points need clearing up, and then I think I will be able to make some sense of this unwelcome intrusion into our political system."

Carstairs needed something to do with his hands. Coffee! The universal cover for unemployed hands and the perfect disguise for tension.

"Annette," he apologised to his guest. "Some coffee, what do you think?"

"Perhaps not at the moment, Jocelyn," Marcia interposed, not wanting to interrupt her vigorous presentation. "Too much to discuss and time marches on regardless."

"As you wish, Marcia, as you wish." Carstairs remained ostensibly cheerful.

"You see," Marcia continued, "I have one or two loose ends to tie up before I can finalise my report (to whom it was left unsaid), and I believe you can help me."

"I can?" Carstairs leant forward.

"Yes. We might start with your minister. New to the position, eager to make a name for himself but yet untried on the battlefield?"

"Battlefield?" Carstairs needed something stronger than coffee.

"Well, perhaps 'battlefield' is a little strong. I meant to imply only that he has yet to be confronted with a significant challenge or the menace of strong opposition or even"—she paused shortly—"an attempt to replace the government."

"Replace the government? You mean a rebellion? You said as much the last time we spoke."

"Exactly. Take the atrocities that have occurred in the country recently." She emphasised his involvement. "The bomb-making criminals in Liverpool,

Birmingham and so on and add to those the shootings in Brighton, the bombings in Peterborough and the London Underground. These are not isolated incidents, but, in my group's opinion, incidents that would lead to civil unrest and widespread dissatisfaction, with an ulterior motive of widespread public alarm and eventually insurgency."

"Ulterior motive? Insurgency?" If Carstairs continued to echo Marcia's words, he would sound like a parrot.

"You are not suggesting that I am, in any way whatsoever, implicated in such a frightful scenario, I hope, Marcia," Carstairs stuttered.

"My dear Jocelyn," Marcia said reassuringly, "nothing like that had ever crossed my mind."

"Good." The answer was short; Carstairs' dignity was re-established.

"You will remember that I did ask you to keep your ear to the ground, listen to rumours, anything out of the ordinary?"

"Of course. And I have been vigilant in that respect. No word has been uttered in my presence that could be remotely linked to any such plot. Of that, I am quite sure." Here, he looked at Annette. For reassurance? For agreement? For endorsement? And Marcia noticed for the first time that Annette had not brought her notebook but sat as an equal participant in the meeting, not as a secretary taking notes.

"So," Marcia brought Carstairs back to the point, "no worries then?"

"Well, not more than the usual office indiscretions!" Annette moved uncomfortably in her seat. "Certainly, as I say, nothing that would lead me to suppose treason—if that's what this is."

"I am so relieved to hear you say that." Marcia allowed her shoulders to drop discernibly, a sure sign of relaxation. There was an easing of tension in the room. "That more or less covers the points I needed to mention today." Now she was preparing to go. "I am sorry to have taken up so much of your valuable time." Marcia moved as if to stand, suddenly changed her mind and remained seated. "Just one other small point. I noticed the last time I was here, you and Sir Brendan were enjoying your conversation. I thoroughly approve of interdepartmental cooperation. Did he mention the wonderful work you had done in apprehending those criminals?"

"I don't think so." Carstairs furrowed his brow in concentration. He looked at Annette, but she was of no help, for she had not been in the room.

"You did not mention Liverpool or Birmingham or Stockport or Felixstowe? Nothing like that?"

Carstairs saw a safety net open. If at some future date, he had to 'remember' the list of bomb-making places, here was his opportunity. "Wait a minute, Marcia…now you mention it, I may have spoken briefly about the police successes."

"You certainly did before the arrests," Annette interjected. "I remember you asking me to get the file…"

"Thank you, Annette. That has cleared up that little mystery." Marcia stood. "What a constructive discussion, Jocelyn. Thank you so much, and of course you, Annette." After the door closed behind her, she hurried down the stairs and out onto Whitehall.

*** *** ***

"Right, Albert, 107. Treble 19, bullseye! It's down to you. Easy!" the captain of 'The Dog and Vicar' public house darts team said. Albert who stepped up to the oche. Most of the customers called it the 'toe line'. 'Ignorant lot' was the captain's opinion.

No pressure! Albert thought. He was in agony; it wasn't his varicose veins; they were in convenient remission, which had allowed him to visit the pub. No, it was the pressure of winning the match. At that very moment, Florrie opened a bag of crisps loudly and started to crunch the contents very loudly. Albert, arrested by the noise, glared at her and automatically threw the dart without looking at the board.

"Treble 19!" The cry went up. Albert stared at the board, not quite believing what he saw. "Bullseye! And that's it!" shouted 'The Dog and Vicar' supporters. *No pressure!* Chatter in the bar stopped. Absolute silence except for the systematic munching of crisps by Florrie, who was oblivious to the tension. Albert concentrated as he had never concentrated before. *Bullseye for game set and match!* He launched his dart; it hit the wire and bounced out. *Now concentrate*, he told himself. Last chance. Last dart. He threw.

"Outer, 25. 82 scored. 'The Carpenters' Arms' to throw. Double 16 for the match!"

"Double 16!" They had won.

"Bugger it," said Albert. His captain did not commiserate, nor did he buy Albert a pint. Instead, Albert's old mate, George, approached.

"Bad luck, Bert. Hit the wire." For a moment, Albert did not reply; this was not because he was overcome by the loss but was rehearsing what he was going to say to Florrie when they got home. And her eating habits.

"Pint?" George offered.

"Thanks, George." Albert accepted the pint.

"Incidentally, heard about the trouble at your end of the village."

"Trouble? What trouble?"

"Aggie's Bookshop."

"Oh, that. Porn, if you ask me."

"Porn? How do you mean?"

"Well, police found a great hulking American and a young girl there. Stands to reason. Took all the books away as well." Albert tapped his nose knowingly. "And a till and a safe."

"A till and a safe? Whatever for?"

"Well, you know the police, and the till was full of money, I bet."

"NO! Not the police, surely!"

Albert tapped his nose again.

At the Cambridge police station, the money from the till had been meticulously counted, the amount certified by a sergeant, and the total amount of £7 and 20 new pence was recorded. Not a penny went astray. Aggie's safe was more difficult. At one stage, a probation police officer suggested local villains be contacted. The duty superintendent made a suitable comment in the young officer's record! The safe was eventually cracked by legal means; the combination was supplied by the maker's firm.

Once opened, the police found a Heckler and Koch submachine gun, the bullets fired from it exactly matching the bullets found in the public house and bodies of those killed in Brighton in October. Also, the fingerprints of Errol Campbell were lifted from the gun. There was no doubt about the identity of the culprit who had committed the murders.

Interestingly, they also found an envelope in which was a sheet of paper listing six or seven names and telephone numbers. After learning the addresses of these people, the list was handed to the Secret Service and eventually to Marcia.

The police were satisfied with the result. Bradley Adams remained in custody; charges were preferred against him, and he awaited a court appearance and, hopefully, help from the American Embassy. Aggie had been transferred to Addenbrookes Hospital, where her condition was still critical. Mercifully, she was unconscious.

*** *** ***

Chapter Twenty-Eight

The driver of an iconic London black cab cruised to a halt in the subterranean garage of a large, well-known, and if truth be told, rather ostentatious hotel in central London. As befitting the circumstances, the driver jumped out, opened the rear passenger door and Marcia stepped down. The lighting here was brighter than most car parks could manage, and therefore the shadows were darker, more defined, more prudent. She paid, there was a short conversation, and she turned to the lift; thus, elevating to the ground floor, she walked across the thick carpet to the reception desk.

The uniformed receptionist inquired, politely, of course, her name and, on being told of the luncheon engagement with Doctor Brooke, directed her to the dining room. The maître d' smiled, acknowledged Julian's wave from a distant table and took Marcia to him. Julian stood, bent forward, kissed her cheek and then stood back to allow the maître d' to help her into the well-upholstered, velvet dining chair.

"Thank you." Marcia made herself comfortable and looked across the table at her dining companion. "Julian, how have you been? You reprobate!"

Julian smiled and relaxed. "Hardly 'reprobate', Marcia. Maybe a little reprehensible, that is all. But I am so glad that you could join me today; it shows that you hold no resentment towards me after I pressurised you to attend that political meeting in north Oxford with Lucas."

"Hardly pressurised me, Julian. It was much more your usual technique of 'manoeuvring' me."

"For which, I am guilty as charged!"

"Undoubtedly."

Cheerfulness in each other's company had been restored; they had known each other over a prolonged period, and much water had flowed under many bridges in that time, and other relationships had interposed, then shattered, but they had never forgotten the early days of youthful exuberance or juvenile mistakes. Both withdrew into their separate memories.

Marcia looked around. The damask wallpaper was a pale lilac; the carpet, a matching shade of grey; the tablecloths starched crisply and laid with heavy cutlery. On their table was a single, fragrant freesia. In November! They read the menus in silence and chose their dishes with care.

"I took the liberty of ordering a bottle of Chablis before you arrived. I hope you do not mind."

"Of course not. That will be perfect," Marcia replied. "My goodness," Marcia exclaimed at last, "look at us now."

"What do you mean?"

"I have been thinking…do you remember the Sunday mornings we walked up The High, down that malodorous alley to that café and read the papers over enormous English breakfasts? What was that café called?"

"Goodness knows. Almost certainly not there now anyway."

"Probably not. We have come a long way since those student days. Drifted apart, now back towards each other again."

Julian frowned. "Yes…many things happened…and of course, Aaron…what a waste."

The silence lingered. Almost on cue, the maître d' approached and asked if they would consider ordering now. Indeed, they would. During their meal, neither referred to the political situation in Britain that had brought them together again or at least allowed them to enjoy one another's company. They ate appreciatively. Over coffee and cognac, Julian finally broached the subject of security.

"The fascist meeting in Oxford. Interesting?"

"Of course. It was yet another example, if one was needed, of the bourgeoning civil dissatisfaction many citizens are experiencing. the speaker was a particularly bigoted, superficial troublemaker. In fact, I was mildly surprised that those present, who I assume were undergraduates or otherwise attached to the university, gave him any credence at all."

"It illustrates how this lunacy permeates all strata of our culture."

"Precisely, but as well, I fear the criminal motivation is behind this fascism."

"Fascism and criminality. Is that not tautology?" Julian had the temerity to ask.

"I am not in the habit of repeating myself, Julian!" Marcia bristled. "What I mean is that this specific fascist movement is being sponsored and promoted by criminals who are not necessarily fascists themselves."

"Criminals using this right-wing propaganda for their own purposes."

"Precisely. And that is what my team and I decided to expose."

"Marcia, we are of one mind. I hoped you would say as much. In fact, I have been waiting for you, and your team, to make sense of this complicated affair. I wish you well in your endeavours, but fear I must return to the Lords this afternoon and listen to a debate concerning transgender legislation. I know nothing of it. But I suppose I will learn."

"You will." Marcia nodded.

"And then, it is my intention to dine this evening with a minister. I need to listen carefully to what he has to say. I will bear in mind your continuing undertaking."

"You are going to insinuate not all is well in the populace?"

"More than that, Marcia. I am going to suggest to him that he and his department listen carefully to any recommendation you may make. In the near future, that is."

"I am grateful, Julian. May I ask a favour…?"

"Depends."

"I wonder if you could listen especially carefully to any worries he may have, particularly in respect to the reliability or otherwise of civil servants in his department or in any other department, for that matter."

"Don't beat about the bush, Marcia. You mean Forsythe?"

"I mean Forsythe."

"I will do better than that. I will ask him directly about Forsythe, in absolute confidence, of course. We do not want that sort of inquiry getting back to Forsythe, do we?"

Julian called for the maître d' while Marcia returned to reception to order a cab and settle the account.

They left by separate exits. In separate cars. With a joint, if loosely defined, purpose.

*** *** ***

That afternoon, Marcia returned to Vauxhall Cross. Julian listened to a debate in the House of Lords, not a mile away.

These days, Marcia visited the MI6 centre infrequently, using it mainly as a base for posts and messages. One of the secretaries hurried in and, after the customary pleasantries, got down to business.

"Marcia. Two things. One has been flagged as urgent."

"Flagged by whom?" Marcia asked.

"Jocelyn Carstairs. He needs to speak to you urgently."

"Does he indeed?"

Marcia thoughtfully surveyed the Thames sliding past: grey and cold in the November afternoon and considered Carstairs. His father, called Kershaw, had been an estate agent's assistant, and Jocelyn had inherited much all that occupation's obsequiousness. He had also a profound and lasting sense of shame of the perceived lowly social position of his parents, and he had changed his name at university but had kept the mortification of his adolescence. Carstairs had compensated for this by becoming boisterous, blustering and, at the same time, always seeking reassurance. He was deeply insecure.

Marca found him unpleasant. But never said so.

"And the other matter?" she asked her secretary.

"Sometime, the boss wants to see you about your specialist team. No urgency there, but he is the boss, remember?"

"Indeed."

The secretary left Marcia to deal with Carstairs.

She called Carstairs on his private landline. And it was answered.

"Jocelyn Carstairs' secretary. May I help?"

"Annette! In the chief's office? How harmonious!"

"Yes." Annette sounded formal, not her usual self at all.

"Is Jocelyn there? He requests an urgent word with me."

"Hold on a moment." Marcia heard the phone placed on a desk, much rustling of papers and a whispered conversation. And then: "Marcia, how lovely! Just the lady we were talking about."

"You wanted a word, Jocelyn? You have kept your ear to the ground? Heard snippets of conversation you want to share with me? You have come across some nefarious activities?" Marcia was deliberately uncomprehending.

"None of those things, dear Marcia." She winced. But he hurriedly realised that such a digression might be useful. But then again, he had not heard anything nefarious. "Bits here and there," he prevaricated. "But the main reason I wanted to speak to you was to correct any false impression you may have gained from when we last met."

Now we get to it, Marcia thought. "Yes?" she said.

"You may have understood from Annette that I had passed on, inadvertently of course, the list of bomb-making sites before they were raided. Someone outside our office."

"Yes. I got that impression."

"Well. It was quite incorrect. Annette did not mean that at all. True, I did have a list of sites but only discussed it with persons inside the ministry and only outside after the raids, not before."

"Is that all?" Marcia smiled to herself. No need to alarm the man more than was absolutely necessary. "I thought Annette sounded chastened."

"Annette…chastened?" As if he did not know the meaning of the word. "Oh!…Chastened!…Oh, no, Marcia, not chastened."

Doth he protest too much? "Well, that's fine then, Jocelyn. A small mistake, a small matter of misunderstanding. Of little importance."

"I'm glad you understand." Carstairs certainly sounded relieved.

Perhaps Annette was in for a four-course meal tonight. And afters! Marcia mused unkindly.

Marcia put down the phone. So, Forsythe had known before the raids. That certainly would have been helpful for the criminals. *Were the trucks there to take away incriminating evidence, not delivering bomb-making materials?*

*** *** ***

The community within Brakeborough had recovered from the 'Oldham drama', as it had become known. News had spread that the murdered person was not local, was a visitor to the estate and had been strangled or drowned or both. And whisper was that the estate was being sold. Whether this was as a direct result of the crime or if Oldham was selling up for other reasons was a matter of intense debate. Marjorie, in the general store-cum-post office, listened. "It was not her place to speculate," she declared, somewhat haughtily. Of course, in private, that was another matter!

The regulars were not so shy in public. "If you ask me"—although no one had—"the place was too big for him. Going to wrack and ruin, parties all the time, up to his neck in debt, I wouldn't be surprised," was Doug's opinion.

"I don't know," Gertie countered. "Had pots of money, didn't he? Plenty to splash out on parties. I think it was down to the police, no mistake. They took a firm hand at last. Drugs. Drink. Now a murder. Makes sense."

"Do you think so, Gertie?" Kelly asked. "The young mothers were saying the place wasn't safe for the little ones. We were going to complain anyway."

"Who to?" Gertie asked.

"And what good would it do?" Doug shrugged.

It appeared the fright accompanying the murder had passed, leaving only an uneasy feeling of resentment in the village. It was most unsettling, but life must go on. Mrs Taylor came in, bought her cigarettes and scratch card, coughed and left without giving an opinion on the business, Oldham's estate, the police or anything else. Frank read the sports page.

Nigel Mountford stayed as a guest at a small hotel in Birmingham. He was far enough removed from Brakeborough to remain a stranger to the community. And that was his intention.

*** *** ***

A newcomer to the office, Philip Kimberly felt friendless. The only chap in a roomful of young ladies did little for his self-confidence. They were pretty, cheerful and competent. He sat at his desk, looking awkward and ill-equipped to deal with customers or life or both. To compensate for this, he turned the pages of his enormous diary and concentrated on today's tasks with vigorous earnestness.

Two appointments:

1. 11:00 hrs: Mr and Mrs Cartwright. Small house, two bedrooms, Selly Oak area. Price £200–250,000. Small garden essential.
2. 16:00 hrs: Roger Lakeland. Selly Oak, Harborne, at a push, four-bedroom, had viewed one. Interested…?

Philip looked up. A tall, well-dressed man, probably in his late 20s, stood with a briefcase at the ready, looking at him. The customer, or should he call him 'client', seemed impatient.

"Can I be of assistance?" Philip tried efficiency.

"I hope so." This was a more forceful Nigel Mountford than the once shy, embarrassed person hiding behind Avril Reynolds in London had been.

"Good."

"Are we looking for a property, sir?"

"I am; I do not know if you are. I have moved to Birmingham only at the weekend to take up the senior post in a local film. I want to view some three- or four-bedroom properties. Preferably Selly Oak, Northfield areas. What have you?"

This is more like it. Some commission if I play my cards right. Aaron thought brightly. He opened a desk drawer and withdrew a folder, upon which was written:

Four-bed; detached, semi-detached or luxury flats

"These are for sale, with immediate closure required." No harm in rushing him a little.

"Good." The word was stated with decisiveness. "If you could give me copies of the particulars on all those properties, I will take them away, browse at my leisure, get to know the area. Am I clear?"

"Of course, sir." Philip was decidedly hopeful. "If I may have your name, and I assume your temporary address, sir?"

"I can do better than that. Have my card. Name, company, mobile number." Nigel produced one of his cards already prepared, and mass produced at Headquarters. If I could have one of your cards, I would be able to speak to you directly.

It was as simple as that. Mountford walked away, briefcase bulging, packed with particulars of properties for sale, the young man's card with the estate agent's name written clearly and a builder's measuring tape. Using his mobile, Mountford rang Oldham's mansion and told the person who answered to expect a representative from Peter Firth, estate agents. He then drove slowly to Brakeborough.

As Nigel approached the gates of Oldham's estate, they automatically opened, which rather negated their purpose. Never mind, he went headlong a drive, through an avenue of leafless trees to the mansion itself. He rang the bell and waited until a butler, in full uniform, opened the door and inquired about his business.

"My company has been approached by…" Here he hesitated, opened his bulging briefcase and extracted a notebook. Laboriously, he leafed through it and continued, "Mr William Oldham to give an estimate of the value of the house and its contents. Here is our card."

PETER FIRTH AND SONS
Selly Oak—Birmingham
ESTATE AGENTS
SURVEYORS and VALUERS
Philip Kimberly

"On the backside, the address and telephone number."

As Nigel opened his case, he made sure the butler saw the notices of properties for sale and the industrial-sized measuring tape. The butler inspected the card.

"Curious this, sir. We were informed only fifteen minutes ago to expect you. Mr Oldham has not informed me of his intent to sell."

"Goodness me, no. That is not his intent at all. Quite the reverse. As I understand it, Mr Oldham is at present considering enlarging his portfolio and needs an estimation, that is all, of his combined wealth."

The relief was appreciable. The butler stepped back and invited Nigel into the house. And what a house! First, the baronial hall—there was no other word for it—had parquet flooring, a stained-glass window, an antique cabinet, a sideboard and a chest standing against one wall. Huge wooden doors led no doubt to the ground-floor rooms. A wide stairway ascended to the first floor.

"I will merely make an inventory of the rooms and measure them."

"The furnishings are beyond my remit; by the look of the hall, that will require expert valuation later."

"May I accompany you, sir, as you go through the rooms?"

"Of course. I would expect you to do so. Don't get too bored; it is not the most exciting of occupations." No harm sowing the seeds of boredom into the mind of the butler.

And they began the exhaustive tour of the rooms. Downstairs and up. As Nigel had hoped, the butler was satisfied his job was not on the line, that the mansion would remain in Mr Oldham's name and life would go on undisturbed. After a while of uselessly watching Mountford measure each room with excruciating exactness, the butler became fatigued and left Mountford to it. Exactly what Nigel wanted! The butler was satisfied; the gold-plated cutlery was locked in the bureau and the safe hidden in a cupboard. No worries on either front. Nigel was looking only to become familiar with the house, not burglary.

An hour or so later, Nigel informed the butler he had finished and to expect an antique furniture expert to call…"I should think within a week." He left with much more than measurements; unexpectedly, he had struck lucky.

*** *** ***

The return flight from Düsseldorf landed at Heathrow at 4:00 in the afternoon, with Marchbanks still handcuffed to Inspector Mayweather. Reginald and Hugo Stratton went with the pair to the Heathrow Airport Police Station in Unit 3 and gratefully handed over their charge to the counterterrorist police who were awaiting their arrival. By 7:00, the same evening, Reginald opened the door to Plantagenet house, pleased to be home.

"Something light, Group Captain?" Mrs Braithwaite asked.

"Thank you. Cold would be fine. Too tired for a full meal."

Diane welcomed him into the 'withdrawing room' and poured him a stiff gin with a splash of tonic, lemon, not lime, and ice. They sat.

"Home at last." Reginald sighed. "Not as young as I once was. No pun intended!"

"No. Nor I," Diane sympathised. "Did it go smoothly, your trip to Germany? Brought Marchbanks back, did you?"

"Worked it out, did you? How do you know about Marchbanks?"

"Sarah told me they found his car at Heathrow. He was bound for Germany, so they said."

"Yes. Germany it was. And they couldn't wait to get rid of the bastard."

"Reginald, really!"

"Mention fascism. Red rag to a bull. Know what I mean?"

"I suppose that is reassuring in a way."

"Trouble is, he's back here now. Let the counterterrorist police deal with him. Anyway, reckon we're close to finishing this business. So, saw his wife? What's her name? Sarah, was it?"

"It was and still is. She came around to tea as planned. This afternoon. A remarkable change in the lady. Cheerful. High spirits. 'Feel fulfilled', her words exactly. Spoke depreciatingly of her husband; I am not sure she will have him back."

"If she does, she'll have to wait a bloody long time!"

"Really, Reginald. Is there any need to swear?"

"My opinion: every need." Reginald helped himself to another gin and tonic. Exceptionally light on the tonic!

*** *** ***

In the Gentlemen's Club off Whitehall, Wilfred was marking the winners and places in today's racing at Chepstow, York and Aintree whilst at the same time taking surreptitious glances at his watch. The library was gradually filling up with evening members, and as usual, Brian, the evening wine butler, was late. Wilfred liked a handover of at least 15 minutes, but today, Brian was 10 minutes late. At last, here he came.

"Evening, Wilfred." Young Brian was oblivious to the time and many other things in life that Wilfred held so dear. And he hadn't done anything about his greasy hair either. Staff were difficult to get hold of these days! The lad was young yet, but still…

"And good evening to you, Brian. Made it last, I see." Wilfred looked at his watch rather pointedly.

"Busy afternoon, Wilfred?"

"Never mind that. Are you up to scratch with important matters of today?"

"Oh, yes, Wilfred. I am up to date." Although Brian was unsure which 'important matters' Wilfred was referring to.

"I do not mean the best vintage bottles laid in the cellar, but who won the 3:30 at Catterick?"

"No idea, Wilfred, but I am sure you have marked all the winners and places in today's races in the paper." Wilfred Davis, a man devoted to this club for 35 years, rolled his eyes and looked at the ceiling. Almost time to leave and face the evening with Mrs Davis.

"Remember, Brian, our gratuities depend upon those results. And, Brian, also in the club, refer to me as Mr Davis, not Wilfred. And this is even more important! This evening, we have Doctor Julian Brooke dining with us. To you, he is to be referred to as 'Your Lordship'. His dining companion is a minister of the Crown, and you will address him as 'Sir'."

What Brian made of all this remains obscure. One thing is certain: he was glad when Wilfred finally decided to leave. Shrugging into his coat in reception, Wilfred bade the porter 'Goodnight' and walked to his bus stop slowly.

Julian entered the club, tired from the afternoon's debate on gender identity, which he had barely understood. His head ached with the intensity of the debate and the ferocity of the emotions revealed. Furthermore, he was lethargic after the luncheon with Marcia. But he had to be awake this evening. A dry sherry and relaxation for a quarter of an hour. Then the minister. He needed to recover, and quickly.

In the library, he had no sooner sat than a young man introduced himself as, "Brian, my lord, at your service"…Enough to frighten poor Julian to death.

"Brian? I thought you were Wilfred," Julian said rather confusingly.

"No, he has gone home. Now it's me." That hardly made matters any clearer. "Do you want to know the winners at Aintree today, my lord?"

Julian looked thoughtfully at the young man. *Is he demented? No, too young. Taking the mickey? No, too forward. Intellectually challenged? Well, it is a possibility.* Eventually, he replied, "Not the winners, just a dry sherry, if you would be so kind."

"Very good, my lord," came the prompt reply.

Five minutes later, the minister appeared, also tired from a parliamentary session, this time on finance, but nevertheless in good spirits. Julian and he chatted amiably for a while in the library and then, at a leisurely pace, adjourned to the dining room. The service there was excellent, and over recent years, the food had undergone immense improvement. Gone was the smell of school, boarding house cabbage; now an eminent chef took care to satisfy everyone's taste. Within reason!

They were shown to a table not too distant from a man of the cloth. A bishop by the look of his purple, Julian surmised.

"This table suitable?" the dinner butler asked.

"Perfect," replied the minister of the Crown. "I like to be close to Christianity. Now then, Julian, how have you been, as a man of leisure in Oxford?" the minister asked.

"Leisure? Don't you believe it. Those undergraduates keep one up to the mark, that's for sure. And this afternoon, I had to sit through an almost incomprehensible discussion, if one can call it that, about gender identification in the House of Lords."

"Oh, yes. I know all about that!" the minister said. But then added, "And people become so emotional about the subject."

"I know, my hairdresser—he's a barber really—has extraordinarily strong views on the subject. But they would hardly have been constructive this afternoon."

"I know. Nevertheless, an important subject."

They concentrated on ordering, and Julian, even now recalling luncheon, ordered abstemiously, the minister rather more robustly: a bottle of sauvignon blanc was a light wine to go with the meal. They returned, thoroughly satisfied, to the library for a cognac and coffee. Brian was the very epitome of servitude.

"Roland. I have a question for you." Julian approached the subject he and Marcia had been discussing over lunch obliquely. "Do you consider the public to be content with government at present, at one with government aspirations, generally at ease?"

"Between you and me, Julian, the answer to all three must be 'no'. But a qualified 'no'. Our aims are laudable; the economy will recover from the dreadful pandemic; Britain will once again be productive. We will thrive; inflation will finally level off."

"That is good to hear, Minister," Julian mused. "But I have heard it said quite forcibly that morale is not well throughout the country."

"Anything specific?"

"Well, yes and no. I know of an extremely perceptive, experienced and qualified lady who has been engaged in examining some disquieting incidents. You know, of course, of the raids nationwide by our police forces and the uncovering of many bomb-making 'factories'. You also know of the atrocities in Brighton, the London Underground and Peterborough. The lady to whom I refer has been actively engaged, together with her team, in discovering a group of entrepreneurs who may well be behind a concerted effort to sow the seeds of discontent within the public and eventually attempt to overthrow not just this government but the constitution. All these apparently disassociated incidents are all part of one conspiracy."

"I think you speak of Marcia."

"I do."

"I thought as much. And I am seriously concerned."

"Good." Now Julian needs only to add his insistence of listening to Marcia, the minister would surely be convinced. "I know she has investigated this field exhaustively. Her assessment of the situation is not only comprehensive but it is, in its way, frightening."

"Thank you, Julian. You are someone I have always listened to with the utmost care during your time in the ministry, and you have been justly rewarded with elevation to the peerage. I will ask to see Marcia's report as soon as it is ready."

"I can ask no more, Minister."

On the strength of that, they ordered another cognac. Eventually, the minister returned to his grace and favour residence, and Julian wearily climbed the stairs of the club and slept soundly in one of the bedrooms reserved for members.

Brian went home. *Wait till I tell Cynthia I spoke to a lord tonight!* It made working there all worthwhile.

*** *** ***

Chapter Twenty-Nine

Nigel Mountford returned to his bungalow in Ruislip late in the evening of Monday, 15 November. Having followed a pantechnicon to Brakeborough, he judiciously chose a hotel at some distance from the village on the outskirts of Birmingham. The establishment was small and provided only the most basic facility, and that was lumpy! He met several furtive couples who neither spoke nor smiled at him, and he was fairly sure they hardly spoke or smiled at each other. Come to think of it, he came to recognise some of the young ladies, but they seemed always to be with a different bloke. It was all most confusing. However, the hotel had one outstanding advantage. It was twenty yards from Firman and Sons, estate agents. He had put that to effective use.

His intrusion into Oldham's mansion had proved fruitful, and he sent an email, with an attachment, to Marcia promptly. It was yet another piece of the jigsaw falling into place.

(Encoded.) **EMAIL and ATTACHMENT:** Nigel Mountford to Marcia.

I have completed an inspection of William Oldham's mansion in Brakeborough, Worcestershire. Although I was accompanied by Oldham's employee during the first part of my inspection, I was left unattended as I walked through the first-floor rooms, i.e., the bedrooms, toilets, etc. It was in the largest bedroom, I assume the master bedroom, that I found the attached letter. SEE: attachment. It appears to be from a Mr Vincent Rodish, a name that means nothing to me, to Mr William Oldham, asking for information and a character reference for Doctor Alistair McIntyre. He has applied for the post of medical director of a clinic named 'The R. and M. Centre', Milton Keynes. If I remember correctly, this is a man Stratton mentioned in connection with Muirhead's Party Committee in Cheshire. If that is the case, then the late Duncan Muirhead must be connected to Oldham through his wife, Mrs Frances, or his brother-in-law, Andrew Stewartson, of Carpel Street and possibly this new clinic.

N.M.
11.11.2021

*** *** ***

The village of Astwelling is sufficiently removed from London to be regarded as 'rural' but close enough for daily commuting to the capital. Unknown to the residents, a large house with the unlikely name of 'The Yards', had been under intense surveillance for some time. It was the country retreat of Sir Bernard Forsythe. The observation on the house involved refugee collection officers with cameras; a unit of counterterrorist police with binoculars and specialist night-vision binoculars and cameras stationed in the copse overlooking the village; and a postal delivery person with an inordinate interest in the letters and parcels addressed to 'The Yards'. Furthermore, GCHQ was monitoring all incoming and outgoing telephonic traffic. To suggest that every movement of the occupants in the house was known to agents of the law would be an understatement.

After considerable discussion and detailed planning, it was decided that armed police would enter the property, using whatever force was necessary, at 15:00 hrs on Tuesday, 30 November 2021, and by 15:15 hrs, every person within the house and garden would be arrested. Those arrested included Forsythe, Stewartson, Oldham, Frances Muirhead, Avril Reynolds, a cook and a gardener. The following day, forensic officers would make a thorough inventory of the contents of the house. Later that same day, unsurprisingly, Avril Reynolds was released without charge. The cook and gardener were given unconditional bail.

The presence of so many police officers in the village caused some consternation among the residents, but forced entry into one of their homes was considered 'vulgar'. The villagers saw themselves as 'gentry'; the younger crowd believed they should be called 'beautiful people', and this type of police behaviour was 'quite gross' if not 'downright obscene'! 'One' could not possibly gossip about it, but if 'one' could not restrain 'oneself', then such phrases as 'OMG!' or 'Dear me!' or 'Well, there you go!' were acceptable. One callous youth, who is the son of the nouveau riche living at the edge of the village, you know, was heard to exclaim, 'Hell's bloody bells!'. He and his family were righteously ostracised.

On the sabbath, the local clergyman preached of stones and not throwing them if 'one' lived in a glass house. He left many of his flock bewildered. Who would be so uncivilised, and in any case, so profligate?

*** *** ***

On Monday, 6 December, Marcia called each member of the team, informing them she was embarking on the final report of their work for Home and Foreign Office records. She reminded each that their contributions had been crucial, telling each to prepare written notes of their investigations and be prepared to bring the notes personally to her at 'The School' over the course of December. "Memories, experiences and intuitions are so much more enlightening than the written word, don't you find?" It would take all of December to gather the statements and write the report.

Christmas was only three or so weeks away, and the 'The School' in Streatham would be closing for a short vacation. Instead of cheerful anticipation, there was an air of despondency in the DuPont household. Marcia and her team had not held any meetings for some time, and they feared 'The School' had run its course and was to be closed. Antoine, who was a non-Christian, had never fully recovered from his father's desertion or the 'bloodless' murder and disappearance of his grandparents, felt the same shame, fear; almost overwhelming emptiness. It had left a feeling of inadequacy that was to be lifelong. News of the shootings in Brighton, the car bomb in Peterborough and the underground outrage in London, together with growing civil unrest, reminded them too vividly of mainland Europe and their assignments in the French counterterrorist police.

Committed anglophiles, they did not want to witness similar incidents in this country; there was still work to be done. Antoine, not expecting visitors, heard a car pull up in the back lane and footsteps approaching the rear entrance. As always in moments of stress, his genitals physically contracted; a heightened reflex reaction, whether of shame, impotence or fear, was irrelevant. He braced himself against the tall dresser with an attitude that he hoped did not suggest belligerence. The door opened, and there stood Marcia, immaculately dressed and smiling, but flushed with the December cold…or something.

"Marcia," he pronounced hesitantly. "*Ca va*? A pleasure to see you. We have missed you and your meetings. We thought you had deserted us." He walked forward, and they shook hands formally.

"Never, Antoine, never."

Delphine heard the voices and came into the kitchen. She immediately stepped over and embraced Marcia, less formally than her husband.

"Delphine, how are you? I was just about to tell Antoine we have completed our investigations; you will be reading the results in the papers later this year—or ,as things stand, probably next year! But it is the culmination of our work that brings me here today."

The two stood silently. Was this to be the end of 'The School'?

"Have you planned your holiday yet?" she asked.

"We had intended to travel to Paris for Christmas," Antoine said cautiously.

"How long?"

"A few days only. If you want us to stay here…"

"Not at all. Not Christmas. Certainly not. But I had thought to use your excellent facilities to complete a report that will be a record of our work here."

"Of course," they said in unison. The relief was obvious.

"Shall we say, I start on Monday, 13 December, and we could all take Christmas away from 20 to 31 December and then start again on Monday, 3 January. Would that be satisfactory?"

They couldn't wait to agree.

"But there is more. What I have in mind is the development of this centre. Luckily, the house next door, which is also detached, as you know, has been bought by my department through intermediaries, as discreetly as possible, and I have agreement from Treasury that we build a passageway between this house and the other. Then, I envisage the development of this house into a specialised unit for my work and my team, which will gradually grow in numbers, and the house next door will be converted into an educational base for learning the crafts needed in espionage, with more accommodation and lecture facilities. What do you say? You will have to expand your roles.

"Not only will you continue your excellent residential care for our young aspirants, but you will also be protectors and guardians of my work. Alterations must be made in this house and will begin on Monday, 13 December and hopefully will be completed by Sunday, 5 January. Those changes to this house are not substantial but are essential. There must be a secure room to store documents and an adjoining room for a bookkeeper or registrar; the kitchen will need to be converted into a reception room, with equipment for a porter or receptionist and so on. I encourage you to speak with the builders to satisfy your needs as well as theirs. Work can start on the house next door when they have finished here, say January. Without fail, we must include proper and comfortable quarters for yourselves. There will also be a substantial rise in your monthly remuneration and pension fund."

Monsieur and Madame DuPont smiled.

*** *** ***

"Reginald?"

Reginald knew a rhetorical question when he heard one. Diane was not asking his name to ascertain whether he remembered it! "Yes?" he replied carefully before taking another mouthful of gin, less carefully.

"You have completed the work with Marcia and the delightful Lucinda, have you not?"

"They are both 'delightful'." Reginald hoped to derail any insinuations.

"So, they may be. However, I think now that you can drag yourself away from their company, we could concentrate on enjoying ourselves together."

"Of course." Reginald was relieved.

"Good. I suggest we take an extended holiday."

"Extended, you say?"

"Yes. Perhaps a month in a warmer clime."

"A month, you say?"

"Southwest India. The Goa."

"The Goa, you say?"

"For goodness' sake, Reginald! Do not keep asking if I have just said something. There is no one else in the room, is there?"

"Don't think so." Reginald looked around the room, somewhat perplexed. *Only a turn of phrase, wasn't it? Perfectly normal! What is wrong with her? Or rather more pertinently, how many gins have I had?*

"So, the Goa. One month. January. What do you think?"

"Excellent idea."

"Good, for I have already bought the plane tickets and booked a hotel. It was well-recommended."

"You have?"

"Reginald! Do not start that again. Are you agreeable to the proposal?"

"Of course, Diane." *Have to be, won't I?*

"Good, so after Christmas."

"So, after Christmas."

Diane looked at him. *How many gins has he had?*

*** *** ***

A week after Marcia broke the good news to Delphine and Antoine, she began her labours: the report for the Home and Foreign Offices. She chose the most elevated room of the house: a loft conversion above the three storeys; it was a room of modest proportions, with a small dormer window that boasted an inappropriately large windowsill, upon which neighbourhood pigeons shuffled, strutted, clicked and cooed contentedly. These reassuring sounds were accompanied by secret rustlings from above the ceiling and may have been caused by small rodents. Marcia found these subdued noises pleasantly soothing.

She sat at a moderately-sized desk, on which her computer and reading lamp stood. There was a chair at the desk, two armchairs, a filing cabinet and an old rug thrown across the wooden floor. With paper, a printer and enough pens to stock a stationer's store, what more did she need? Well, organisation and a recognisable timetable of events would be a start. But life was never easy.

A seagull with a yellow, hooked bill, beady eyes and an aggressive demeanour had the temerity to land on the sill and disrupt the pigeons' tranquil rhythm of life. This caused considerable ill-feeling among the local birds, and war was declared. It was the first time Marcia had had witnessed a feather being torn from a seagull, and she sincerely hoped it would be the last. The seagull properly chastened, flew away, and Marcia returned to her toils.

By lunchtime at the café, she had five files assigned and labelled for essential stages of the investigation. She would start in earnest this afternoon. Lunch was ready downstairs, the break welcome.

The pigeons on guard and the unseen creatures patrolling above, Marcia soon felt comfortable. The 'Introduction' would deal with Muirhead's premature death on a golf course in the wilds of Worcestershire, miles from where he should have been and his wife's false declaration of any knowledge of this sporting venue, the essential events that had started the whole business. It was quite straightforward; only Marcia's loose jottings and cryptic notes in her diary needed rewriting on the computer and printing. It took all afternoon. Tomorrow, she would begin to disentangle the branches of the 'Muirhead Association', and for that, she would need Lucinda.

Lucinda answered her mobile. "Hallo, Marcia. I've been expecting a call. Want me at 'The School'?"

"Morning?"

"I'll be there."

Good as her word, Lucinda arrived at 'The School' early the next morning; she climbed the stairs and accepted an invitation to sit.

"Can we start immediately?" Marcia began.

"Certainly," and in a rare show of impatience, Lucinda added, "that's what I'm here for."

Marcia noticed the pique. Or was it merely nervousness? Either way, she made no comment. "This place is certainly out of the way," Lucinda continued. "And bang in the middle of all these houses. Clever."

"Clever?" Marcia was now intrigued.

"Reminds me of Carpel Street."

"I suppose there are similarities. In fact, Carpel Street is the subject I would like us to discuss."

Lucinda tried to get herself comfortable in the old armchair but apparently didn't succeed, for she suddenly jumped up, came across and leant against the desk. "I played it badly. Almost from the word go. Too trusting, too naive, too bloody stupid." It was direct, almost a challenge—but Marcia knew it was also a petition for tolerance. Lucinda was embarrassed!

"You are too hard on yourself. How were you to know that the MP for whom you worked, and incidentally was well-thought-of, could be involved with a scheme as frightening as this?"

"There were letters to a mysterious 'Muirhead Association' I was not allowed to touch; I was driven to Lyfen on a bloody motorbike no less and 'invited to stay' in that godawful bookshop…"

"I'm not here to soothe your troubled brow," Marcia said curtly. Then more placidly added, "But what I am here for is to put together pieces of evidence and find a coherent and complete picture. And you have added appreciably to that picture. From the Muirhead Association in Carpel Street, you have shown a direct link to Lyfen and to Brakeborough. More than that, the murder of Errol

Campbell on Oldham's estate, his relationship to Duncan Campbell and the shootings in Brighton. Not a bad tally for one so new to the service."

Lucinda returned to her armchair; Marcia was too long in the tooth to be fooled. Lucinda might be pacified, but she was yet a long way from being convinced. It was part of the learning curve. Sometimes painful.

*** *** ***

The morning then went relatively evenly, and when they went down for lunch, Marcia had her file on the Carpel Street Association well underway. That was a solid start. Downstairs was mayhem; builders everywhere and dust in more places than could reasonably be expected. Delphine had prepared a cold spread under cellophane, of course, and neither Marcia nor Lucinda refused a drop of white wine. The conversation eased, and Marcia was able to put Lucinda's embarrassment into perspective. As often was the case, Marcia had listened more closely to her intuitions. Oldham was central to the enterprise, not Muirhead; Aggie's Bookshop was important not only for the safekeeping of incriminating evidence but also as headquarters for Marchbanks' university clubs and even far-right political reasoning.

She returned to the loft. Lucinda went home. Reassured?

Marcia started early the next day. She was expecting Hugo Stratton in the afternoon, but for the morning, she settled down, concentrating on the overall picture, trying and as yet not discerning a definite progression of events. Her concentration was such that the rustlings and cooing of the pigeons were dismissed from her mind; even the unpredictable percussion of hammering bricks receded from her awareness. Then a subtle change in sound from below brought her out of the absorption of work. Laughter, a new voice, male, insistent; more laughter. Then:

"Hell, are you doing with that door?"

More laughter.

"Okay, you win. Looks better with a bloody great hole in the wall."

More laughter. Some muttered backchat, followed by heavy footsteps on the stairs and there stood the bulky figure of Group Captain Reginald Young. "Morning, Marcia. Thought you might need me sometime—just passing, thought I'd drop in." He came into the room, selected one of the armchairs and sat. "Long way up here, don't you know?"

Several thoughts came to Marcia's mind. *Just passing? Seemed unlikely. Needed to see him? Certainly, but not today. What was all the hilarity downstairs?* But she actually said, "Good to see you, Group Captain; make yourself comfortable; it is about time for a coffee, in any case."

She called down to Delphine; coffee was ordered.

"Wrapping it all up, are we?"

"I have made a start; your contribution will be most welcome. Now that you 'have just dropped in', perhaps you would give me your general overview."

"Overview? Not quite with you, know what I mean?"

"I think so. Just your impressions of the investigations."

The coffee arrived, helping Reginald out of a tight spot. *Impressions? Devil does she mean?*

Marcia poured the coffee and handed Reginald a cup. After a lot of wriggling, squirming and searching of his back pockets, Reginald produced a hipflask and tipped a good measure of whisky into his coffee. "Marcia?" He waved the flask about. She declined the offer graciously.

"Reginald, what do you make of our efforts so far?"

"Lot going on, for sure." Reginald was playing for time, trying to put their investigation straight in his mind. "Took a while to be accepted. But doesn't matter, I suppose."

"I apologise. The service is a fellowship really; perceived outsiders are treated with reservation. Understandable, the nature of our work."

"You said 'my impressions'—those were my first, rather intimidating impressions!"

"But now accepted?" A pause, after which Reginald agreed. Marcia presumed she had his permission to move on. "Your input has been crucial and led to important decisions. Take, for example, your attachment to Mendel Partners. That excellent report highlighted the seriousness of the Muirhead-Oldham relationship, which in turn motivated our interest in Brakeborough. Need I go further?"

"That's true enough. You think that is the centre of the whole thing?"

"Not exactly the centre. I believe it is the conduit through which funds are transferred to this country from abroad, monies that finance various revolutionary cells in this country. It is the combined efforts of these disparate groups that make up the single threat."

"Seems far away from 'impressions'."

"Not really, Reginald. Facts incorporated with intuitions are the fundamental base for understanding a conspiracy as complex as this. In a sense, this has been a tour; various communication pathways and widely dispersed groups make up a network of a malign conspiracy, like a spider's web, with the trap woven by the unseen killer. If the spider is sufficiently hidden, victims must depend on secondary evidence, even hunches, to identify the predator."

Reginald considered this for a while and then seemed to make up his mind. "Right, Marcia. These are my rough notes on what I've seen and done. When I say rough, I mean rough!" He passed over a loose-leaf folder holding several sheets of paper and one or two envelopes, upon which hurried notes had been jotted down. Later, Marcia was to find an unpaid bill in one of the envelopes.

"This looks extensive. Thank you. But impressions…?"

"Right. Brakeborough. Close community. Oldham is an outsider"—he gave a meaningful look—"but tolerated because he employs some villagers. Not liked, not disliked. The post office is the hub."

"Disinterest?"

"Not exactly. More, none of our business."

"Nobody knows what goes on behind his walls." Marcia was pleased; this is unquestionably the type of information she needed. "And the murder?"

"No idea. Shook the village but unsolved. He was the brother of Duncan Campbell awaiting trial. So probably Brighton. But that brings me to another nasty piece of work: Maurice Marchbanks. Now, he puts a whole new light on things. Absolutely self-centred; he and wife came for a meal at our place; had no idea how to act—kissed Mrs Braithwaite! Can you believe it? Same night deserts his wife, turns up in Germany, lodging with a far-right bloke in a place called Viersen. Police there were glad to be rid of him. They're still embarrassed about Nazis."

"So, we hear of right-wing extremist talk. I also had an unfortunate experience, this in Oxford. Far-right rubbish." Marcia realised this was the first time she had spoken of the meeting in Summertown to anyone other than Julian Brooke.

"Finally, Siobhan in Cambridge." Reginald neared the end of his involvement. "Now here, I thoroughly agree with your take on 'impressions'. At first sight, Siobhan is a member of the Lyfen group. On second sight, had been besotted with Marchbanks. On third sight, disillusioned. Wants no more of him or them. But hugely important in that she reported the kidnapping of Lucinda.

Talking of a village, reminds me, do you know Diane read something in the paper today. Made a fuss, no idea why. Said to mention it to you."

So, just passing! Marcia thought, but said, "I have always held your wife's opinions in the highest regard."

"You have?" Reginald sounded genuinely surprised. "Well, she noticed that the clinic where that unexplained death occurred—Phoenix Clinic, I think it was called—is to be opened again. To be called 'The R. and M. Centre'. Odd name."

"Now I have a much fuller picture. If we are talking of fine art, then I have a much clearer and satisfying picture. I can empathise with the artist, follow his line of thinking. Do you know, if we can beg another coffee from Delphine, I will have a drop of your firewater; that is the correct expression, is it not?"

"It is." *Did she giggle?*

*** *** ***

The same afternoon, it was the turn of Hugo Stratton and Avril Reynolds. They were accustomed to Marcia's interest in a person's subjective response to situations, and Annette described Carpel Street in detail, its connection with Brakeborough when Mountford had followed the pantechnicon, the condominium in Park Lane when Avril had followed Stewartson there, and Lyfen, about which Marcia knew about anyway but had little to add with regards to reactions or fundamental passions. Hugo had a different take. He reminded Marcia that the Earl of Kingsworth was met at Northolt Airfield by Stewartson and possibly Frances Muirhead. "And don't forget Wesley. Smelt a rat by the name of Forsythe but ran a mile when I showed interest." But there was more.

"You may or may not be aware of my wife's background. So, forgive me if I relate something you already know. Krystina was born and brought up in Krakow, in the Jewish district. It's an hour's train journey from there to Auschwitz-Birkenau. I think it was her great-grandfather who made that journey during the German occupation during the war. Like many, he didn't return. Although Krystina doesn't practise the family's faith now, that murder and thousands more from Krakow have left a personal hatred that runs deep. It goes without saying that it has influenced my own attitude. When I went with Reginald Young and Inspector Mayweather to Viersen, I found it difficult. The only redeeming feature was the acute embarrassment and lingering hatred the German police showed towards Marchbanks and their own fascists."

"And Marchbanks?"

"Difficult to tell. He said nothing. Reginald reckons he's a psychopath, so feels no remorse. I think he might have been belatedly sorry for his involvement in such an organisation."

"That is precisely the sort of comment I find so useful. Thank you, Hugo."

*** *** ***

Only Mountford to be seen, and she could write a full, and she hoped, an uncompromising report.

Nigel duly arrived the next day, on Thursday, 16th. "It's like a sandstorm down there," he began. "And how do you put up with the noise?"

"I have got used to it. I don't notice now."

While these preliminaries were taking place, Marcia had fished out Nigel's email. "Fascinating, Nigel. And another puzzle. But the only one we need to keep an eye on, for now. What do you think?"

"The same. If Oldham is the main channel for money and the underlying strategy for this organisation, then two things. The first is that he has disappeared; the second is that it was easy to get into his mansion."

"With regards to your first observation, somewhere in Reginald's notes"—she shuffled the said notes, apparently with little success—"he mentions seeing Oldham with Stewartson in his club, and I believe he has just been arrested in Forsythe's country house."

"Is that right? Well, he was not well protected in his Brakeborough mansion; the butler soon left me to my own devices, more interested in his own job."

"Not close, the butler and Oldham?"

"Doubtful."

"That is especially useful, Nigel. It gives me some insight, at least, into how this branch of the organisation operated. Only as an employer-employee. The staff were not participants in any conspiracy, merely hired hands. They were not threatened by your presence?"

"Not at all."

"Thank you, Nigel; with the rest of the team, take the rest of the month off. You all have earned it."

"Thank you, Marcia; the experience has been stimulating…is that the right word?"

"It is for me!" Marcia looked around the papers scattered over her desk and on the floor; folders at the ready to be filled with chronological notes; a computer poised to begin her final report. And she needed peace for that.

"Thanks for the time off, Marcia. We'll all see you in the new year. I'll go down and fight my way through the dust."

Marcia set to. She was on her own, generally pleased with the work. The conspiracy, to all intents and purposes, had been shut down, in this country at least. It had turned out that the organisation was like an onion: as you peeled away one layer, another was exposed below. But you had to complete a full dissection, get at the roots, or the thing might grow again.

Politics and politicians depended on the public, and the public had come to depend on the politicians. She and her team had drawn attention to the malign nature of this political movement; surely, the public would now understand. The team had proved its value; the future of 'The School' was assured, even enlarged. That was enough to go on with.

*** *** ***

Chapter Thirty

The report, dignified with the impressive, if not imaginative, title 'S02/3C4/1', was exhaustive. Not only were there accounts of the members' investigations but there were six appendices describing: the right-wing meeting in Summertown, Oxford; a list of members of the 'Lyfen Club'; the 'Muirhead Association'; the 'Oldham/Muirhead/Forsythe Connection'; and various correspondence' that mentioned, among other items, a letter from Vincent Rodish, who was previously unknown; the last appendix recorded the vital part played in the release of Lucinda Clayton from incarceration in Lyfen by Siobhan Behan.

The report clearly described the as yet unidentified consortium of financiers with access to enormous resources and the development of a country-wide scheme to displace democracy. It was further reported that the condominium in Park Lane had been sold and was now empty, awaiting a buyer(s). Of the Earl of Kingsworth, there had been no sighting, therefore he was presumed abroad. In a sad post-script, it was noted that Agatha of Aggie's Bookshop had died, and a last post/post-script reported that no country had yet claimed Bradley Adams. He languished in prison.

The report was considered to be extremely comprehensive by all who read it, which included branches of the secret services, top civil servants, ministers of the Crown, and, it was rumoured, even the prime minister. How Julian Brooke had come to read the report was something Marcia felt it wise not to ask. But read it he had, and on their next meeting, he congratulated her generously. He then murmured quietly, "I have reason to believe Jocelyn, after an exhaustive inquiry, has resigned."

In the corridors of Whitehall, there was talk of honours, but they came to nothing. Instead, 'The School' was promoted to 'The French Language Academy', as if it had become more prestigious after a long labour and difficult delivery of the report. When the team reassembled in January 2022, the two houses were joined by a covered walkway, the front gardens incorporated into one large carpark, and a discreet sign proclaimed 'The French Language Academy proprietors M and Madame DuPont'.

There was still an area for parking cars in the back lane, and on entering their old premises through what had been the kitchen, the members of Marcia's team were startled to be accosted by a uniformed receptionist and their passes examined. The house, if not palatial, had been modified and was well-staffed with secretaries, registry officers and so on. Marcia kept the top room for herself. Odd that; the most spartan accommodation, but perhaps she had become attached to the pigeons, liked the view, or as Stratton drily remarked, "You remember those bloody wooden chairs downstairs?"

The luxury condominium near Park Lane has stood empty since December 2022; some interest has been shown in buying the property, but the price is reputed to be astronomical. Estate agents and banks are reluctant to make the details public, and it is assumed that the financial strictures that beset the country in 2023 will be a hindrance to potential buyers.

Not so in Buckinghamshire. Alfred Morris, you will remember, the farmer inclined to shout his views to all and sundry in the village public house, had got hold of some disturbing news.

"Know that place down the road, closed after that death?"

The faces of the regulars turned towards him. "That place, the place that closed down these last three months? What about it?"

"I'll tell you 'What about it!' Bloody reopening, isn't it? A new director, bought by someone overseas. Advertising for nurses. That's what's going on!" Alfred drank the last of his beer, banged his glass on the counter and waited. In vain. Nobody was going to buy that old crab a beer.

"And shut up." This was from the postman, who was trying to sleep.

"All very well telling me to shut up. What if some of those idiots come and take advantage of your wife? What then?" But Alfred remembered the postman's wife, and not even those idiots would…"No offence, mate," he mumbled.

That was the first the village had heard of the clinic reopening. And the name Alistair F. McIntyre meant nothing to them at that time.

Printed in the USA
CPSIA information can be obtained
at www.ICGtesting.com
LVHW012031090224
771462LV00003B/22